'Not yet. Let's just go on like this. Please, Terry.' She squeezed his hands tightly. 'If you can meet me from work sometimes and we can go to the pictures once a week ... that would be all right. Let's just do that. For the time being, anyway.'

'All right,' he agreed. 'And now I suppose we'd better go, or you'll be in trouble for being late home from work.' He drew her closer and they stood still, both trembling a little. 'Can I kiss you, Patsy?'

For answer, she moved a step nearer and lifted her face. He could feel her hair brush against his cheek, and his heart kicked. He bent his head and moved gently until his lips found her cheek, and then her lips. They bumped noses, giggled a little, and then seemed to find the right place to settle.

Their first kiss was exploratory and tender; the second more ardent. When Terry let her go, they were both breathless.

'I'm not giving you up, Patsy,' he murmured, keeping his arm around her waist as they moved on along the narrow path. 'You'm my girl now. It don't matter what your father says – he can't alter that.'

Lilian Harry's grandfather hailed from Devon and Lilian always longed to return to her roots, so moving from Hampshire to a small Dartmoor town in her early twenties was a dream come true. She quickly absorbed herself in local life, learning the fascinating folk-lore and history of the moors, joining the church bell-ringers and a country dance club, and meeting people who are still her friends today. Although she later moved north, living first in Herefordshire and then in the Lake District, she returned in the 1990s and now lives on the edge of the moor with her ginger cat and two miniature schnauzers. She is still an active bell-ringer and member of the local drama group, and loves to walk on the moors. Her daughter and two grandchildren live nearby. Visit her website at www.lilianharry.co.uk or you can follow her on Twitter @LilianHarry

BY LILIAN HARRY

April Grove quartet

Goodbye Sweetheart
The Girls They Left Behind
Keep Smiling Through
Moonlight & Lovesongs

Other April Grove novels

Under the Apple Tree
Dance Little Lady

'Sammy' novels

Tuppence to Spend
A Farthing Will Do
A Penny a Day
(*also a Burracombe series novel*)

Corner House trilogy

Corner House Girls
Kiss the Girls Goodbye
PS I Love You

'Thursday' novels

A Girl Called Thursday
A Promise to Keep

Other wartime novels

Love & Laughter
Three Little Ships
A Song at Twilight

Burracombe novels

The Bells of Burracombe
A Stranger in Burracombe
Storm Over Burracombe
Springtime in Burracombe
An Heir for Burracombe
Secrets in Burracombe
Snowfall in Burracombe
Weddings in Burracombe

Other Devon novels

Wives & Sweethearts

Weddings in Burracombe

LILIAN HARRY

An Orion paperback

First published in Great Britain in 2013
by Orion Books
This paperback edition published in 2014
by Orion Books,
an imprint of The Orion Publishing Group Ltd,
Orion House, 5 Upper St Martin's Lane,
London WC2H 9EA

An Hachette UK company

1 3 5 7 9 10 8 6 4 2

A CIP catalogue record for this book
is available from the British Library.

ISBN 978-1-4091-2797-0

Typeset by Deltatype Ltd, Birkenhead, Merseyside

Printed and bound in Great Britain by Clays Ltd, St Ives plc

The Orion Publishing Group's policy is to use papers that
are natural, renewable and recyclable products and
made from wood grown in sustainable forests. The logging
and manufacturing processes are expected to conform to
the environmental regulations of the country of origin.

www.orionbooks.co.uk

To all my good friends who gather round the
'bellringers' table', in the Peter Tavy Inn

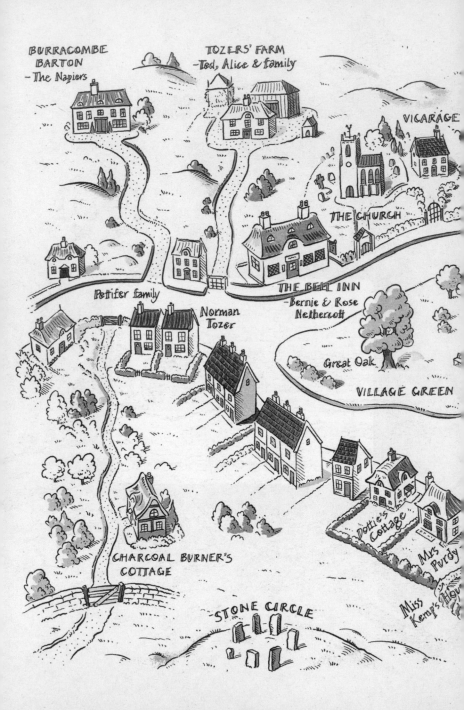

Chapter One

I t really was a rainbow wedding.

Hilary Napier, standing with her father, the village squire, and her brother Stephen at the end of the family pew in the village church, turned her head to watch Stella Simmons proceed up the aisle. She moved slowly, but she was on her feet and walking, as she had been determined to do ever since that day in early January when she had promised Felix Copley that she would, after all, marry him.

The seven bridesmaids followed her, bringing smiles from the congregation. Hilary smiled too, knowing that Stella had really wanted a quiet, simple wedding, with her sister Maddy and perhaps one or two smaller children to follow her. During the planning, though, it had become clear that keeping the number of bridesmaids down was going to be a difficult task; and to prevent an overpowering mass of one single colour they had finally settled on a mixture.

The idea of a rainbow – intended to brighten the January day originally fixed for the wedding – had been Felix's, and a colour was chosen to suit each bridesmaid. Now, six months later than originally planned, it brought the glowing brightness of June into the church.

Stella, at the head of the procession on Frank Budd's arm, was transformed into a beacon of clear white light in front of this blaze of colour. In a sheath of oyster satin, fitted closely from neck to waist and swirling out to a rippling circle of rich cream, she appeared even more slender than before the accident that had threatened to rob her of so much, and more than one person wiped a tear from their eye at the sight of her radiant face.

Her bouquet was of simple June flowers – foxgloves, campions and bluebells, frothed with Queen Anne's Lace and meadowsweet, all gathered from the hedgerows near the church. The lychgate and church door were also festooned with garlands of the same flowers, so that the simple beauty of the country lanes flowed seamlessly in through the ancient oak door. The church was lit by the sunshine streaming through the plain glass windows, while the bright colours of the bridesmaids' dresses were like patterns cast through stained glass.

Maddy, Stella's younger sister, and their friend Val Ferris came first, Maddy wearing the blue of a spire of delphinium and Val in the glowing red of a rose. They were followed by the two fourteen-year-olds, Maureen Budd and Felix's niece Pearl (known to her family as Button), in yellow and indigo, and Pearl's cousins, five-year-old Julie and Vivienne, in soft green and a violet so pale it was really lilac; and, finally, Janice Ruddicombe, the little girl chosen by her schoolmates from the class Stella taught, looking so much like an exotic flower in her dress of deep burnt orange, with a rosette tucked into her shining dark hair, that the limp caused by her heavy built-up boot passed without notice.

The brilliant cavalcade stopped as Stella reached the head of the aisle and Felix turned towards her. Hilary was close enough to hear him catch his breath and her eyes swam again at the tender delight in his eyes and the answering glow on Stella's face. For a tiny space of time there was no sound in the little church and she wondered, briefly and painfully, whether she would ever share such a moment with the man she loved; then, taking a determined grip on herself, she focused all her thoughts on the couple at the altar steps.

The bells, rung from behind the wrought-iron screen and gates at the west end, had ceased as Stella entered through the south door, and the swelling notes of the organ now faded to a trembling echo of their harmony. Like Hilary, the entire congregation seemed to be holding its breath and the two who were about to be married to be enclosed in the shining iridescence of a bubble.

Even through her own heartache, Hilary could wish them nothing but joy.

Chapter Two

Buarracombe, January 1954

It had been a relief to the whole of Burracombe when Stella Simmons, so badly injured in the accident with the Dartmoor ponies on that dark, cold December night, had finally agreed to marry Felix Copley.

'So the poor little maid's come to her senses,' said Stella's landlady, Dottie Friend, wiping a tear of relief from her eye with the corner of her pinafore when the little group came back from the hospital in Plymouth to give her the good news. 'Thank the Lord for that.' She reached up to put her arms around the young vicar standing just inside the door of her little cottage. 'Oh Felix, my dear, you must have wanted to go down on your knees and give thanks right there in the hospital when she told you.'

'I did,' he said feelingly. 'And while I was there, I proposed to her all over again, just to make sure. I'm not letting her get away this time.'

'He had witnesses, too,' Stephen Napier said, laughing. 'Hilary and Maddy and me – we all saw it. And we heard her say yes, so unless she wants to be sued for breach of promise ...'

'Mr Stephen!' Dottie exclaimed in horror. 'What a thing to say! Sued, indeed. Now, don't all stand there in the doorway, cluttering the place up. Sit down and have a cup of tea before you go back to the Barton. I dare say that's where you're all going, isn't it?'

'Not me,' Felix said, lifting the fat black cat off one of the sagging armchairs and sitting down with it on his lap. 'I'll have to be getting back to Little Burracombe, and before that I want to slip into the vicarage to see Basil and Grace and tell them the news. But I'll have a cup of tea first, please.'

'I won't stay,' Hilary said. 'I need to go home and see how my father is. I just wanted to come in and tell you first.'

'Oh, we'll stay for a bit,' Maddy said, reluctant to leave their old friend on her own so soon. 'There's so much to talk about now. We've got a wedding to plan again!'

'Well, not for a while,' Felix said. 'Stella's got a long road to travel before she can walk up the aisle, I'm afraid. I had a word with the doctor afterwards and he says it's going to take several months. They've got to be sure her broken leg's healed before they can know for certain if the paralysis really has gone, and then she'll have to learn to walk again, almost as if she were a baby. I don't think the wedding can be before June at the earliest.'

'We can still plan it,' Maddy said. 'It will be good for her to think about bridesmaids' dresses and flowers and things, not to mention her own dress. It'll give her something to do if she's got to be in hospital all that time.'

'As long as we don't tire her out,' Felix said, clearly still anxious.

'Of course we won't. It will only be short visits, and I'll have to be at West Lyme most of the time anyway – the Archdeacon has given me quite enough time off. And Stephen's got to come all the way from the air base at White Cheriton. But we'll come whenever we can, won't we, Stephen?'

Stephen nodded and accepted a cup of tea from Dottie. 'She'll probably get tired of seeing our faces at the door.' He glanced at Felix. 'How are you going to get there every day, Felix? It's not so easy without a car. I know there are trains and buses, but they take a long time, and you've got a parish to look after as well.'

'I've been thinking about that,' Hilary said, before Felix could answer. 'I don't see why we shouldn't lend him the little Austin. I hardly ever use it now – Travis and I share the Land Rover for estate work – and with Dad not able to drive until Charles Latimer says so, I can always use the Armstrong-Siddeley. It's quite all right,' she went on firmly as Felix began to object. 'Don't forget, if you hadn't kindly offered to go to Exeter to fetch Rob from the train, you'd never have had the accident in the first place. It's the least we can do. I don't know why I didn't think of it sooner. Anyway, there's to be no argument. I'll arrange the insurance and it's yours for as long as you need it.'

4

'That's really very kind of you,' Felix said. 'Thank you so much. It will make an enormous difference.'

'And you're not to use it just for visiting Stella,' she told him. 'Use it for your parish work as well. I know some of your parishioners live miles away and if you have to cycle to them it'll take you all day.'

'I shall be thoroughly spoilt,' he protested. 'I won't want to give it back at all if I get used to such luxury.'

'You'd have had a car already if Mirabelle hadn't been smashed up,' she pointed out. 'Anyway, your living is in the Burracombe gift, so it's for my father to say if you should have a car, and I think I know what he will say. I doubt if we'll be wanting it back. You won't want Stella overtaxing herself when she's your wife.'

Stephen laughed and Hilary gave him a stern glance, while Maddy punched him on the arm. Dottie lifted the teapot and offered to refill their cups, but Hilary shook her head.

'I'll be off now. I'll see you two later,' she said to Stephen and Maddy. 'You're coming for supper, aren't you? Dad will want to hear all the news.'

Her brother was stretched out in the other armchair, looking as if he'd settled in for the evening, but he nodded and said, 'We'll be there. I've got to go back to the airfield tonight, but I don't need to leave until half past eight. I'll drop Maddy back here then, if that's all right,' he said to Dottie. 'She's decided to go back to West Lyme on the early train tomorrow, so if she can stay here she can have the rest of the evening with you.'

'Of course it's all right. You know I love to have the maid here – both of them.' Dottie wiped her eyes again. 'It sounds as though it'll be long enough before Stella comes walking in through the door again, the dear of her.'

'But at least we know she will,' Maddy said comfortingly. 'When we left here this morning, none of us had any idea – or that she'd have changed her mind about marrying Felix. Now everything's different again – and for the better.'

Felix stood up and put the cat gently back on its cushion. 'I feel as though I've lived through a hundred years since this morning,' he said. 'Almost like the prince breaking through the thorny hedge to find his Sleeping Beauty.' He paused for a moment, considering, and then said in a tone of surprise, 'In fact, I think that's just what *has* happened. Maybe that's what the old fairy tale is all about – breaking through the thorny hedge of our doubts to be awakened by love. Do you know—'

'I think I feel a sermon coming on!' Stephen broke in with a grin. 'If you go over to Little Burracombe next Sunday, Dottie, you'll hear the whole thing in full. Go on, Vicar – go back and torment your own parishioners! We've got better things to think about. You're not the only man here who's engaged to one of the Simmons sisters, you know.'

Felix laughed. 'So I'm not. But you're right, I should go.' He turned to Hilary. 'I think perhaps I'll leave visiting the Harveys until tomorrow. They're bound to want me to stay to supper and to be honest I just want to go home, have a cheese sandwich and go to bed. I'll beg a lift to the end of your drive, if I may. I can walk down the footpath and across the Clam from there.'

'Indeed you will not,' she said firmly. 'I'll take you round by the main road. And tomorrow you can collect the Austin.' She kissed Maddy. 'I'll see you later. Thank you for the tea, Dottie.'

'And you won't just make yourself a cheese sandwich, either,' Dottie said, equally firmly. 'There's the best part of a cottage pie left in my larder – you can take that back with you and heat it up. You want something hot inside you in this cold weather.' She went to the larder, took out an enamel dish and put it in a basket. 'You can bring the pan back tomorrow.'

Hilary opened the door and went out. Felix kissed Maddy too, shook hands with Stephen and then put his arms around Dottie's plump figure.

'You're such a comfort, Dottie,' he said. 'I don't know what we'd do without you. Now, I'm going to the hospital again tomorrow and I'd like you to come too. You will be able to, won't you?'

'Go on, you don't want me with you,' she said, giving him a push. 'You and Stella will have far too much to talk about.'

'We'll want you as well,' he said firmly. 'Stella will want to see you. Don't forget what Maddy said just now – there's a wedding to plan, and dresses to talk about!'

Hilary took Felix to his vicarage in the village across the river, then drove back. She felt suddenly tired and dispirited. The excitement of

Stella's improvement had buoyed up her spirits, but, now that she was alone, her own troubles came seeping back into her mind like a cold grey mist, and she wondered if things would ever come right for her.

For her and David, she amended, as she turned off the main road into the narrow lane that wound for a mile to Burracombe. The situation was even worse for him. She didn't yet know how serious his wife's condition was – all he'd been able to tell her during the hurried phone call that morning, just before she'd had to leave for the hospital, was that Sybil had had a stroke. It might be a minor one, from which she would recover quite quickly, or it might be serious enough to disable her for the rest of her life. For all Hilary knew as she approached the drive of the Barton, Sybil might even be dead.

The thought struck as cold as ice into her heart. Horrifying though it was to find herself considering it, she could not help knowing that if Sybil died, the way would be left clear for herself and David to marry, without the scandal of a divorce, which, although Sybil herself had demanded it, would involve him in the distasteful process of providing 'evidence'. Evidence that would ruin his career as a doctor and, if – *when* – they married, Hilary's reputation simply through association, as well as, quite possibly, her father's health. Having a daughter married to a divorced man – a disgraced doctor at that – would be a shame he would never be able to tolerate.

And if Sybil didn't die? The speculation slid into her mind as appallingly as the other. I *can't* be wishing her dead, Hilary thought with a sense of self-disgust. Yet she could not help the thoughts crowding in upon her. Suppose Sybil remained helpless for years, as people with strokes often did? Hilary knew that Sybil's lover would be unlikely to marry her or take over her care in those circumstances. She would remain David's wife, and David would never be able to leave her.

The whole situation seemed impossible and, not for the first time, Hilary wished that she had never gone to the reunion where she had met David again, so many years after their first affair during the war. It had been brief and unfulfilled then, since they were both committed to other people, but on this second meeting their feelings had overpowered them and Hilary had found herself unable to hold back. She had cast all her scruples, all her inhibitions and all her upbringing to the winds and flung herself, part joyous and part guilty, into David's waiting arms.

Neither of us was cut out for this, she thought sadly. Neither of us is the type to have affairs, to be unfaithful. It's been worse for David than for me, because he had Sybil, even though she was never faithful to him. What must he be going through now, seeing her suffer and knowing that whatever happens it will be even harder for us both – but especially for him?

Suddenly, she knew that she needed to talk to someone else about this. Val was the only one who knew about David, though she did not yet know about Sybil's stroke, nor about the demands she'd been making for a divorce. Hilary hesitated, then drove past the gates of Burracombe Barton and turned back to the village, pulling up outside Jed's Cottage, where Val and Luke Ferris lived with their baby Christopher.

'Hilary!' Val said, opening the door. 'I've been wondering if you might pop in. How is she?'

Hilary stared at her for a moment before realising that she meant Stella. 'Oh, a lot better,' she said, following Val into the tiny back room and dropping into a chair. 'Well, maybe not a lot, but it's made a great deal of difference.' She told Val about the returning sensation in one of Stella's feet. 'I think he's trying not to show it – he just said it was a good sign – but the doctor's obviously very optimistic, and Felix is over the moon. Mainly because it seems to have brought Stella to her senses and she says she'll marry him after all.'

'Oh, that *is* good news!' Val exclaimed. 'So why are you looking as if you've lost a shilling and found sixpence?'

'I'm not, am I? Well, perhaps I am feeling a bit like that,' Hilary admitted. Then, quite without warning, her features crumpled and she covered her face with her hands. 'Oh *Val* ...'

'Hilary!' Val dropped to her knees beside her friend and put her arms around her. 'Whatever is it? Do you think there's something the doctor's not telling you? D'you think Stella knows it's worse and is just being brave? What—'

'No – no, it's nothing like that. It's not Stella at all.' Hilary lifted her face from her hands and felt in her pocket for a hanky. She blew her nose, wiped her eyes and said shakily, 'I'm sorry. I didn't mean to break down like that. But there's nobody else I can talk to. It's – it's ...' Her face crumpled again and she shook her head speechlessly.

'It's David, isn't it?' Val said quietly, taking hold of her hands. 'What's happened to him, Hil?'

'Nothing's happened – to him. But Sybil . . . Val, she's had a stroke!'

'A *stroke*? Oh my Lord.' Val sat back on her heels. 'How bad is it?'

'I don't know. I'll have to try to phone him tonight. I only found out just as we were leaving for the hospital, and that was all he had time to tell me.' Hilary shook her head again. 'I didn't even have time to think about it until I'd taken Felix back to the vicarage. It hit me on the way. I just had to come and talk to you. There's no one else . . .' Her voice trembled. 'I don't know what's going to happen now. He won't be able to go through with the divorce, anyway.'

'The divorce? What divorce?'

'Sybil wanted it,' Hilary said wearily. 'She'd found someone else – she's had a lot of lovers over the years, but this one wanted to marry her. But she didn't want to be the guilty party, of course, so David was going to have to do it.'

'And involve you?' Val stared at her, shocked. 'Hilary, that's awful!'

'No, he wouldn't involve me. He knew what it would mean. I'd have done it, mind,' she added fiercely. 'I wouldn't have cared about myself. But there's Dad to think about. The scandal of it all – it would be in the newspapers, all his friends would know, the whole village would know. It could kill him. I couldn't do that, even if David had let me. And I wouldn't let him do it the other way – a hotel room with some woman, and a maid giving fabricated evidence. It's so *sleazy*, Val.'

'So what . . .?'

'We didn't know,' Hilary said wryly. 'We were still talking about it. But something was going to have to be done, because Sybil had found out about us. Or suspected, anyway, and that's the same thing, because David wouldn't lie about it. And now . . .' She shrugged. 'Now, I just don't know. I don't even know if she's still alive. If she is, David will have to look after her. He won't have any choice.'

'But what about the other man?'

Hilary lifted one shoulder again. 'I don't suppose they'll see him for dust. Who would want to take on an invalid? Anyway, David's her husband. He's responsible for her, and he won't duck that. He's not that sort of man.'

'No,' Val said thoughtfully. 'No, he's not. Oh Hilary, what an awful mess.'

'It always was,' Hilary said drearily. 'Right from the start – when

9

I first saw him at the reunion. When we first met, all those years ago in Egypt. It was always a mess – and yet it always seemed so right for us to be together. But nobody else will understand that. I don't understand it myself, Val.'

'I know,' Val said, thinking of the difficult start her own relationship with Luke had had. 'Oh dear, Hilary, I wish I could say it'll all turn out right in the end, but I can't. I just can't see what's going to happen.'

'At least that's honest,' Hilary said. 'I'd rather that than have you say you're sure it will be all right, when you can't possibly know.' She drew in a deep breath. 'I ought to go home. Maddy and Steve will be in soon for supper, and Dad will be wondering where on earth I've got to.'

'There's someone with him, is there? Mrs Ellis?'

'Yes, but she'll be wanting to get home. I can't keep on taking advantage of her – she's not a nurse, after all.' Hilary rose to her feet. 'Oh, why does everything happen at once?'

'I don't know, but it always does.' Val gave her friend another hug. 'Don't let it get you down, Hilary. Ring David as soon as you can and find out what the situation is, and come down and let me know when you get a chance. I'll be thinking of you. Remember, I'm always here – or not far away, anyway.'

'I know.' Hilary gave her a grateful smile. 'I don't know what I'd do without you to turn to.'

'You've got more friends than you realise,' Val told her. 'But I know what you mean – there are some things you don't want to tell all and sundry. Anyway, you go home now and try not to worry too much. It's not going to make any difference to what happens to Sybil.'

Hilary nodded and went to the door. Outside, it was growing dark and she shivered and drew her coat more tightly around her. The early stars were obscured by flying rags of clouds and, as she glanced up at them, a thin, spiteful wind seemed to strike to her very bones. She wished she had worn a thicker coat, then wondered if it would have done any good anyway. It was as if there were no coat thick enough to keep this kind of cold from her heart.

It's like a portent, she thought. An omen of worse to come.

Chapter Three

Hilary reached the Barton to see all the lights on and, despite the cold, the front door wide open. Anxiously she hurried up the steps and into the hallway to find Mrs Ellis just emerging from the drawing room, where her father Gilbert Napier was now spending most of his time.

'I'm sorry to have been so long,' Hilary began, and then stopped short as she saw the housekeeper's face. 'Why, Mrs Ellis, what's wrong? Is it my father?' A wave of fear swept over her and she put out a shaking hand. 'He's not had another attack, has he?'

Mrs Ellis shook her head. 'It's not your father, Miss Hilary,' she said, and Hilary drew a quick breath of relief. But it was obvious that the housekeeper was upset, and she took the woman's arm and led her towards the kitchen. Closing the door behind them, she pressed her gently into a chair at the big wooden table and said quietly, 'What is it? What's happened?'

'It's my old mum,' Mrs Ellis said, her mouth working as she tried to keep from crying. 'She've had a fall and broken her arm. Her right one, too. My hubby took her to the hospital since I couldn't leave here, but I'll have to go to her now. I'm real sorry, Miss Hilary, but—'

'Of course you must go,' Hilary exclaimed, fresh waves of guilt washing over her. 'You ought to have gone at once. I'm sure someone would have come ...' She wondered who, knowing that the housekeeper was too loyal to call on just anyone to look after the Squire. 'Anyway, I'm here now, so you go and see your mother. How bad is she? Was there any other damage?'

'I don't rightly know. A few bruises, I dare say, and at her age

... If you don't mind then, I'll be off right away. She's in Tavistock hospital, so I can catch the bus if I hurry.'

'No, of course you mustn't go on the bus. There must be someone who will take you. The Tozers – there's bound to be someone around.' They'll begin to think they're running an ambulance service, she thought wryly. 'Or Travis – he'll probably be in the back office now. Do you know if he's come in?'

'I thought I heard him a while ago. But he'll be busy ...'

'Not too busy for this,' Hilary said firmly. 'I'd take you myself but I don't like to leave my father on his own. Wait here.' She ran through the house to the outer office, where the estate manager, Travis Kellaway, usually came last thing in the afternoon to make notes about the day's work and check on what might have cropped up during the day. To her relief, he was there, his head bent over a pile of government forms. He looked up as she burst in and began to say something in an exasperated voice, then stopped.

'What is it?' He was half on his feet. 'He's not had another—'

'No – no, it's not Dad. It's Mrs Ellis – her mother's had a fall and been taken to hospital. Could you take her there, please? She's in Tavistock. I'd go myself but I've only just got back from Plymouth.' She leaned on the desk and put her hand to her forehead, remembering how she had asked Val why everything happened at once.

Travis came round the desk and put his arm across her shoulders. He held her firmly for a moment, then said quietly, 'Of course I will. You go and make yourself a cup of tea and sit down – you look all in. Did you say you've only just got back? How is Stella?' He turned away and took his coat off the hook on the door.

'A lot better, thank God. She has some sensation in her feet and she seems much more optimistic. Oh, Felix is borrowing the Austin – I said I'd arrange the insurance for him.' She looked distractedly at the filing cabinet. 'I ought to do that at once. I'll need to ring the broker.'

'I'll do it when I come back. Is Mrs Ellis's husband around? Should I fetch him?'

'He took the old lady to the hospital, so he'll be there. You can come straight back. I think it's just a broken arm, but at her age ... She must be about eighty-five.' Another thought struck her. 'She won't be able to live alone for a while – if ever again. And I don't think there are any other children able to look after her. I'll need—'

'You need a cup of tea,' he said again, firmly. He patted his pockets for the key of the Land Rover. 'Go and make one, Hilary. Now.'

She smiled faintly. 'I'll have to make sure Dad's all right. I haven't even seen him since I came in.'

'I have. I looked in only half an hour ago and he was snoring his head off. You can have a few minutes to yourself.' He looked at her seriously. 'You need it, Hilary. You look as if you've had quite a shock.'

More than you know, she thought ruefully, but she nodded and said, 'Yes, all right. It's no use going in to see him in a state. And I'll have to think about what we're to do if we're going to be without Mrs Ellis for a while. She'll need to be with her mother ...' She put her hand to her forehead again and Travis took her by the shoulders and steered her out of the office.

'Go and fetch her. And tell her not to come back until she's ready. Jennifer will come and help you.'

'Jennifer? Will she really?'

'Of course she will. I'll call in at Wood Cottage on the way – it won't take us more than a few minutes. Then I can collect her on the way back.'

'Oh no!' Hilary exclaimed. 'You mustn't do that. She'll be busy – we can't impose ... I can manage perfectly well tonight. Mrs Ellis would have been going home anyway.'

'Tomorrow then,' he said. 'Here's Mrs Ellis now, with her coat on and ready to go.' He smiled at the housekeeper. 'Don't worry about a thing, Mrs Ellis. We'll be at the hospital in less than twenty minutes. Now, remember what I said, Hilary – a cup of strong, sweet tea and feet up for a quarter of an hour at least. I'll come in and see you when I get back.'

'Yes. All right. Thanks.' She watched as he led the anxious housekeeper towards the back door, and then made her way to the kitchen. Travis was right, tea would help to soothe the immediate shock. But in the long term?

It was going to take a lot more than a cup of tea to solve all the problems that seemed to be piling up around her.

Before making her tea, Hilary peeped into the drawing room to see her father. As Travis had said, he was dozing in his big wing chair with a rug across his knees, so she withdrew quietly and returned to the kitchen.

While the kettle came to the boil, she lit a cigarette and stood gazing out of the window. Hilary didn't often smoke but she had started while in Egypt during the war, when everyone smoked, and usually had a packet handy in case she felt the need. She felt it now, and lit another to have with her tea, which she carried to the table to drink. She rested both elbows on the scrubbed wood and smoked while she waited for the tea to cool.

What was she to do without Mrs Ellis? She knew she'd been guilty of taking advantage of the housekeeper's loyalty during the past weeks. First Marianne and her family coming for Christmas, then her father's second heart attack, and now this ... There was no doubt that they owed the poor woman time off to look after her mother, but how was Hilary to manage?

It's not just during the past few weeks either, she realised. We never replaced Jackie Tozer when she left to go and work at the Duke of Cornwall hotel in Plymouth. And I've been so keen to keep my hands on the reins of running the estate, I haven't been doing as much as I used to. We've been overworking Mrs Ellis for months.

Well, there was no help for it now. They would have to find help, not only in the house but also in looking after her father. It wasn't that he needed nursing care as such, but he certainly needed someone to be on hand when Hilary was out, and unless she gave up some of her estate work and stayed at home, there should be someone to take on the housekeeping and cooking tasks as well.

Unless she gave up some of her estate work ...

She groaned faintly and stubbed out her cigarette. Have I worked so hard and fought so much with Dad just to give it all up now? she asked herself. In principle, it need only be temporary – but would it stay that way? It had all happened before, when her mother was ill and she'd had to come home to look after her and take on running the household. It had taken her years to assert herself as someone capable of so much more. Was it all to be thrown away now?

She considered Travis's suggestion that his wife Jennifer should come to help. That was all very well, and Hilary knew she would be immensely grateful, but it couldn't be considered permanent. Jennifer had her own life to live and Hilary had wondered once or twice lately if she and Travis were about to start the family they both wanted. With a late marriage, there was never much time to delay. In any case, even if Jennifer was willing to help out until Mrs Ellis came back – if she did come back – there was still the question of extra help to fill the gap left by Jackie far too long ago. Someone who would help with the housework and be able to cope with an often irascible semi-invalid. Where were they to find someone like that, at short notice?

She was still sitting there when Stephen and Maddy came in, banging cheerfully through the back door and into the gun room. She heard their chatter as they took off their coats and turned quickly, half rising to her feet as her brother entered the kitchen.

'Hullo, having a cuppa and a ciggy?' he said. 'Don't blame you. It's been quite a day.'

You can say that again, Hilary thought, but all she said was, 'I'm afraid supper's going to be a bit late. Mrs Ellis has been called away – her mother's had a fall and broken her arm. I was just about to rustle something up myself.'

'Oh, poor Mrs Ellis,' Maddy exclaimed. 'I remember her mother – she used to sell apples at her front gate. She made us all toffee apples once. You must remember, Stephen.'

'I do. Haven't seen her for years now. She must be nearly a hundred years old.'

'Eighty-five,' Hilary said. 'The thing is, I don't know when Mrs Ellis will be able to come back. She'll need to look after the old lady. I'll have to look for a temporary housekeeper. And someone else, too, a young girl perhaps, or an older woman who wouldn't mind helping with Dad. There's too much for one person.'

'Well, let's get supper ready and think about it,' Maddy said. 'What was Mrs Ellis making, do you know?'

'I've no idea,' Hilary said, feeling suddenly helpless. 'I've hardly had time to think.' She passed her hand across her forehead. 'It seems to have been all illness and hospitals lately. Look in the oven – she might have left something there.'

Maddy opened the doors of both the ovens in the Aga and shook her head. 'Nope. Nothing here. Look in the pantry, Steve.'

'There's a pie,' he reported. 'Could be a meat pie, perhaps. Then again, it might be apple. Is there any way of telling, short of breaking into it?'

'She does different crimping round the edges,' Hilary said, and he brought it over to the table to show her. 'Meat, I think. I'm not sure I remember which way round it is now.' She felt tears come to her eyes. 'Oh, it's awful how much we depend on her!'

Stephen stared at her. 'No it isn't. She's our housekeeper. We pay her to do this. Hil, whatever's the matter? You look as if the sky's fallen in. It's only a pie.'

'It's *not* only a pie! It's – it's everything, all coming at once. Abe Endacott buying his farm. John Wolstencroft – Dad wants him here as soon as possible to make those changes to his will. That means an overnight stay, the spare bedroom to get ready, dinner to think about. Dad won't want me giving him beans on toast! And other things too ... things you don't even know about.' She caught herself up and bit her lip. 'I'm sorry. I'm being stupid. Of course it doesn't matter whether it's meat or apple. Look, dig a knife in and see how it comes out.' She blinked and rubbed her eyes as her brother went to the drawer for a knife. 'There. Meat. So all we need do is put it into the oven and do some vegetables.'

'They're done, except for potatoes,' Maddy said, emerging from the pantry. 'Cabbage and carrots. Come on, Steve, let's do a bit of spud-bashing. It'll be ready in no time and we'll eat out here, shall we? Oh – what about your father?'

'I don't expect he'll mind. We often have kitchen supper. I'd better go and see how he is and tell him about Mrs Ellis.' Hilary got up, leaving her brother and Maddy cheerfully peeling potatoes together. They look so happy, she thought, pausing at the door. None of these things seem like problems to them. And they're right, really. It's just that whatever I do, the thought of David overshadows everything. David and Sybil ...

Stephen glanced round suddenly. For a moment, they stared at each other, and Hilary knew that he was aware there was something troubling her. What had she said? *Things you don't even know about ...* She'd hoped he and Maddy had missed that, but Stephen at least had noticed. And he intended to ask her what she had meant. His steady gaze told her that.

Could she tell him about David? Would he understand? After his experience with Marianne, she thought he might. Yet she wasn't at all sure that she wanted to confess, even to her brother. Val already knew, and the more people who learned the truth, the more dangerous it became.

She turned away and went quickly through the door, closing it behind her.

Chapter Four

'Patsy Shillabeer,' Felix said.

'Patsy who?' Hilary asked. Felix had heard about Mrs Ellis's mother and called in after morning service, on his way to Sunday dinner with the Harveys. He had found Hilary still racking her brains about how to get help in the house. 'Is she one of the Shillabeers from Town Farm?'

'That's right. Their eldest. She left school last summer and found a job in Pillar's, in Tavistock, but her father didn't like her working in town so she's had to leave. Not very happy about it either, by all accounts.'

'I don't suppose she is. What's Percy Shillabeer got against Tavistock? It's not exactly a den of iniquity, and Pillar's is a respectable newsagent's shop.'

'You know that,' Felix said, 'and I know that, but maybe Percy knows something different – or thinks he does! Anyway, the girl left just before Christmas and now she's kicking her heels at home. Well, not kicking her heels – her father and mother find her plenty to do around the farm – but certainly wishing she were somewhere else.'

Hilary gazed at him. 'D'you know much about her? D'you think she'd be suitable?'

'She seems a pleasant, quiet sort of girl,' he said cautiously. 'I saw a bit of the family when I was helping John Berry, before he died. The father's something of a Tartar – very strict. He used to be Chapel until he fell out with the minister. The mother comes to church as often as she can and usually brings the children with her. Patsy seems to be quite a help to her.'

'The mother probably won't want her to get another job, then,' Hilary said gloomily. 'She'll be too useful at home.'

17

'It's worth a try,' he said encouragingly. 'Would you like me to look in on my way back?'

'Oh Felix, would you? It would certainly be a load off my mind. And tell them it would be a permanent position – even when, or *if*, Mrs Ellis comes back, I still want her to have more help.'

'Do you think she might not come back, then?'

Hilary spread her hands. 'I don't know. The old lady's going to need quite a lot of care and attention when she comes home, which will probably be in the next few days. And it's not as if they really need the money – Mr Ellis has got a good job at the railway and she's been thinking about retiring when he does, in a year or two. I wouldn't be surprised if she decides to call it a day now.'

'Well, I'm a great believer in crossing bridges when you come to them,' Felix said encouragingly. 'I'm sure she'll give you ample notice if she does decide to retire. Meanwhile, I think Patsy would take some of the load off your shoulders, and if Jennifer Kellaway comes in as well—'

'Oh, but I can't impose on Jennifer. Not for more than a few days, anyway. I really do need to find somebody else for the cooking and general running of the household. I can do a lot myself, of course, so it needn't be full time, but I must have somebody.'

'Yes.' Felix gazed at her thoughtfully and seemed about to speak, then changed his mind and got up. 'Well, I promise I'll give it some thought. Now, I must go or Grace Harvey will think I don't like her roast pork and apple sauce, and that's very far from the truth. And then I'm going to Plymouth to see Stella. Thank you again for the loan of the car, Hilary. You're sure it's all right about the insurance?'

'Oh yes, you can drive it on yours until I get it sorted out. It shouldn't take more than a few days.' She smiled at him. 'Look on it as your own, Felix. It's the least we can do. And give Stella my love.'

'I will.' He paused and then stepped nearer and gave her a quick kiss on the cheek. 'Bear up, Hilary. You look as if you're carrying the woes of the world on your shoulders. It's not really that bad, you know.'

'No,' she said, smiling faintly, 'I don't suppose it is.'

She watched him go and then drew in a deep breath. Now, at last, it might be an opportune moment to ring David and find out how he was. And how Sybil was, too; whether she was still alive, or whether he was even now a widower.

'She's still deeply unconscious,' David said, his voice weary. 'Her doctor can't say if she'll ever come round. It depends where the bleeding is in the brain.'

'Can't they tell?'

'Not accurately, no. All we can do is wait for her to wake and then see what the effects have been. But the longer she's unconscious, the worse the outlook is. She could be completely paralysed – unable to move, unable to speak, unable to do anything.'

'Oh David.' Hilary felt a wave of helpless misery sweep over her. 'And could that last a long time?'

'Yes, it could.' He sounded as hopeless as she felt. 'Hilary – darling – I don't know what we're going to do.'

'We can't do anything,' she said miserably. 'You can't leave her now. Unless the other man ...'

'Oh, he's out of the picture completely. He was upset, of course, but what can he do? He can't be expected to take on an invalid. Anyway, she's my wife and my responsibility.'

Hilary was silent for a moment. Then she asked, 'Has he seen her? Did he come to the hospital?'

'Yes. I contacted him and he came at once.'

'You've *met* him? But that must have been awful.'

'It was a bit awkward,' he acknowledged. 'But I could see he cared for her. It wasn't the time for recrimination. We just had to be objective about it.'

'*Objective?* With Sybil lying unconscious?'

'It was the only way. It wasn't easy, but what else could we do? To tell you the truth, I felt sorry for the chap. Almost as sorry as I'd have felt for him if it hadn't happened and he'd ended up married to her.'

It was the first time Hilary had heard any hint of bitterness in his voice. She rested her elbow on the desk and leaned her head on her hand. 'Oh David ... What are we going to do?'

'I don't know,' he said. 'I really don't know.'

There was a silence. Then she said, 'So he's gone? He's not coming back?'

'Probably not. I made it clear that I was taking full responsibility, as her husband, and that there was no place for him. If she recovers enough to want to contact him, she'll do so – but I don't think it's likely.'

The tiny flicker of hope that his words had lit in her heart dwindled and died. But even if it did happen, she thought, they would be no further forward. A divorce would be just as impossible as it had been before – more so, in fact. David was even more firmly chained to his wife, whether she recovered or not.

'I can't see any way out of this,' she said at last. 'We're never going to be together. We'd better stop now.'

'No!' His cry of anguish tore at her heart. 'Darling, don't say that. I can't go on at all if you're not there. Just to talk to – to meet sometimes ...'

'David, you know we can't do that.'

'We can. We must.' His voice was desperate. 'If only two or three times a year – something to keep us both going. A couple of days in London. We can both do that. Please, Hilary.'

'And what if someone sees us? One of your patients – someone who knows you? It could destroy your career.'

'London's a big place.'

'Not too big for Ted Tozer's brother Joe and his son Russell to have seen us last time. Twice – once in Piccadilly Circus and once in Hyde Park. And they're staying at the farm, practically next door to me. It might be *your* next-door neighbour next time.'

'Somewhere else, then. We can't let it end like this.'

'David, we have to. You've got Sybil to think of now. You say you told this other man that you were taking full responsibility for her as your wife. That means ...' She drew a deep breath. 'That means keeping faith with her. Even if she's not capable of appreciating it.'

'She never did appreciate it,' he said, the bitterness back in his voice.

'I know. But it's different now. She's completely dependent on you.' She paused again and added quietly, 'For better, for worse.'

'In sickness and in health,' he agreed wryly. 'We don't have to quote the whole marriage service. I know it all too well. But can't we meet just as friends? Can't I ever talk to you again? Are you really saying all that's over?'

Hilary hesitated. There was a bleakness in his voice now that made her feel afraid. She had a sudden picture of David's life as it had become – as desolate as the high moors that lifted behind the valley of Burracombe, as dark and featureless as they appeared in winter, when the gorse had ceased to flower except for the odd bright spot of gold that gave rise to the old rhyme, *When gorse is out of season, kissing's out of reason*; when the heather had lost its royal purple and the bracken had dwindled to a few dun stalks and the sky was ominous with lowering clouds that threatened the harshness of January and February and a bitter chill that seemed to last for ever.

It was those spots of gold he was asking for, no more. Could she deny him those? Could she deny herself?

'Ring me again, David,' she said quietly. 'Just to let me know how she is. But no more than that, please. And not too soon. I don't think I could bear it.'

Felix was as good as his word and brought Patsy Shillabeer and her father to the Barton to see Hilary on Monday morning. Patsy was a thin, pale-skinned girl with hair so fair it was almost silver. It hung down past her shoulders, as straight as a yard of pump-water, as Alice Tozer would have said. Her one claim to beauty was a pair of huge grey eyes with a glint in them that almost matched the silvery gleam of her hair, fringed with long black lashes.

She must take after her mother, Hilary thought, taking in the sturdy bulk of her father with his black hair, shot with grey, and dark eyes. They held hers with a hint of challenge and she thought that this was not a man to be trifled with. Not that she intended to trifle with him, or indeed have anything much to do with him. It was his daughter she was thinking of employing, not him. She wondered why he, rather than the mother, had accompanied the girl.

'So you're looking for a job,' she said to Patsy, seating them both at the kitchen table. Jennifer Kellaway was there too, chopping vegetables for a beef casserole. 'I understand you worked in Pillar's for a time.'

'That's right, she did,' her father answered for her. 'Did well, too. All my youngsters know how to do a proper job of work. Been brought up that way.'

'So why did you leave?' Hilary asked, and again the father replied.

'I didn't like some of the people she was having to mix with. You get all sorts in a newsagent's, buying their papers and sweets and all that. *And* cigarettes. I don't hold with smoking. Nor strong drink. I wasn't having any daughter of mine mixed up with that kind of thing.'

Hilary gazed at him, wondering guiltily if her own cigarettes were on view. She'd smoked one or two out here in the kitchen on Saturday afternoon. But then she remembered putting them back in her handbag and breathed a sigh of relief.

She turned back to Patsy, hoping that the girl would be allowed to speak for herself. 'And do you think you'll like being in service?'

'She'll like it,' her father said grimly. 'If she knows what's good for her.'

Hilary felt slightly helpless. It didn't look as if she was going to get a word out of the girl while her father was here. She caught Felix's eye and looked hastily away. Another idea came to her.

'Suppose we give each other a trial,' she said brightly. 'You stay here for today and see how you like it. And I'll be able to have a chat with you and see if you're suitable.' She glanced at Percy Shillabeer, hoping he wouldn't insist on staying too, but to her relief he seemed to find this acceptable.

'You'll pay her for her time, I take it?'

'Of course,' Hilary said. 'And we can discuss her hours and pay as well.'

'Eight in the morning until six at night,' he said inflexibly. 'And her dinner thrown in. She can have her supper at home with the rest of us. One pound ten shillings a week, more if you wants her at weekends. And if you wants her wearing a uniform, you'd better see to it yourself. We got nothing of that sort at home.'

'Yes, of course,' Hilary said faintly. 'Well, that seems very satisfactory. I'll let you know if she's suitable when you come to collect her at six.' She had given up addressing her remarks to Patsy herself.

'She'll be suitable,' Percy Shillabeer stated with a dark look, and Hilary half expected him to add *if you know what's good for you.* 'Her mother and me have made sure of that.'

'Yes, of course,' Hilary said feebly, wondering if anyone ever had the temerity to stand up to this man. She moved towards the back door and he took the hint and put on the cap he had removed when he entered.

As he went out, he turned and gave his daughter one of his threatening looks. 'You behave yourself, mind. You'm only on trial, and if I finds out you been giving Miss Napier any of your lip, you'll have me and your mother to answer to.'

Lip? Hilary looked at the girl with some surprise. But Patsy seemed no more inclined to speak than she had when her father was present. She sat at the kitchen table, staring down at her hands, a deep blush rising up her neck and spreading over her face, and Hilary felt suddenly sorry for her. She went over and laid her hand on the girl's shoulder.

'I'm sure you'll suit us very well,' she said gently. 'Now, why don't you start by helping Mrs Kellaway with the vegetables, and then I'll show you round the house and explain what you'll be expected to do. It'll be rather different from working in the newsagent's shop.'

Patsy looked up at last and met her gaze, and Hilary was struck again by how attractive her eyes were. They seemed to light up the thin, pale face. 'I think 'tis lovely, Miss Napier. I've never been in a house like this before. I hope you'll let me stay and work here.'

Why, her voice is as sweet as a lark's, Hilary thought. I wonder if she can sing too. She's a dear little thing, and if something were done to that hair and she had a pretty dress on, she'd look quite different.

'I'm sure we will,' she said, smiling. 'But we've got to give each other a fair trial first. Let's wait until this afternoon before we decide, shall we? I'll leave you now to help Mrs Kellaway while I go and do some of my own work.'

She slipped through the green baize door to the house, followed by Felix. In the hall, she turned to him and said, 'What a sweet little thing she is! And what an awful father. No wonder she's like a church mouse when he's around.'

'He is a bit overwhelming,' Felix agreed. 'Brought up Chapel, as I told you, and came to the Church of England after some sort of falling-out. But he sticks by his Chapel principles and he's a good man, if a trifle strict. I'm surprised you don't already know him.'

'Well, I do slightly, but he's not one of our tenants so I've never really had anything to do with him. I hope she turns out to be a good worker. I'd like to keep her on, if only to get her out of his way for a good part of each day.'

'Oh, I'm sure she will,' Felix said gravely, and added with a twinkle, '*If she knows what's good for her.*'

Hilary laughed. 'You're as bad as ever, Felix! It's obvious you're not nearly as worried about Stella as you were. It's good to hear you joking again.'

He smiled, then grew grave again. 'I do feel more myself. But we've got a long way to go yet, Hilary, and it's poor darling Stella who is going to have to do all the hard work. She'll still be in plaster for two or three more weeks but she's going to have to start doing exercises soon and learning to walk again. It's not going to be easy for her.'

'She'll have you and all of us to support her,' Hilary told him as they reached the front door. 'That's what will help her most.'

She saw him off and made her way to the office, already considering her day's work. Her first task was to ring John Wolstencroft's office in Exeter to arrange his visit to change her father's will. They could put the legal process of selling Abraham Endacott his farm into action at the same time.

The news that Gilbert had decided to bequeath the estate equally to herself and Stephen after all had come as a complete surprise and she wondered whether he would really go through with it. He had been so set on leaving everything to his half-French grandson Robert, who had turned up suddenly out of the blue, just as if Rob's father Baden, Hilary's elder brother, had never been killed in the retreat to Dunkirk and had lived to inherit. There was a logic in this, for Rob would have been the natural successor, but his life had been too different, his existence not even known to the family until recently, for him ever to feel at ease with Burracombe and its ways, and he was old enough now to have developed his own interests and ambitions.

It had been difficult for Colonel Napier to come to terms with this. Rob was physically so like Baden, whose death had brought such grief, that Gilbert had come almost to regard him as his son. He had tried, without quite realising it, to force Rob into the same mould, and it was not until the unhappy boy had run away from school and tried to make his way back to France, resulting in the accident that had nearly robbed Stella Simmons of her life, that Gilbert had been shocked into the understanding of what he had done.

Even so, Hilary and Stephen had both been surprised by his declaration, and she still wasn't sure that he really meant it. I hope Father's not going to turn into one of those people who change their wills with the weather, she thought. But John Wolstencroft is a good man. He won't let him do anything silly. Letting Abe have his farm is a sensible idea. It's too far from the rest of the estate. And Stephen and Maddy will be glad of Steve's share of the money when he comes out of the

RAF. It'll help them to be independent, whatever they decide to do.

David, never far from her thoughts, came once again to the fore and she wondered what support he was receiving. Whatever it was, she knew that it was hers he yearned for most; yet how could she give it to him, other than by telephone? And even that she was denying him, asking him not to ring again too soon.

I'm being cruel, she thought. Maybe it is wrong to keep up our relationship, but what harm can it do to Sybil now for him just to talk to me? If it helps him, surely it must help her too. Or am I being disingenuous?

She would telephone him again herself. Not tonight, maybe not tomorrow, but soon. She had seen how Felix had suffered during these past weeks, and although David's situation was different, the suffering was as deep. She could not let him go through it alone.

Chapter Five

'The dear maid,' Alice Tozer said when her daughter Val came up to the farm to give her the good news that Stella would almost certainly walk again. 'Brave as a little lion, her be. 'Tis no wonder poor Felix didn't want to let her go.'

'It's going to be a long job,' Val said. 'One leg's still in plaster and she'll have to learn to walk again. But she'll do it, now she's made up her mind. And at least it means Dottie's got more time to finish our bridesmaids' frocks!'

'I'm not so sure about that,' Alice said a trifle grimly. She finished ironing one of Ted's work shirts and folded it neatly before taking up a blouse belonging to her mother-in-law. 'Not if her's going off to America with Joe and Russell and our Jackie. A good six weeks she'll be away, and that's if her don't decide to stay there and turn herself into another auntie for you.'

'Mum!' Val protested, laughing. 'You don't really believe there's any chance of that, do you?'

Alice stood the iron on its heel and looked at her. 'After what I've seen these past few months, I'd believe almost anything,' she stated. 'What with that young French tacker turning up at the Barton and looking to inherit the whole blessed estate over Hilary and Stephen's heads, and Jennifer Tucker coming out here to look for her father and finding out 'twas the last person any of us would have thought, and our Jackie holding us to ransom over going to America herself, no matter what me and your father thought about it – not to mention young Maddy Forsyth getting engaged to Stephen Napier when us all thought that was over long ago – well, after all that, the idea of Dottie marrying our Joe don't seem nothing out of the way at all. They was

26

sweet on each other before he went off to America in the first place, back in 1919 – sweeter than us realised at the time, I reckon.'

'Go on,' Val said, still smiling. 'They're both in their sixties now. They won't be thinking of getting married.'

'I don't know what *you* think they might be thinking of, then,' Alice said tartly. 'And sixty's not too old to be marrying anyway. Look at that couple over to Mary Tavy, getting married in their eighties!'

'Yes, and look what you said about them,' Val replied. 'Ought to know better at their age – wasn't that it? Honestly, Mum, I don't think you need worry about Dottie and Uncle Joe.'

'It's not them I'm worrying about,' Alice said darkly, going on with her ironing. 'They'm big enough and ugly enough to make up their own minds, as the saying goes. It's our Jackie that bothers me – as you well know.'

Val sighed. The discussions about her younger sister Jackie and her trip to America to stay with her uncle Joe and his grown-up children, Russ and his sisters, had gone on and on, round and round in circles, until at last Jackie had worn their mother and father down and got her way.

In some ways, Val knew, Alice was almost as excited as Jackie herself, helping with the planning, writing to Joe's daughters, learning more about the New York State town of Corning where they lived, but when she stopped to think about what it meant to herself, she felt her heart sink and knew that her deepest fears were that Jackie would find herself in some kind of trouble, so far away from her family and everything that was familiar to her. Or even that she might decide to stay there and never come back.

Val understood this. A mother herself now, she knew that the thought of her son Christopher's ever leaving her was like a pain in her heart. But she knew too that it was almost inevitable. Children did grow up and leave their parents. Uncle Joe had done so himself, her own husband Luke too – although he'd not actually gone abroad. And her brother Brian, now in Germany in the army, didn't seem likely ever to return to Burracombe to live. And since the war, it had happened even more, with people now emigrating to countries like Canada and Australia. Why, even Stephen Napier had been talking of emigration when he finished his National Service and left the RAF.

'Uncle Joe will look after her,' she said comfortingly. 'And she's going to stay part of the time with his daughters. They won't let her come to any harm.'

'They don't know our Jackie, though, do they?' Alice pointed out. 'Headstrong as a clutch of kittens, she be. Me and your father have never been happy about her going off to live in Plymouth, and now to think of her thousands of miles away in America ...' She held up a large bed sheet. 'Help me fold this up, if you don't mind.'

Val rose and laid Christopher down in his pram, which was standing near the back door. She took one end of the sheet and together they folded it so that it was a manageable size for ironing.

'Yes, but for all your worrying, Jackie never came to any harm in Plymouth, did she?' she said. 'If you ask me, she's grown up quite a lot through being responsible for herself and it's been good training for going away. I think she's got more sense than you give her credit for, and you ought to trust her.'

Alice bridled. 'You sound as if you think it's a good thing for a young girl to go away from her family.'

'Well, maybe it is. Things are different now, Mum. People do move about more and young women are getting more independence. After all, a lot of us had to do it during the war. I did. Hilary Napier did.'

'Hilary Napier's a different class from us. She'd been to boarding school, for a start. And I don't know as it did *you* a lot of good, going off to Egypt the way you did.' She gave Val a meaningful look, and Val groaned inwardly, regretting yet again that she'd confessed to her mother about her affair with Luke during that time, and its tragic consequences. There were some things it was better for a mother not to know. And she knew that Alice herself was well aware of this – no doubt she'd kept a few secrets from her own mother – and this was the source of her worries about Jackie.

'I think you just have to trust her,' she repeated. 'Otherwise you'll never have a minute's peace. She's going, Mum, and that's really all there is to it.'

Alice sniffed but said no more, and Val reverted to the subject of Stella, or rather to the consequences of her accident.

'How does young Robin like the new schoolmistress? She looks a bit of a battleaxe for an infant teacher.'

'Face like a bag of spanners, that's how our Tom described her,' Alice agreed. 'And I know Joanna's not very keen on her, but you know what Joanna's like since baby Suzanne died – hardly likes to let either Robin or Heather out of her sight. Tom tries to make sure she gives the little tacker some independence – he's five years old, after all, so he needs to find his feet. As for Miss Watkins she's got plenty of experience by all accounts – been in a few schools, they say – so she must be all right, I suppose.'

'Been in a few schools? That doesn't sound so good – as if she moves about rather a lot. Maybe they didn't like her.'

'Well, she seems to have settled in Tavistock now, so we hope she'll stay. Comes in on the bus each day.' Alice gave the sheet its last fold and rubbed the iron over it, frowning a little. 'Mind you, Robin don't seem all that keen to go to school these days, but I reckon they'm all missing Stella. They did love her.'

'Mrs Warren did a good job of helping before Christmas,' Val observed. 'I was quite surprised by her. And Mrs Harvey was lovely. What a shame neither of them was able to go on teaching when they were younger.'

'They both got married and had husbands to look after, that's why,' Alice said tartly. 'And quite right too. I hope you don't think of going back to nursing when Christopher gets bigger.'

'We'll have to see, won't we?' Val said equably, knowing that she and Luke would make up their own minds about this. Jackie wasn't the only one in the family who knew her own mind. 'Anyway, Christopher's not going to be the only one. It'll probably be years before I'm free to do anything like that, and I'll be too old by then.'

Alice paused, her iron suspended over one of Ted's handkerchiefs, and stared at her. 'Why, however many do you mean to have? After what happened to you this time, I'm surprised you're considering any more at all.'

'Eclampsia's not something that happens every time. And Luke and I both want more. Not just yet, though,' she said, casting a fond glance towards the pram. 'We want to enjoy Christopher for a while longer first.'

'Well, that's something.' Alice held up her iron suddenly, as if addressing a crowd and calling for silence. 'But I'll tell you who I think *is* expecting, and that's Jennifer Kellaway!'

'Jennifer? Are you sure? She hasn't said a word to me and I saw her only a few days ago.'

'I don't reckon she's said anything to anyone yet, not even her own hubby, but I saw her in Tavi pannier market last Friday and I thought then she'd got a look about her. You know, I can always tell.'

Not always, thank goodness, Val thought, remembering Jackie's scare with Roy Pettifer a few years ago. But then Jackie hadn't been pregnant after all, so she wouldn't have had the 'look' that Alice noticed.

'Well, I know Jennifer and Travis are keen to start a family fairly soon,' she said. 'But we'd better wait until it's official before we mention it to too many people. You know what happened when Ivy Sweet saw them looking in the jeweller's window in Tavi, and the village had them engaged and the wedding date set before they got back to the village. Jennifer told me she thought Jacob would never forgive them for not telling him first, even though that was what they meant to do.'

'You don't catch me gossiping,' Alice said a little stiffly. 'Especially not to the likes of Ivy Sweet.'

Val grinned. 'I'll put the kettle on, shall I? You've nearly finished your ironing and Dad'll be in soon to have a cup before he starts milking. And then I'll have to be getting home, to get my husband's tea ready, like the good wife I am.'

Alice looked at her suspiciously, as if she thought Val was mocking her, then smiled. 'All right, maid, you do that. I can't say I'm not ready for a cup.' She looked at the pile of freshly ironed clothes. 'You know, the worst thing about ironing is that you finds a lot of mending to do as well. I don't know what your dad does to his working shirts, but all the sleeves have got tears in them.'

'He works in them, I suppose,' Val said, pumping water at the sink to fill the kettle. 'They get caught on brambles and things.'

'In January? I'd have thought he'd have too many jumpers and jackets on for brambles to get through to his shirt sleeves. Anyway, the brambles have all died down long ago. Oh well, just one of life's many mysteries, I suppose, and it'll give me something to do this evening while I'm listening to *Take It From Here*.' She folded the last hanky, gave it a final rub and added it to the pile, then set the iron on the wooden draining board to cool down. 'I'll just fold up this board and put it away and then I'll have a sit-down. Your gran will be down soon too.'

Val made the tea and got out the biscuit tin. It was filled with fresh biscuits made by Minnie, who still liked to do her bit around the house – or at least, in the kitchen. At almost ninety, she had been persuaded at last to have an afternoon rest on her bed, but apart from that, she had declared her intention to wear herself out rather than rust away, and Val knew it gave her a lot of pleasure to see the family enjoying her baking just as they'd always done.

Jennifer's helping out at the Barton this week, she thought. I wonder if Hilary's noticed anything. Maybe I'll stroll up there one afternoon, to see how they're getting on without Mrs Ellis. They probably need some more help. And it would be nice to know if Mum's right. It will be lovely if Jennifer really is expecting a baby.

Joanna Tozer had walked down to the school to meet Robin, with Heather in the pushchair. It was a cold afternoon and the little girl was well wrapped up in a coat and bonnet knitted by Alice. Her round, cheerful face smiled at her mother over the mound of blankets Joanna had piled on top of her, and Joanna wondered if she ever missed her sister Suzanne. Did babies know they were twins, and did Heather realise that her twin had disappeared from her life? We'll have to tell her one day that Suzanne died suddenly in her pram when they were both tiny, Joanna thought. I wonder how she'll feel about it. Perhaps it would be better not to tell her. It might frighten and worry her.

Other mothers were waiting at the school gate and greeted Joanna as she appeared. Maisie Crocker was looking tired but cheerful enough as she waited for her own twins, George and Edward, and Maggie Culliford looked as if she'd been thrown together in her old grey coat, too skimpy for this weather, with her hair in a tangle round her thin face. She was expecting yet again, Joanna noticed. How many would that be? Eight? Nine? Nobody seemed to know how many children the Cullifords had, they came along so fast, and each new arrival stretched the family's tight purse strings even closer to breaking point. It was no wonder Arthur, who never had a proper job, eked out their precarious living by poaching.

The school door opened and the children tumbled out. The infants – aged from five to seven – came out fifteen minutes earlier than the bigger children and made straight for their mothers, most of them waving sheets of paper with crayoned pictures on them. George and Edward Crocker, who were identical and took advantage of it, hadn't put on their coats, so their names could be seen knitted boldly across the fronts of their jumpers. This was supposed to help their teacher identify them, but since they were perfectly capable of swapping jumpers in the school lavatory, it could never be relied upon. When Stella had been teaching them she had more or less given up and treated them as one boy, even though she had been told this could damage them psychologically. Stella's opinion was that the Crocker twins were too tough ever to be damaged, psychologically or otherwise.

Betty Culliford came out looking remarkably clean and tidy, for a Culliford, and made her way daintily across the playground. Like her older sister Shirley, Betty was quite a bright little girl and had been repaying the extra attention given her by Stella, but today she looked miserable and hid her face in Maggie's coat.

'Whatever be the matter, maid?' Maggie asked, looking down at her. 'Not been in trouble, have you?'

'We've all been in trouble,' said the Crocker twin wearing the 'George' jumper. 'For talking while we was supposed to be doing our pictures.'

'I thought you were allowed to talk then,' Joanna said, watching Robin coming slowly towards her. He looked a bit downcast too. 'Surely Miss Simmons let you talk to each other when you were crayoning.'

'Yes, but Miss Watkins don't. Her don't like us talking any time unless it's to answer questions. Us has to stand in the corner if we do.' George grinned. 'Only trouble today was, there wasn't enough corners!'

'Maybe someone ought to say something to her,' Joanna said doubtfully. 'It does seem rather hard to expect these babies to stay quiet all that time.'

'I got to go and see her,' Maggie Culliford said. 'I want to ask if she can take my Billy in early. He's not five till July, but what with two other little ones at home and another little stranger on the way, it'd make things a sight easier for me if he was at school too.'

'It's Miss Kemp you ought to ask,' Joanna said. 'She's the head teacher. Miss Watkins is only temporary anyway – she wouldn't be able to say.'

'I suppose so. I'd better wait a bit then, till her class comes out.' Maggie shivered and Joanna felt sorry for her. She looked cold and underfed, despite her thickening waist, and Joanna wondered how she could possibly cope with yet another baby in that tumbledown little cottage at the end of the village. Maggie tried her best for the family, there was no doubt about that, but she received little help from her feckless husband, and she always had a cigarette hanging off her lip. Joanna had heard Joyce Warren speak to her quite sharply about it once, when Maggie had been in the shop asking for her weekly bill to be put on the slate, and told her that if she stopped smoking, she'd have more money for important things like food for the children, but Maggie had simply told the solicitor's wife that it was her one pleasure and she didn't mean to give it up. She was rolling herself a fresh one now, her fingertips stained orange from the nicotine, and Joanna turned away and held out her hand to Robin.

'Come on, Robin, don't be so slow. It's too cold to stand about.' She looked at him more closely. 'Have you been crying?'

'A bit,' he muttered, and wiped his nose on his sleeve.

'Don't do that! Use your hanky.' She softened her voice. 'What's the matter? You haven't fallen out with your friends, have you?'

He glanced over his shoulder. Miss Watkins was standing at the door, watching Maggie Culliford walk across the playground. Robin shook his head.

'What is it, then? Have you been in trouble? Has teacher been cross with you?'

His eyes filled with tears but he wouldn't answer. Joanna sighed. 'Well, I don't suppose it was all that much. She'll have forgotten about it tomorrow. Let's go home. Great-Granny's made some of your favourite biscuits.'

They walked back through the village with some of the other mothers. Heather clamoured to be allowed out of her pushchair, and Joanna unfastened her reins and let her toddle beside her. The other children skipped ahead of them, but Robin walked slowly, holding the handle of the pushchair. Joanna glanced at him once or twice but knew he wouldn't tell her what had happened. She felt a pang of sadness. Robin was only five, but already he had begun to grow away from her. He had his own life now, his school life, where she could not enter. He was no longer her baby.

She thought of her mother-in-law, having to watch her youngest child go off to America, and understood a little of what Alice must be feeling. The day would come when Robin would leave as well. Of course, he might decide to stay on the farm, as they all hoped he would, but these days you never knew what might happen. Farming was changing, just as everything else was now, and the war seemed to have hurried the changes along. People didn't always stay where they'd grown up. Joanna hadn't herself – she'd come here as a Land Girl and then fallen in love with Tom when he'd come home from the war, and stayed. But Tom's brother Brian hadn't returned. He was still in the army, stationed in Germany, and although he was due to come out soon, he might well decide to stay on for a further term. Even if he left, he wouldn't be coming to make his home in Burracombe.

'What sort of biscuits?' Robin asked suddenly, and she looked down at him, bemused. 'What sort of biscuits did Great-Granny make?' he repeated impatiently, and Joanna laughed.

'I'd forgotten I said that. Orange shortbread and melting moments, with oats on. And we'd better hurry up, because your auntie Val was there when I came out, and you know she likes them too.'

Robin quickened his steps and Joanna smiled, feeling relieved. Whatever it was that had happened in school, he'd forgotten it now. As she'd thought, it couldn't have been anything very serious. If it had been, Miss Watkins would have told her.

Chapter Six

Patsy Shillabeer started work at the Barton straight away. She was, Jennifer told Hilary, a good little worker, although very quiet. She'd obviously been accustomed to helping her mother around the house and could cook quite well too. And she had nice, pleasant manners.

'She'll probably be more use to you than I am,' Jennifer said with a smile. 'I only ever had a little two-up, two-down house in Devonport to look after before I married Travis.'

'And a good job as a buyer at Dingle's,' Hilary said, feeling guilty. 'Honestly, Jennifer, we really are imposing on you. I'll have to find someone else to take Mrs Ellis's place.'

'Has she said when she'll be coming back? Not that I mind helping out – it's just that ... well ...' A pink flush rose into her cheeks.

'You want to be in your own home, enjoying your own life and getting Travis's dinner ready, not ours.' Hilary nodded. 'I quite understand. I would never have dreamed of asking you if he hadn't suggested it.'

'Really, I don't mind,' Jennifer repeated. She hesitated, then said, 'We weren't going to tell anyone yet – it seems too soon. But I think I ought to tell you. I'm expecting a baby.'

Hilary stared at her, remembering that the thought had passed through her own mind and then been forgotten. 'A baby! Oh Jennifer, that's marvellous. When? How long have you known? And whatever are you thinking of, standing there doing our ironing? You ought to be sitting down – putting your feet up. You shouldn't be working here at all.'

Jennifer laughed. 'Don't be silly. I'm perfectly fit and well, and it's

35

early days yet, not even three months. I'm not due until August. And we didn't know until last week, not for certain. Well, I didn't – Travis didn't know until last night.'

'Last night? I haven't seen him since yesterday. Will it be all right if I congratulate him? He won't mind your telling me?'

'No, of course not, but we'd like to keep it quiet for a bit. All the same, I don't think I'll want to work here for too long. There'll be so much to do getting ready. So if you know when Mrs Ellis is coming back ...'

Hilary sighed. 'I don't, not really. I don't think she knows herself. She came in yesterday evening and we had a talk. Her mother's really very frail now and the accident has shocked her quite a lot. Mrs Ellis says she seems to have shrunk overnight. I don't think she's going to be able to go back to her cottage, and that means she'll stay with the Ellises, and Mrs Ellis isn't going to be able to leave her to come and work here. Not for the same hours, anyway. So it looks very much as if I'll have to look for a new housekeeper.'

'Isn't there anyone local who would be suitable?' Jennifer asked thoughtfully. 'Or are you going to advertise?'

'I'll have to, I think. Both the local papers and the *Western Morning News*. And perhaps *The Lady*. But usually people who look there want a live-in post and we haven't had anyone living in for years. And I can't advertise until I know for certain what Mrs Ellis wants to do.'

'Well, I'm happy to help out for a month or two,' Jennifer said. 'And if Patsy's as willing as she seems, she can do a lot of the cleaning work. I'll just do the cooking and organising.'

'And you won't do all of that,' Hilary said warmly. 'I can take the time to do quite a lot. Look, if you'll come in about eleven and do lunch and get things started for dinner, I can see to the rest. You can go home in the afternoon then. It's just so that my father gets regular meals and has someone to keep an eye on him when I'm out. Would that be all right?'

'That'll be ideal,' Jennifer said. 'Thank you, Hilary.'

'I'm the one who should be thanking you! And I'll pay you the same rate as Mrs Ellis, of course.'

'Oh, but ... I wasn't thinking of pay. I'm glad to help.'

'Of course you must be paid. A day or two of help in an emergency is one thing, working regular hours is quite another.' Hilary glanced

36

at her watch. 'Speaking of which, it's almost time you were going home now, so I'll finish the ironing, and if you tell me what you've done towards supper, I'll finish that too. And then you can go straight back to Wood Cottage and put your feet up, like expectant mothers are supposed to do!' She paused. 'I haven't even asked you whether you're hoping for a boy or a girl!'

Jennifer laughed. 'We haven't got as far as that ourselves. We're not even used to the idea of a baby yet. As long as it's fit and healthy, I don't think we'll mind what it is.'

'No, I don't suppose you will,' Hilary said. She looked at her friend for a moment and then came over and gave her a kiss. 'I'm so pleased for you. I really am. I think you're the luckiest people in the world.'

Travis too thought they were the luckiest people in the world. He told his wife so that evening when he came in from work to find her in the kitchen, taking a casserole out of the oven.

'And how's the mother of my child?' he asked, swinging her off her feet the moment she put the dish on the worktop. 'Oops – I suppose I oughtn't to be doing this sort of thing now. I should be treating you like porcelain.'

'Don't be silly. I'm not made of eggshells. You're as bad as Hilary, she wanted me to sit down and put my feet up even though I was in the middle of ironing.'

He frowned. 'I must say, I agree with her. You shouldn't be standing up for hours – won't you get varicose veins? I'm rather sorry I suggested that you go and help out now – I wouldn't have done if I'd known about the baby.'

'Well I'm glad you did. They really do need the help, and Hilary won't take advantage.' She told him the arrangement they had made. 'Patsy Shillabeer seems a really good little worker, and she's got nice manners too. She'll suit them very well.'

'Let's hope they suit her father too,' Travis observed. 'I don't know him all that well, but he seems a pretty domineering sort of character to me. Keeps all his youngsters on a tight rein.'

'I can't see him having anything to complain about at the Barton.' Jennifer lifted the pan of potatoes from the hob and carried it over to the sink to drain. 'She'll be as well looked after there as she is at home. As long as she can cope with the Colonel when he's in one of his moods.'

'He's getting better all the time,' Travis said. 'Can't wait to get his fingers back in the estate pies again. I was rather hoping Dr Latimer would tell him to retire and leave it all to Hilary and me – not that he'd take any notice.' He frowned as he sat down at the kitchen table. 'Have you noticed anything about Hilary, by the way?'

Jennifer brought the casserole to the table and went back for the potatoes. 'What sort of thing?'

'I don't really know how to describe it. I mean, she's had a lot on her plate lately, what with the French family coming for Christmas and the Colonel's heart attack, and now Mrs Ellis having to take time off ... But it seems to me there's something more than that worrying her. She doesn't seem to have her heart in the estate the way she did. It's as if there's something much deeper on her mind.'

'Maybe she's still worrying about Rob and the inheritance,' Jennifer said. 'But you're right – she does seem a bit distracted.'

'It's something to do with these trips to London,' Travis said thoughtfully, putting a piece of beef into his mouth. 'I've even wondered if she's thinking of leaving Burracombe and starting a new life somewhere else. She thought of it before, you know – she told me she was hoping to be an air hostess, just before her father had his first attack and she took over the estate.'

Jennifer stared at him. 'She wouldn't do that, surely! Not with things as they are now. She loves running the estate.'

Travis shrugged. 'I wouldn't have thought so. But there's definitely something. Maybe she'll talk to you, now that you're going to be there every day.'

'Maybe,' Jennifer said. 'But I think she's more likely to talk to Val Ferris if she needs to talk to anyone. They've been friends for years. And it's really none of our business anyway.'

'No, it isn't – unless it affects the estate.' Travis looked at her. 'And then it could become very much our business.'

'Thank you, Patsy,' Hilary said as Patsy prepared to leave. 'You've done a very good day's work. It's going to be a pleasure having you work here.'

''I like being here,' the girl said shyly. 'It's a lovely house.'

'I hope you won't mind helping to look after my father, too. It's really just a matter of giving him his meals and keeping an eye on him when I'm not here. He can be a bit difficult sometimes but you mustn't take any notice of that.'

'Oh, I don't,' Patsy said with the smile that lit her face. 'He reminds me of my grandad. All mouth and no trousers, my mum says.'

Hilary laughed. 'Well, perhaps you'd better not let him hear you say that! He'll probably be nicer to you than he is to me, anyway. It's just his illness that makes him bad-tempered, when he can't do the things he wants to do.' And his natural short temper as well, she thought. Gilbert Napier had never been known for his ability to suffer fools gladly. But Patsy wasn't a fool – just rather quiet and mouselike.

'My dad's bad-tempered most of the time,' Patsy said cheerfully. 'We're used to it in our house.'

Hilary looked at her and felt sorry for the girl, not much more than a child, who had grown up with bad temper in the house. I'll make sure Dad treats her properly, she thought. No biting her head off. He's to mind his manners, even if she is working for us. *Especially* because she's working for us.

'Oh, I ought to tell you,' Patsy said as she began to put on her coat. 'There's something wrong with the electric socket in Mr Stephen's bedroom. I tried to use the vacuum cleaner in there and it made a sort of buzzing noise and sparks flew off, so I unplugged it quick.'

'Goodness! You're lucky you didn't get a shock,' Hilary exclaimed. 'I'll get Bob Pettifer to come and see to it at once.'

Patsy nodded. 'I used the one in the room next door instead – the lead stretched that far so it wasn't no problem.' She wrapped a long striped scarf round her neck and pulled on a pair of gloves that matched the stripes. Hilary guessed that she had knitted them all herself. 'Well, I'll see you in the morning, Miss Napier,' she said cheerfully, and went to the back door to put on her wellingtons.

Hilary watched as she took a torch from her pocket. 'Will you be all right, walking back on your own? It's very dark this evening and you've got to cross the Clam. Perhaps I should take you round in the car.'

'My stars, no! I'll be right as rain. It's no more than twenty minutes and it's not even icy tonight. I've got a good torch. And Father said he'd walk down to meet me if he was back home in time.'

'All right then,' Hilary said doubtfully, still not altogether happy about letting the girl go out by herself in the dark to walk down the footpath, across the footbridge and up the other side of the river to Little Burracombe. Fortunately, the Shillabeer farm bordered the river, so she didn't have too far to go. On a summer evening it would be a pleasant walk, but at this time of year it was fully dark long before her day's work was over. The village people were used to walking in the dark, though, and the paths were clear enough. Patsy didn't seem worried about it, anyway.

The door closed behind her and Hilary turned back indoors, thankful to have found such a good and willing worker. Now all she needed was a reliable woman as housekeeper. She was fairly sure that Mrs Ellis would not be coming back, unless it was to work part time as Jennifer was doing now. Perhaps that will be enough, Hilary thought, if I do more myself. But that would mean time taken away from the estate work, and I know what would happen. The house would gradually take over – especially if Father never gets any stronger than he is now. I'd be back where I started before I knew what was happening.

She sighed. It all seemed too difficult. As Travis was saying to Jennifer at just that moment, it was as if her heart wasn't wholly in the estate any more. And she knew just why that was.

Her heart was in Derbyshire, with David Hunter.

Chapter Seven

'The letter came by the afternoon post,' Alice told Val, her face flushed with delight. 'I had to run down here and tell you straight away. Your father and Tom had just started milking, so I popped in to tell them too.' She peeped into Christopher's pram, which was standing in the tiny cottage living room. 'Your uncle Brian's coming home! What do you think about that?' She straightened up again. 'Dead to the world, the dear of him. Your dad's some pleased, I can tell you.'

'I bet he is. And what about Tom?'

'He didn't say much, but I reckon he was pleased too, to know his big brother's coming home soon. It's such a long time since we saw him. And Peggy, too.'

'Didn't Brian say she'd rather be called Margret?' Val asked, giving the name its German pronunciation. 'He said it was only him that calls her Peggy.'

'Well, I reckon her'll have to get used to it if they mean to spend much time in Burracombe,' Alice said with a laugh. 'You'll never get folk hereabouts to get their tongues round saying it like that. Anyway, Peggy's friendlier.'

Val wasn't so sure. On his last visit home, Brian had been rather protective of his German wife and her feelings. Not that that was really surprising, considering the two countries had been at war not that many years earlier and feelings still ran high amongst some of those who had lived through two such wars.

Still, they weren't likely to stay long. If Brian was indeed coming out of the army, he would be looking for a job, and there weren't many around in Burracombe.

'I suppose they'll be looking to move to Plymouth or Exeter to find work,' she said thoughtfully. 'He'll want something in engineering, won't he?'

'I dare say, but there'll be no hurry for that. He'll have his pay for a while and he won't have any expenses while he's with us. We don't want to push him out the minute he's arrived, Val.'

'No, of course not. I didn't mean that. It'll be good to see him. It's years since we had any time together – not since before the war, really. He's always been away.'

'Nearly fifteen years.' Alice nodded. 'He wasn't much more than a boy when he went, and now he's in his thirties. He'll find it strange being in Civvy Street again. But he hasn't always been away, Val, has he? He's come home on leave at least once a year since the war ended.'

Val nodded, but she still didn't think her soldier brother would want to stay long in Burracombe. He wouldn't fit in here any more, she thought. His life had been so different, and although there was room at the farmhouse (or would be, once Joe and Russ had departed for America), there wouldn't be much for either him or Peggy – *Margret* – to do once they'd been here for a week or two.

'When does he say they'll be arriving?'

'Week after next.' Alice beamed, and then her face fell. 'Two days after our Jackie goes to America with Joe and Russ. Oh, what a shame!'

'Seems a good thing to me. At least you'll have their bedrooms free.'

'Brian and Peggy'll only need one.'

'Yes, but they're bound to have a lot of stuff with them, if they're coming back to England for good. They'll need another one to put it all in.'

'It's just a pity they won't see each other,' Alice said regretfully. 'Especially for our Jackie, not seeing her big brother after so long. Why, she was only four when the war broke out, not even at school, and now she's an independent young woman – or thinks she is – going off travelling the world.'

Val laughed. 'Only to America, Mum.'

'Well, isn't that the world? And we don't know that it's going to end there.' For a moment, Alice's worry about her daughter overcame her, but her joy at Brian's return quickly superseded it. 'I just think it's a pity she'll miss him after all this time.'

'She'll be back in six months,' Val said comfortingly, hoping this was true. 'And if Brian and Peggy are going to settle near here, they'll see plenty of each other then. Anyway, you ought to be thinking about those bedrooms. Have Uncle Joe and Russ finished the wallpapering?'

Alice chuckled. 'Yes, at last! That wallpaper was bought to get the rooms ready for when they came, and they've ended up doing it themselves for our Brian. Well, it'll be nice to have it all fresh for them, so it's not wasted. And how's my little boy, then? Waking up, are you?' She bent over Christopher's pram again. The baby opened his eyes, saw his grandmother, smiled and stretched out his arms. Alice laughed and picked him up, cradling him against her.

'He's a lovely little boy, Val. I think you're right, it's not good for a kiddy to be the only one, but I hope you'll give yourself a bit of time with him before you has any more. You never get that time with just one baby again. 'Tis never the same for the others.'

Val looked at her thoughtfully, wondering if Alice was thinking of her own firstborn, Brian. She was barely two years younger than her brother, so her mother would have been pregnant again by the time Brian was little more than a year old. Val, Tom and Jackie had never had their mother's undivided attention.

'I don't know that we felt any different, though,' she said. 'Whatever children have, they think that's normal. We were happy enough.'

'I'm glad to hear it! But I was thinking more about you, and the time you have to enjoy your baby. You never get so much with the others as you do with the first.'

'I'm afraid that's all too deep for me!' Val said with a laugh. 'I'm just grateful for having Christopher at all, and I'll feel exactly the same about any others we might have. But it won't be yet, Mother, so don't worry about it. Try to persuade our Brian to start a family instead, once he's back in England. How long have he and Peggy been married – nearly seven years, isn't it? And not a sign of any children yet.'

'I suppose it's difficult for them, with her being German. If they were born over there, they'd be German too, and Brian wouldn't want that, so maybe they've decided to wait till they're living here.'

'But Peggy – Margret – might not want them to be English,' Val said. 'I'm not sure you're right anyway, Mum. Wouldn't they be both?'

Alice stared at her. 'How could they be? You've got to be either one or the other, surely. Anyway, I don't know that your father and me would want our grandchildren to be German.'

43

She was beginning to look upset, and Val felt uncomfortable. She said peaceably, 'Well, it's for them to sort out for themselves. Maybe they don't want children at all, but it's not really any of our business, is it?'

'Not our business? Of course it's our business! It's me and your dad's grandchildren. It's our *family*.' Alice's face was reddening and Val felt even more uncomfortable. Her mother laid Christopher back in his pram. 'I think I'd better go home. I just came down to bring you some good news, not start an argument. I might walk along to the school and meet Joanna and Robin. At least someone will be pleased our Brian's coming home!'

Val jumped up. 'Mum! Don't go like that. I never meant anything – I don't even know what I said to upset you. Of course I'm pleased they're coming home.' She laid her hand on her mother's arm. 'Don't let's fall out, Mum.'

Alice looked at her, and her face softened. 'I'm sorry, maid. It's just – well, I don't know what it is, but every little thing seems to upset me these days.' She took a hanky from her coat pocket and dabbed at her eyes. 'I flew at your dad this morning just because he asked for a bit more fried potato with his breakfast. Asked him if he didn't think I fed him proper. He looked that struck, you'd have thought I'd hit him. I don't know what's come over me.'

'I do,' Val said. 'It's Jackie, isn't it? You're still worrying about her. Honestly, Mum, I'm sure she'll be all right. Uncle Joe will look after her.'

'I know.' Alice sighed. 'And I don't know that I am all that worried about her, to tell you the truth. It's just the thought of her being so far away that upsets me. She's my youngest, Val – my baby. I never thought she'd want to leave us.'

'You can never really know what anyone will want to do. And it's not that she wants to *leave* us – more that she wants to go and see new things. There is a difference, Mum. You know, I think she'll be more homesick than she realises.'

'I do want her to enjoy it.' Alice sniffed. 'I don't want to be selfish over it, honestly, Val.'

'Of course you don't.' Val gave her mother a hug. 'Look, you go now and meet Joanna and tell her the news about Brian. It'll cheer us all up. And he'll still be around when Jackie comes back. She *will* come back, you know – I'm sure of it.'

Alice nodded and dabbed her eyes again. She gave Val a wavering smile. 'I know. I am, too – I think. Anyway, she's going now and that's all there is to it. I'm sorry I flew off at you like that, Val.'

'It's all right, Mum. Off you go now.' Val gave her mother a little push through the door, watched her walk up the street and then went back indoors, shivering a little as she closed the door against the cold January wind.

'I hope we're right about Jackie,' she said to her little son, picking him out of his pram again. 'And I hope our Brian coming home isn't going to cause problems. But I've got a nasty feeling it might ...'

Jackie Tozer was disappointed that her brother wouldn't be arriving until after she'd left for America, but her excitement had mounted to such a pitch that almost nothing could distract her attention for long. Joe Tozer too was sorry to miss his nephew by such a short time, but it couldn't be helped. The tickets were booked and paid for, the packing almost done, and there was nothing left but goodbyes.

Ted had arranged a special practice night on the bells. Joe, who had never had church bells to ring while he'd lived in America, had regained all his old skills and was almost part of the team again, and Russell had tried his hand and said he'd have liked to continue with it if only the Corning churches had such bells. After the ringing, they all went to the Bell Inn, where Bernie and Rose had laid on a special party table of sausage rolls, sandwiches and cakes for anyone who wanted to come and wish the travellers luck. The whole Tozer family was there, with the babies in Rose's bedroom so that Val and Joanna could come as well, and Dottie Friend was the star of the evening.

'Us'll miss you proper,' Norman Tozer told her. 'Come back a real Hollywood pin-up, you will, won't lower yourself to pulling pints for such as we. That's if you comes back at all,' he added with a sidelong glance at Joe.

'Don't be dafter than you got to be,' Dottie retorted. 'I'll be back before you know I'm gone. I'm only going for a month, as well you know.'

'Six weeks, with the journey there and back,' he pointed out. 'And I bet our Joe puts up a fight before he lets you board that old ship to come home. That's if he don't come back with you. Don't reckon us've seen the last of he.'

'Use your mouth for eating this sausage roll and stop talking so far back,' Dottie said, handing him a plate. 'It's the last of my baking you'll be seeing for a few weeks.'

'I'm surprised you had time to do any baking today,' Miss Kemp said. Like many of the other women, she rarely frequented the Bell, but this was Dottie's farewell party and couldn't be missed. 'There must be a hundred things to do before you go tomorrow. And what's going to happen to your cat?'

'Bless you, Miss Kemp, I done all they. Everything's packed and ready, and all I got to do is walk out of the front door. And Mabel Purdy's going to look after my Albert, he won't hardly know I've gone.'

'I'm sure he'll miss you, all the same. And the village will certainly miss you and your cooking.'

'We will,' agreed Dottie's cousin Jessie Friend, from the village shop. 'What's George Sweet going to do without our Dottie's cakes to put in his window?'

'He'll have to get Ivy to make 'em,' someone said, and there was a general laugh. Ivy Sweet, although married to the village baker, was not noted for her cooking. Dottie looked a little anxiously towards the bar, where Ivy's red hair could be seen amongst the others, but she didn't seem to have heard and Dottie moved on quickly with the plate of sausage rolls.

'Here, you didn't ought to be doing that,' Alice said, taking the plate away. 'You'm a guest here tonight. Go and sit down, and I'll get you a drink.'

'I've got one somewhere.' Dottie looked around to where Joe was sitting, with two drinks in front of him, in the inglenook, where a log fire was blazing. 'Dear me, look at the man. Honestly, it's not as if he's not going to be seeing enough of me for the next few weeks!'

'Joe'll never see too much of you,' Alice said quietly. 'You know that, Dottie.'

Dottie looked at her. She had always tried to deny this, even to herself, but now she couldn't. The noise of the party seemed to recede, leaving herself and Alice in their own small oasis of silence. She said, 'I do know, Alice, and to tell you the truth, I don't know what I'm going to do about it. Half of me wants to give in and say I'll marry him, and half of me says I can't leave Burracombe – not for good. And for all he says he'll come back, it wouldn't be right – not with all his family there. Sometimes I wish I'd never agreed to go to America, and that's the truth.'

'Perhaps you'll find it easier to decide when you're there,' Alice said. 'Seeing him on his home turf, so to speak. I've known that make a woman's mind up more than once.'

Dottie nodded and smiled at her. They looked at each other with understanding, and then someone else touched Dottie's arm and she turned away. Alice passed on with the sausage rolls and the noise of the party flooded back into Dottie's ears.

Bernie Nethercott rapped on the bar with the handle of a large knife. 'Let's have a bit of hush! I wants to propose a toast. Has everyone got summat in their glass? Well then, lift them up good and high and say, "Here's to our Dottie! Good health, safe voyage, and come home soon!"'

'Come home soon!' everyone echoed, and Dottie blushed and raised her own glass in thanks.

'I'll be back before you can turn round,' she promised, and then caught Joe's gaze across the crowded room.

At the look in his eyes, her heart thumped as it hadn't since she was a girl, walking out with him on those summer evenings so long ago; and for the first time she wondered whether there might be a serious chance of her breaking the promise she had just made.

It was a large party that set off next day for Southampton, where the travellers were to embark on the great ocean liner *Queen Elizabeth*. There were six of them altogether, as well as all the luggage, and it needed two vehicles to carry them all. Joe, Russell and Dottie went in the car Joe had hired at the beginning of his trip to England back in October, while Ted, Alice and Jackie followed in the farm truck. Jackie had turned a little mutinous when she'd realised this, but Ted had told her in no uncertain terms that he'd spent quite enough already on this trip of hers, which he'd never been in favour of anyway, and he wasn't spending even more on hiring a posh car just so that she could arrive at the docks like the princess she seemed to think she was these days. He would have said even more but he'd caught his brother

47

hiding a grin, and Jackie had backed off quickly, obviously realising she'd gone too far.

'I'll give it a good wash before you go,' Tom told her. 'You won't need to be ashamed of coming from farming folk.'

'I'm not ashamed!' Jackie denied quickly, but Ted turned his head away and she knew she'd been in danger of hurting him. She went to him and laid her hand on his arm. 'Honestly, Dad, it's not that – it's just that I didn't want our stuff to get dirty. I'm really grateful for all you've done. I'll wash it myself.'

In the end, she and Tom had tackled it together, with Tom doing the lion's share, and it looked cleaner today than it had since the day it had arrived on the farm. Ted piled Jackie's luggage into the back, along with some of Dottie's, and they crammed themselves in, with Jackie perched amongst the cases. The two-vehicle cavalcade set off along the street, with half the village lining their way to wave goodbye.

'My stars,' Alice said. 'I feel like the Queen herself. You'd better wave, Jackie, it's you and Dottie they've come to see. Me and your father will be back tomorrow.'

Jackie said nothing and her mother turned to look at her. 'Why, what are those tears for, maid? You couldn't wait to be off half an hour ago. Don't tell me you'm having second thoughts.'

'She'd better not,' Ted growled. 'Not after all this hoo-ha, not to mention the money we spent.'

'I'm not.' Jackie sniffed. 'It's just saying goodbye to everyone, that's all. And all these people coming out to see us off. Mind you, I reckon it's Dottie they've come to see more than me.'

'Not all of them,' Alice remarked. 'I can see Roy Pettifer there, and I don't reckon he's looking that down in the mouth because Dottie Friend won't be around for a bit. Nor Vic Nethercott, neither – he don't look best pleased.'

'Oh, them!' Jackie said impatiently. 'I don't have time for them now – stick-in-the-muds, never been anywhere.'

'Jackie! However can you say that? Roy spent all that time risking his life in Korea, and Vic was over in Germany for some of his National Service. You can't call them stick-in-the-muds.'

'They never took themselves there, did they? They just went where they were told. And now they're back, they never think of going anywhere further than Plymouth. I don't understand it. I don't understand why anyone should want to stay in Burracombe all their lives when they've seen a bit of the world.'

Alice said nothing, but her heart sank. Jackie was confirming her worst fears – that once she'd been away from Burracombe she would never want to come back. She turned to look ahead, at the road, and tried to keep her own tears from falling. The parting early tomorrow morning was going to be one of the worst moments of her life, and she didn't know how she was going to get through it.

Chapter Eight

'**P**erhaps you'd better check all the other sockets in the house while you're about it,' Hilary said to Bob Pettifer. 'Just in case there's a problem with any more. I hope it doesn't mean rewiring,' she added anxiously. 'We've only had electricity in Burracombe for a few years. It can't need doing again already.'

'It's probably only that one, but best if I check the others as well.' The young electrician hesitated. 'Would it be all right if I brought my brother Terry along to give me a hand? He've just started his apprenticeship and it's good experience for him. Us don't get the chance of working in a big house like this very often.'

'No, that's quite all right. I've seen him around the village, haven't I? He looks a bit like you.'

'More's the pity,' Bob said with a grin. Tall and spindly, with a long, rubbery face and ears that stuck out almost at right angles to his face, Bob was by no means the best-looking young man in the village. Not that it ever seemed to bother him – he was a cheerful soul who bore his friends' ribald taunts with equanimity. Hilary hoped his brother was just as easy-going.

'Looks aren't everything,' she said. 'You've got a nice, honest nature, Bob, and that will take you a long way. Better than looking like a film star nobody likes.'

'Oh, everyone says I do look like a film star,' he told her, and then twisted his rubbery face up and added, 'Boris Karloff!'

Hilary laughed and let him out of the back door. He was coming back next morning, she told Patsy as she returned to the kitchen, and bringing Terry with him. 'You probably know him from school.'

'Not really, miss. He's a bit older than me, and anyway, he went to Dolvin Road school.'

Hilary looked at her. 'Which school did you go to then, Patsy?'

'The grammar school,' Patsy said with some surprise. 'I thought you knew that, miss.'

'No, I didn't. I just thought ...' Hilary hesitated. 'I mean, if you went to the grammar school, why are you here? You could have got a job in an office, or gone on to be a teacher.'

'Father wouldn't ever have allowed that,' Patsy said. 'He likes us all under his eye. That's why he took me out of Pillar's.' She picked up her duster and went out of the kitchen, leaving Hilary to wonder if young women would ever be able to escape the restrictions placed upon them by men. If it wasn't their fathers, it was their husbands, refusing to allow their wives to work because they believed it was an assault upon their pride if they weren't seen to be the sole provider for their family. Look at the struggle she'd had herself to persuade her father to allow her to run the estate – and even then he'd brought Travis Kellaway in to manage it with her. And yet we did so much during the war, she thought. We drove buses and ambulances, we flew aircraft, we looked after barrage balloons and anti-aircraft guns, we worked on canals and in factories and on farms – we did almost all the jobs that had been done by men, only to be pushed back to the kitchen when the men came home. We don't seem to have gained an inch.

She sighed and went through to see her father. He was picking up now after his attack and growing restive at being told to take life easy. As usual, he started to grumble the minute she walked into the drawing room.

'Charles Latimer's turning into more of an old woman than ever. I'd be better off having Mrs Warren looking after me. At least she'd find me something to do.'

Hilary smiled. 'Joyce Warren finds something for everyone to do, but it doesn't mean it would be good for you. Try not to get annoyed about it, Father. If you do as you're told now, you'll be all the better for it later. It's only for a few weeks.'

Gilbert huffed and then said, 'That new girl seems a nice little thing. Got good manners – doesn't answer back like young Jackie Tozer used to.'

'Jackie's got a lot of spirit. You know she's off to America today?'

'You told me. Don't know what Ted Tozer's thinking of, letting a girl that age go jaunting about the world on her own. Bound to lead to trouble.'

'She won't be on her own. She'll be with her uncle and cousins.'

'All the same . . .' he said, as if he were already thinking of something else. 'When's Stephen bringing Maddy here to see me again?'

'Not for a week or two. He's used up all his leave and Maddy's had a lot of time off in the last few weeks to see Stella. She said she'd just slip up by train at the weekends when Steve can't make it – she can see Stella in the afternoon and then go back the same day.' She smiled. 'And I expect when Steve does get a few hours off, they'll want to spend them together. They've got a lot of time to make up.'

Gilbert grunted. 'Thank goodness the boy's come to his senses at last. Thought he was going to let her slip through his fingers.'

Hilary opened her mouth to say that it was Maddy who had been hanging back – Stephen had never been in any doubt that she was the girl for him. But there was no point in arguing about it, so she said merely, 'It's been a difficult time for them. She's had to come to terms with losing her fiancé, young Sammy Hodges. It was terrible for her to actually see him killed by that lorry.'

'If Stephen had had his wits about him, she'd never have been engaged to the feller in the first place,' Gilbert stated. 'Would never have met him.'

'They knew each other as children, you know that,' Hilary said quietly. 'It was a tragedy, Father, and I hope you'll never say anything like that to Maddy herself. She'd be terribly upset.'

'Well of course I won't. What d'you take me for?' he demanded, and Hilary forbore to tell him. Instead, she remarked merely that she was going to the office now to sort out today's post and would then be out all day.

'What would you like for lunch? An omelette? Some soup?'

'Invalid food,' he snorted. 'I'll have both. I assume that's allowed?'

'I think that will be all right,' Hilary agreed meekly and went out, closing the door behind her and leaning on it for a moment. He'll never change, she told herself, so there's no use expecting him to. And his heart's in the right place after all. At least, I think it is!

*

52

Patsy was cleaning the bathrooms when Bob Pettifer arrived next day with his brother Terry. She knew them both by sight, but had never really spoken to either of them. The last time she had seen Bob was when he had fallen off the slippery pole crossing the Burra Brook during the Coronation celebrations, setting up a splash that had soaked half the onlookers.

Terry was a few years younger than Bob and about eighteen months older than Patsy. That made him just over eighteen. He had the same long, rubbery, face, freckles and jug ears as his brother, and the same bright eyes and cheerful grin. He and Patsy almost collided on the landing as she came out of the bathroom to meet him trailing after Bob carrying a heavy toolbox.

'Sorry,' he said, stopping just in time. 'I didn't know there was anyone up here. Here, aren't you Patsy Shillabeer?'

'Yes, and you're Terry Pettifer. Miss Hilary said you were coming. It's that socket in Mr Stephen's bedroom.'

Terry knew that because Bob had told him, but he wasn't ready to let Patsy disappear too quickly and he said, 'You'd better show us. Don't want to be messing about with the wrong one.'

Patsy glanced at him. She liked the look of him despite his ugliness. It was a nice sort of ugly, she thought, and although his smile was crooked, it was a real smile and made his blue eyes crinkle. She felt herself colour up a little as she said rather shyly, 'It's in here, by the bed.'

Bob was already there, kneeling on the floor by Stephen's bed. Without looking round, he said, 'You took your time, our Terry. Been flirting with that Shillabeer maid, have you?'

Patsy's face grew even hotter and she cast a quick sideways glance at Terry, who grinned back without any sign of embarrassment and answered, 'You'd better ask her, Bob, she's right here beside me.'

Bob turned his head and rolled his eyes, looking even more like a church gargoyle. He gave his brother a withering look and said to Patsy, 'You'll have to make allowances for him. He was at the back of a long queue when manners was handed out.'

'If I was, you were there behind me,' Terry retorted. 'Don't you know no better than to stand up when you're talking to a lady?'

'I'd better go,' Patsy said. 'I've got work to do.'

'And so have we,' Bob told her. He stood up and stuck out his hand. 'It's Patsy, isn't it? I play cricket with your cousin Jonas.'

'I know.' Neither Burracombe nor Little Burracombe had a team of its own, so cricket was one of the few activities that brought the two rival villages together. They played on a field near Little Burracombe church, but their fixtures were as hit and miss as their playing. It had been rumoured that Felix Copley, who had played for his school, was hoping to join them in the summer and would improve the standard; but with Stella having been so badly injured, nobody knew whether her fiancé would have the time now.

'He's not a bad bowler, your Jonas,' Bob remarked. 'And I've seen you down the field a time or two, watching the game. Our Terry's not interested in it, more's the pity,' he added casually, with a sidelong glance at his brother.

'I am!' Terry contradicted at once. 'I'm thinking of joining come summer. You'll come and watch me, won't you, Patsy?'

'I don't know. I might.' Still blushing, she turned towards the door. 'Anyway, you know which socket it is now, don't you?'

Bob grinned. 'Pretty well, I think, thanks. We'm checking them all over the house, so we'll be around for a day or two. Probably bump into you again, eh, Terry?'

'Expect so,' Terry said, but Patsy never saw the appreciative glance he gave her as she escaped on to the landing.

'Not if she sees you first!' Bob said with another grin. 'Reckon you got your work cut out there, Terry, specially with your looks. Now, open up that toolbox and let's see what us've got here.'

Terry did as he was told, but he kept his thoughts to himself. He didn't agree with Bob that he had his work cut out to make friends with Patsy. He hadn't missed those blushes, and after a couple of days in the same house, he thought there was a chance she might agree to go to the pictures with him one evening. Or maybe to the Saturday night hop in Burracombe church hall. He could see her home afterwards, down the footpath and over the Clam ...

He was startled out of his daydreams by his brother giving him a friendly cuff over the head. 'Wake up, you dozy blighter! We got work to do here, remember? I ain't running a lonely hearts club.'

'If you were, you'd be the only member,' Terry retorted. 'When are you going to get yourself a girlfriend, Bob?'

'When I find one short-sighted enough not to see my ugly mug.

And that goes for you too. I saw you making eyes at young Patsy just now. You might as well forget it – her dad's got her on a tight rein and he's not going to let her waste herself on an apprentice with a face like a toby jug.'

'Hold on,' Terry protested. 'Don't gallop on so fast, our Bob. I'm thinking of asking her to go to the pictures with me, that's all – not walk down the aisle.'

'One thing leads to another,' Bob said. 'And talking of leads, we'm here to do a job of work, so let's get on with it.'

Patsy, cleaning Hilary's room, heard their voices but not their words. She dusted the bookshelf, remembering the way Terry had looked at her with those bright blue eyes. I don't think he's ugly at all, she thought. Funny-looking, yes, with those big sticking-out ears, but not as much as Bob, and not in a way that makes you not want to look at him. In fact, quite nice really, in a friendly, homely sort of way.

She wondered whether they'd have a chance to talk again while the two brothers were working in the house.

Chapter Nine

You could see the *Queen Elizabeth* from the main road entering Southampton. The dock was so close that she seemed to be almost on the pavement, towering over the traffic. The two cars stopped for a moment and the occupants stared up at the huge black hull, the sparkling white superstructure and the two red funnels. After a long moment, Jackie broke the silence, her voice awed.

'I can't believe I'm going on that enormous ship. I'll never be able to find my way round.'

Alice shook her head. She looked dismayed, as if the full meaning of Jackie's departure had just hit her.

'I can't believe it either. Oh Jackie, are you sure? You don't have to go, not if you change your mind.'

'What, after me and our Joe spent all that money on the ticket?' Ted demanded. In fact, Joe had paid more than half, despite Ted's protestations, but it had been a lot of money all the same.

Alice turned on him. 'Yes, if she don't want to go. It'd be worth it just to have her stop at home where she belongs. You just say, Jackie, and never mind your dad.'

'I'm not changing my mind,' Jackie said. 'I was just a bit taken aback by how big it is, that's all. I think it's really exciting. There'll be famous people on board too – film stars, even. You never know who I might meet.'

Alice moaned slightly and Ted said, 'You needn't get any ideas in your head about going off to Hollywood. Corning's where you're going, and where you'll stop if you got any sense, which I'm beginning to wonder. And Joe'll make sure you toe the line – I had a long talk with he last night after you'd all gone to bed. Anyway, what film star's going to look twice at a Devon maid, never been further than Plymouth in her life?'

'I have!' Jackie said indignantly. 'I went to London, remember, to see the Festival of Britain.'

'On a day trip in a charabanc, with the rest of the village round you.' Ted started the truck again. 'Anyway, us can't stop here all night chewing the fat. We got to find this hotel our Joe's booked us into and get a bite to eat. Got an early start in the morning.'

'I wish I could go aboard this minute,' Jackie said, gazing longingly at the great ocean liner, and Alice blinked away the tears. It was clear that Jackie had no idea at all what she was doing to her mother by being so eager to fly the nest and go halfway across the world. She'll learn one day, Alice thought. When she's a mother herself, she'll know what it's like to have to step back and let her children go. It's something we all have to go through, I suppose, but knowing that don't make it any easier.

Now that the day was almost here, she wished it were over. The sooner she goes, the sooner she'll be on her way home again. This time next year, she'll be home again, her travels behind her, and ready to settle down.

Perhaps ...

The hotel was comfortable enough, but nobody got much sleep that night. Jackie was in a fever of excitement, while Alice spent most of the night in tears and Ted found it hard to console her, especially since he wasn't finding much consolation himself in his own words. He'd said too much about his feelings about the trip for any words of comfort to sound anything but hollow. Eventually he just put both arms around his wife and drew her close so that they lay together, sharing their thoughts and feelings silently, until in the end they both fell asleep.

Joe also was having doubts. This whole enterprise had started from a casual remark one day when he and Russ had met Jackie in Plymouth and taken her out for lunch. It had never been intended seriously, but Jackie had seized upon the idea and, like a terrier with a rabbit, refused to let it go. The arguments that had followed had very nearly spoiled his trip home to see the family, the first for over thirty years, until Ted had finally given in. Now Joe was wondering if he'd done right in agreeing to bring his headstrong young niece to America. Suppose she refused to stay in Corning and went off on her own? Suppose she fell for some guy and decided to make her life with him? In less than two years she could get married without her parents' permission. What control would Joe have over a young woman who was prepared to stand up against her own parents? He was only her uncle and had no real authority at all.

Ted and Alice will never forgive me if anything happens to her, he thought, and wished he had never made it easier for her by offering to have her to stay as long as she liked, either with him or with his daughters. They would all look after her, he knew that – but did Jackie want to be looked after? He didn't think so.

The bright spot for Joe was that Dottie was coming as well, but even that brought worries. Joe and Dottie had been sweethearts long ago, when they were young together, and he'd believed that she would follow him anywhere. But she hadn't. She'd chosen to stay in Burracombe, and the hold the village had on her now, in her early sixties, was even greater than it had been then. He knew that she meant this to be no more than a visit, and although he hoped she would change her mind, he realised that the chances weren't high. Dottie, at least, was likely to be using her return ticket before the summer was out. For one thing, she'd promised to be back for Stella Simmons's wedding to that young vicar, and Dottie didn't break promises.

Dottie herself was also lying awake, thinking of the huge ship they had seen on their way in to Southampton and wondering if she would ever be able to manage to spend five days at sea aboard such a monstrous vessel. Like Jackie, she didn't think she would ever learn to find her way around and feared that, once having said good night to Joe on the first evening, she might not clap eyes on him again until they arrived in New York.

And suppose she were seasick? That would put him off her good and proper. Nobody looked their best heaving into a bucket, and she'd have to take her teeth out too. I just won't let him in the cabin, she thought. I'd rather die by myself with no one to see.

Worse still, she would have to come back all by herself. Jackie Tozer was supposed to be coming home, but not as soon as Dottie and in any case Dottie shared Alice's doubts about whether she would return at all. That young woman had both itchy feet and a mind of her own and, once out of her father's control, there was no saying what she might do. Dottie had seen young women like her during her time in London, when she worked as dresser for the famous actress Fenella Forsyth, and knew that a place like Burracombe was never going to be enough to hold Jackie.

Not like it held me, she thought, remembering how she had refused to go with Joe to America. She'd regretted it later, but now she had lived too long in the village to want to uproot herself to a new life. It would be like transplanting an old tree, with roots that twined themselves around every little rock and stone in the earth. Dottie was twined around Burracombe and Burracombe around her, and that was all there was to it. They belonged together. And it wasn't just the place – it was the people. The Tozers, the Nethercotts, the Pettifers. Jessie and Jeanie Friend, her cousins who ran the post office, and their brother Billy, who was, in village terms, 'simple'. Miss Kemp and the schoolchildren. Jacob Prout and that nice Jennifer Kellaway who'd thought once that she might have been his daughter and, even when the truth was known, still looked on him as her dad. Even grumpy old Mabel Purdy and bossy Mrs Warren. Even, thought Dottie with a slight smile of surprise, Ivy Sweet with her artificially ginger hair, dyed to match her little boy's. As if everyone didn't know about her wartime flirtation with that Polish airman over to Harrowbeer, that she'd met while working in the pub in Horrabridge! Even George must know, if he wasn't blind, although he'd never said anything.

Most important of all were dear little Maddy, whom Dottie had fostered during the war, and her sister Stella. It had taken some persuading for Dottie to agree to leave Burracombe while Stella was still in hospital, and it was only when she was convinced that Stella would get better and marry Felix that she gave in. 'As long as I'm back in time for the wedding,' she'd said firmly, and Joe had agreed.

And so she would be, she thought, turning over in bed for the umpteenth time. I'll be back in time to finish the frocks and ice the wedding cake. And I'll watch her walk up the aisle to marry Felix. Even if I have to make Joe come back too.

And yet ... Suppose he didn't come back. Suppose when she said goodbye to him again, it really was for ever. In her heart, Dottie suspected that Joe was now as tightly bound to Corning as she was to

Burracombe, and that they would never be truly together, and she felt a hint of the sadness that was to come.

The parting was every bit as emotional as they'd all dreaded. As they stood together near the bottom of the gangway, Alice could no longer hold back the flood of tears that had been gathering inside her ever since she opened her eyes in the hotel bedroom, and she sobbed as she hugged her daughter for the last time. Ted frowned, rubbed the bridge of his nose and then blew it very loudly on the fresh hanky Alice had insisted he take, and held Jackie firmly for a minute or two before letting her go with a gruff 'You mind and be a good girl, now, and remember what me and your mother have always told you. Do what you know's right and don't do what you know's wrong. And have a good time.'

Jackie was on the point of making a cheeky reply when she caught her mother's eye, and suddenly her own tears were flowing too. She choked and tried to smile, but her face twisted instead and she clung to both her parents, her shoulders heaving.

'I didn't know it would be like this,' she wept. 'Oh *Mum* ...'

'You don't have to go,' Alice said, a tiny bubble of hope rising inside her.

'No, I *want* to go. It's just ... Oh Mum, I'm sorry I've been such a toad. I never meant to upset you.'

'I know, my bird, I know.' Alice patted her shoulder. 'You just forget all about that and enjoy yourself. And come back to us soon.'

'I will. I will,' Jackie promised fervently, and stepped back as Joe, who had been shaking his brother's hand, came to give Alice a hug.

'You'll have to come over next,' he said. 'Once your Jackie and Dottie have broken the ice, so to speak. My girls would love to see you.'

'Don't talk about ice,' begged Alice, who could remember the disaster of the *Titanic*. 'Just get there safely and send us a postcard the minute you arrive.'

'We'll do better than a postcard,' Russ said, bending to give her a kiss. 'We'll cable you when we get home.'

Dottie came then to give Alice a hug and shake Ted's hand. 'I'll keep an eye on the maid, don't you fret,' she said out of Jackie's hearing. 'And she's a sensible young woman. She won't go far wrong.'

Alice was slightly startled to hear her daughter referred to as a 'young woman'. To her, Jackie was still a little girl, the baby of the family, a maid. Perhaps I ought to have given more account to the fact that she's growing up, she thought. Still under twenty-one, but as Dottie says, a young woman just the same.

Well, twenty-one or not, Jackie was going to be responsible for herself from now on. You couldn't hold Joe to account for whatever she chose to do once she was in America. As Ted had said, they must just trust her to know right from wrong and act as they'd brought her up.

The activity around the ship and gangway had increased and the moment had arrived for the travellers to go aboard. There was no time for more now than a final quick hug all round, and then Joe was shepherding his little flock up the steep wooden gangplank. They paused at the top and turned to wave, and Ted and Alice waved back, hardly able to see through their tears. Then the gangplank was drawn up and those ashore were directed out of the way as the great ship made ready to depart.

'Oh *Ted* ...' said Alice as the immense bulk began to move slowly away from the jetty. Both ship and shore were lined with a mass of people, all waving and calling last-minute messages that nobody could hear. A band was playing and streamers were being thrown; some people were laughing and excited, some in tears like Alice and Ted. Some turned and walked away, unable to bear it for a moment longer, and others watched stonily as if their emotion had frozen inside them.

'She will be all right, won't she?' Alice whispered at last, clinging to her husband's arm.

'Of course she will. Our Joe'll take care of her. You don't need to worry, my dear.'

But as they watched the great liner move slowly away down Southampton Water, the same thoughts were in both their minds.

Would Jackie really be all right, so far from home? And would she ever come back to Burracombe again?

Chapter Ten

There was plenty to distract Alice and Ted when they returned home after seeing Jackie off to America.

'I don't know what's the matter with Robin,' Joanna said after they had recounted all the details of their journey. 'He said he'd got a tummy ache and he did look a bit pale, so I let him go back to bed and sent a note to Miss Kemp to say he wouldn't be in school. But an hour later he came downstairs looking as bright as a button and said he was all right. I thought he'd better stay home till dinner time to make sure, but after dinner he said he felt poorly again so I put him on the settee. I can't think what it is. It seems to come and go.'

'He's eating all right, is he?' Alice asked anxiously. 'He had two slices of your gran's fruit cake for tea, I noticed.'

'I know, that's what seems so strange. And now he's outside helping her feed the chickens, as happy as Larry.'

'Children get these things,' Alice said comfortingly, knowing that Joanna was naturally inclined to worry after her baby Suzanne, Heather's twin, had died unexpectedly in her pram less than a year ago. 'He's a hardy little chap, he'll be right as rain in the morning.'

She turned her attention to other matters. Brian and his wife Margret (or Peggy) would be here next week, and she wanted to be sure that everything was ready for their arrival. Joe and Russ had redecorated the two spare bedrooms, but they still needed tidying and the bed must be made up and cupboards cleared. Then there were meals to think about – a big family meal on the day they arrived, and cakes and pies to be baked in readiness for the first few days, when no doubt there would be more talking going on than cooking.

She wondered what Brian's plans were. He'd been in the army for so long, it would seem strange to him to be in Civvy Street again. He was an engineer, so he wouldn't have much trouble finding a job, but it wouldn't be in Burracombe, probably not even in Tavistock. Plymouth was more likely. Well, that wasn't too far away, not when he'd been in Germany all these years. You could get there on the bus or the train. She had no doubt that they would be seeing plenty of Brian and Peggy in the future.

Robin woke with a tummy ache again the next morning and looked so wan and unhappy that Joanna sent him straight back to bed. She came down to breakfast looking worried and said she thought she might send for Dr Latimer to come and have a look at him.

'Why not ask our Val to pop up?' Alice suggested, but Joanna shook her head.

'It might be something really serious. That infantile paralysis that Janice Ruddicombe had, or rheumatic fever or – what do they call it? Meningitis. It's so hard to tell. I don't want to take any risks.'

'No, of course you don't. Tell you what, I'll walk round with a note for him straight after breakfast. I need to go to the post office anyway. I've got a letter to post to our Jackie.'

'Already? She won't even be halfway across the Atlantic yet.'

'No, but I'd like it to be there waiting for her when she arrives.'

'You should have posted it before she went then,' Tom observed, helping himself to more fried potato. 'It's the *Queen Elizabeth* and the *Queen Mary* that the post goes on.'

'Is it? I didn't know that.' Alice looked disconcerted. 'Well, it still needs to go as soon as possible. It'll catch the *Queen Mary* anyway.'

As soon as she had finished breakfast, she took the letter and the note that Joanna had scribbled for the doctor, and set off. At the bottom of the farm drive she met Jacob Prout, who was clearing culverts. He straightened up when he saw her.

'All get off all right, then?'

'Yes, we saw the ship go down Southampton Water. I got to admit, it were a proper sight. You'd never believe how big it is, Jacob. I've seen plenty of pictures, but they'm nothing like the real thing.'

He grunted and rested on his long-handled shovel. 'Dare say you were a bit upset, saying goodbye to your youngest.'

'Yes, I was, but you got to let them go, Jacob. Even the girls, these days. It's not like when we were young and maids did what their parents told them.'

'Boys too,' Jacob said. 'Come the time us was leaving school, your dad would already have been to see about a job for you. 'Twasn't no use you saying you didn't want to be a carpenter or a stockman or whatever he'd got fixed up, you just went and did it. Until the war came along and changed it all, anyway.'

'It's the last war that's changed things most,' Alice said. 'I know women got the vote and that after the Great War, but they still gave the men their jobs back. This time, they've not been so keen. Look at our Val, carrying on nursing even after she was married, till little Christopher was on the way. And Hilary Napier, thinking she could run that big estate all on her own. And our Jackie, off to America and living her own life, to all intents and purposes, before she'm twenty-one. And there didn't seem to be a thing me and her father could do about it. It was like we weren't even there to have a say.'

From what Jacob had heard, this wasn't quite true – Ted and Alice had had plenty to say – but he let it pass. He changed the subject.

'Have you seen my Jennifer lately, Alice?'

'She were at the WI meeting last week. Why?'

'You'd have seen her without her coat on, then. I just wondered if you'd noticed anything.'

Alice looked at him. She knew quite well what he meant, but it wouldn't be seemly to put it into words. She said cautiously, 'I might have done. Have her said anything to you, then?'

'Not as such, no. But I'm expecting her to any day. Not that there's anything to *see*, exactly – not yet. It's just a sort of feeling I got.'

Alice nodded. 'I wouldn't be at all surprised, Jacob. Anyway, I can't stand here chattering, I got a note to take to the doctor from Joanna. Our Robin's a bit poorly.'

'Is he now?' Jacob gave her a quick bright glance. 'Just in the mornings, is it?'

'Yes it is, now you mention it,' Alice said, surprised. 'Why?'

'He ain't the only one,' Jacob told her. 'There's quite a few of they little tackers sending in notes of a morning. Tummy ache, most of them, but some says it's their heads.'

'Dear me!' Alice exclaimed. 'There must be something going round.'

'Not so much going round,' he said darkly, turning back to his work. 'More like in the school the whole time. I might be wrong, mind, but it ain't like it was when young Stella were there. And that's all I'm saying.'

Alice stared at him for a moment, then hurried on. She wasn't sure what Jacob had meant by that, but if there was some germ that the children were catching, it ought to be seen to. Mrs Dawe, the cleaner, was the one to talk to, but Alice knew she wouldn't take at all kindly to the suggestion that the school was dirty. It was difficult to know what to do. Perhaps she might mention it quietly to the doctor when he came to see Robin. There was no sense in alarming Joanna, after all.

'Now, you make sure you keeps an eye on him,' Maggie Culliford told her daughter Betty. 'I know you can't sit next to him, but you can look after him in the playground. He's only little and he might get picked on.'

Betty pushed out her bottom lip but said nothing. She took her brother's hand and led him across to the school door. Billy hung back a little, looking over his shoulder at his mother, but she waved encouragingly and he went inside.

Maggie was just turning away, with Jeanie clutching one hand while she held the handle of the battered pushchair with the other, when Miss Watkins, the teacher who had taken Stella's place, came out. Maggie paused and Miss Watkins approached her.

'I see Miss Kemp agreed to letting him start early,' she said in her rather grating voice. 'I hope you've made sure he can take himself to the lavatory and blow his nose properly.'

'My kids can all look after theirselves,' Maggie said, affronted. 'They has to, when there's so many of them.'

'Yes,' Miss Watkins said, glancing at the two smaller children. She was a plain-looking woman with sallow skin and straight black hair that hung down past her cheeks. Already she had a reputation for strictness and the children didn't seem to come home with as many pictures as they had when Stella was teaching them, but she had made it clear from the start that she believed in concentrating on the three Rs and that less time would be devoted to play.

'Well?' she said, as Maggie hesitated. 'Was there anything else you wanted to tell me?' Her tone was abrupt, as if she didn't think Maggie could have anything useful to say.

'Only that I hope you'll keep an eye on him, like,' Maggie said. 'He's only four and I don't want him frightened by the bigger children.'

'If you think I don't know how to look after small children ...' Miss Watkins began in a dangerous tone, and Maggie took a step back.

'It's not that. It's just that our Billy – well, he's small for his age and he's still a bit of a mummy's boy and—'

'Perhaps he shouldn't be in school, then,' the teacher said tartly. 'But since Miss Kemp's agreed, there's not much I can do about it. He'll have to take his place with the others. But you can rest assured there'll be no bullying in *my* class, Mrs Culliford. That's something I do not tolerate.'

Maggie mumbled her thanks and retreated, pulling Jeanie with her. The little girl took hold of the handle of the pushchair and whined at her mother not to go so fast, and Maggie slowed her pace.

'Sorry, my flower, I didn't mean to pull you over. I hope our Billy will be all right. That teacher don't seem as nice as poor Miss Simmons. She'd have made sure he'd wouldn't be picked on.'

'Can we have some sweets?' Jeanie asked as they approached the village shop. 'I got that penny you gave me yesterday.'

'What penny? I never gave you no penny.'

'Yes you did, when I went to Sunday school with our Betty.'

Maggie stopped. 'I gave you a ha'penny, not a penny. It was for your collection. Didn't one of the big children come round with a bag when you were singing a hymn?'

'Yes, Wendy Cole did, but she never said I had to put anything in it. I thought it was for getting pennies out, so I put my hand in and took one. I've still got the ha'penny too,' Jeanie added earnestly. 'I'll buy some sweets for Freddie as well, if you like.'

Maggie stared at her, then gave a short laugh. 'Well, if you'm not a chip off the old block! All right then, I suppose you might as well spend it now, but next week you put it into the bag, and no taking pennies out. I don't want folk saying I'm bringing my kiddies up to pinch things.'

'I didn't pinch it ...' Jeanie began, her face starting to crumple, and Maggie pulled her close for a moment.

'Of course you didn't, not really. You just didn't understand. But you do now, don't you? Come on then, let's see what Mrs Pettifer's got for a penny ha'penny, and I'll get meself some more fags while

I'm at it. Your dad went off with my packet this morning and left me short.'

They went into the village shop, where Edie Pettifer was serving Bert Foster, the butcher, with a *Daily Sketch* and a quarter of toffees. They seemed to be in the middle of a conversation, but as Maggie opened the door Edie handed over his change and he took it quickly and turned away. He gave Maggie a brief nod as he passed her and nearly fell over Freddie in his pushchair just outside.

'Well, you ought to look where you'm going,' Maggie said as he began to complain. 'I can't leave him halfway up the street, can I, and there's no room to bring him in here.' She turned back to Edie. 'Ten Woodbines, please, and Jeanie here wants a penny-ha'porth of sweets. Choose what you want, Jeanie, and don't take all day about it. I just left our Billy at the school,' she said to Edie. 'Miss Kemp let him start early seeing as I'm a bit pushed. I suppose you know I got another on the way.'

'I see that,' Edie said disapprovingly. 'How many will that make? And when's it due?'

'Nine, unless it's twins, and I reckon it'll be around the middle of July. Can't be too sure because I never got regular again after Freddie, if you know what I mean. I was breastfeeding, see. But that's what I think, going on when I started being sick.'

'And how are you keeping?' Edie handed over the green cigarette packet, keeping an eye on Jeanie while she did so. You never knew with these Culliford children. She'd caught the oldest boy, Jimmy, red-handed once with a Mars bar he hadn't paid for, and with a father like theirs it wasn't surprising they didn't know right from wrong. The girls didn't seem so bad – Brenda, the biggest, was at the secondary modern school in Tavistock, and Miss Kemp spoke well of Shirley and Betty – but it was just as well to take no chances.

'I'm not too bad,' Maggie said, answering her question. 'The sickness is the worst. It don't seem to be passing off like it usually does. I generally get over it by three months. And I'm getting more tired than before. That's why I asked if Billy could start school. It's a help not to have him under me feet for a few hours each day.'

'It'd be more help if that man of yours gave you a bit more consideration,' Edie said tartly. 'Nine kiddies in your situation! You wants to have a good talk to him, you do.'

67

Maggie shrugged. 'He's a man, isn't he? Come on, Jeanie, have you made up your mind yet? I can't stand here all day.'

Jeanie asked for an ounce of toffee crunch with a liquorice strip for Freddie, and Edie weighed out the few sweets, put them on a square of blue paper and made it into a cone. 'There you are, my bird, and don't eat them before your dinner. Oh, hello, Mrs Warren,' she added as Joyce Warren came in. 'And what can I do for you?'

Maggie went out into the village street. She hadn't missed Edie's reference to her 'situation'. I suppose she means my Arthur never having a proper job, she thought. But that's not his fault, if nobody will give him one. He's a good worker when he puts his mind to it. The trouble was, he didn't always feel like putting his mind to it. He'd go down the pub and have a few pints too many, wake up in the morning with a thick head and turn over and go back to sleep. Or he'd be out half the night poaching and not wake up till gone nine, when most men had been at work for an hour or two already. Or he'd have words with the boss or foreman and get the sack. It was just the way he was, and there was nothing anyone could do about it.

Maggie had known Arthur all her life. They'd grown up playing in the fields and woods together, a gang of them, and as they'd got older they'd taken to meeting on the bridge by the ford of an evening. Gradually they'd paired off and started slipping away and going for walks on their own, and that was how she'd come to be married to Arthur Culliford – Jim, as he was known then – by the time she was seventeen, with their first baby on the way.

They'd called the baby Jimmy, after his dad, and Arthur had then decided to use his second name. It sounded older, he'd said, more like a father ought to be. It had taken a while, and his mother still called him Jim sometimes, but people had got used to it pretty quickly, just as they'd got used to the untidy appearance of the cottage they rented from the Squire and to the constant stream of babies born there.

Maggie walked slowly along the street. They'd need a new push-chair when the new kiddy got to walking stage, she thought. This one was nearly falling to bits and it squealed like a cat with its tail trodden on. Better get Arthur to put a drop of oil on it when he came home.

'Can I eat my sweets now?' Jeanie asked, looking at Maggie's shopping bag.

'No. You heard what Mrs Pettifer said. Not until after dinner.'

'But I'm hungry.'

'You should have eaten your bread and milk then, instead of just messing about with it. I had to give it to the cat in the end. And stop dragging your feet – walk properly.'

'What's for dinner?' Jeanie asked, dragging her feet even more.

'I don't know yet. Baked beans on toast, maybe. You like that, don't you?'

'No.'

'Well you did last week,' Maggie said, exasperated. 'Come on, Jeanie. I got all the washing to do. Our Billy'll be home before we are at this rate.'

'I wish I could go to school,' Jeanie said mutinously. 'Why couldn't I?'

'Because you're not old enough,' Maggie snapped. I wish you could go too, she thought, you'm more trouble than a barrowload of monkeys. But there was no use wishing – Jeanie was only three, for all she was as bright as any five-year-old if chattering the hind leg off a donkey was any sign, and Miss Kemp would never agree to it. It had been hard enough to persuade her to take Billy.

Maggie wondered how he was getting along. He was the most timid of all her children. It would be nice if this new baby was a boy. Billy could be an older brother to him then. It might bring him out of himself.

I didn't go much on that Miss Watkins, thought Maggie. Boot-faced old hag, for all she's probably no older than me. I hope she don't pick on him because he's so little.

She shoved the pushchair through the gateway. It was about time Arthur mended that gate; it was hanging off its hinges, and now that Freddie was on his feet, he could wander out at any time and be down by the ford getting drowned before you could say knife. There was that old motorbike still in bits too, that Arthur had got from some chap in Tavistock and thought he could mend and sell for a few pounds. Anyone with half an eye could have seen it was never going to go again, and now there it was with its petrol tank laying on the beaten earth beside it and its engine all to pieces and going rusty. Freddie could hurt himself on that too. She'd found him out there only yesterday, his hands all covered in oil and his thumb stuck in his mouth, crying because it tasted nasty.

69

She walked round the side of the cottage and pushed open the peeling back door. Arthur had been going to paint it sometime and had even got half a bucket of paint that Bernie Nethercott had had left over from doing up the outside of the pub, but it had stood there so long now that a thick skin had developed on top of the paint and the bucket had filled up with greenish water. That was another thing Freddie could get into if she didn't watch him.

Arthur was sitting at the kitchen table, reading yesterday's *News of the World* and eating bread and marmalade. He was wearing a grubby striped shirt with its sleeves rolled up and a greasy waistcoat. His swarthy face was unshaven and his dark hair needed a cut. Maggie looked at him with disfavour.

'Any tea in the pot? I just took Billy to school.'

Arthur nudged the pot towards her with his elbow. The cup she'd used earlier that morning was still on the table and she poured in some milk from the bottle, then poured some more into two enamel mugs and gave them to the children. She took Freddie out of his pushchair and set him on the floor.

'Go and play with your bricks,' she said to them, and helped herself to tea and a slice of bread. 'Did you hear what I said, Arthur?'

'Yes. You said you took Billy to school. So that's all right, then.'

'I hope it is. I didn't take to that new teacher at all. She's not a bit like Miss Simmons.'

'Pretty little piece, Stella Simmons.' Arthur was still immersed in the sports pages.

'Well, nobody could say that about Miss Watkins. Proper hatchet-faced she is, and got a nasty look in her eye. I don't reckon she's all that nice to the kiddies, and our Billy's only four. I'm wondering if I done right to send him.'

'He'll be all right. Toughen him up a bit. You'm too soft on him.'

'I'm trying to bring him up decent,' Maggie retorted, lighting one of her Woodbines and spreading margarine on the slice of bread. 'I want him to know what 'tis like to work for a living. Which he won't learn from his father.'

Arthur slapped down his paper. 'I work for a living! I work bloody hard – when I get the chance. It ain't my fault nobody round here'll give me a steady job for a regular wage.'

'Ain't it? So you going off poaching every night got nothing to do with it? And picking up stuff in that sleazy little pub in Tavi and selling it in the market when you know full well it's been pinched, that got nothing to do with it neither? It's a wonder you ain't had the coppers round here a lot more than you have already. I tell you, Arthur, I live in fear of a knock on the front door. If you get put in prison again, I don't know what we'll do.'

'I ain't going to prison,' he grunted. 'You know Squire turns a blind eye to a rabbit being took now and then, and now he and Miss Hilary got that Kellaway toeing the line, nobody takes any notice. I don't hear you saying no when I brings one home under me coat, anyway.'

'I can't afford to, can I? A bit of rabbit stew's the only meat meal the kiddies get some weeks.' She drank some tea and then took a long drag on her cigarette. 'I mean it, Arthur. Go careful, for pity's sake. We got another mouth to feed come July. People are saying we got too many already and I don't want any of them to end up in the workhouse.'

'The workhouse? Why should any of them end up there?'

'It's what happens if people think they'm not being taken proper care of. It's true, Arthur. I've seen them there, when I went to visit Father after he went in. Little tackers no bigger than our Freddie, all in blue smocks and crying for their mothers. It nearly broke my heart.'

'Well it ain't going to happen to ours,' he said firmly. 'And our Jimmy'll be leaving school come July and getting a job himself. He'll bring fifteen bob or so in every week. Anyway, I got to go now. It might surprise you to know,' he went on heavily as he rose from the table, 'that I got a *job* to go to today. A job of work, carrying bricks for one of the builders in Tavi. So I'll be coming home tonight with money in me pocket. And I got to catch the bus in ten minutes, so if you can put a couple of bits of bread together with some fish paste, and a bottle of tea, I'll be on me way.'

Too surprised to speak, Maggie did as she was told. She put the sandwiches in a brown paper bag and poured the rest of the tea from the pot into an old beer bottle. Arthur pushed his arms into his working jacket and shoved the packet and bottle into his pockets, then shouldered his way out through the door. He paused, and looked back.

'Don't you worry about our Bill. It'll be the making of him, getting to school early. Now, you put your feet up and have a rest and I'll be back on the four o'clock bus for me tea.'

Maggie stared after him. She looked round the cluttered kitchen at the newspapers piled in one corner, the washing hung untidily on a wooden clothes horse round the meagre fire, the dishes from last night's supper pushed to one end of the table to make room for this morning's sketchy breakfast, and gave a short laugh.

'Put me feet up and have a rest!' she said aloud. 'Huh! Chance'd be a fine thing.' Then she shrugged and said, 'Suppose I might as well, all the same, while the kids are quiet. I won't get much chance later on.'

She sat down again, lit another Woodbine and pulled the *News of the World* across the table. In a few minutes she was immersed in the latest scandal and Billy, Miss Watkins and the hazards that awaited Freddie in the garden were forgotten.

Chapter Eleven

John Wolstencroft had made his visit and returned to Exeter to draft Gilbert's will before Hilary was able to hear David's voice again.

He rang late one evening, after her father had gone to bed. She went to the hall to answer the phone, and gripped the receiver tightly as she heard his voice.

'David!'

' I had to ring,' he said, sounding very far away. 'How are you, darling? Is it all right to talk?'

'Yes, but ... Hold on, I'll go into the office.' She put down the receiver, wishing that she had a telephone in her bedroom, and hurried through to the office, hoping that the call would not be cut off. To her relief, he was still there. 'How are you, David? How's Sybil?'

'Much the same. Still unconscious – she could stay like this for weeks. Months.' His voice shook. 'Years. Her parents have been up from Worcester to see her. Her mother's distraught.'

'How awful for them,' Hilary said sincerely. Whatever she knew, or thought, about Sybil, it must be terrible for parents to see their child in such a condition. 'But what's going to happen if she doesn't come round? Will she just stay in hospital?'

'Not where she is, no. If there was nowhere else for her to go, she'd have to be moved into some kind of nursing home.'

'What do you mean – if there's nowhere else for her to go? Where else *could* she go?'

'Well, she could come home,' he said bleakly. 'I'm her husband. Naturally, I'm the one to take care of her.'

'You? But David – you're a doctor—'

'And therefore more qualified than most husbands. And the house can be adapted – she can have the main bedroom, so that there's room for nursing equipment and so on. I'd have to have a nurse in, of course. Two or three, I suppose, taking turn and turn about. I couldn't be here all the time.'

'That's what I mean. You've got a busy life. How can you take on an invalid who can do nothing for herself? Even with nurses . . .'

'I'm no busier than any other working man,' he said quietly. 'No more so than a factory worker on overtime, working twelve hours a day. And such a man wouldn't be able to afford the care I can pay for. And I already have "taken her on", Hilary – the day we got married.'

'Yes, but . . .' Her voice trailed away. She knew he was right. It was perfectly feasible for David to care for his wife at home, and she knew that he cared also for his marriage vows. He had already, against his own nature, broken those that demanded that he keep himself only to his wife, but he would honour his promise to keep her in sickness. He would never abandon her now.

'What about her parents?' she asked with a flutter of hope. 'Wouldn't her mother want to take her?'

'I'm sure she would. She's never liked me much as it is – she's Sybil all over again. I think Harold has quite a difficult life. But it's not possible. Beatrice has severe arthritis and uses a wheelchair. Besides, it's my job.'

'Yes, I know.' The tiny tremor of hope died. 'Oh David, I'm so sorry.' It was pitifully inadequate, she knew, but what else could she say? 'I wish there was something I could do,' she added, feeling that that was not much better.

'Just be there,' he said. 'Just let me ring you sometimes, to talk, to know that you're with me in your heart. Just – just agree to meet me occasionally, so that I can see you and touch you, if only for a little while.'

'David, we've talked about this already.'

'I know. You think we should stop. But how can I go on, with all this around me, knowing that you're there and I can't talk to you? Hilary, please. We were meant to be together – you know that. And if we can't, who could grudge us just a few moments now and then. Just to see your face, touch your hand, hear your voice. I won't ask more than that, I promise. Please, darling. Please.'

She could not deny him. Knowing that she wanted it as badly as he, she could not deny his need. She leaned her forehead against her palm and said, 'In a little while, then. Not yet. I can't leave my father yet. And you can't leave Sybil – not until you know for sure what's going to happen, whether she's coming home or not. But in a few weeks – when the weather's better and I can risk going away – maybe then ...'

'It will be an eternity,' he said. 'But as long as you promise ...'

'I don't have to promise,' she said quietly. 'I can't. And neither can you. We just have to trust.'

'Just at this moment,' he said, 'I feel as if you are the only thing in the whole world that I *can* trust. I feel as if I'm in a shifting sea, with currents pulling me in every direction, and you are like a rock.'

'And you're my rock too,' she said, for his description matched exactly her own turmoil. 'We'll be two rocks together, standing against the tide.'

He laughed suddenly. 'We'll be writing poetry next! Oh Hilary, you don't know how much good it does me to talk to you. I can ring again, can't I? Soon?'

'Yes,' she said softly. 'Ring again – soon. Good night now, my love.'

'Good night, darling,' he whispered, and added, 'I love you.'

As gently as if she were giving him back his hand, she replaced the receiver. For a moment or two she sat very still. It came to her that she should be wondering if she had done the right thing, but this time there was no doubt in her heart. The image of twin rocks in a turbulent sea rose strongly before her, and she put out her hands, as if to cling to their jagged surfaces. Then she brought them back slowly to cover her face, and the tears that seeped between her fingers were as salty as that storm-lashed tide.

'That Glenn Miller picture's on in Tavi next week,' Terry Pettifer remarked to Patsy next morning when he and Bob came to continue their checking of all the electrical sockets at the Barton. They had already discovered a few faults, and Hilary wanted to be quite sure that everything was safe. 'You wouldn't like to come and see it with me, would you? It's James Stewart.'

Patsy was standing on a chair, dusting the curtain rail in the spare bedroom. She turned and looked down at him. 'I might.'

'Would you?' He flushed with delight and she hastened to correct him.

'I only said *might*.'

'Yes, but you will, won't you? It's really good and it's got lots of his music in it. You like Glenn Miller music, don't you? "In The Mood" and all that.' He winked.

Patsy ignored his wink. 'It's all right. A bit old-fashioned, though. I mean, he died years ago, in the war. I'd rather have Dean Martin or Tony Bennett.'

'What about Doris Day? I bet you like Doris Day. *Calamity Jane*'s coming soon – we could go and see that too.'

'I haven't said I'll come to this one yet.' Patsy stepped off the chair. 'Anyway, my dad'll never let me.'

'Don't ask him, then. Say you're going with one of your friends.'

'That's telling lies!'

'No it's not. I'm one of your friends, aren't I? I would be if you went to the pictures with me, anyway.'

Patsy laughed, and he went on, encouraged. 'Come on, Patsy. Say yes. I don't want to go on my own.'

'Oh, so that's the only reason you asked me, is it?' she retorted, tossing her head. 'Billy No-Mates, are you? Got no other friends of your own?'

'Plenty,' he said. 'But none I want to take to the pictures.'

'I'll think about it,' Patsy conceded, starting to polish the chest of drawers. 'I'm not sure I can manage next week. What night were you thinking of?'

'Any night. Tuesday or Thursday would be best, for the late bus back. It goes to the Little Burracombe turning as well.'

'It comes here first, though. I'd have to go the last bit on my own. My dad don't like me walking from the stop in the dark.'

'You wouldn't have to. I'd see you home and then walk back across the Clam.' Terry had no intention of saying good night to Patsy on the little bus that rattled through the villages taking people home from Tavistock. 'Honestly, Patsy, I'd look after you. Say you'll come.'

Patsy regarded him. Some of her objections were genuine ones – her father wouldn't agree for a moment to her going to the pictures with a boy, especially one he hardly knew. But she knew perfectly well that it would never occur to him that she might be in any danger walking the short distance from the bus stop to the farm at night through the quiet lanes of Little Burracombe. Patsy had her own reasons for not wanting to say good night to Terry on the bus, and they were very similar to his.

'All right,' she said, rubbing lavender wax into the mahogany chest. 'I'll come on Tuesday. But I'll have to be home by ten. Dad don't like me being out any later than that.'

'That's all right.' Like all the other boys who were beginning to think about taking girls out, Terry was used to a curfew. Fathers, who you'd think would know better if they remembered their own youth, generally set a time for their daughters to be home, just as if nothing could happen that shouldn't until then. But Terry wasn't intending to do anything he shouldn't anyway. How own father had drilled it into him that you didn't mess about with respectable girls like Patsy Shillabeer.

They grinned a little self-consciously at each other and then Bob called out from another room and Terry winked again and scurried back to his work, while Patsy went on polishing, a small smile playing about her lips.

It was the first time a boy had asked her out. Did that mean Terry was now her boyfriend? She felt a small bubble of excitement rising inside her. All right, so he wasn't the best-looking boy in the village, but since they'd both been working at the Barton, she'd grown to like him. And really, he wasn't all that ugly. In fact, he wasn't ugly at all. Not when you got to know him.

Patsy thought she might like to get to know Terry Pettifer even better.

'There's definitely a hint of romance in the air,' Jennifer told Travis as they sat down to their shepherd's pie that evening. 'Patsy's got a real sparkle in her eyes, and wherever Terry and Bob happen to be working, she finds excuses to go and do a bit more cleaning and polishing. They have their sandwiches in the kitchen and she asked Hilary off her own bat if she could make them a pot of tea, even though I'd have done it anyway. I've got a feeling he's asked her out one evening. There was talk of that film, *The Glenn Miller Story*. I said we were going and she was rather keen to know which night!'

'Doesn't want us to see them, I suppose,' Travis said, amused.

'Well, it probably won't last. You know what these young romances are – they soon fizzle out.'

'Yes, and Bob told me they'd have finished all their checking by the end of the week, so Terry and Patsy won't be seeing each other every day. It would be a shame if they didn't enjoy it for a while, though. I don't think Patsy's had a boyfriend before.'

'Well, they're both pretty young. I can't imagine her father will be too pleased about it.'

'I don't think he's going to know,' Jennifer said. 'Not that there's anything to know anyway. They're only going to the pictures.' She smiled. 'The first boyfriend I had, when I was about fifteen, used to ask me to go to the pictures with him and then say he'd meet me inside! We had to arrange which row we'd be in because the B film would have started and it would be dark.'

'Why on earth did he do that?' Travis asked, helping himself to more carrots.

'So that I'd pay for myself, of course! I don't suppose he had much more money than I had, although he did have a morning paper round, but boys are always expected to pay for girls, aren't they?'

'Well, I hope he bought the sweets.' Travis grinned. 'And let's hope our baby is a girl, so that we don't have to give her extra pocket money when she starts going out with boys.'

'We'll have to pay for her wedding, though,' Jennifer pointed out, and he groaned.

'It's nothing but expense, having a family! How on earth do people like the Cullifords manage?'

'They don't. They live in a state of chaos in a poor house, and get by on whatever Arthur can earn.' She glanced at him sideways. 'Or poach.'

'Don't remind me! I'll never forget the way that little girl of his cried out when that gun went off when we were up in Top Woods after poachers. Thank God it was no worse than a broken arm, though that was bad enough. And I've never been entirely convinced he wasn't part of the gang. It was just too much of a coincidence, him being there as well.'

'I think it *was* coincidence, though. Arthur may be a bit of a ne'er-do-well, but I think both he and Maggie are fond of their children. I don't believe he would ever have taken her poaching.'

'He's taken that eldest boy of his, though,' Travis said grimly. 'Jimmy, isn't it? I'd swear I saw the pair of them skulking home along the hedges early one morning last September.'

'Well, you know what Colonel Napier said. Give him a bit of leeway. He's one of their tenants and what harm if he does take a rabbit or two, or even a pheasant? He might sell them at the odd back door around the village, but he's not taking them into Tavistock or Plymouth by the sackload. And most of them go to feed all those children – they'd starve otherwise.'

Travis grunted, and she knew this was something they'd never entirely agree on. Like the gamekeeper, Travis would have liked there to be no poaching at all on the estate.

They had come a long way from Patsy and Terry's little romance, she reflected. She and Travis could talk for hours without boring each other, simply because they were so at ease together and could discuss so many things, and even disagree without letting it come between them.

I used to think I was quite happy, living on my own and reading or listening to the wireless for company, she thought. But being married to Travis is so much better!

Chapter Twelve

O nce she had regained the sensation in her back and legs, Stella began to make good progress. It was hard and certainly more painful, but whenever she began to think it was too much to bear, she would remind herself of what it had been like not to be able to feel anything at all. Those dark days and nights when she had believed she would never walk again and could not be a proper wife to Felix were a time she recalled with horror. The pain she suffered now was nothing in comparison with the misery she had felt then.

'I'm sorry I was so horrid to you,' she said to Felix as he sat by her bed, stroking her hand. 'I must have made you really miserable.'

'It wasn't your fault,' he said, smiling tenderly at her. 'You weren't yourself. You'd been unconscious for so long, you didn't really know what had happened to you – it must have been like a nightmare you couldn't wake up from. No wonder you were confused.'

'I didn't feel at all confused. I felt absolutely certain that I couldn't marry you.'

'A sure sign of being confused,' he said with a grin. 'There was never any question of it – not in my mind.'

'I thought I'd be in bed for the rest of my life. How could I be a proper wife to you? I'd just have been an encumbrance.'

'Now, you're not to start talking like that again,' Felix said sternly. 'For one thing, you would never be an encumbrance, and for another, it's not going to happen. You're going to be walking again before we know it, and we'll be getting married as soon as you feel ready. Only don't take too long to feel ready,' he added. 'I'm finding it very difficult to manage without you.'

'Go on – I bet you've got crowds of women beating at the vicarage

80

door, bringing you cakes and wanting to cook you meals.'

'That's what I mean,' he said, thinking of Tessa Latimer, whose attentions had been a little too seductive, and Olivia Lydiard, the naval commander's wife who seemed to want to take him over. 'They won't leave me alone – I need you there to protect me.'

Stella laughed, and he thought how good it was to hear her happy, infectious chuckle once more.

'You must miss Dottie and her cakes and scones,' she said. 'Has anyone heard from her yet? Shouldn't they have arrived in America by now?'

''They'd have arrived in New York at the end of last week, I think. But then they've got to get to Corning, where Joe and Russell live. I don't know how long that would take. I'm sure they'd have written the moment they arrived, though. I expect Alice will hear soon and she'll lose no time in telling everyone else.'

'Poor Alice,' Stella said. 'She was really anxious about Jackie going off like that. But Val told me that Brian's coming home soon, so that will cheer her up.'

'Tomorrow, I think. I don't hear so much about Burracombe now, of course, but I saw Basil yesterday and he told me that's what he'd heard. He and Grace send their love, by the way.'

'That's nice. I wonder if they'll come to visit me one day, when they've got time. I feel much more like seeing people now. For a while, when I was so miserable, I didn't want to see anyone at all, but now I'd like everyone to come in – even the Crocker twins!'

'I think that's going a bit far,' Felix said with a grin. 'They'd set your recovery back by at least a month. But perhaps one or two of the children could come, if Miss Kemp would bring them. Who would you like most to see?'

Stella considered. 'Shirley Culliford, I think, and Betty as well. And Janice Ruddicombe, since she's going to be my bridesmaid. And I mustn't miss out the boys – what about Robin Tozer? He could come in with Val and Joanna. I'm only allowed three visitors at a time.'

'The girls are going to have to come in separately as well, then,' Felix pointed out. 'Why not just have Shirley and Janice, and have Betty and another child later on?'

'I think Betty would like to come in with her sister. I'll ask Val to bring Janice and Joanna can bring Robin. And the first thing I'll do when I'm allowed home is go to the school and see all of them.' She glanced at Felix's face. 'What's the matter?'

'Nothing,' he said, squeezing her hand and using his other hand to brush at his eyes. 'It's just – hearing you making plans for seeing the children, and for when you come out of hospital ... I was beginning to think you'd never talk like that again.'

'So was I,' she confessed. 'But let's not think about that any more. There is one thing worrying me, Felix. Where am I going to go when I do come out? I can't expect Dottie to look after me, even if I could manage her stairs, and she might not even be back from America anyway. And I can't come to you – not before we're married.'

'If we had someone living in the vicarage with us ...' he began, but she shook her head.

'I can't think who we could ask to do that. Anyway, it's not the way I want to start our life together. I want to do it properly – going to church and getting married, and then going back to live in our own home for the first time. But I just don't know where I can go in between.'

'When do you think you'll be coming out?' he asked, and she shrugged.

'I don't really know. Not until the plaster's off my leg, anyway. That should be in about a fortnight. The leg will be quite weak at first, too. I might have to stay even longer.'

'We've got time to think about it, then. Don't worry, darling. I'm sure there'll be plenty of people willing to have you to stay until you can manage Dottie's stairs again. Of course,' he added hopefully, 'we could always get married the minute you come out, just quietly as you really wanted, and then you could come straight to the vicarage.'

'Indeed we couldn't! I've got used to the idea of a big wedding now and we couldn't possibly disappoint all those people. Think of all the preparations that have already been made because we were supposed to be getting married just after Christmas – the sewing and baking and everything. Dottie's taken an enormous amount of trouble with my dress, and some of the bridesmaids', *and* she's made the cake. And there are all your relatives too. And Maddy. And—'

'All right, all right!' he exclaimed, holding up both hands. 'It was just a thought. But we'll have to arrange a date soon. What about Easter?'

'No, you're far too busy then, and so are your relatives. Whitsun would be better. Whit Monday – that would be nice. It's a bank holi-day, so everyone would be able to come, and the Pentecost services will be over, and the girls at school will all be in white dresses. It's usually warmer by then, too.'

'Whit Monday,' Felix said thoughtfully. 'That sounds ideal. And it gives you lots of time to recover.' He leaned down and kissed her. 'I'm looking forward to it already!'

The bell for the end of visiting time rang then and they kissed goodbye. Felix walked out of the hospital with a jaunty step, feeling happier than he had since before that terrible accident at the beginning of December. Stella was on the mend, she was cheerful and optimis-tic, and making plans for the future. For their future, together. It was something he had begun to think would never happen.

He got into the little Austin that Hilary had lent him and started the engine. The cold, dark day seemed suddenly light and filled with the promise of spring. It would not always be winter. Whitsun would come, and with it a new life for himself and Stella.

Not only that, he had a very good idea as to who might be pleased to take her into their home until such time as she could return to Dottie's cottage.

Brian Tozer and his wife were, as Felix had said, due home the next day. Preparations at the farmhouse were complete, cakes and pies baked, a large joint of beef ready to be roasted, and the bedroom fit, as Ted observed, for the Queen and Prince Philip themselves.

Ted and Alice had left in good time to meet the train in Tavistock. They drove up Kilworthy Hill and along Quant Park into the station yard, where coal was being loaded on to a lorry ready to be delivered to local homes, and crossed the bridge to the down platform. The train was coming direct from London and would be continuing to Plymouth. It chugged into view at last, arriving at the platform with a hiss and a snort and a cloud of steam, and for a few minutes nobody could see a thing. Then the steam cleared and Alice ran forward with a cry.

'There they are! Just getting off – go and help them with their lug-gage, Ted, before they get carried on to Plymouth. Oh Brian, it's some good to see you.' She gave her son a hug, tears pouring down her face, then turned to the blonde woman standing by his side. 'And Margret, too – or can we call you Peggy?'

'Brian calls me Peggy,' her daughter-in-law said a little stiffly. 'It is an endearment between us.'

Alice looked at her a little uncertainly, not knowing whether this was a yes or a no. 'Well, it'll be nice and friendly for the family too,' she said, deciding upon 'yes'. 'Anyway, let's make sure we've got all your bags before the train starts again. My stars, you got enough to fill the truck three times over.'

'We had to bring everything, Mum. What else were we supposed to do with it?'

'I know, my bird, I know. I'm not saying you shouldn't have. We'll find room for it all. But however did you manage on the train? Anyway, never mind all that, let's get it across the bridge and take you home. It's *so* good to have you back,' she chattered on as they gathered up suitcases, canvas grips and Brian's kitbag. 'Just a shame you couldn't get here before our Jackie went off to America. We had a letter from her yesterday by the afternoon post. Said the crossing was lovely – they went on the *Queen Elizabeth*, you know. Dottie Friend went as well, though we never thought she would, but our Joe persuaded her somehow. He'd like her to stay there but she never will, her heart's in Burracombe, always has been and always will be. I'm not so sure about our Jackie, though. Me and your dad—'

'All right, Mum,' Brian interrupted. 'We can hear all that later. You haven't even asked us if we had a good journey.'

Alice stared at him, then put her hand to her mouth and laughed. 'No more I have! Whatever must you be thinking of me, Peggy my flower? I must have left my manners at home. It's because I'm so pleased to see you, that's what it is. Well, did it go all right, then? You managed getting through London with all these bags? I can't even lift this kitbag of yours.'

'We managed very well, thank you,' Margret said. 'Brian is very good at such things.'

'I dare say he is. He was always the one to take charge even when he was a little tacker, and now he'm a sergeant … Not that you are any more, are you, Brian? Not now you've left the army.'

'Once a soldier, always a soldier,' Ted declared as they dumped their burdens beside the farm truck. 'Now, stop your chatter, Alice, and let's get all this stowed. We got a lot to do on the farm and I don't want to leave Tom working on his own too long.'

'I'll do my bit, once we've settled in,' Brian declared, throwing his kitbag into the back as if it were full of feathers. 'I haven't forgotten how to farm.'

'You'll be welcome,' Ted said, getting into the driving seat. 'Not that you'll be with us long, I doubt. You'll be looking for a job, though I can't say there's much in Burracombe.'

Brian helped his wife in to the back seat and Alice took the front, beside Ted. The truck trundled out of the yard and down the steep hill into Tavistock and across the square.

'Doesn't change much, does it?' Brian remarked. 'Same old town hall, same old church ... Looks as if it's been asleep ever since we were here last.'

'No reason for change,' Alice said. 'It's not as if we got any bomb damage, not like Plymouth – fair flattened, that was ...' She bit her lip and glanced over her shoulder at Margret, but the German woman was staring out of the window and appeared not to have heard. Alice gave herself a stern reminder not to talk about the war. It was bound to be a sensitive subject, and best avoided.

The weather had been dry for the past few days and there were only a few patches of snow left on the tors as they drove out across the moor towards Burracombe. They dipped down into the sheltered bowl where the village lay and turned up the track that led to the farm. Val and Luke were walking towards the house, pushing Christopher in his pram, and Ted slowed down to pass them. They looked round and waved cheerfully, and Alice wound down her window.

'Here we are, safe and sound. Here's your little nephew, Brian – first time you've seen him, isn't it? He's a real little Tozer, though some folk think he takes more after his father.'

'He'll grow out of that, with any luck.' Luke grinned and held his hand up towards Brian's window. 'How are you, Brian? Hello, Peggy.'

'Margret,' Brian said, but nobody heard him because Christopher caught sight of his grandmother at that moment and let out a crow of excitement. Brian reached through and shook Luke's hand briefly, and Margret gave him a cool smile. Val looked at them both a little doubtfully, and stepped back.

'We can say hello properly when we get indoors,' she said. 'It's too cold to stand about here and I expect you want to get out of that truck. It's not exactly a Rolls-Royce.'

'It's good enough for us,' Ted said, but he drove on and parked in the yard, by the small barn. They all scrambled out, and Luke hurried along to help with the luggage. Val manoeuvred Christopher's pram into the big kitchen and parked it by the staircase, and they all crowded in, festooned with bags and cases, which they dumped on the floor.

'They'd better go upstairs right away or us won't have room to move,' Alice began, but Minnie was getting up out of her chair by the range, her wrinkled face wreathed in smiles, and Brian went straight across to take her in his arms.

'Hello, Gran. How are you? You look younger than ever!'

'Go on, you know I'm getting on for ninety,' she said, giving him a push and then a kiss. 'I must say, you'm looking as well as ever. Army life suits you. And how's Peggy, then?' She held out her arms to the tall blonde woman. ''Tis a pleasure to welcome you, my dear, and you've met us all before so you've got to make yourself right at home. You'm one of the family, after all.'

Margret smiled and offered her cheek to be kissed, then turned to Brian.

'Your mother is right. We should take our luggage upstairs, and I would like a wash.' Her English was good, though accented, and her voice rather deep.

'The big spare room's all ready for you,' Alice said, fluttering around them. 'And you can use the one next door for your things. It's our Jackie's room really, but she'll not be wanting it for a few weeks.'

'I thought you said she'd gone to America for a few months, not weeks,' Brian said, swinging his kitbag on to his shoulder and lifting a heavy case. 'That's if she comes back at all.'

Val gave her mother a quick look and said hastily, 'Of course she'll be coming back. Why shouldn't she?'

Her brother shrugged. 'Why should she? There are a lot more op-portunities in America than there are here. Jackie's a bright kid – I wouldn't blame her if she decided to emigrate. Plenty of people do these days.'

He clumped up the stairs, followed by Margret with two more cases. There was a silence in the kitchen and then Val said, 'He doesn't really know anything about what Jackie'll do, Mum. She said she'd come back, and she will.'

But Alice's bright joy in her son's homecoming seemed to have evaporated. She turned away and went to open the oven door and peer in.

'This joint's ready to come out now. I'll get the vegetables on and it'll all be ready by the time they come down. Lay the table, will you, Val, and give our Joanna a call. She ought to have finished dressing Heather by now. And sit you down, Luke, you'm making the place look untidy standing in the middle of the floor like that.'

'I'll go and tell Tom dinner's nearly ready,' Luke said, with an uneasy glance at his wife, and went out.

By the time the family was all in the kitchen and seated round the table, greetings over, vegetables in their dishes and the joint of beef carved, the atmosphere had been restored. Brian was the centre of attention as he told them stories of his life in the army in Germany, and Margret sat beside him, smiling and praising everything that was put in front of her. The roast beef was followed by apple pie, spiced with cloves and served with a large dish of clotted cream made by Alice from their own milk, and the feast finished off with a pot of tea.

'Peggy'd rather have coffee,' Brian said as Alice passed round the cups.

'Oh – I'm sorry, I ought to have thought. We've only got Camp.'

Brian made a face. 'That's not coffee! It's all right – we've got some in one of our cases. I'll go up and get it.'

He went upstairs and again there was a small silence. Tom, who had been quiet while his brother was holding court, said, 'You'll have to start shopping in Creber's, Mother. They're the only shop in Tavi likely to stock the sort of coffee Peggy's used to.'

'Of course they aren't. Underwood's will have it.' Alice turned to her daughter-in-law. 'That's the big grocery store in Tavistock. They send Bob Perry round once a week for our shopping list and it's delivered next day. I'll put coffee on this week's directly. I like a cup myself now and then.'

'We'll all start drinking it now,' Val said with a smile. 'You'll be getting us into bad habits, Peggy!'

The German woman looked at her, a small frown creasing her brow. 'Bad habits?'

'Well, you know what I mean,' Val said, and turned as Christopher stirred in his pram. 'Hello, someone else wants a drink. But I bet *he* doesn't want coffee!'

87

Chapter Thirteen

'It was a lovely picture,' Patsy said as she and Terry left the Carlton cinema in Tavistock. 'I liked the music, and James Stewart's really nice. But it was so sad at the end, with all the children round the Christmas tree not knowing their daddy was never coming home. I wonder what really happened to him?'

'I expect the plane he was in was shot down,' Terry said. 'There's nothing else it could be, really. Must have been queer for James Stewart playing that part when you remember he actually did fly planes in the war.'

'Did he?'

'Yes, he came to England and flew Liberators over Germany from Norfolk. Our Bob told me. He did his National Service in the RAF, that's how he knew.'

They walked along Plymouth Road to the bus stop. The bus didn't go all the way to Little Burracombe, but stopped on the main road, giving them a mile to walk. Patsy looked up at the church clock.

'We've only got half an hour before I've got to be in. We'll have to walk ever so fast.'

'It's a pity they don't have the small picture on second,' Terry said. 'We could come out before the end then. It's bad enough trying to get out before they play the national anthem and you all have to stand up till it finishes. Your dad won't mind a few minutes after ten, will he?'

'You don't know my dad! If I'm not through the door by ten, he'll be coming down the road with a torch, looking for me.'

'But if he knows you were going to the pictures ...'

'He thought I was going with Susie Crocker and we always go at five o'clock. Well, we did when I worked at Pillar's.'

'But you can't do that now that you're at the Barton. Didn't you tell him you were going later?'

'He said to mind I was in by ten just the same. Oh, here's the bus.' They jumped aboard and climbed to the top deck. 'It only takes about ten minutes to get to the Little Burracombe turning. We should just make it.'

The bus trundled at an unhelpfully sedate speed through the town and out to the main road. Patsy sat tensely in her seat, hardly feeling Terry's hand as he took hold of hers. When he'd done that in the cinema, after quite a long time of almost touching it and then slowly letting his fingers stray over hers before taking a firmer clasp, she'd been so excited her heart had thudded and a tingle had run right up both arms, but now she was more concerned with the progress of the bus. It stopped at the Burracombe turning at last, and she was out of her seat and down the stairs almost before Terry could let go.

'Only just over a quarter of an hour,' she panted as they set off along the lane. 'We'll have to run some of it.'

Terry, who had been hoping to linger on this stretch, scurried along with her, trying to hold his torch steady to light the way. It would never do for Patsy to fall over and be even later. But Patsy knew the road well enough and was ahead of the beam most of the way, so he put it out. He might need it for crossing over the Burra Brook, on the narrow footbridge of the Clam, after he'd seen her home.

'What's the time?' she gasped breathlessly as they came to the gate of the Shillabeer farmhouse. 'I haven't got a watch.'

'How does he expect you to keep to time if you haven't even got—' But Patsy squealed with impatience and he got his torch out again to look at his wrist. 'It's two minutes to ten, Patsy—'

'Oh, thank goodness!' She dragged the gate open and scrambled through. 'Thanks ever so much, Terry. It was lovely.'

'Patsy!' He caught her arm. 'Don't I even get a good-night kiss?'

'Terry, there's no *time*.' She leaned over the gate and gave him a hasty peck which landed somewhere between his nose and one ear. 'I'm ever so sorry – I've *got* to go!' A rectangle of light showed as the farmhouse door opened and she gave a squeak of dismay as it was blocked by a burly figure.

'Is that you, Patsy?'

'Yes, it's me, Dad.' She pushed Terry frantically away and he ducked down behind the gate. 'I'm coming.'

'Have you got someone with you?' The figure began to approach down the path.

'No – no, I walked home by myself. I had to stop for a minute – there was something on the road, a fox, I think. I almost bumped into it in the dark.' She was hurrying up the path as she spoke, gabbling her excuses. 'I'm not late, am I? I made sure I'd be home before ten.'

'Well, you are, but only just. Cutting it a bit fine – you'd better make sure you leave earlier next time. Come on, indoors with you, your mother's just making the cocoa and then you'd better get straight to bed.' He stood back to let Patsy go in and then stayed a moment in the doorway, the broad shape of his body turning slightly as if he were casting his eyes about the path and down to the road. Terry, still lurking behind the hedge, drew back and edged away into the darkness.

The farmer gave a grunt and went back into the house, closing the door behind him. Terry waited a moment or two, as if hoping that Patsy would appear again, maybe at an upstairs window, but there was no sign and he made his way slowly on along the lane towards the path that led down the field to the Clam and over to Burracombe.

It wasn't going to be easy courting Patsy Shillabeer, but he was determined to try. Plenty of fathers were strict with their daughters. Once old man Shillabeer had become accustomed to the idea and got to know him, Terry was sure he'd come round. Fathers wanted to get their daughters settled with a decent young man, after all, especially if the young man had a trade.

Patsy had no such hope. She drank her cocoa, answered a few questions about the film and whether she'd seen anyone she knew, and then went upstairs to bed. Once inside, she threw herself down and began to cry.

She was quite sure that Terry Pettifer would never ask her out again.

'Whatever's the matter with Patsy?' Hilary asked Jennifer next morning. 'She hasn't got a word to say for herself and she looks as if she's been crying half the night. There's nothing wrong at home, is there?'

'Only the fact that she lives there,' Jennifer answered grimly. 'It's that father of hers. He's so strict. Last night was the night Patsy was going to the pictures with young Terry, and she told me they had to run nearly all the way from the bus stop to get home by ten. They had no time to say good night and she hadn't told her dad she was going with a boy, so she had to make Terry hide. She thinks he'll never ask her out again.'

'Oh dear!' Hilary said. 'Young love! It really feels like the end of the world, doesn't it?' So does older love, she thought wryly. She'd heard no more from David, and her mind was constantly distracted by wondering how he was getting on and what Sybil's condition was. Every time the telephone rang, she jumped, until both Travis and her father noticed it. Gilbert reacted in his usual way by asking testily if she was expecting the Devil to ring her up, while Travis gave her a thoughtful look and asked if she was more worried about her father than she had admitted.

'Dr Latimer hasn't said anything else, has he?' he asked, and Hilary shook her head.

'No, just that Dad's got to take things easy for quite a while yet. He doesn't like it, of course, but I'm used to coping with him. Why d'you ask?''

'It's just that you seem rather worried lately, and I don't think it's the estate. I don't want to pry, Hilary, but if you need anyone to talk to at any time, or any help ... It wouldn't go any further.'

Hilary looked at him and smiled. 'No, I know it wouldn't. Thanks, Travis. There isn't anything anyone can help with, though. I think I'm just a bit run-down – what with Stella's accident, and Dad's heart attack, and winter dragging on. Losing Mrs Ellis has just been the last straw.'

'Have you heard anything from her?'

'She's coming in later today for a talk.' Hilary sighed. 'I think I know what she's going to say, too. I can't see how she can leave her mother to come and work here, certainly not for the hours she used to do. I'm going to have to look for someone else. I can't continue to impose on Jennifer, especially in her condition.'

'I think she's happy to go on for a few weeks,' he said. 'It's convenient that I can bring her here in the mornings and take her home in the afternoons. It's not as if she's got to walk miles.'

'I still need to start looking,' Hilary said. 'It might take months to find the right person.' And who knows what the situation between

David and me will be by then? she wondered, rubbing her forehead. 'Anyway, let's get these papers finished before Mrs Ellis comes. I can't make any decisions until I've talked to her. She might even want to come back.'

As she had suspected, however, the housekeeper had come reluctantly to the conclusion that she would have to give up work. 'I'd hoped to carry on until my hubby retires,' she said apologetically, 'but with Mother the way she is ... I just can't see any way round it, Miss Hilary. That accident has really shaken her up. It's not just her arm – that'll mend – but she seems to have become so forgetful. She was getting a bit that way before, but she's worse now. And she gets in such a huff if I'm not there. I've left her with my Bert now, and he's as good as gold with her, but I know when I get back she'll treat me like a young girl coming in too late at night. Even when her arm's healed, I don't think she's going to be any better in herself.'

'I'm so sorry,' Hilary said sincerely. 'That must be awful for you. Well, you mustn't worry about us. We'll be very sorry to lose you, but I can see there's no possibility of your coming back to work. We'll pay you your month's wages, and of course there'll be some extra ...'

'Oh, I don't expect that! Not when I'm letting you down like this.'

'You're not letting us down at all,' Hilary said firmly. 'You've worked really hard for us, and often stayed late or come in to help when we've had visitors. And I've been feeling very guilty that we never got anyone else to help you when Jackie left. You deserve a thank-you and that's what you shall have. Now, please don't say another word, and don't worry about us. You've got enough on your plate. Now that I know you're definitely not coming back, I shall look for someone else. And do come back to see us now and again – I'd like to keep in touch.'

'That's main good of you, Miss Hilary,' the housekeeper said, wiping a tear from her eye. 'I've been happy here and I'm real sorry to leave. And I'll want to know how the Colonel is getting along. Would it be all right if I went to say goodbye to him?'

'Of course.' Hilary took her along to the drawing room, where her father was settled with the day's newspapers, the two old Labradors snoring at his feet, and left them together. When Mrs Ellis returned to the kitchen she was wiping her eyes again.

'He was so nice, Miss Hilary. Said I'd saved his life, if you please! I'm more sorry than I can say that it's worked out this way.'

'So are we,' Hilary said. 'But that's life, isn't it – while we're expecting it to go smoothly, it has other plans! Now, Jennifer's made a pot of tea and if you've got time, I want you to sit down and have a cup with her and explain anything she needs to know about the house. Patsy's about somewhere, but she seems to have settled in well so I don't think we need bother her.'

'She's a good girl,' Mrs Ellis said, sitting down at the big table and accepting the cup Jennifer handed her. 'As long as that father don't take her away like he took her out of Pillar's. A right martinet he is. And I tell you what, Miss Hilary, when you do get someone new, I'll come along if you like and show them what's what. It's the least I can do.'

Hilary thanked her and went back to the office. She'd been hoping to get away from the house today, to go round some of the tenant farms with Travis, but the winter afternoon was already growing dark. There wouldn't even be time for a ride on Beau to clear her head.

I hate winter, she thought. At least, I'm beginning to hate this winter. It's gone on too long and, apart from that snowfall before Christmas, it's been too dark and dreary. Like life itself.

As she'd commented to Mrs Ellis, it was never safe to think you could make plans. Life always seemed to intervene.

'All right if I walk you home, Patsy?'

Patsy, just coming out of the Barton drive, stopped with a gasp. 'Is that you, Terry?'

He emerged from the shadow of the oak tree that stood at the gate, and touched her arm. 'Of course it's me. How many boys do you expect to be waiting for you, then?'

She gave a nervous little laugh. 'You just took me by surprise, that's all. I didn't think ...' She stopped.

'Didn't think what?'

'Well ... after the other night, I didn't think you'd want to bother with me again.'

'Why not?'

'Oh, you know ... After me having to dash off like that. I felt awful. But if Dad had seen you ...'

Terry peered at her in the darkness. 'Why, what would he have done?'

'Sent you packing, that's what. With a flea in your ear.'

'I've had plenty of those in my time,' he said cheerfully. 'But I don't see why. Wouldn't he be pleased you'd got someone to see you back late at night? He don't really want you walking along the lanes by yourself, do he?'

'He wouldn't want me being seen home by a boy,' she said bitterly. 'He wouldn't want me going out with a boy at all.'

Terry was silent for a moment. They walked along side by side, not touching for a few moments; then he took her hand.

'It don't seem right, you not telling him. Suppose I came to see him, ask if I can take you out and promise to bring you home on time. Would that do?'

Patsy squealed. 'No! You mustn't do that! He'd go mad.'

'Strikes me he *is* mad,' Terry said grimly.

'He's not. At least, I don't think he is. He's just strict.'

'But that's silly. You've got to be able to go out and enjoy yourself. Can't your mum do nothing?'

'You don't understand,' Patsy said wearily. 'You see, Dad was Chapel for a long time, and they're more strict than church. He doesn't even go in the pub. He quarrelled with the minister years ago and came over to Church of England, but he seemed to get even stricter. We're not allowed to have the wireless on on Sundays, or play cards or anything. And now the new vicar's come and he's so friendly and easy-going, Dad's talking about leaving the church as well. I don't know what he'll do then. And nothing Mum says will make any difference. It'll just make him worse.'

'But what's all that got to do with us?' Terry asked, bewildered.

'He just doesn't approve of girls my age going out with boys. He says I've to wait till I'm twenty-one. It's why I left Pillar's. There was a boy used to come in there ... Nothing ever happened, but Dad heard about it and I had to leave.'

Terry stopped. They were at the footpath that led down to the Clam and across to Little Burracombe. He took hold of both her hands and said, 'I'm not going to let that stop me seeing you, Patsy. I really like you and I want to get to know you better. I've been thinking about you ever since we went to the pictures together.'

'I've been thinking about you too, Terry,' she whispered.

'So what are we going to do about it?' he asked. 'I'd like to meet you like this every afternoon and see you home. That'd be something. But I can't always leave work this early – I could only do it today because we were doing a job at Mrs Warren's and we finished sooner than we expected, and Bob said I could get off. Anyway, I want to take you out properly, all above board.'

'I don't see how you can,' she said wretchedly. 'Not with my dad the way he is. I'm sorry, Terry. I can't see what we can do, unless I tell him I'm going with my friend, like I did the other night.'

'But what about when he finds out?' Terry asked. 'It'll be all the worse then, when he knows you've been telling him lies.' Patsy was silent and he added, 'You can't keep it a secret for ever.'

'We can for a while,' she said pleadingly. 'Just for a while, and then we'll see what happens.'

He sighed. 'All right. For a while. But I really think it'd be better if I came to see him. He could see then that I didn't mean you any harm.'

'Not yet. Let's just go on like this. Please, Terry.' She squeezed his hands tightly. 'If you can meet me from work sometimes and we can go to the pictures once a week … that would be all right. Let's just do that. For the time being, anyway.'

'All right,' he agreed. 'And now I suppose we'd better go, or you'll be in trouble for being late home from work.' He drew her closer and they stood still, both trembling a little. 'Can I kiss you, Patsy?'

For answer, she moved a step nearer and lifted her face. He could feel her hair brush against his cheek, and his heart kicked. He bent his head and moved gently until his lips found her cheek, and then her lips. They bumped noses, giggled a little, and then seemed to find the right place to settle.

Their first kiss was exploratory and tender; the second more ardent. When Terry let her go, they were both breathless.

'I'm not giving you up, Patsy,' he murmured, keeping his arm around her waist as they moved on along the narrow path. 'You'm my girl now. It don't matter what your father says – he can't alter that.'

Chapter Fourteen

'The doctor can't find anything wrong with him,' Joanna said to her mother-in-law. 'Says he's the picture of health. I said he ought to come round here and see him in the mornings when I'm trying to get him out of bed to go to school. He doesn't look the picture of health then.'

'Well what does he think's the matter, then?' Alice asked, setting a cup of tea in front of her. Joanna had taken Robin to the doctor three times now, and still there didn't seem to be any answer to the intermittent headaches and tummy pains the little boy was suffering from. 'Perhaps you ought to ask to see a specialist.'

Joanna drank some tea. She drew in a deep breath and said, 'I'll tell you what he thinks it is. He says Robin doesn't want to go to school.'

'Doesn't want to go to school?' Alice echoed in amazement. 'But Robin loves school. He couldn't wait to start, and he was doing so well, up to Christmas.'

'That's the point. He loved it when Stella was there. It's this new teacher.' Joanna shook her head. 'Dr Latimer didn't put it in so many words, but I'm pretty sure he thinks she's at the bottom of it. Robin's not the only one, you see. There's a lot of the babies getting these tummy aches and so on. Some of the other mothers have been talking about it too.'

'But what's she doing to them?' asked Minnie, who was in her usual chair by the fire. 'Is she smacking them? Surely if she wasn't treating them right, Miss Kemp would know.'

'I don't think it's anything like that. She said at the beginning that she believed in being strict and teaching the children their three Rs and all that, and a lot of people thought that was a good thing. Stella

96

did let them do a lot of painting and singing, and then there were the plays and pageants and things like that. It was no wonder they liked being there. I think Miss Watkins has come as a bit of a shock. And Stella's so pretty – they all rather idolised her.'

'It's true Miss Watkins is no oil painting,' Alice remarked. 'But that shouldn't make any difference. It's the teaching that matters.'

'We never got no painting or drawing when I was at school,' Minnie put in. 'Copperplate writing, that's what we had to learn, and hours and hours of spelling and dictation, and learning our tables and mental arithmetic. When we left school at fourteen, we had to know all that. And plenty of history and geography, as well. I could tell you the names of the longest rivers in the world now, if you were to ask me.'

Joanna smiled. She finished her tea and went to the sink to start peeling the potatoes. 'I think Mother's right, Granny. It's the teaching that's important. Stella's a good teacher and the children like her. Miss Watkins may be a good teacher too, but if they don't like her, and don't want to go to her lessons, what's the good?'

'But they got to go,' Minnie said. 'It's the law.'

'They don't have to go if they're ill,' Joanna said.

'But are they really ill? I know Robin seems poorly, but if you look back at last weekend, he didn't have no headache on Saturday or Sunday. You thought it was because he was getting better, but what happened on Monday? He said his tummy ached so much he wouldn't get out of bed.'

'He was as white as a sheet,' Joanna said defensively. 'He couldn't have been putting it on.'

'I'm not saying he did.' Minnie put out a wrinkled hand. 'All I'm saying is, he *thinks* he's got a pain but he hasn't really. It's all in his mind because he don't want to go to school, and if you ask me that's worse.'

Joanna was silent for a moment. She put the peeled potatoes into a saucepan and filled it with water. As she carried it to the range, she said, 'So what can we do?'

Minnie shrugged. 'I wouldn't do anything. He'll get over it in his own time. So will the others. You got to learn to take the rough with the smooth in this life.'

'But he's miserable.'

'I think Granny's right,' Alice said. 'If you give way to him over

97

this, he'll be the same next time he's got to do something he don't want to do. He's bound to come up against teachers he don't like. It's all part of learning. Don't take too much notice and he'll come round. It's not as if he's the only one.'

'I could have a word with Miss Kemp,' Joanna said, unwilling to let it go. But Alice shook her head firmly.

'If you ask me, that'll just make it worse. Miss Watkins won't take kindly to being interfered with and her'll be even harder on the kiddies. You don't want that.'

Joanna sighed, crumpled her lips together, and went back to the sink to wash the cabbage. After a bit, she said, 'Well, I'll give it another week or two, but if he's no better then, I will speak to her. I don't see why Robin should be made miserable. He's always been such a happy little boy.'

'And so he will be again,' Minnie said comfortingly. 'This is just one of those things. I'm not saying it isn't a pity, mind, but he'll be all the better for being a bit tougher. He'm a lovely little boy, but he got to grow up like the rest of us.'

The door opened and Brian came in, followed by his wife. They took off their thick coats and boots and came over to the fire. Margret shivered extravagantly and put out her hands to the flames.

'It's very cold out there.'

'I thought you were used to the cold,' Joanna said. 'You get a lot more snow than we do.'

'It's the raw damp here,' Brian said. 'It feels colder. In Germany they get dry cold. Much healthier.'

'I'm surprised you didn't decide to stay there,' Joanna remarked casually as she chopped carrots. 'You seem to like it so much more.'

He turned and looked at her. 'What's that supposed to mean?'

'Nothing,' she said, surprised. 'I was just saying, that's all. It's Peggy's home, after all.'

'For about the hundredth time,' he said, 'it's Margret. I'm the only one who calls her Peggy.'

There was a short silence. Joanna, Alice and Minnie looked at each other, while Margret stared steadfastly into the fire.

'I'm sorry,' Joanna said at last. 'I didn't realise that. You should have said.'

'I've tried. Nobody ever listens.'

'Well, we'm listening now,' Alice said peaceably. 'I'll tell the others. But we've got used to saying Peggy, so you mustn't mind if we forget now and then.'

Brian said nothing. He moved over to the table. 'Any tea in the pot?'

'I'll make some fresh,' Alice said, getting up. 'And some coffee for Peg— Margret, I mean. Sit you down now, maid, you look shrammed with cold. Have you been far?'

'We walked up to the Standing Stones,' Margret said. 'It was very windy and very cold.'

'It's always cold up there,' Joanna said. 'It's because it's higher than the village.'

'Yes, I know that,' Brian said. 'I lived here until I was called up.'

Joanna put the pan of carrots on the range. 'I'll go and wake Heather up now,' she said to Alice. 'And then I'll find Tom and tell him dinner will be ready soon. The cabbage will only take a few minutes.'

She went upstairs and Brian raised his eyebrows. 'What's the matter with her?'

'She'm worried about Robin,' Alice said. 'And you were a bit sharp with her.'

'Well, she seems to forget I was part of this family before she came along. And if you ask me, that boy's spoiled. That headache of his is just put on because he doesn't want to go to school.'

'It's a bit more than that,' Alice said. 'Joanna says a lot of the kiddies are the same, and it's because they don't like the new teacher.'

Brian snorted. 'They're a lot of namby-pambies then! They wouldn't be allowed to get away with it in Germany. Off to school at seven in the morning and working hard at their desks before English kids are out of bed. They know a thing or two about discipline there.'

'And look where it got us,' Minnie said, and there was a sudden silence. Margret turned abruptly and went out of the kitchen, and Brian's face darkened. Alice got up quickly and went to the range.

'That beef casserole looks ready to me. I'll put the cabbage on. Go out and tell your father, will you, Brian? He'm in the big barn, or was when I came in from seeing to the hens.'

Brian went without another word, and Alice turned to her mother-in-law.

'You shouldn't have said that, Mother. You know what we agreed.

Tidden easy for Peg – Margret, I mean – to come here and we got to make it comfortable for her.'

'I know, maid, but it's not easy for us neither. You and me, we been through two world wars and we know who caused 'em. Sometimes my tongue just runs away with me.'

'Well, try not to let it.' Alice poked the potatoes and carrots with a fork. The cabbage was coming to the boil and she took the dinner plates from the side of the range and set them out on the big kitchen table. 'Now, let's just try to have our dinner without any more argufying. I must say, our Brian do seem a bit ready to take offence these days, and as often as not, there's none meant. He seems to have forgot how we chi-ike each other in this family.'

'He've been away too long,' Minnie said. 'He've got used to other ways and he've got a foreigner for a wife. It's bound to have had an effect. But you'm right, Alice, 'tis up to us to make allowances, and it's not for long, after all. Once they've had a bit of a holiday and got tired of the place, they'll be off again. Burracombe's not going to be enough for Brian, not now he've seen a bit of the world.'

Alice put the big, heavy casserole on the table in front of her place, and then dished up the vegetables. She put the pile of plates ready to serve and went to the staircase door.

'Margret! Dinner's ready. Is Joanna still up there? I didn't see her go out.'

'You had your back turned,' Joanna said, coming in with Tom behind her and Brian and Ted crowding into the stone porch. 'We're all here.'

'That smells good,' Tom said, shucking off his boots and padding across the kitchen. He gave his grandmother's wrinkled cheek a kiss. 'I bet you've been slaving all morning getting our dinner ready.'

'I done a bit,' Minnie said, smiling. 'And Joanna done her share too, not to mention Alice. It's been a hive of industry here, while you folk have been out enjoying yourselves.'

'Peg offered to help too,' Brian said at once. 'She was told she wasn't wanted.'

Alice paused, the serving spoon held ready above the casserole.

'She wasn't told that at all, Brian. You two are on holiday, that's all. Us don't want to make you work. Now, sit down and let's enjoy this, before it gets cold. Pass this plate to your Granny, Tom, and help her to some vegetables, and let's put the wireless on. It's *Workers' Playtime* and Arthur Askey's on.'

The meal continued, with the background of jokes and laughter easing the atmosphere. But Alice could see that her elder son was still aggrieved, while her younger had raised his eyebrows at Joanna and rolled his eyes. She sighed. The two boys had always been at odds, even as youngsters, but she'd hoped now they were grown men they'd have got over their differences. It didn't seem as if they had.

It was so good to have Brian back, she really didn't want anything to spoil it.

Chapter Fifteen

'I wants a word with you.'

Miss Watkins stopped abruptly on her way out of the playground. Maggie Culliford was standing at the gate, arms akimbo, a belligerent look on her face and the inevitable cigarette drooping from her lip.

''Are you talking to me?' the teacher asked frostily.

'Well, I don't see no one else around. I been waiting ever since the big children came out. Thought you were settled in for the duration.'

'I had work to do,' Miss Watkins said stiffly. 'I like to prepare for next day before I go home. But I can't stop now, my bus will be along soon.'

'It's not here yet,' Maggie said stolidly. 'You got time to tell me what you'm doing to my Billy.'

'Your Billy? What are you talking about? I'm not doing anything to him.'

'So why don't he want to come to school of a morning?' Maggie demanded. 'Every morning it's the same. Headache, tummy ache, feeling sick, and when he thinks he've got away with it, all of a sudden he'm better. Now don't you tell me that ain't because he's afeared of coming to school.'

'Frightened of school? Of course he's not frightened of school. What an idea! He's playing you up, that's what he's doing, Mrs Culliford, and from what I've heard about his brothers and sisters, it's no surprise.'

Maggie drew in a deep breath and her eyes flashed.

'What do you mean by that?'

'Why, everyone knows about your children,' the teacher said

contemptuously. 'The bane of the school. Why Miss Kemp makes so much of Shirley and Betty I can't imagine. Very ordinary little girls.'

'My Shirley's one of the cleverest girls in the school!' Maggie shouted, taking a step nearer. 'She were Pageant Queen and she's done well in her exams. And Betty was in the pantomime too, and never forgot a single word. You wants to watch your tongue.'

Miss Watkins gave her a withering look and stepped away. 'And you need to watch your manners. I'm afraid I can't tell you why your Billy is pretending to have headaches. It seems to be something of a craze amongst the children, like playing fivestones or two-ball. In a week or two they'll have thought of something else. I've seen it all before.' She brushed past Maggie and set off for the bus stop by the village green. 'There's my bus.'

Maggie opened her mouth to retort, but the teacher's square, stocky figure was already bustling away and climbing aboard the little bus that trundled twice a day round the villages. Maggie's mouth clamped shut and she gave a snort of fury before turning to go home and almost bumping into Janet Madge, Billy's mother, who was on her way home from the shop with a full basket.

'Did you hear what she said? Did you hear? Called my Shirley and Betty *ordinary little girls*, and said my kiddies were the bane of the school! My Jim, and Brenda that she never even met, and our Joe, and little Billy that's only just started in the babies' class. The cheek of it!'

'She's probably getting mixed up with my Billy,' Janet said with a grin, resting her basket on the low wall. 'I'd be quite relieved if that was all she said about him.' She gave Maggie a closer look. 'Here, you look proper upset. You don't want to take no notice of her. She's only here for a term or two anyway, till they find someone better.'

'That's long enough to put my Billy off school for life. It's not fair – he's only a little tacker and Miss Kemp said he could start now, so's to make things easier for me, and here's Miss Stuck-Up making them harder. It's not just mornings, it's in the night when he wakes up crying. I've half a mind to take him out of school again, but with two other little ones at home it's just too much for me. And there'll be four when the baby comes.'

'How are you going to manage in the holidays? You'll have them all home then.'

'My Brenda will help. She's a marvel with the little ones. And

Jimmy will take Joe and Billy round with him until he starts work. Anyway, I'll be all right once this lot's over.' She patted her stomach. 'I don't usually have any trouble when I'm expecting, but I seem to get so tired this time. And I'm sure I'm bigger than usual.'

'Well, it won't help to make bad friends with the teacher,' Janet said. 'You want her on your side, not against you. You won't have done your Billy no favours at all, the way you went on at her.'

'Well, maybe, but she got me so riled. I've got half a mind to speak to Miss Kemp about it. She never used to have much time for us Cullifords but she've come round a bit lately – mind, that's Miss Simmons's doing more than anything. It were a bad day for Burracombe school when she had that accident.'

'We were going to lose her anyway,' Janet said. 'She'd have been married by now and living over to Little Burracombe. We'd still have got landed with Miss Watkins. But why not let it go, Maggie? She won't be here long. There'll be a new one come summer and your Billy will have found his feet by then.'

'And who's to say they won't make this one permanent?' Maggie demanded. 'She might be here on probation, as they call it – last time I heard the word probation was when our Jimmy had to go to court for taking one of Squire Alford's pheasants backalong – but that ain't to say they won't give her the job proper. Suppose nobody else applies? And her lives handy in Tavistock now.'

'I reckon us'll cross that bridge when us comes to it,' Janet said. She heaved her basket on to her arm again. 'I got to go now. My auntie Mary's coming round to tea and her always expects scones fresh out of the oven.'

'You ought to get them from George Sweet,' Maggie said. 'I do, when I can afford them.'

'I tried that once but she knew the difference straight away. I reckon that must have been one of the times Ivy made them!' Janet grinned again and walked off down the street.

Maggie went on her way. She was still angry with the teacher and determined to do something about it. It was all right for Janet Madge, her Billy was in Miss Kemp's class, where the children went when they were seven, and he was a tough little chap anyway, but her own Billy was just a baby still. The teacher ought to take a bit more care with him.

It's daft to say it's just a craze, she thought. Kiddies don't have crazes like that – all crying with tummy pains or headaches at school time. None of them like her. She's making them all miserable, and it's time something was done.

'I just don't know what we *can* do,' Miss Kemp said worriedly. 'She's an experienced teacher, and if her ways aren't ours, that doesn't mean they're wrong. She doesn't shout at them, or I'd have heard through the partition. The worst I've heard of her is that she doesn't let the children paint or draw as much as Stella used to. I can't reprimand her for simply making them work!'

'It does seem to be more than that, though,' Basil Harvey said. The school governors were meeting in his drawing room at the vicarage. They had all heard of the dissatisfaction with the new teacher and had decided that it must be discussed. Basil looked at Dr Latimer. 'You say that a lot of the smaller children are being brought to you?'

'That's right,' Charles Latimer said. 'At first I thought nothing of it. Children do get tummy aches or even headaches, and it's the time of year when I expect colds and flu and so on. None of them seemed really ill, so I just let them have a day or two at home and they seemed to get better. But then more and more came along, not once but two or three times, and I began to wonder if I had an epidemic on my hands. In the end it dawned on me that all the mothers were saying the same – the children complained of the symptoms in the mornings and got better as the day went on. And they were never ill at weekends!'

'She must be doing something wrong,' Basil said. 'You've never had this problem before, have you, Miss Kemp?'

'Never. Not in these numbers, anyway – you usually get one or two children who find it hard to settle. When Henry Bennetts started, he was forever running home to his mother, but once he made friends with Micky Coker, he was quite all right. Not that they were always an easy combination,' she added wryly, and they all laughed as they remembered some of the mischief the two boys had got into over the years. 'But they're good boys at heart and doing well at school in Tavistock.'

'There's never been anything like this,' Constance Bellamy affirmed. 'I've been in Burracombe longer than any of you – I started in the village school at the turn of the century, when old Mr Randle was headmaster, and he was a martinet if ever there was one. The cane was never out of his hand. But he never touched the little ones, nor the girls. And in all those years, I never remember the little ones being afraid of going to school.'

'Are they really afraid?' Basil asked in concern. 'Is it as bad as that, Miss Kemp?'

'I can't honestly tell you,' the head teacher confessed. 'I feel guilty for saying it, but as far as I can see, the children are quiet and well-behaved – maybe a little *too* quiet and well-behaved. Apart from the Crocker twins, of course, and they seem to be a match for anybody. It's as if once they're at school, they work hard enough and they're certainly learning, but they just don't want to come in the first place.'

'She's very strict,' Basil said. 'I've noticed that myself when I've come into the school to talk to them. She only has to look at them and they sit at their desks like mice, their arms folded.' He thought for a moment, his round, pink face creased like a baby's. 'I don't like to use the word, but I might almost say they seem rather – well, *cowed*.'

'Well, that's not good,' Constance said forcibly. 'Someone needs to talk to her. Perhaps we should call her to a meeting.'

'I don't think we should do that just yet,' Basil said. 'It might be a bit too heavy-handed. Miss Kemp, I'm afraid it seems that it should be you. Could you have a word?'

Miss Kemp looked unhappy. 'I don't see what I can say, without having something more concrete to mention. She'll simply point to their writing, which is certainly coming along well, and their reading and sums, and ask what my complaint is. And if I say it's because so many children seem to be ill in the mornings, she'll say either it's the time of year or they're putting it on, or that the children of Burracombe are soft and spoiled!'

'Perhaps a gentle word,' Basil suggested. 'They could have one or two afternoons a week that aren't lessons – painting pictures for Stella, or going on a nature walk if it's fine enough. They *are* only little, after all. A day at school is often too much for such young children at the start.'

'Especially Billy Culliford,' Miss Kemp said. 'I agreed to him starting early to help his mother in her situation, but I'm afraid it's making things worse. The poor little chap looks as white as a sheet sometimes.'

'Yes, he's the one I worry about most,' the doctor nodded. 'And

Mrs Culliford needs the respite. He seems an amenable little boy, but it must be a help for her to have him at school. I'm not altogether happy about her, to tell you the truth.'

'She's got too many children, that's her problem,' Constance said grimly. 'Always been a no-good lot, the Cullifords. Arthur's father was, and so was his grandfather before him. They'll never change.'

'I'm hoping they will,' Miss Kemp said. 'Shirley and Betty are coming along nicely and I'd like to see Joe and Billy do the same. Well, Basil, I'll do as you suggest and have a quiet word, but I'm not sure it will do much good. Miss Watkins has her own way of doing things and I doubt if she'll change them to suit me. But I suppose we must make a start somewhere. By the way, I didn't leave my old purse here last time I came, did I? It's a brown leather one I use for the dinner money.'

'I don't think so. I'll ask Grace if she's seen it. Was there much in it?'

'Hardly anything – a few pennies, perhaps. I thought it was in my desk, but it's not there – it's probably at home somewhere.' Miss Kemp rose to her feet. 'I'll let you all know how I get on. To tell you the truth, I'm rather afraid of Miss Watkins myself!'

They laughed again and she went out. Basil turned back to the doctor.

'Miss Kemp is all right, isn't she? She does seem a little forgetful just lately.'

'Oh, I don't think there's anything in that,' the doctor said easily. 'She's had a lot to worry about, with Stella's accident and a new teacher coming in – it's enough to try anyone. She'll be all right once the weather improves – we all will.' He got up and helped Constance from her low chair. 'I'll see you home, Miss Bellamy. It's almost dark.'

'And what of that?' the old lady demanded. 'I've walked these lanes a thousand times in the dark. But if you insist ...' They followed Miss Kemp to the front door and Basil saw them down the steps. As he closed the door he met his wife, collecting the teacups from the drawing room.

'Well, we had a good chat over it all,' he told her, 'but I don't think we've heard the last of it yet. Miss Watkins is rather like a force of nature – immovable and irresistible. I really don't know what any of us can do about her.'

*

Maggie Culliford's problems were not over when she reached home.

Picking her way through the cluttered scrap of front garden, she found her husband Arthur wiping his boots on the doormat. His old bike was in the hallway and she scraped her leg on one of the pedals and exclaimed in annoyance.

'Why don't you take it round the back? I'm always telling you. And what have you done with the pram?'

'It's in the front room. I couldn't take me bike round the back because there's a load of logs there that I brought home. I thought you'd be pleased.'

Maggie squeezed past the bike, saying nothing. It was true they were almost out of firewood and she'd been putting off lighting the old kitchen range until it was nearly dark the past few afternoons. She saw that Arthur had already lit it now and felt grateful, but suspicious.

'Where d'you get that from then? I asked Jacob Prout for some this morning and he said there wasn't none around, and wouldn't be till a tree blew down.'

'That was just him being awkward. There's plenty around if you know where to look.'

'Oh? And where did you look?' She lifted the kettle to see if there was enough water in it for a pot of tea and set it at the side of the range. It was the only fire in the house, as they seldom lit the one in the front room, where there was no furniture; instead the room was used for things like the pram and bits and pieces that Arthur found and thought he'd do up and sell. The children played in there too, crawling on the floor with a few wooden bricks and old tin cars and such that other children had discarded.

'Never you mind where I looked,' Arthur said, coming in and throwing himself into a sagging settee that he'd salvaged when the Warrens had bought a new three-piece suite after the war. 'I got it, that's the main thing, and there's a good pile of it, if you want to see. What's more, there's a nice fat pair of rabbits in the scullery. I'll skin 'em for you a bit later.'

'Rabbits! Arthur, where have you been? I hope no one saw you, taking wood and rabbits. I can't be doing with any more trouble.' She went to the little lean-to scullery and looked at the rabbits. They would make some tasty dinners, it was true, but she was always afraid that Arthur would be had up again for poaching. Mr Kellaway more or less turned a blind eye these days, after being told to by the Squire, but that didn't apply to other landowners in the area, and none of the gamekeepers would let Arthur off if they caught him. He'd already done two short terms in prison – a month each time – and it meant no money coming in for weeks. Two rabbits wouldn't last them if that happened again.

'You will be careful, won't you?' she said, coming back with a couple of cups and a jug of milk from the meat safe outside the door. 'I mean it, Art. I don't know what I'd do if you got put inside again. I wouldn't be able to do any cleaning work, not the way I am now.'

'I'll be all right, my bird, don't you worry.' He bent forward to unlace his boots. 'Anyway, you'll be pleased to know I got some more work in Tavi, on that new garage they'm building. So that'll be a regular wage coming in.'

'Oh Arthur, that is good news!' She gave him a kiss and then poured the tea and handed him a cup. 'You won't need to do no more poaching, then.'

'Well, maybe.' He gave her a sly wink. 'I won't say that if a rabbit or a pheasant runs out in front of me I won't knock it on the head, to put it out of its misery, like. And if that happens, it'd be a shame not to make use of it. But I won't be going out at night specially. Not often, anyway.'

Maggie pursed her lips and regarded him, shaking her head. 'You'm a bad man, Arthur Culliford, there's no two ways about it. I reckon you'd still go out poaching if you was a millionaire and owned all the land there is.'

'It wouldn't be poaching then, would it!' he said, and grinned. 'Not that you might not be right all the same. There's nothing like it, you know, Maggie – being out in the fields and woods, everything quiet except for the owls and maybe a fox calling for its mate, and the moon shining down ... That's when a man feels more himself than any other time. That's what men was *made* for – hunting for food for their women and children. It ain't right for those with money to set 'emselves up above the rest of us and say what we're to do with the grub that the good Lord provided for us all. That's why I go poaching. That, and because if I didn't us'd starve to death in this country that was meant to be fit for heroes to live in.'

Maggie sat down beside him, stretching out her legs and regarding her swollen ankles.

'Well, you'm my hero, Arthur,' she said, lifting her cup to her lips. 'Just be careful, that's all I say.'

Chapter Sixteen

'I t's a long time since young Stephen's been home,' Gilbert Napier grumbled to his daughter at Saturday breakfast. 'Forgotten the way here, has he?'

'I don't think so,' Hilary answered mildly, helping him to bacon and eggs. 'He did tell us he wouldn't be able to get away so much. He took a lot of leave over Christmas, remember, and now that he and Maddy are finally engaged, he obviously wants to spend as much time as possible with her.'

'He could bring her here. I dare say they're going to see her sister in Plymouth.'

'Maddy is. She comes up at least once a week by train, but she goes straight to the hospital and then back again to West Lyme. She says she took a lot of time off as well, and she's trying to make it up. The Archdeacon is very kind, and he's Felix's uncle so he's concerned about Stella too – he and his wife drove up one day to see her   but Maddy is supposed to be working for him, and she doesn't want to take advantage.'

'Hm. Well, next time you write to either of them, remind them that there's a sick old man here who'd like a visit now and then.'

Hilary laughed outright. 'A sick old man! Honestly, Dad, you're a real hypocrite at times. If Charles tells you to take things easy you bite his head off and call him an old woman, but when it suits you to be pathetic, you're a sick old man. You can't have it both ways.'

'I can have it any way I like. You're allowed a bit of leeway when you reach my age and have had two heart attacks. Anyway, I'd like to see Stephen again, and little Maddy. I miss having a bit of young life about the place.'

And I'm not young, then? Hilary thought wryly, but she looked at her father with a touch of both pity and anxiety. It was Rob he was really missing, she thought – the young grandson so recently discovered who seemed now to have disappeared from their lives to go back to his own in France. Gilbert had held such high hopes that the boy, who so closely resembled his father Baden, would grow up to take his place on the estate, and although he had eventually accepted the fact that Rob's background was too different and his own ambitions in another direction, it had been a bitter disappointment for him.

'I'll tell Steve,' she said, making up her mind to persuade her brother to bring Maddy to Burracombe at the first opportunity. She would like to see them herself anyway. Just at present there seemed to be so few people she knew who were truly happy. Even Felix's joy that Stella was improving was tempered by his concern for her as she slowly learned to walk again. As for herself – she could only hope for infrequent phone calls from David, none of which seemed to hold out any hope for their own future.

Like her father, she felt it would be good to have some young, happy life around the house.

Still, there was some happiness at the Barton. Jennifer was flourishing in her pregnancy and still able to help as housekeeper, for at least a couple of months, and little Patsy seemed to have changed completely from the mouse-like creature who had first joined them. Her skin glowed, her fair hair gleamed and her large grey eyes shone, and she seemed to skip around the Barton as she carried out her duties.

Hilary and Jennifer had agreed that it must have a lot to do with young Terry Pettifer, who had been seen more than once sauntering along the lane near the end of the drive at around the time Patsy left to go home.

'It's sweet to see,' Hilary said as she took the breakfast dishes out to be washed up. 'I just hope she doesn't get too hurt when it comes to an end.'

'We all have to get hurt sometime,' Jennifer said, and they looked at each other, neither knowing what hurt the other had suffered but acknowledging that it must have happened. 'Not all young romances come to an end, though. Look at Ted and Alice Tozer. She told me once that they fell in love the minute she walked through the door when she came to the farm to work as a maid, and there was never anyone else for either of them, before or since.'

'They were very lucky,' Hilary agreed. 'I hope Patsy is just as lucky. She's a nice young girl.'

She went to the office to tidy up some papers. There seemed to be more and more government documents arriving just lately. Half of them were irrelevant, but they still had to be read and often answered. Travis complained that it was a waste of time, and Hilary agreed, but that didn't make any difference to the fact that it had to be done. She had taken to setting aside Saturday mornings for this task, and as she looked out of the window at the heavy grey clouds that hung like bruises in the sky, she thought perhaps it wasn't such a bad job after all.

Patsy and Jennifer both left for the weekend at noon, but when Patsy brought her a cup of coffee at eleven, Hilary raised her head from her work and said, 'Good Lord, look out of the window – it's snowing! I didn't notice it before.'

'You've been busy,' Patsy said, setting the cup down on a spare space between the papers. 'It's been snowing for near on an hour.'

'Has it really?' Hilary got up and went to the window. 'Heavens, yes – it must be over two inches deep already. Patsy, you ought to have left sooner. Get your coat and go now – you know how deep it can get down by the river.'

'Oh no, that's all right. I don't need to go before my time.'

'Of course you must.' Hilary glanced at the girl's face. 'Or were you going somewhere else from work?'

Patsy nodded. 'I'm going to Terry's house for dinner, and then we're going to the pictures in Tavi.'

'Oh – well that's all right, then. So long as you don't get stuck in Tavistock. Terry will see you home afterwards, won't he?'

Patsy smiled. 'Yes, he's a proper gentleman, Terry is. If only ...' She stopped, and coloured a little.

'If only what?' Hilary asked gently, sensing that the girl wanted to tell her something but needed a little encouragement.

'If only Father would let him come to the house,' she said in a rush. 'But he won't hear of me going out with a boy, so we got to keep it secret, see. You won't say anything, will you, Miss Hilary?' she finished anxiously.

'Well no, not if you don't want me to. But if he ever asks me directly – I couldn't lie to him, Patsy.'

'Oh, I wouldn't ever ask you to do that! Nor would Terry. He's all for going to see Father and telling him straight, but I'm frightened of what Father might do.'

'Why, what do you think he might do?' Hilary asked in alarm. 'He wouldn't hurt you, surely?'

'He might hurt Terry. He do have a bit of a temper on him when he's crossed. And he'd never let me see him again. He'd stop me working here and keep me at home and I'd never see anyone at all.' Patsy raised huge, frightened eyes to Hilary's shocked gaze. 'Please, Miss Hilary. Please don't say anything.'

'I won't,' Hilary promised, shaken. And I thought my father could be a bit of a tyrant at times, she reflected. The poor child. She looked at the girl again and said gently, 'I'm sure it will turn out all right, Patsy. Fathers usually come round in the end, and I'm sure he only wants the best for you. Terry's a nice young man and he'll see that.'

'I don't know how, when he never sees him at all,' Patsy said dolefully. 'But it can't last for ever, can it? I can do what I like when I'm twenty-one – it just seems an awful long time to wait.'

She went out, leaving Hilary to sip her coffee and stare out of the window at the falling snow. I'm not the only one with difficulties, she thought. An hour or two ago I was thinking that Patsy was one of the happy ones in the house, and now I realise that underneath it all she has a real problem.

Was there anyone, anywhere, who could claim to be truly happy?

'It's so lovely to see you,' Maddy said, tucking her arm into Stephen's as they walked along the beach at West Lyme, with the black Labrador Archie bounding along in front of them. 'I missed you last weekend.'

'I missed you too. I wish we could get married, so that we don't have to be apart. Why don't we, darling? Why do we have to wait?'

'Because it's nice to be engaged for a while,' Maddy said, but her tone was wistful. 'And because your father would think there was something odd if we got married too quickly – not to mention the busybodies of Burracombe, casting suspicious glances at my waistline! But mostly because I can't get married without Stella at my wedding, and that doesn't look likely to be possible for months.'

'We'll tell her to hurry up when we see her tomorrow,' Stephen said, throwing a piece of driftwood into the sea for the dog to retrieve. 'It's nice of the Archdeacon to let me stay in their spare bedroom.'

'I did wonder if we should be going to Burracombe,' Maddy said. 'Your father might be feeling neglected.'

'Dad feeling neglected?' Stephen gave a hoot of laughter. 'Dad makes sure he's never neglected!'

'Still, he does like to see you as often as possible. Perhaps we ought to go next time you have a forty-eight-hour pass.'

'Mmm, perhaps.' Archie brought back the stick, dropped it on the wet sand and stood there wagging his tail and grinning. 'Oh, all right then,' Stephen told him. 'But this is the last time. It's too cold to stand around here – we're going home for cinnamon toast in front of the fire.'

They turned and strolled back along the beach. The clouds were gathering towards the west, covering the blue sky and bringing a sudden icy chill that made Maddy shiver and pull her coat more closely around her. Stephen put his arm around her shoulders and held her close as they walked along, and she leaned her head against his shoulder.

'I wonder how Dottie and Jackie are getting on in America,' she said presently. 'I haven't heard anything yet.'

'You'll probably get a letter from Dottie this week. It takes time for the post to arrive. I expect she's baking Joe a batch of scones at this very moment.'

'I hope she comes back. You know, Alice Tozer says they were sweethearts years ago, and nobody really knew why she didn't go to America with him.'

'There you are, then,' Stephen said, taking the piece of driftwood from the dog and keeping hold of it. 'I wouldn't be at all surprised if she stayed there this time. I think he'll persuade her quite easily once she sees what it's like. No, Archie, I told you, that was the last time. It's no use jumping at me like that. Get off – you're all wet.'

'Oh, I'm sure you're wrong. Dottie will never leave Burracombe now.'

'People do. But we'll see. Anyway, I'm more interested in us. You'd come to America with me if I decided to emigrate, wouldn't you?'

Maddy slanted a look up at him. 'I'd be more likely to go if we'd discussed it and decided together.'

'Well of course! That's what I meant. I wouldn't do anything you didn't want to do too. But would you think about it?'

'I thought it was Canada you were thinking of.'

'Yes, it is,' he said thoughtfully. 'And I really am quite serious about it. Especially now that Father's giving me and Hilary the money from the farm he's just sold. It would help us to set up the air freight business. But if you really didn't want to go ...'

'I think it sounds very exciting,' she said, hugging his arm. 'A new life in a new country! But I'd have to be sure Stella was going to be all right. And I'd want to be able to come home to see her as often as possible – not leave it for years and years like Joe Tozer did. And you'd have to come back to see your father too. He's already lost one son, and it doesn't look as if Robert is going to make his home here after all, so you can't abandon him completely. He really would feel neglected then.'

'It would be expensive,' he said doubtfully. 'And not so easy at first, while we're building up the business. But I promise it will be something we'd start planning for from the start. I think you're right, Maddy – we shouldn't just go away and never come back again. Burracombe is a part of us both. We can't turn our backs on it.'

They came to the path that wound up the cliff to the Archdeacon's house, and paused for a kiss.

Maddy smiled into his eyes. 'Do you know something, Stephen? I don't know how anyone could ever turn their back on Burracombe.'

Terry and Patsy were turning their backs on Burracombe at that very moment, but only to trudge through the snow to the main road, to catch the bus to Tavistock for their afternoon at the cinema.

'Your mum wasn't too keen on us going, was she?' Patsy remarked, clinging to Terry's arm. 'I suppose the snow could get worse this afternoon, and we might not be able to get back.'

'Go on, we'll be all right. If the bus don't run, us'll catch the train. They can always get through and we can get off at Burracombe Halt and walk over the Clam. I'll make sure you'm home by eight, never you fear.'

'We should have plenty of time for that,' Patsy giggled. 'The picture finishes at six o'clock.'

'There you are, then. We could walk all the way home in that time if us had to.' They plodded along in silence for a while, the flakes whirling around their heads and settling on their eyelashes. Presently he said, 'Where does your dad think you are today?'

'Over at Auntie Mary's, helping her with the twins.' Mary Crocker and Patsy's mother were cousins. 'I do go sometimes to give her a hand, so nobody thought to question it. They're little devils, but they're quite good with me. We play ludo and things like that.'

'So this afternoon you'll be throwing snowballs and making snowmen.' She laughed and nodded, but Terry went on more seriously, 'I don't like all this, though. Going behind your mum and dad's backs. We ought to have it out in the open. We'm doing nothing wrong, after all.'

'We are as far as my dad's concerned.'

'But we're *not*,' he insisted. 'He must know that. He courted your mother, didn't he, before they got married? He must know you'll want to do the same.'

'But we're not getting married, are we?' she said. 'We've only been out together a few times.'

'Well, that's long enough to know,' he said, and they both stopped and stared at each other through the mass of whirling snowflakes. 'I didn't mean to say it yet, but I reckon you'm the girl for me, Patsy, and if you feel the same, I'd like to ask you to marry me.'

Patsy stared at his long, rubbery face. His ears stuck out so far that each had a little pile of snow gathering on top of it, and his hair was standing up like sparrows' feathers over his head. But his eyes were serious and steady, and she felt her heart quiver.

'What do you reckon?' he asked when she didn't answer at once. 'Or didn't you want me to say nothing?'

'No,' she stammered. 'I mean – yes. I just never thought ... I never dreamed you were thinking that way. We've only been going out a couple of weeks. I thought we'd wait years before we thought about getting wed.'

'I don't want to wait years,' he said. 'I reckon I knew the minute I first saw you. I don't want to take the chance of some other chap getting in first.'

'I don't think there's much chance of that,' she said quietly. 'I felt the same way when I first saw you.'

'You mean that's a yes?' he exclaimed joyously. 'You'm saying yes?'

'I reckon I must be,' she said, and laughed suddenly. 'I reckon I am!'

'Patsy!' He caught her against him and began to kiss her face. The snowflakes swept about them and Patsy tasted them against her tongue as she opened her mouth for his kiss, and knew that for the rest of her life she would sense the same magic whenever she saw snow begin to fall. Tears came into her eyes and brimmed over, and Terry drew back suddenly and stared at her with concern.

'You'm crying, my bird. Whatever be the matter? Not sorry already, are you?'

'Not sorry at all. It must be because I'm so happy. Oh *Terry* ...'

'I'm happy too,' he said, drawing her close again. 'But I'm not going to cry about it. I want to shout it from the rooftops.'

'No! You mustn't do that! It's got to be a secret.'

'A secret?'

'Yes! My dad – we can't let him find out. I don't know what he'd do.'

'But he've got to know,' Terry expostulated. 'We want to get married. We can't do that without his permission. My dad's too, come to that.'

'I don't suppose he's any more likely to give that than mine is,' Patsy said dolefully. 'We're both too young. We're going to have to wait, Terry.'

'Four years?' he exclaimed. 'We can't wait that long! We just can't!'

They walked on, their hands clasped, the euphoria of the moment evaporating. Then Patsy said, 'Don't let it spoil things, Terry. I was so happy when you asked me. Let's just be like that.'

He stopped and kissed her again. 'You'm right, sweetheart. There's nothing anyone can do that can spoil that for us. And it don't really matter how long we got to wait, or if we have to keep it secret, because *we* know, and that's the main thing.' He paused for a few minutes. 'All the same, I do reckon I ought to tell your dad we'm going out. He's going to find out sometime.'

'All right. But not yet.' She squeezed his hand. 'Let's keep it to ourselves for a little while longer.'

The snow was falling faster and thicker than ever by the time they reached the main road. The bus was twenty minutes late and crawled slowly into Tavistock, where there was almost no traffic. Terry hesitated outside the cinema, looking uneasily at the white flakes swirling down from the dark clouds.

'I dunno, Pats. I'm wondering if us ought to give it up and go home now, while us can.'

'Oh no! You said it would be all right – we could catch the train.'

'I know, but it looks worse now. Suppose they decide not to run the train at all. We could be stuck in Tavistock all night.'

'Don't let's give up now,' she begged. 'I've been looking forward to seeing this picture. And it's only for a couple of hours – it won't be that bad if we go straight back when we come out.'

'I was going to take you for tea at Perraton's,' he said regretfully.

'We'll do that next time. Anyway, the snow might have stopped by the time we come out and we could still do it then. Come on, Terry, if we don't go in soon we'll miss the start.'

They went inside and Terry paid for two tickets. There were still a few seats in the back row and they settled down close together. Terry put his arm around Patsy's shoulders and gave her his other hand to hold. She snuggled against him.

'I wish they had double seats, like they do in the big cinema in Plymouth,' she whispered, giggling.

Much as she had wanted to see the film, if she had been asked afterwards what it had been about, she couldn't have answered. Close and warm in the shelter of Terry's arm, she watched in a dream, the images floating past her half seen, the music no more than a background to the emotions that swirled about her like the snowflakes outside. Terry had asked her to marry him! They were engaged, even if nobody knew it, even if she had no ring to wear. I don't need a ring, she thought. I don't need anything now I know Terry truly loves me. I don't even mind waiting – not really.

The only fly in the ointment was her father. When would they ever be able to tell him? When could they be a properly engaged couple, with everyone knowing, saving up for their wedding and a home of their own?

As she sat there, conscious only of Terry's arm about her, her feelings began slowly to change and a new strength entered her heart. She thought of Hilary's dismay when she had heard of Percy Shillabeer's rigid ways. It's not right, she thought. Terry and me ought to be able to go out together properly. I ought to be able to ask him home to tea, or Sunday dinner. And now we're engaged, he ought to be able to ask Father's permission.

She turned her face to Terry's, but before she could say anything, he sensed her movement and kissed her, and she said no more until the film had finished and they were walking out again into the snow.

Chapter Seventeen

The snow reached West Lyme as the afternoon light began to fade, when Stephen and Maddy were settling down to their tea and cinnamon toast in front of Maddy's fireplace. There was just one table lamp alight, casting a soft glow to aid the flames, and it was not until Maddy got up to draw the curtains that she noticed the flakes brushing against the windows.

'It's snowing!'

'Good Lord! Much?' He jumped up and came to stand beside her, his arm around her waist. 'It's quite heavy. And it's settling fast – look, it must be an inch deep already.'

'Isn't it lovely!' Maddy said dreamily. 'We haven't had snow since before Christmas. I didn't think we were going to get any more.' She leaned against him. 'We'll be able to build a snowman.'

Stephen said nothing and she glanced at him in surprise. 'What's the matter?'

'Only that if it carries on like this, we won't be able to go to Plymouth. And I may have to think about going back to the base early.'

'Oh no!' She gazed at him in dismay. 'I hadn't thought of that. But they'll understand, won't they, if you're snowed up?'

'I rather doubt it,' he said wryly. 'I'm in Her Majesty's Services, don't forget. Being on duty is supposed to be my first priority.'

'But we're not at war now.'

'Doesn't make any difference. And I had a lot of leeway a few weeks ago –coming home when Dad was ill and all that. I can't take any chances, darling. I don't want to be in jankers for the next month!'

Maddy turned away and went back to the fire. 'I suppose that's it, then,' she said dismally. 'I won't be able to go to see my sister, and you'll have to go back first thing in the morning.'

'Not even that, I'm afraid,' he said, coming to join her. 'I ought to go now, while I can. Just in case it gets any worse.'

'Oh Stephen! Can't you say you didn't know? After all, if we'd drawn the curtains before it started ...'

He shook his head, smiling. 'But I do know, don't I? I'm sorry, sweetheart. I'll have to go. And you might still be able to go to see Stella, if it turns out to be nothing much. You can catch the train, like you have before.'

'But I wanted to go with you,' she said childishly. 'Oh, why does everything have to be spoilt, just when it was so nice!'

'Come on, it's not that bad.' He took her in his arms. 'It's just one weekend, that's all. There'll be plenty more. By the time we've been married a while, you'll be pleased to see the back of me!'

'I never will. Anyway, we'll be old then. I want to see you *now*.' Stephen said nothing, but pulled her a little closer, and after a moment she drew in a shaky breath and said, 'I'm being selfish, aren't I? Like I used to be when I was a child, and ... and after Sammy died. I thought I'd got over that.'

'You're not selfish,' he said gently. 'You're my darling, sweet Maddy and you're disappointed, that's all. And so am I. But I've still got to go, I'm afraid.'

'I know. I won't make any more fuss. But you ought to have something more to eat than cinnamon toast before you leave.' She glanced uneasily at the window and the flakes falling thickly outside. 'Are you sure it's safe? I don't want you to have an accident.'

'I'll be careful,' he promised. 'I've put winter tyres on the car, and I've got chains if I need them. And it's best to go before it gets worse. It might not be safe if I put it off.'

'I wish we *had* drawn the curtains earlier,' she muttered, and then held up her hands. 'It's all right – I'm not going to start again! You'd better get your things together and I'll do some scrambled eggs. I'll make you a flask of coffee to take with you too.'

There was a knock on the door. Maddy's flat was part of the Archdeacon's house, but it was treated as her own private space and nobody entered without permission.

'Come in,' she called, and the Archdeacon's wife put her head round the door.

'I'm terribly sorry to butt in on you, but we wondered if you knew it was snowing,' she began, and Maddy and Stephen glanced at each other ruefully and then laughed. 'Why, what's so funny?'

'I was just wishing we'd drawn the curtains earlier so that we wouldn't know,' Maddy said. 'But you'd have made sure we did anyway.'

'I'm sorry – we just thought ...'

'You thought right,' Stephen told her. 'I'll have to go back straight away.'

'Yes, that's what my husband said. What a shame. And you were going to see Stella tomorrow as well, weren't you?'

'I still will, if the trains are running,' Maddy said. 'I don't suppose it'll last anyway. You know what snow is like – six inches deep in the morning and all gone by the afternoon. We'll probably be cursing ourselves for panicking tomorrow.'

'Better that than incarcerated and not allowed off the airfield for a month,' Stephen said, going through the door. 'I'll get my stuff together.'

'And I'll do those eggs,' Maddy said, turning to the tiny kitchen. 'Thanks for coming to tell us, Mrs Copley. I hope I didn't sound ungrateful. I'm being rather silly over Stephen having to go back so soon.'

'Not silly at all. You're bound to be disappointed.' The older woman hesitated, then said, 'You know, that's a very nice young man. And if you don't mind my saying so, he seems to have grown up a lot since he first started coming here. He seemed rather spoiled then.'

'We both were,' Maddy confessed, getting a saucepan and some eggs from her cupboard. 'Though I don't really know why Stephen should have been – he's always very much aware of being second best in his father's eyes. Still, we've both improved since those days. When I look back and remember what I was like ...!' She shuddered.

Mrs Copley laughed. 'You weren't that bad! But you've had to grow up quickly.' She looked at the younger woman compassionately. 'You've been through things none of us would like to experience, although a lot had to, during the war. But losing your fiancé wasn't because of the war – that was because of someone else's actions entirely. That must have been very hard to bear.'

'It was. But I've got Stephen now. He waited for me all that time and I'm not going to let him go.' Maddy paused as she beat the eggs in a bowl. 'I suppose that's why I hate it so much when he leaves me.'

Mrs Copley nodded with understanding. 'He'll be safe, dear. He's a careful driver and he's sensible to leave before the snow gets any worse. And here he comes now, so I'll leave you to your supper.'

She closed the door and went downstairs. Those two need to be married, she thought. They're still very young, but they've been through too much. They need to be together.

'There, you see,' Terry said as he and Patsy got off the train at Burracombe Halt. 'I told you we'd be all right. We'll go home for a cup of tea before I take you back.'

The snow had eased a little and the train, running along the branch line from Launceston to Plymouth, had got through without too much trouble, although it was slightly late. But it was still only just six, and Patsy wasn't expected at home until eight.

'We mustn't stop too long,' she said nervously. 'It's starting again and it'll take us longer to walk through deep snow. But just a cup, if your mother doesn't mind.'

'Of course her won't mind. She likes you. Told me I could invite you round any time.' He grinned. 'To tell you the truth, I think she's pleased any girl will look at me, with my ugly mug!'

'You're not ugly!' she protested. 'Not to me, anyway.'

'Well, you know what they say – love's blind.' He tucked her hand into his pocket. 'I was thinking, back there in the pictures – we'm not likely to forget this day in a hurry. It's the happiest day of my life, Pats.'

'Oh Terry.' She paused. 'Mine too. But the day we get married will be even happier. It just seems such a long way away.'

'You've got to let me talk to your father,' he said.

'I know, but not yet, Terry, please. You saw what he's like. He'll half kill us both and he'll never let me out of the house. Look, I'll talk to Mother. She knows the best way to deal with him.'

'Does she?' Terry thought of the wispy, downtrodden little woman who came into the village to do her shopping, lugging it all the way back over the Clam with only the youngest children to help her, because – it was said – her husband wouldn't let her go into Tavistock. 'Well, I'll be patient for a while but I'm not waiting four years till we're both twenty-one. He've got to see sense before then.'

'Yes,' Patsy said, and felt a return of the unexpected determination she had felt in the cinema. 'Yes, he has. I don't want to wait either. I don't see any point in it. We're engaged now and there's nothing he can do to change that, and it's our lives we're talking about, not his. We'll talk to him soon, Terry. Only we'll do it together. It's time he realised I'm grown-up now and want to live my own life.'

'Patsy! That's the first time I've heard you talk like that.' He stopped and threw his arms around her. 'I love you, Patsy Shillabeer. I really, really love you!'

Mrs Pettifer was, as Terry had said, pleased to see Patsy again and made them both sit down to a late tea of sardines on toast followed by a dish of junket. The cottage room was warm and cosy, and Bob kept them entertained with his impressions of famous film and radio stars. He seemed able to twist his rubbery features into almost any shape and Patsy was helpless with laughter when he finally got up from the table and said he was going to the pub to have a game of dominoes with his friend Reg. He pulled on an old army greatcoat he'd got from the second-hand shop in Tavistock and went to the door.

'Here, that old snow really means it,' he called back, peering out. 'You'd better get young Patsy back over the river, our Terry, or she'll be having to stop the night.'

'Oh no, I mustn't do that!' She jumped up and ran to get her coat from the hooks by the door. 'And look at the time! It's nearly half past seven. I didn't realise ...'

'It's all right,' Terry said, helping her into her coat and shrugging into his own. 'We'll get there in time. Anyway, he'll surely realise it takes you longer to walk through the snow. He'll expect you to be a bit late.'

'He'll say I should have left sooner.' Patsy turned to Mrs Pettifer. 'Thank you for the tea, it was lovely. And the dinner, too. I'm sorry to rush off like this.'

'That's all right, my flower. You don't want to get into your father's bad books. Now, you remember, you'm welcome any time. You don't have to wait to to be invited.'

She kissed Patsy, and then gave them both a gentle push out into the swirling snow. They set off along the narrow village street, Terry lighting their way with a big torch which shone a yellow light on to the smooth white surface. There were a few footprints to show that some hardy souls had gone along to the Bell Inn, but it seemed that most of the inhabitants of Burracombe were staying indoors.

Patsy and Terry walked as fast as they could, their arms linked. The snow crunched beneath their feet and the wind blew icy spicules against their cheeks. As they left the road and took the stony, uneven track leading down to the narrow bridge over the river, which everyone called the Clam, the way became more and more slippery and their progress slower. Patsy clung to Terry's arm and squeaked as her feet slid, and he stopped and steadied her.

"'Tis no good rushing, Patsy. Us won't get there any sooner if one of us falls and breaks an ankle.'

'I know, but ...' They crossed the wooden footbridge safely and began to climb up the other bank. 'Nearly there now,' she panted thankfully. 'Oh Terry, I—'

A figure suddenly loomed up in front of them, huge and misshapen in the wavering light and swirling flakes. Patsy gave a little scream and clutched Terry's arm even more tightly, and he stopped, startled and alarmed.

'Who's that?'

'Who's *that*?' the figure demanded, and Patsy uttered a little cry of dismay. 'Who be you, out on a night like this with my daughter? Come on – speak up!'

'Father!' she whispered. 'It's Father!'

For one long, dreadful moment they all stood there, staring at each other. Then Percy Shillabeer shot out a massive hand towards his daughter.

'Come here! Come here this minute!'

Patsy shrank back against Terry. 'Father, don't. We've done nothing wrong.'

'Nothing wrong? And ain't telling lies to your mother and father wrong? What happened to the Ten Commandments, what you been taught since the day you were born? What happened to *honour thy father and thy mother*? And if you've broke that one, what else have you done that ain't *wrong*?'

'Nothing! We've done nothing!'

He snorted, then turned his attention to Terry.

'And what about you, out all hours with my daughter that's always been brought up respectable? Where've you took her today when her was supposed to be helping my wife's cousin Mary? When were you thinking to bring her home?'

'We'm on our way home now, Mr Shillabeer,' Terry replied steadily. 'And we've been to the pictures in Tavistock and then back for a bit of tea with my mum and dad. We haven't done nothing we shouldn't have done.'

'You have! My Patsy was supposed to be at Mary Crocker's, and she never even went there. If I hadn't gone round to fetch her because of the snow, I'd never have known. How many other times have you and her been out somewhere, and me and her mother thinking she were somewhere else? Well? Because I doubt this were the first.'

Terry and Patsy glanced at each other, and the angry farmer caught the glance and gave another snort. 'Thought so! Well I'll tell you this now, this is the end of it. You'll not see each other again. Patsy's my daughter and under my control, and I'll say who she sees and who she don't see, *and* where she goes and doesn't go, so make up your minds to it. No more little jaunts to Tavistock, nor anywhere else. Now, come you home, my lady, and see what's waiting for you there.'

He reached out again and this time caught Patsy's shoulder in a rough grip. Again she cried out, and Terry stepped forward angrily.

'Let her go! You'm hurting her.'

'And what if I am? What business is it of yours?'

'It's my business because Patsy's my girl,' Terry retorted. 'I been wanting to come and see you about it.'

'You'd have been wasting your time. Patsy's not going to be any-body's girl, not for a long while yet. Now you get off home before I takes my stick to you.'

Terry stood his ground.

'You can't stop us seeing each other.'

'I can and I will!' The farmer's voice grew even angrier. 'And I'm not going to stand here in the snow argufying about it.You'll not see Patsy again, and that's it and all about it, and if I see your ugly face this side of the river again you'll be sorry. Get off home! Patsy, you come here.'

But Patsy too was standing her ground. Frightened and humiliated as she was, she had a temper to match her father's. It rarely surfaced, but now it came surging through her, so strong and fierce that it seemed almost to lift her off her feet. Her heart thudding, she raised her chin and looked him in the eye.

'I won't! Not until you say I can go on seeing Terry. We love each other. We're going to be married.'

The silent, white world seemed to pause; even the snow seemed to stop whirling about them as the words fell into the air. Patsy stared at her father, hardly able to believe that she had spoken them, and she felt Terry move suddenly beside her. He gripped her hand tightly.

'*Going to be married?*' Percy Shillabeer repeated at last, in a slow, thick voice. 'What nonsense be you talking now, maid?'

'It's not nonsense, Mr Shillabeer,' Terry said. 'I asked her today and she said yes. We know we can't be wed for a while, but—'

'For a *while*! You can't be married *ever*! Why, you'm just children, the pair of you – still wet behind the ears. Had your heads turned by all these pictures you been going to see, no doubt. Well, there's an end to it. You'll not see each other again.'

'Father, we're engaged . . .'

'You'll be engaged when I say so!' he bellowed. 'And it won't be to this apology for a church gargoyle – it'll be to someone with a bit more to him. Someone that works at a proper job, on the land, not fiddling about indoors with bits of wire. Now, come on home. I've had enough.' He shot out his hand and caught Patsy's shoulder again, jerking her towards him. 'Your mother's waiting for you. And you, Terry Pettifer, you get back to your home. I'll have something to say to your father next time I see him.'

He pulled roughly at Patsy's arm and she turned her head towards Terry. 'Better do as he says. But I'll see you again soon. I meant what I said.'

'You'll mean what you say when you'm twenty-one, and not a minute before,' her father growled. 'Until then, you'm under my authority, and don't you forget it.'

He dragged Patsy away along the lane and Terry stood for a moment watching them out of sight. It was no use resisting any more. The farmer was bigger and stronger than he was, and both Terry and Patsy were uncomfortably aware that he had the law on his side. After a few minutes, Terry shivered, suddenly aware of the cold, and turned to walk miserably home.

Percy Shillabeer hadn't won, however. As he trudged along the track and over the Clam, Terry made up his mind that whatever the angry farmer said, he could not put an end to what had happened between himself and Patsy. He could not unmake the promise Patsy had given him, nor change Terry's determination. Somehow they would continue to see each other, and one day they would be married.

Nothing on earth could prevent that.

Chapter Eighteen

'I never took it!' Billy Culliford cried. His face turned red and his lips trembled. 'It wasn't me! I never stole Janice Ruddicombe's penny!'

He stood in front of Miss Kemp's desk, tears streaming down his cheeks. The two teachers looked at him and then at each other.

'You're quite sure?' Miss Kemp asked, turning to Miss Watkins.

'I told you. I saw it in his hand. I don't know what he did with it after that, but he definitely had it.' Miss Watkins turned her eyes on the little boy before them. 'Billy, you know it's naughty to tell lies. Tell Miss Kemp the truth.'

'But I never!' he protested. 'It must have been someone else. I'm not a thief, miss, I'm not.'

'Sometimes it happens by mistake, Billy,' Miss Kemp said gently. 'Perhaps you picked it up meaning to give it back, but didn't get the chance. Is that what happened?'

'He picked it up, but not by chance,' Miss Watkins said. 'It was deliberate theft.'

Miss Kemp frowned at her. 'Please. I don't like that kind of language in my school. And give Billy a chance to answer. Now, think very carefully, Billy. Is that what happened?'

He hesitated, then glanced at the infant teacher. She had pursed her lips tightly together and he quailed at the sight of her frown. Then he shook his head.

'No, miss. I never picked it up. I never even saw it.'

'Well, that certainly isn't true! The other children told me that it rolled right across the floor after Janice dropped it. They all tried to catch it – including Billy Culliford. And if he'll lie about that—'

'Miss Watkins, *please!*' Not for the first time, Miss Kemp longed to have Stella back, with her gentle ways and obvious affection for the children. This woman didn't even seem to *like* them. 'Let me speak to Billy, if you don't mind. Perhaps it would be better if I had a word with him on my own.'

Miss Watkins hesitated, clearly reluctant to go. Miss Kemp waited, and with a shrug, the teacher left the classroom. Miss Kemp turned her attention back to Billy.

'Now, Billy, tell me what you think happened.'

The little boy looked up at her. His face was grimy and streaked with tears, his hair could have done with a wash and his jumper had a hole in the front and unravelling cuffs. But his gaze was clear and honest.

'I never stole Janice's penny, honest, miss. I never even seen it. I heard her shout out about it but we were all out there in the lobby and I was by the door. She were right over by the window. I couldn't have stole it.'

'Miss Watkins says it rolled across the floor.'

'It never come near me, miss.'

'Do you think Miss Watkins saw it?'

'I dunno, miss. She could have. She were right near me, so if it did roll that way ... But I never saw it, miss. I didn't, honest.' The tears began to flow again. 'Please, miss, don't send me to prison.'

'Of course I won't send you to prison. Little boys like you don't go to prison anyway, so stop worrying about that.' She gazed at him for a moment, then sighed. 'All right, Billy, you'd better go now. I expect your mother's at the gate wondering where you are. Now, it doesn't look as if we'll ever know what happened to Janice's penny, but obviously somebody did pick it up and keep it, and as we know, that's stealing just as much as if you take a penny from someone's coat pocket. I shall speak to everyone about it in the morning. But you're not to worry about it any more. Run along now.'

Billy scampered out of the door, and a moment later Miss Watkins reappeared.

'I see you've decided to believe him, then.'

'Without any further evidence, I have to,' Miss Kemp replied. 'He's turned out his pockets and it's clearly not there. I can't strip him. I think you must have been mistaken.'

The infant teacher flushed a dull, ugly red. 'Perhaps you think I took it.'

'Don't be ridiculous,' Miss Kemp said sharply. 'Of course I don't. But I won't have small children suspected and bullied.'

'Bullied?'

'Yes, bullied. The poor child was terrified he'd be sent to prison. Did you tell him that would happen?'

'No! I simply told him that thieves go to prison, and if he thought I meant him, that's a clear sign of a guilty conscience. I tell you, I saw the penny in his hand.'

'I'm afraid I don't think you did. I think you were mistaken. But in any case, I intend to leave it at that. If he did do it, he's had a bad fright and is unlikely to do it again. I shall speak to the whole school tomorrow and I want no more to be said about it.'

'So he's going to get away with it. Well, I warn you, we're storing up trouble for ourselves. I've seen it before. Once a child like that—'

'A child like what?' Miss Kemp interrupted dangerously.

'You know what I mean! From the sort of family he comes from – I've seen their cottage, I've met the mother. Down-at-heel, slatternly, always got a cigarette hanging off her lip, more children than she knows what to do with ... And the father no better than a petty crook, by all accounts, in and out of prison for poaching. Of course the children will grow up the same way.'

'Billy is only four years old,' Miss Kemp said, with slow emphasis. 'And his sisters Shirley and Betty are doing well and are a credit to the school. Their clothes may not be as clean and smart as those of someone like Wendy Cole, whose father is in the Civil Service, but they do their best and they're bright little girls and as honest as the day is long. I see no reason why Billy shouldn't do every bit as well. But he needs encouragement, not bullying, and *I will not have him*, or any other child, frightened by threats of prison. Is that understood?'

The younger woman stared at her for a minute, the flush deepening on her cheeks and neck. Then she tossed her head and shrugged.

'If you say so, of course. You are the headmistress, after all.'

'Yes, I am,' Miss Kemp said. 'And if there are any more cases like this, with money or possessions disappearing, I want them referred straight to me. I am not happy about the way you handled this, Miss Watkins, and if anything like it happens again, I shall be telling the school governors so. Now I think you'd better go, or you'll be missing your bus to Tavistock.'

Miss Watkins turned on her heel and marched out of the classroom, her shoulders stiff with anger. Miss Kemp watched her and sighed. She had not intended to make an enemy of her colleague, but she very much feared that she had done so. However, she was not prepared to have the children in her care either frightened or unjustly accused, and she was angry that Billy, the youngest child in the school, seemed to have been singled out.

She went to the window and gazed out. The snow of the weekend had almost all gone now, leaving a ridge of dirty slush along the edge of the narrow stream that ran down the side of the road. In the gathering dusk, she could see Billy with his mother, Maggie Culliford, walking slowly away from the gate. The woman looked tired, she thought, and heavy with the coming child. Miss Watkins had a point, of course – neither parent seemed properly equipped to manage their own lives, let alone those of their children. But that simply meant that it was up to their neighbours to give what help they could. You couldn't live in a village and just pass by on the other side.

We must be very careful whom we select when Miss Watkins' appointment comes to an end, she thought. We certainly can't take her on permanently.

But what had really happened to Janice Ruddicombe's penny?

'I dunno what's the matter with him,' Maggie said to Joanna Tozer. They had met in the butcher's shop, where Maggie had gone for sausages and Joanna for lamb chops for the family's dinner. 'Crying his eyes out, he'd been, when I fetched him out of school. Wouldn't tell me a thing, but I reckon that teacher's at the back of it somewhere.'

'Robin doesn't like her either,' Joanna said. 'It's a shame, when they all liked Stella so much. She gave the little ones a really good start.'

'I can see our Billy going the way of his brother,' Maggie said despondently. 'That Mr Billington, he was headmaster when my Jimmy and Brenda started, and he frightened the life out of them. They never took to learning after that. It wasn't till Jimmy got to St Rumon's and started to learn about plumbing and carpentry that he picked up at all, but he never properly caught up.'

Joanna said nothing. She'd heard about Mr Billington's strictness, of course, and he had been a familiar figure in the village before he retired and Miss Kemp took over, but plenty of other children had managed to learn their lessons during his regime. From what she'd heard, Jimmy Culliford had spent a lot of his schooldays playing truant and roaming the woods with his father at night. He'd been had up for poaching more than once, and was on probation even now. She said goodbye to Maggie and went home.

'It's the way they'm brought up,' Alice Tozer said when Joanna told her about the conversation. 'Families like the Cullifords are always in and out of trouble. Those two girls, Shirley and Betty, would be the same if Stella hadn't taken the trouble she did over them.'

'Maybe that's all they need,' Joanna said thoughtfully. 'Someone to take a bit of interest in them. Half the village doesn't even know which is which of Maggie's children, unless they're in trouble.'

Minnie was sitting by the range, knitting a cardigan for Heather. Her hands were getting very arthritic now and her movements were slow, but she insisted on keeping up her knitting and sewing. She looked up and joined in the conversation.

'Cullifords has always been like that. Arthur's father was the same, and Maggie's was no better. And look how they ended up. 'Tis in their blood.'

'How did they end up?' Joanna asked. 'I've never heard anything much about them. Arthur's mother's still alive, isn't she?'

'Yes, but she's very frail now,' Alice said. 'Lives over the other side of Top Wood – don't you remember all that trouble when young Betty got hurt when Travis Kellaway was looking for poachers backalong? Arthur said he'd been over to see his mother that night and was taking a short cut back.' She sniffed in a believe-it-if-you-like fashion. 'His father died a few years ago. Never had two pennies to rub together. And Maggie's dad had to go to the workhouse.'

Joanna stared at her. 'The workhouse? The one in Tavistock?'

'That's right. Up top of Bannawell Street. He was an old curmudgeon, that one. Gave Maggie and her sister a terrible life, and drove their mother into an early grave. He finished up living in a sort of lean-to shack at the end of that row of miners' cottages over to Horndon before he went to the workhouse.'

'Couldn't his daughters have looked after him?' Margret asked suddenly. She was standing at the kitchen table, cutting bread and spreading it with butter. 'In Germany we don't send our old people to live in tiny shacks or – what did you call it? A workhouse? What work do they have to do?'

''I don't really know,' Joanna said vaguely. 'Making mailbags, I think – or is that the prison? And isn't there a laundry there? I think it's closing soon, anyway. People don't need it now they get pensions.'

'In Germany,' Margret said again, 'we look after our families ourselves.'

There was a brief silence, then Alice said mildly, 'So do we – some of us, at any rate. We're not sending Granny to the workhouse. Not as long as she can make herself useful here, anyway!'

'That's right,' Minnie said, starting another row of knitting. 'There's always plenty for me to do. Alice sees to that!'

They laughed, but the German woman remained serious. Before anyone could speak again, the door opened and Brian came in. He stamped some slush off his boots and took them off at the door.

'Someone tell me the joke?' he asked, hanging his coat on one of the hooks.

'It is not a joke,' Margret said. 'We were speaking about old people and the way they are treated here. I said it was different in Germany.'

'I see.' His eyes went from one to another of the women. 'And you all thought that was funny?'

'No, it wasn't like that,' Joanna said. 'It was something Granny said, that's all. Is Tom coming in soon?'

'He's just finishing off in the milking parlour. Didn't want my help any more.' Brian came over to the range and held out his hands to the glowing coals. 'I got the feeling I was in the way.'

'I don't suppose you were,' Alice said. 'Tom and your father are always glad of a hand.'

'Even the long-lost brother's!' Tom remarked cheerfully, entering at that point. 'As long as he does as he's told!'

'I only suggested—'

'I know, I know.' Tom came over to warm his hands too. 'The experience of all those years in the army. I dare say you did a lot of milking there. Shove over a bit and let me see the fire, will you?'

It was all said jocularly enough, but Alice glanced at them uneasily. There had always been an undercurrent between the two, even as boys, and she didn't want any friction now, when Brian was here on his first long visit since before the war. Tom, however, was grinning in his usual friendly manner; he'd always been one for jokes and banter. Alice relaxed and brought jars of fish paste, Marmite and home-made raspberry jam to the table. She poured some hot water into the big teapot, then moved the kettle to the hotplate to bring it to the boil before she made the tea.

Margret said nothing. After a moment or two Brian said, 'I'll go and change out of this work clobber and have a wash. OK if I take the kettle with me?' He picked it up, still half full of hot water, and went upstairs. Margret got up and followed him.

'You'd better have a wash as well,' Joanna said to Robin, who was on the rag rug in front of the fire with Heather, playing with his set of wooden bricks. 'Tea'll be ready soon. Come on, the two of you.' She shepherded the two children into the scullery. 'Cold water won't hurt, just for your hands and faces.'

Alice glanced over at Minnie, still knitting peaceably in her chair.

'It's a shame about that little Culliford kiddy. I wonder if he did take that penny.'

'As likely as not,' Minnie said. 'He'm only a baby still – don't hardly know the difference between right and wrong. But I don't like the sound of that teacher. I know I were only a nursemaid, but I've had plenty of experience with little ones over the years, and 'tis my belief they do best with a bit of kindness, like young Stella used to give them. 'Tis no use shouting and scaring them, they'll never do their best work.'

'It's our Robin I worry about,' Alice said in a low voice, glancing at the scullery door. 'I know Tom and Joanna want him to do well at school. It's all very well to say he don't need much education if he'm going to take on the farm one day, but us don't know he will, do us? Things are changing, and Ted reckons they'll change even more. What with tractors taking the place of horses, and more and more machinery, farming's going to be a lot different by the time Robin grows up. Education's important whatever you are.' She shook her head. 'I reckon we've had the best of it, Mother, even with two world wars to live through. I don't envy the youngsters like Robin and Heather and little Christopher – I don't really.'

Chapter Nineteen

'He says I'm not ever to see Terry again,' Patsy wept as she sat in the Napiers' kitchen.

'Oh Patsy,' Jennifer exclaimed in dismay. 'But perhaps he doesn't really mean it. He was just angry.'

'He's always angry – and he did mean it. You don't know my father. Once he's said something, he doesn't change his mind.'

'But he can't prevent you from seeing your friends.'

'He can.' The girl raised a woebegone tear-stained face. 'He's going to come and meet me every day when I finish here and make sure I don't see Terry on the way home. And I'm not allowed out in the evenings, and at weekends only if he says so, and if he knows where I'm going. And if I go anywhere, he'll take me there and meet me afterwards. I can't see anyone he doesn't want me to see.'

'But what's wrong with Terry? He's a nice boy.'

'Father doesn't want me going out with boys,' she said drearily. 'It's not just Terry.'

Jennifer gazed at her. It seemed unbelievable. This was how fathers behaved in Victorian times, not in the 1950s. Girls and women had done so much to achieve their independence. How could anyone seriously expect to keep a girl in chains these days?

'I honestly don't think he's allowed to do that,' she said at last. 'Legally, I mean. I know you're under his authority until you're twenty-one – you can't get married without his permission, and that sort of thing. And you can't vote or sign legal documents. But I don't think he can go that far. In fact, I think you're allowed to leave home at sixteen if you want to.'

Patsy stared at her. 'Is that really true? I could leave home and he couldn't make me go back?' For a moment, her face lit up, then her expression sagged again. 'But how can I do that? I've got no money, only what I earn here. Where would I live?'

'I don't really *know* that's true,' Jennifer said hastily, realising that she might have gone too far. 'Obviously it wouldn't be easy.' She saw the despair return to Patsy's big grey eyes. 'But I think you could go to court and ask them for permission. You'd have to convince them you could look after yourself, of course.'

Patsy pressed her lips together and stared despondently at the floor. 'I don't see how I could do that. Not without somewhere to live. And I can't ask anyone to take me in, not with Father the way he is.'

Jennifer suppressed a small sigh of relief. For a moment she'd been afraid that Patsy would turn to her for help, and she didn't fancy having Percy Shillabeer turning up on her doorstep demanding the return of his daughter.

''Terry's the only one who can do anything,' Patsy said. 'And I don't even see what he can do, specially if I'm not allowed to see him. I don't know what to do.'

'Nor do I,' Jennifer said honestly. 'All I can tell you is that nothing lasts for ever. Things do change and sometimes they change sooner than you expect. I can't believe your father will keep this up for four years. He's bound to give way eventually.'

'He could keep it up for ever,' Patsy said gloomily. 'And Terry will get fed up and meet someone else, I know he will, and I'll never get married. I'll *never* be able to get away!' Her voice rose in a wail.

Hilary came into the kitchen at that point and stared at them in surprise. 'Whatever's the matter?'

Jennifer gave Patsy a quick look and then explained, 'Patsy's father says she's not to see Terry Pettifer again.'

'Oh dear.' Hilary gave the girl a compassionate glance. 'But surely he'll come round in a little while.'

Patsy shook her head, and Jennifer said, 'She doesn't think so. She really is very upset.'

'So I see.' Hilary looked at the girl again and asked, 'Why has he done this? You've been out with Terry several times, surely, and he didn't mind. Has something happened to set your father against him?'

'He didn't know,' Patsy wept. 'I told him I was going to my friend's house – or to help Auntie Mary. He only found out when he came to meet me when it snowed on Saturday and I wasn't there.'

'Oh.' Hilary digested this. 'Well, it never helps to tell lies.' She was uncomfortably aware that she had told a number of lies to her own father about her whereabouts when she'd visited London recently. A reunion or shopping trip when in truth she had been going to meet David ... 'But I'm not blaming you,' she added quickly. 'We all do things when we're in love that we mightn't do otherwise.' She was aware of Jennifer's eyes on her and went on doggedly, 'The thing is, what are you going to do about it? Is it really serious between you and Terry?'

Patsy nodded. 'He's asked me to marry him,' she whispered, and then, lifting her head and speaking in a stronger voice, 'We're engaged.'

'Engaged!' the two women said together, and then Jennifer said, 'But how can you be, without your father's permission?'

'I don't need his permission to say yes to Terry,' Patsy said with a flash of rebellion. 'If he asks me and I say yes, we're engaged. And there's nothing Father can do to change that.' Her shoulders drooped and she said, despondent again, 'That's if Terry can put up with not seeing me for four years. '

'It won't come to that,' Hilary said. 'He can't keep you a prisoner all that time.'

'But we don't want to wait four years!' Patsy cried. 'We want to get married *now*! Well, sooner than four years, anyway.' She looked at Hilary. 'What if I came here? Live in, like servants always used to. I could have one of those rooms in the attic. I'd work ever so hard,' she went on eagerly, 'and you wouldn't have to pay me so much. Could I, Miss Hilary?'

Hilary stared at her, nonplussed. 'Well – no, Patsy, I don't think you could. For one thing, you'd need your father's permission and with things as they are, he'd almost certainly refuse. And for another, I couldn't agree to your deceiving him about Terry. There's my father to think about as well. He's not well enough for that kind of trouble. I'm sorry.'

Patsy's shoulders sagged. 'Oh well. I didn't really think you'd let me. I suppose I'll have to write to Terry then, and tell him it's all off. I can't ask him to wait all that time without even seeing each other.'

'Don't do that,' Hilary said. 'I'm sure something will happen to change your father's mind. Terry's a nice boy from a decent family.

Your father can't really have anything against him. He'll come round, you'll see.' She hesitated, then said, 'There's no reason why he *should* let you get married, is there?'

'Not if you mean ...' Patsy blushed. 'No, of course not. Me and Terry haven't done anything like that. I just wish we had!'

'Well, it seems to me you'll just have to be patient,' Hilary said. 'Fathers always find it hard to realise their daughters are growing up.' I'm not sure my own has completely realised it, she thought wryly. 'Give it a few months and you'll find he'll be a bit more ready to accept it. Now, I really must get on. Jennifer, I came to tell you that we've had a reply to the advertisement. A Mrs Curnow. She's coming to see me the day after tomorrow. We'll give her lunch and, if she seems suitable, would you mind showing her round the house? I have to go out in the afternoon to see one of the tenants who's worried about his sheep.'

'Yes, that'll be all right,' Jennifer agreed. 'Curnow? Sounds Cornish to me.'

'I think it may be. She writes from Bude. She's coming down by train, so I'll meet her at the station and then be home again in time to take her back. Unless she's so dreadful that I take her back straight after lunch! There's no point in spending an afternoon showing her round if she just won't do.' She turned to the door, then looked back at Patsy. 'Now, try not to worry too much, Patsy. I'm sure things will turn out all right in the end. We all have trouble with our fathers when we start to grow up!'

Patsy looked at her as if to imply that Hilary didn't know what trouble was, but nodded and said rather dully, 'I expect you're right, miss. I'll go and carry on with the bedrooms then, shall I, Mrs Kellaway?' She picked up the box with the handle that held all her dusting and polishing equipment, and departed.

'Poor girl,' Hilary said when she'd disappeared. 'It's all so dreadfully intense at that age, isn't it? But he'll probably come round. Or she and Terry may forget all about each other in a fortnight. He's her first boy, isn't he?'

'As far as I know,' Jennifer said. 'But I'm not sure you're right about this, Hilary. Patsy's the sort who falls for one man and carries a torch for him for the rest of her life. And she's not the little mouse we all took her for. I don't think she'll let go so easy.'

At dinner time, Jennifer gave Patsy a sheet of notepaper and an envelope so that she could write to Terry and tell him not to meet her after work. *If you do*, she wrote in her neat, careful handwriting, *Father will take his whip to you, for sure. I'm ever so sorry, Terry, but I don't see what we can do, but I still love you and always will. Your loving Patsy xxx*

'I'll pop it through his letter box when I go down to the village shop,' Jennifer said. 'Unless you'd like to walk down yourself? You might even see him.'

Patsy shook her head. 'And someone might see us and tell Father. I don't want to get Terry into any more trouble. Anyway, he's working over to Whitchurch all this week, he told me. He probably wouldn't have got back in time to meet me as it was.'

Jennifer took the letter and put it into her shopping basket. There was no wind, but it was a cold, cloudy afternoon and she wrapped her winter coat around her and walked quickly. She met Maggie Culliford just past the turning to the Tozers' farm.

'Hello, Maggie, how are you keeping?'

The other woman looked at her cautiously. 'Not too bad, I suppose. How about you? They tell me you'm in the family way too.'

Jennifer blushed. 'Now who told you that? We were planning to keep it a secret for a while.'

Maggie gave a short laugh. 'In Burracombe? Thought you'd know better than that by now. Anyway, some people can tell when a woman's expecting just by looking at her face. Don't ask me how. Jacob Prout always seems to know before I do meself.'

'Jacob didn't tell you?' Jennifer said, alarmed. After the hurt the old man had experienced when news of their engagement had flown like wildfire around the village, she and Travis had determined that he should be the first to know about their coming baby. We'll have to go and see him at once, she thought. This evening. If the news has got as far as the Cullifords . . .

'No, 'twasn't him. Come to think of it, I don't know that anyone did tell me. Maybe I just recognise the look, being that way meself.' She glanced at Jennifer's figure, swathed in her winter coat. 'You don't look like you'm showing yet.'

'I'm not. Look, you won't mention it to anyone else, will you? Not until we've had a chance to tell Jacob.' Maybe he's already noticed and is waiting for us to tell him, she thought. 'After that, you can tell who you like – not that they'll be all that interested.'

'Oh, they'll be interested all right. But I won't talk out of turn.' The two women looked at each other and Jennifer felt a sudden, unexpected warmth towards the poacher's wife. Maybe she wasn't so bad after all. Travis had little time for her husband, but it wasn't Maggie's fault if he couldn't keep a job and went out at night stealing other people's pheasants. As Jacob Prout had commented once, every village had its Culliford family living from hand to mouth in a ramshackle cottage with too many children and never enough money. In days gone by, men like Arthur had been forced to poach to prevent their children from starving, and many had been hanged for it. At least the worst he could expect now was a month in prison, and even that would be bad enough for Maggie and her family.

'You're looking tired,' she said. 'Are you getting enough rest?'

Maggie laughed bitterly. 'With my lot? Chance would be a fine thing. And getting Billy into school early haven't helped much. In trouble from the day he started, he's been, and it's all that new teacher's fault. Picks on him, she does.'

'Oh, surely not. Maybe he's having a bit of trouble finding his feet, him being so much younger than the others.'

'You'd think she'd take more care of him then, wouldn't you?' Maggie demanded. 'But that's not her way. Accused him of stealing, she has! Four years old and branded as a thief! If that's not picking on him, I don't know what is.'

'Stealing?' Jennifer said, horrified. 'But why?'

'That little Janice Ruddicombe dropped a penny in the lobby and Miss Watkins swears our Billy picked it up and kept it. Poor little toad was crying half the night. It took me hours to get it out of him, he was so upset. Kept asking me if he'd go to prison.'

'Poor little chap,' Jennifer echoed feelingly. 'And did they find the penny?'

Maggie shrugged. 'Not that I know of. I went straight in and had it out with Miss Kemp this morning and she told me she'd had a word with old Bootface and told her not to make accusations without she got proof. Other than that, she ain't going to do nothing. Reckons the penny must have rolled behind the cubbyholes where the kiddies put their wellingtons. I don't s'pose you've ever been in there, have you? It's like that set of pigeonholes Jessie Friend got in the post office, only bigger – takes a hang of shifting.'

Jennifer nodded, and Maggie went on bitterly, 'Course, I knows why she got it in for Billy. Same as everyone else – because he's a Culliford. They think because my Arthur and our Jimmy been in trouble a time or two, all the little'ns is bad. Never mind our Shirley being Pageant Queen that time and our Betty doing so well. And that's only because Miss Simmons took the trouble with them. Crying shame, it is, what happened to her – not that we weren't going to lose her anyway, when she marries the young vicar.'

A spiteful wind suddenly gusted along the lane and Jennifer shivered and pulled her coat more tightly around her. 'I hope you get it sorted out, I really do. Billy seems a sweet little boy.'

'He is. But he won't stay sweet for long if that dried-up old maid don't leave him alone.' Maggie glanced up the farm track. 'I thought I'd have a word with Joanna Tozer about it. Her Robin's come out in tears once or twice, I've heard. Maybe Miss Kemp'll take a bit more notice if a few of us gets together over it.'

The two women parted and Jennifer continued along the lane to the centre of the village. The great oak was bare of leaves now, its branches bowing and swaying in the blustering wind, and there was nobody on the seat that had been set beneath it years ago to commemorate the end of the war. She paused by the Pettifers' cottage and dropped Patsy's letter through the door.

Maggie was right, she thought. The name Culliford was a bad one in the village and Arthur's reputation was, as the Bible said, visited upon his children. But did it have to be like that? She made up her mind to mention it to Travis. She'd noticed him watching the older boy, Jimmy, with some suspicion when they had encountered him once or twice on walks. Maybe he was being as unfair as Miss Watkins.

Or, as Maggie called her, old Bootface!

Chapter Twenty

'I've had a letter from Dottie,' Stella told Felix when he arrived for visiting time a week or so later. She had been moved from her previous ward and was now in a room with six beds, all occupied by people who were learning to walk again. Most of them were older and had suffered strokes and one had had a brain injury resulting from a fall from a horse.

'They say she'll never be the same again,' Stella had told Felix on a previous visit. 'It's so sad – she's only thirty. It makes me realise how lucky I am. All I had was a broken bone or two and some bruising to my spine. I'll soon get over that.'

'It seemed a lot worse than that at the time,' Felix said, but he was relieved to hear her talking so optimistically.

'What does Dottie say?' he asked, and Stella gave him the letter. He read it through, smiling at her description of American kitchens and the new recipes and cooking methods she was learning from Joe's daughters. 'If anything persuades her to stay, it won't be Joe,' he commented. 'It'll be his kitchen!' He read further. 'She certainly seems to be enjoying herself. And Corning sounds a nice little town.'

'The countryside sounds quite English,' Stella said, taking the letter back and putting it away in her bedside locker.

'It does. More like the area around the Forest of Dean and Herefordshire than the moors here. I should think it's very attractive. Not at all like the endless prairies and Wild West canyons that I think Dottie was half expecting.'

'Do you think she will stay there?' Stella asked.

'She'd better not! She's got to come home to finish your wedding dress.' He leaned a little closer. 'Shouldn't we start to make plans for the wedding soon? I know June seems a long way away, but it's less than five months now. We ought to book the Bedford Hotel for the reception, and let everyone know. June's a very busy month for weddings and Whitsun will be especially busy, and you know how many relatives I have in the Church.'

'No, I don't,' she said. 'I've never been able to count them. But you're right, we ought to start thinking about it. At least I can do something to help, even here. I can write invitation envelopes for a start.'

'There are an awful lot,' he began doubtfully, but she interrupted him.

'And I've got an awful lot of time. I can't be learning to walk again every minute of the day. Why don't you get the new invitations printed as soon as you can and bring them in, so that I can make a start? And ask Val to come in. She knows most about the bridesmaids' dresses, after Maddy. She could see if they still need anything done to them. I'd better write to Auntie Jess as well, and make sure they'll be able to be here. With Uncle Frank giving me away and Maureen being a bridesmaid, we can't have it without them. And—'

'Whoa! Stop!' Felix protested, digging in his pocket for a notebook and pencil. 'Let me write this down.' He flipped the pages to find a blank sheet. 'Invitations ... Val ... Notepaper for letters – have you got enough?' He looked at the little pile of envelopes waiting for him to take away and post. 'You seem to be writing a lot of letters.'

'Yes, I think that's all. Oh, you'd better see Basil as well. As soon as possible.'

'Basil? Why him especially? The whole village will know soon enough – probably even before I get home.'

'Because we're going to be married in his church,' she said patiently. 'In Burracombe. We don't want to find the church is already booked on Whit Monday and we can't be married there after all, do we?'

He looked at her dumbly. 'I suppose not. But I don't think it's very likely. There aren't that many young women in Burracombe thinking about getting married, as far as I know. I'm sure it will be all right.'

'And in Little Burracombe?' she asked, and again he stared at her. Stella sighed and rolled her eyes. 'Have *you* got any weddings coming up? You don't want to find you've promised to officiate at someone else's wedding on the day we want to get married ourselves!'

'Oh – no, of course not. I'll check as soon as I get home. But I'm sure it will be all right. I don't know of *anyone* planning to get married in Little Burracombe in the next few months.'

Patsy carried her box of dusting and polishing tools upstairs to go through the bedrooms. She had not heard from Terry since writing the letter to him a few days earlier, and was beginning to think he really had given her up. Even though she'd told him it had to be all over between them – at least until she was twenty-one – part of her had hoped that he would not simply accept it. How could he, if he really loved her? And yet what could he do?

She didn't want him coming to the farm to confront her father. Percy Shillabeer was a big, strong man with a hot temper and had already threatened to horsewhip Terry if he dared set foot on the land. And now that he was bringing her to the Barton every morning and waiting at the gate every afternoon to walk grimly beside her all the way home, there was no chance of even a snatched meeting. Once or twice Patsy had thought she'd caught a glimpse of someone lurking in the bushes and wondered if it was Terry, but if it had been, he had melted away into the dusk on seeing Percy, and she'd been relieved. Terry could end up hurt and her father in trouble with the police, and where would that get any of them?

If only I could see him, she thought. If only we could talk long enough for me to know what he really feels. If only I could tell him my plan . . .

Instead of driving straight up the main road to Little Burracombe, Felix turned off to the bigger village and brought the car to a halt outside the vicarage. Basil Harvey was just coming through from the churchyard and stopped to welcome him.

'Have you come for tea? Grace will have the kettle on, and I dare say there'll be cake or scones. There usually is.'

'Tea in Burracombe wouldn't be tea without cake or scones,' Felix said with a sly glance at the vicar's rotund figure. 'I still miss Dottie's teas. There always seemed to be something hot coming out of the oven whenever I went there.'

'That's because you knew how to time your visits!' Basil told him. He opened the front door. 'Mind you, we all miss Dottie. She's so much a part of the village that she's left a big gap. Grace and I are hoping she won't decide to stay in America.'

'What am I hoping?' Grace Harvey asked, coming through from the kitchen. 'I missed the last bit. Oh, hello, Felix, have you come to tea?'

'Apparently.' Felix smiled, slipping off his coat and hanging it on the coat stand. 'If that's all right.'

'Of course it's all right. I've just taken some scones out of the oven.' She stopped as both men started to laugh. 'Whatever's so funny about that? And what were you saying about me hoping for something?'

'We were talking about Dottie,' her husband told her. 'About how she always seemed to be taking scones out of the oven whenever Felix went there. And hoping she won't decide to stay in America.'

'Oh yes, we're all hoping that,' Grace said. 'Felix, why don't you come through to the kitchen? It's warmer there.' She turned to Basil. 'I did light the living-room fire but it's smoking again.'

'I'll go and have a look at it,' he said. 'No, Felix, you go with Grace. I can manage it.'

'He *thinks* he can manage it,' Grace observed as she led Felix into the big warm kitchen. 'As often as not we end up sitting out here listening to the wireless. And why not? It's comfortable enough, and it saves fuel if we don't keep the other fire going. The range throws out enough heat to keep the chill off the whole house if we leave the kitchen door open at night.'

'It's really cosy,' Felix said, looking at the two rocking chairs drawn up on either side of the big cooker. 'Vicarages are such huge places, aren't they? Nobody could possibly keep them really warm.'

'It's because we were always expected to have big families,' she nodded. 'Six or eight, at least! Now, you sit there, Felix, and tell me how Stella is. You've been to see her, I expect.'

'Yes, I'm on my way home now. She's had a letter from Dottie, by the way – I meant to tell Basil but he got distracted by the living-room fire.'

'My fault,' she said with a smile. 'I should at least have let you both get indoors before bombarding him with complaints. It sounds as if he's coming back. How did you get on? Oh ...'

'Not very well, I'm afraid,' Basil said, coming through the door. He had several black smudges on his round pink face and his hands were black. He went to the sink and Grace hastily turned on the tap for him to wash. 'It's completely out now. I think we'll have to leave it for tonight.'

'It doesn't matter. We'll stay out here and ask Jacob to come in and have a look at it. Probably the chimney needs sweeping. It gets birds' nests in it,' she explained to Felix.

'Not in February!' Basil said, mopping at his face with a tea cloth. 'But it does seem to be blocked by something.'

'Would you like me—' Felix began, but Grace shook her head vehemently.

'Certainly not. Jacob understands our chimney. He'll deal with it. Now, come and sit at the table, both of you, and have some tea. Basil, please don't hang that tea cloth back on the rack, it's all over soot. Give it to me.'

They settled themselves round the table. Grace had laid out a plate of bread and butter, with fish paste and raspberry jam to spread on it, and the scones were there together with half a fruit cake. She poured them all tea and then said, 'Felix was telling me that Stella's had a letter from Dottie.'

'Has she? And how is the dear girl? We were both so pleased when we heard she was getting better.'

Felix understood this to be a delicate reference to Stella's despair when she had thought herself permanently paralysed. He nodded.

'Yes, she's doing really well now. We're starting to plan the wedding again.'

'Oh, that *is* good news,' Grace exclaimed. 'She must really be feeling better, then.'

'Yes. She's doing exercises to start learning to walk again. Apparently, after such a trauma as she suffered, the muscles seem to forget. And of course her leg is still in plaster, which doesn't make it any easier.'

'So when will she be coming out of hospital?' Basil enquired. 'People do come out when they're still in plaster, don't they?'

'Oh yes, that's not the reason she's still there. It's more to do with the damage to her spine. It does seem to have been mostly bruising, but they need to make sure, especially as there was some paralysis to start with. But we think she should be out in two or three weeks' time. It depends how her walking goes.'

'It could be around the beginning of March, then,' Grace said. 'And when are you planning the wedding?'

'We thought Whit Monday.' He looked at Basil. 'That's why I called in – Stella told me I'd got to make sure the church was free that day.'

'That's a good idea,' Grace said. 'The children won't be in school that day – I know Stella wants them to be there.'

'Whit Monday,' Basil said thoughtfully. 'A bank holiday – the whole village can celebrate. Yes, that will be very nice. I'll put in in the diary straight away.'

'And Dottie will be back by then,' Grace added. She looked at Felix and said, 'Have you decided where Stella is to go when she comes out of hospital, if Dottie isn't back?'

'Well, not really. And even when Dottie is back, the stairs might be a problem. I do have one or two ideas, but I haven't actually asked anyone yet. I did think she could come to my vicarage if we had some-one to live in for a while, but she says no – she wants to walk through the door as my wife. Except that of course I shall carry her,' he added.

'And who were you thinking of asking?' Grace enquired, fixing him with a stern look. 'Us, I hope.'

Felix looked at her. 'Would you? There's no one I'd rather ask, but it seems an awful imposition.'

'Of course it's not an imposition!' Grace exclaimed. 'I'd be most upset if you didn't ask us. It's the obvious place for her to come. Then, when Dottie's home, she can go back to the cottage as soon as she's ready. But she can stay here as long as she likes, and welcome.'

'More than welcome,' Basil agreed, putting the last slice of fruit cake on his plate. 'Grace and I have already discussed it and if Stella can put up with us, we'd really like to have her. It will give her a chance to see what life in a vicarage is like, too.'

'That may be more of a risk than I'm prepared to let her take,' Felix said ruefully. 'I was hoping to keep the truth from her until it was too late.'

They laughed, and Grace removed the cake from her husband's plate and cut it in half. 'You've already had one slice and three scones. Give Felix half. He's probably starved over in Little Burracombe.'

'With Olivia Lydiard on my doorstep every other day with an invitation to supper, and half the single ladies of the village bringing me casseroles?' he demanded. 'Chance would be a fine thing! How did you manage to keep all those predatory females at bay when you were single, Basil?'

'I took the line of least resistance,' the vicar told him, smiling. 'I married the first one through the door!'

Chapter Twenty-One

Percy Shillabeer could prevent his daughter from seeing Terry while she was not at work, but he could do nothing about what happened while she was actually inside the Barton and, when Hilary decided that she needed some more electrical work done, Bob Pettifer was more than sympathetic towards his brother's pleas to be allowed to come and help.

'I don't 'zackly need a mate,' he said. 'But I reckon 'tis good for you to see a job done proper. And you knows the house and its wiring now, so it might not be a bad idea for you to come along.'

Hilary had told Jennifer the pair of them were coming. 'I shall be out for the day. As far as I'm concerned, I've simply asked the electrician to send someone to correct that flickering light in the cellar. I don't know who he's going to send and I don't want to know.'

'I understand.' Jennifer smiled. 'And you don't want to know if I send young Patsy down to the cellar with their tea?'

'I definitely don't want to know that!' Hilary said, and they both laughed. 'Now, before they arrive, I want to talk to you about Mrs Curnow. I need to make a final decision today. I think we both liked her best of the three applicants, didn't we?'

'Well, it isn't for me to say really,' Jennifer said. 'I'm not going to be here. But she seemed a sensible, pleasant body, and she's had nursing experience too, which is what you need. And she's willing to live in – it's either that or go and live with her sister in St Columb and find a job she can go to daily, and that might not be easy.'

'I got the impression she's not awfully keen to live with her sister anyway,' Hilary said. 'At least, not just yet. I certainly liked her better than Miss Smith – she's never lived in the country, probably frightened of cows, would never fit in here. And the young one struck me as being a bit flighty. She had good references and seemed a hard worker, but I think she's looking for a husband!'

Mrs Curnow had impressed them both with her quiet, pleasant personality and excellent references. She had looked around the house with Jennifer and had lunch with her and Hilary, and had been taken to see Colonel Napier, who had pronounced her a decent little woman whom he would be happy to employ.

Probably this surprisingly ready acceptance had been partly due to the fact that her late husband had been a colour sergeant in the army, and she had worked in the NAAFI. While still in her late thirties, she had been widowed when he was killed in Korea, and had been forced to supplement her pension by taking a variety of housekeeping jobs, two involving nursing care.

'I'm not a proper nurse,' she'd told Hilary. 'But I'd have been one if I'd had the chance. I've always enjoyed looking after sick people, and the district nurse at my last place taught me a lot. I'll be able to do most things for your father if he needs help.'

'At least she won't try to bully me like that hatchet-faced woman who came in when Charles insisted I needed someone here at night,' Gilbert had grunted when she had gone. 'Not that I need a nurse anyway. Not a babe in arms, for God's sake.'

'Of course not, Father, and nobody's saying you need a nurse. It's just in case anything happens when I'm not here. It's sensible to have someone on hand who knows what to do.'

The two or three other applicants had been turned down without interview, and Hilary had more or less made up her mind. After a few more minutes of discussion with Jennifer, she said, 'That's settled, then. I'll write to her tonight. She said she could start at the beginning of April – sooner, if we need her. I think in that case I'll ask her to come halfway through March. Then you can put your feet up and think about your baby.'

'That'll suit me,' Jennifer said. 'It's been nice working here and the extra money will come in very useful, but it'll be good to be home all day again. I'll be able to get on with all that knitting and sewing.'

Hilary smiled, then glanced at her watch. 'I must be off. I'm supposed to be in Exeter by ten thirty, and Bob and – I mean, the electricians will be here at any moment. I'll see you later, Jennifer.'

She whisked out of the door and was just turning out of the drive when she spotted the electricians' van coming the other way. I didn't even see who was driving, she thought, smiling a little at her self-deception. Whatever happens at the Barton today is nothing to do with me. Nothing at all.

'Oh Terry!' whispered Patsy, clinging to him in the shadowy cellar. 'I thought you'd forgotten all about me.'

'Forgotten you! I'd never forget you, Patsy.' He kissed her face, over and over again. 'I've been going out of my mind wondering what to do. How long d'you think your dad is going to keep this up? Don't he have no farm work to do?'

'Plenty, but he manages to take time off to see me to work and back home again,' she said ruefully. 'And I can only go out at weekends if he knows where I'm going and who I'll be with, and he makes sure I'm telling the truth. It's like being in prison.'

'I don't know as he've got the right to do that. Didn't you say Mrs Kellaway told you you could leave home at sixteen? Or go to court or something for permission?'

'Yes, but how can I do that when I've got no money and nowhere to live? I asked Miss Napier if I could live in here, but she says she can't be involved because of her father. She's gone out today just so she don't know you're at the Barton. I mean, she does really, but she hasn't seen you and nobody's said you'd be coming with Bob, so she can tell Father that if he asks.' She drew back a little and looked at him in the dim light. 'There's only one way I can think of, but I don't know if you'll want to do it.'

'If it's a way we can be together, I'll do anything,' Terry told her. 'You know that, Patsy. I love you.'

'Well then.' She took a deep breath. 'I think we'll have to get married.'

Terry stared at her. 'Whatever be you talking about? How's your father going to let us get married when he won't even let us go to the pictures together?'

'I mean, we'll *have* to get married. You know ...' She gazed at him, trying to convey her meaning, and then whispered, 'Have a baby.'

Terry drew in a sharp breath. 'A *baby*? But we've never ... I wouldn't ever do that to a girl. Specially not you. And your dad would go mad.'

'I know he would, but he'd let us get married all the same. It's the only way, Terry.' Her eyes beseeched him. 'You know Jean Parracott from Lamerton, two or three years older than us, who got in the family way just before she turned sixteen? Her dad let her get married on her sixteenth birthday and she lives in rooms in Tavistock now with her husband and baby, happy as Larry. Got another one on the way, so I heard. We could do that, Terry.' She stepped into his arms again and pressed her face against his shoulder. 'We could be together, with our own baby, in our own little home. I wouldn't mind if it's rooms to start with. You've got a good job, we could manage. It's the only way.'

'I'm only an apprentice ...'

'But you've got a *trade*. You'll always have work. I know it won't be easy to start with, but we'll be together.' She lifted her face to his. 'It's what we want, isn't it – to be together?'

'Yes, but ...'

'You said you'd do *anything*,' she reminded him.

There was a silence. Bob had gone up to the kitchen when Patsy brought Terry's tea down, but he'd told them he would only be a quarter of an hour. They weren't supposed to take tea breaks at all, and Terry knew he'd be clattering down the steps in a few minutes.

'I'll have to think about it,' he said at last. 'I can't rush into this without thinking a bit. There's my mum and dad as well. Father's always said he'd turn me out if I got a girl into trouble, and your dad will take a horsewhip to me.'

'But this is *us*,' she urged him. 'All that will be over soon, and your mum will get round your dad. She likes me, and you know what they say about babies, they bring their love with them. They might even let us stop with them for a while to start with. Please, Terry. Otherwise I can't see we'll be able to be together for years.'

'I'll think about it,' he said again. 'I promise that. I can't do no more now – our Bob'll be back any minute. But even if I say yes, how are we going to manage? And suppose it don't work first time?' He felt his face grow hot. 'Some people, *married* people, go years before they have a baby.'

'That's because they don't want one. Jean said she and her boy only did it once. And I'd sneak out after everyone's gone to bed, we could go in the barn. It would work, Terry, I know it would.'

A voice sounded loudly above them, at the top of the cellar steps. 'Thanks for the tea, Mrs Kellaway. I'll tell young Patsy to bring back Terry's cup. I dunno what they'm doing down there, got talking I dare say ...' Stamping noisily on the stairs, Bob descended, to find his brother and Patsy standing decorously apart while Terry hastily drank his cold tea. 'All right, you two. That's it for today. You'd better get back to work, Patsy, and I hope you got something sorted out, because I can't string this job out any longer. We'll be finished in half an hour.'

'That's all right, Bob,' Patsy said, her face pink. 'Give me your cup, Terry.' She stepped close to him again and whispered in his ear, 'Eleven o'clock Friday night, by our barn. I'll be waiting ...'

She took the cup and scurried up the stairs. The two brothers looked at each other.

'She's a nice young maid,' Bob said. 'You want to hang on to her, Terry. With our looks, neither of us is going to get many chances.'

'I know,' Terry said. 'And I want to keep her, Bob, I really do. But I dunno – I never thought having a sweetheart was going to be as tricky as this. I didn't really.'

Hilary had never expected love to be as difficult as it was either.

David had now rung her two or three times, late in the evening, but there had been no change in Sybil's condition, and she wondered miserably if there ever would be. It was weeks now since her stroke, and she'd been in a coma ever since. People could go on like that for years, David had told her, and while she was like that he could not possibly leave her. Nor if she gets better, Hilary thought dismally. She'll never be really well again, her parents can't take her, her lover has gone and she'll obviously never find another. That would probably be the worst part of it, as far as Sybil herself was concerned. She had no more love for David than he had for her, but they would be chained together for the rest of their lives.

She thought of this as she came home that evening. The drive across the moor to Exeter had shown her the first hints of the approach of spring. Snowdrops were brightening the hedgerows and spreading sheets of white light in the woods that bordered the lanes near Teign Bridge. Some of the hawthorns were already showing a tinge of green and in the village gardens she could see the nodding cups of hellebores and even a few early primroses. Camellia bushes were smothered in white and pink flowers, incongruous but cheering against the cold grey skies, and when she paused and turned off the engine at Holne Bridge, she could hear birds singing.

It won't always be winter, she thought, getting out of the car to look at the tumbling waters of the Dart river. Spring is coming to Devon again; why shouldn't it come to us as well? Stella's getting better and she and Felix will be married sometime in the summer. Dottie Friend and Jackie are having a wonderful time in America and Dottie at least will come back – well, we hope she will; I'm not so sure about Jackie! The Tozers have got their elder son back, for a while anyway. Jennifer and Travis are over the moon about their new baby. Mrs Curnow will be here soon and life will be easier again, with both her and Patsy to look after the house so that I can attend more to the estate. And Stephen and Maddy are engaged and happy at last. It's been a horrible winter, but spring is coming to all of those, so why not to David and me?

'So did the electricians come?' Hilary enquired after Patsy had gone home.

Jennifer smiled. 'They did indeed. But you don't want to know who they were, do you? The cellar light's mended, anyway.'

'Patsy certainly looked a lot happier. I'll have to see if there's anything else needing attention. Are you off now too?'

'Yes. Travis is collecting me – I think he's just arrived. There's a meat pie ready to go in the oven about half an hour before you need it, and the potatoes, carrots and cabbage are all in pans. I mixed up a sponge pudding earlier too; you just need to add the eggs and tip it into the bowl with some jam.'

'You're a wonder,' Hilary said gratefully. 'I hope Mrs Curnow can live up to the standard you and Mrs Ellis have set. I'll go in and see Father. He hasn't given you any trouble, I hope.'

'Not a bit. He came out and sat at the table for a while, watching me work. We had a good chat. And then Dr Latimer called in, so they went back to the drawing room – he's still there.'

'Oh, that's good.' Hilary went through to the drawing room, where the two men were sitting deep in conversation. The doctor looked up as she came in and rose to his feet, holding out his hand.

'Hilary, my dear, how nice to see you. We don't seem to have bumped into each other much lately. How are you?'

'Oh, you know – much as usual. Tired of the winter.' She gave him a kiss. 'But there are snowdrops coming out and some of the gardens nearer Exeter have got quite a lot of colour in them. So spring's definitely on its way.'

'Sit down and let me look at you,' he ordered. 'You're looking tired. Is anything the matter?'

The suddenness of his question took Hilary by surprise, and to her consternation she felt her cheeks flush and tears come into her eyes. She pulled her hand away from his and said quickly, 'Of course not. I'm as fit as a flea. Whatever could be the matter?'

He looked at her thoughtfully. 'You probably need a tonic. Not surprising, with this old curmudgeon to deal with. Come and see me at my surgery.'

'There's no need—' she protested, but her father butted in.

'Do as you're told, Hilary. You're always telling me to follow this old woman's advice, now it's time for you to see what it feels like.'

'But I'm perfectly all right.'

'I'd like to see you anyway,' Charles persisted, and she shrugged and said, 'All right. I'll pop in sometime. But there's really nothing wrong with me.'

'Hmm.' He turned back to her father. 'I'll be on my way now, Gilbert. Remember what I said. A few more weeks of taking it easy and you'll be able to do all you want to do – within reason, of course. But you've got to be sensible.' He looked at Hilary. 'Don't bother to see me out. I know the way well enough by now. You sit down by the fire and have a cup of tea.'

He departed and Hilary did as she had been told. But as she sipped her tea, she found herself wondering just what it was he wanted to see her about. He seemed happy enough about her father's progress, and her own health was in perfect order. It was true that she hadn't been sleeping well, but she was sure that didn't show on her face.

I'll drop in sometime and see about that tonic, she told herself, but even as the thought crossed her mind, she knew that she probably wouldn't.

Chapter Twenty-Two

'You know,' Brian Tozer remarked to his brother, 'there's a lot we could be doing with these barns.'

'We're doing a lot with them now,' Tom said. 'We keep feed in them during the winter, and the horses are stabled in the smaller one.'

'That's what I mean. They're wasted.'

'Wasted?'

'Yes. Feed, horses – they're a waste of space. I've been drawing up some plans ...' He turned away to go back towards the house. 'I think I'll have a word with Dad about it.'

'Here, what is all this?' Tom moved swiftly to keep up with him. 'Plans for what? And who asked you to draw up plans anyway?'

'Nobody did, for the simple reason that you're all living in the past here. Farming's moved on, little brother. In another ten years' time horses will be out of date. Then what will you do with your barns of feed and your stables? Let them fall down because you can't think of anything else to do with them?'

'What would you do with them, then?' Tom demanded.

'I'll tell you when I've talked to Dad.'

They were almost at the back door and Tom gripped his brother's arm. 'Wait a minute. Dad and I are equal partners in this farm now. Anything you say to him, you say to me as well.'

Brian turned and looked at him. He had always been the bigger of the two brothers and his shadow, thrown against the back door by the yard light, seemed to make him loom over Tom. He smiled.

'I'll say it to you both together, then. And we might discuss this business of being equal partners as well. I don't remember any legal agreement being drawn up about it. Even if I was away in Germany, fighting for my country, I think I'd have remembered that.'

'I did my share of fighting as well,' Tom said quietly. 'But when the war was over I came back, to pull my weight at home. The army was never my career. Farming's that.'

Brian laughed and pushed open the door. Minnie and Margret were knitting in the wheel-back armchairs each side of the range and he went over and gave them each a boisterous kiss, then stood warming his hands at the fire. Tom went to the sink to wash his hands.

'I must say, 'tis nice to see you two getting on so well,' Alice remarked. 'And Peggy – sorry, Margret, I can't get used to that, m'dear, you'll have to forgive me – knitting here so peaceful with your gran. It's just as if she were always here.'

'Just as if she always wants to be, anyway,' Tom remarked, and dried his hands on the roller towel behind the door. 'Better get used to it, Mother, they're here to stay.'

'Oh, I don't think so. Brian wants to get back to his own work and I'm afraid he won't find that in Burracombe. Not that you aren't welcome to stay as long as you like,' she added to her elder son. 'And your dad and Tom are glad of your help round the farm, that I do know.'

The two brothers exchanged expressionless glances and Tom went through to his and Joanna's own living room. They were spending more and more time there these days, but as Alice remarked to Ted when he commented on it, they were a family of their own now, with their two children, and it was natural they should want to spend some time by themselves.

'Val popped in this afternoon,' she said now. 'We had a lovely hour with her, and Christopher's a real bundle of joy. Having a good laugh with Margret over some of our sayings, wasn't she, m'dear?'

'She thought it was very funny,' Margret agreed. 'I find it difficult to understand some of the things you say. Calling little children "toads" – it seems a strange way to show affection. 'And "terrifying" when you mean teasing. I think you must have a very different sense of humour from us.'

'Well, maybe us do,' Alice said peaceably. She knew that Tom was of the opinion that Margret had no sense of humour at all, and that Brian had lost the one he'd once had. That was why it had been such a pleasure to hear him laughing as the two brothers had come in just now. She desperately wanted the family to get along well together, especially if Brian and Margret were to stay long. They'd given no hint as to when they'd be leaving for Brian to find work, and as yet he didn't seem to be making any efforts in that direction. Well, why should he, when he had a welcome here in his own home and was making himself so useful about the place? Full of new ideas, Ted had said, though where he'd got them from in the army was anybody's guess.

'Robin seems to be settling down a bit better at school now,' she remarked, bringing the kettle over to the range. 'Joanna thinks Miss Kemp's had a word with that new teacher.'

'Children are spoiled here,' Margret said. 'Ours have to go to school earlier than yours and work hard when they are there. They would not dare to make the fuss Robin makes.'

Alisce started to slice the loaf of bread she'd made that morning. 'The poor little tacker was really miserable. I don't see as it does any good to send a kiddy to school crying.'

'Ours would not cry,' Margret stated.

'Well, maybe our Joanna's a bit sensitive over her kiddies, having lost one,' Minnie said. 'That's something that never leaves you.'

'Plenty of people lost children in the bombing,' Margret began. 'In Dresden—'

Alice intervened quickly. 'We've all lived through the war – me and Gran and Ted have been through two. It's best not to bring that up. That wool's a pretty colour, Margret. Show me the pattern again.'

Margret gave her a brief look and held up the sheet of paper she had cut from *Woman's Weekly*. The pattern was for a lacy jumper and the wool was a very pale green. She had finished the front already and was now halfway up the back.

'That'll set off your hair a treat,' Alice said. 'It'll look lovely on Easter Sunday, if you're still here.'

'Still here?' Brian said. 'Why shouldn't we be?'

'No reason,' Alice said, startled by his tone. 'You know you'm welcome to stop as long as you like. I was just saying – in case you weren't, like.'

'If you want to get rid of us ...'

'Don't be daft! Of course us don't want to get rid of you.' She stared at him in dismay. 'Don't take everything the wrong way, Brian. Now, come away from that fire, I want to make some tea. I dare say we all need a cup.'

'I was just coming out to make one myself,' Joanna said, appearing through the door. 'Hello, Brian. Tom says you've been helping with the milking.'

He nodded. 'As much as I'm allowed. I'm hoping I'll manage to get it right one day.'

Alice laughed. 'Go on with you, you never forget how to milk a cow! You don't want to take no notice of Tom – he was always one for a joke, you know that.'

'Oh, I remember Tom and his jokes,' Brian agreed, taking a chair at the table. 'When do you think Dad will be in?'

'You'd know more about that than I would,' Alice said, bringing the big brown teapot to the table and standing it on its trivet. 'You've been outside with him. I expect he'll be in soon for his tea – why?'

'I want to have a bit of a meeting. All the family. There's things I think we need to talk about.'

Alice gazed at him doubtfully. 'What sort of things?'

'Family things. Farm things. I've been away a long time. I'm not sure what my place is here any more.'

'This is your home,' Alice said steadily. 'D'you need to know more than that?'

'Yes, I do. Anyway, it won't hurt to have a bit of a talk round the table. It's not a ringing practice night and there's nothing else on as far as I know, so let's make it this evening.'

'We'd better get our Val back, then. The farm's her business too, in a way. She and Luke can bring Christopher in his pram.'

'Luke?' Brian said. 'I don't see any need for him to be here. He's got his own job.'

'Well, Val then. 'Twouldn't be right to have a family meeting without her. Maybe Tom can run down and tell her before supper.'

'Yes, he can do that,' Joanna said. 'I'll take a couple of cups of tea in and some bread and jam, and he can have that first.' She looked uncertainly at Brian. 'It's all right for me to be there, is it?'

'Of course it's all right for you to be there!' Alice exclaimed before he could reply. 'You'm a part of this farm and this family same as the rest of us, and don't let me hear nobody say any different.' She looked at Brian. 'I don't know what it is you got in mind, but us have all

160

worked and lived happy together here for years, and I don't see that changing. As long as there's work for all, there's room for all. Tozers' farm has always been a family concern and so it will always stay.'

'Before we go any further,' Brian said as they settled themselves round the table after supper, 'can we agree to stop all this criticism and back-biting that's been going on?'

Val turned in astonishment. 'Who's been criticising?'

'You all do it,' he said. 'Scoring points, making people feel small, criticising everything we do – it's upsetting Peggy and it's upsetting me. We're not used to it and we'd just like it to stop.'

'But what have we said? Give us an example.'

He shook his head. 'There've been so many. Almost every time you open your mouths. You do it all the time.'

There was a silence. The others looked at each other, and Tom said angrily, 'Seems to me you've lost your sense of humour, our Brian. Don't they never chi-ike each other in the army no more? There was plenty of that going on when I was serving.'

'What goes on between squaddies in the mess is nothing to do with what goes on in a family,' Brian retorted. 'It's making us feel we're not welcome and we don't like it. That's all.'

Val took a deep breath. 'Well, if you think anything I've said was intended to make you feel criticised and small, all I can say is, it was never meant that way, and I'm sorry.'

'There's no call for you to feel unwelcome, neither,' Alice said sharply. 'This is your home, same as it's Tom and Joanna's and our Val's whenever she walks in through the door, and you'm all as wel-come as each other and no need to feel otherwise. I thought I'd said that often enough.'

'I don't want to cause an argument,' Brian said. 'I just want you all to stop.'

'But we're not *doing* anything!' Tom exclaimed, exasperated. 'Any-thing we've said that you think's meant as a criticism is just a joke, that's all. There's no need to take offence.'

'Oh yes,' Brian said, 'it can be *cloaked* as a joke. But we're not daft – we know the difference between a proper joke and one that's meant to be nasty. Anyway, I said I don't want an argument, so let's leave it there, shall we? Now that you know how we feel.' He put his arm protectively around his wife's shoulders.

'So anything we say is an argument, is it?' Tom demanded. 'You can say what you like – tell us off for things we never even knew we'd done – and we're not allowed to say a word, because that's *arguing* and nobody must argue with Brian. Because *Brian's* always right and what *Brian* says goes. Is that what it is?'

'You see?' Brian said. 'That's just what I wanted to avoid. Now you're just making things unpleasant.'

'*I'm* making things unpleasant?'

'Just leave it. You've all heard how we feel. There's no need to say anything more. Just stop your so-called funny remarks and we'll all get on a lot better. I don't like seeing Margret upset, that's all.'

'But nobody's been upsetting her! Not deliberately. It's all in her mind, the way she takes things. Val's right, it wasn't meant, and in any case Val's apologised, even though she doesn't know what she's done. Why can't you leave it at that?'

'That's exactly what I'm asking you to do!' Brian shouted. 'Why can't *you* leave it at that?'

Ted rose to his feet. 'That's enough, both of you. Scrapping like a couple of schoolkids. Whatever's got into you both? Brian, nobody's set out to hurt or upset anyone – Tom's right there. It might have been better if you did as Val asked and told us what it is we do that's caused all this, but if you won't, you won't. Now, I think it would be better if we just got on with this meeting you want us to have. You might have forgot, but tonight's the night I do the football pools and I want to get on with them.'

Tom opened his mouth, but Joanna laid her hand on his arm. He closed it and sat glowering at the fire, while the rest of the family sat in an uncomfortable silence. Ted looked at his elder son and said, 'Well?'

'All right then,' Brian said. 'It's the farm. The way you're running it now, you're losing money. If you're not already, you will be soon. Farming's changing and you've got to change with it. I think it's time we sat down and decided which way we're going to go next.'

'We?' Tom began dangerously, but Ted raised a hand to silence him.

'Go on, Brian. Which way do you think us should go?'

'Machinery,' he said. 'That's the way farming's moving. Horses will be dead and buried in ten years' time. Sooner on a lot of farms. You'll be using tractors, harvesters – machines that will do all the work men and horses do now, and do it faster and better. And if you don't do that, you'll get left behind.' He leaned forward, his face eager. 'It's better to be out in front, and that's where we could be if we set our minds to making changes now.'

'Here he goes again,' Tom said. 'We. *We!* What's it all about? I thought me and you were the farmers here, Dad.'

'And so we are, but Brian has a stake in it too, as does Val. Jackie too, come to that. When your mother and me go, it'll be left to the four of you, fair and square, so maybe 'tis only right we talks about it now.' He looked at Brian. 'But I dunno about this machinery idea. Seems to me—'

'Hang on a minute,' Tom broke in. 'Leave it to us all equal, you mean?'

'That's what I said.'

'But that's going to be impossible! Me and Jo will have done all the work and all we'll get is a quarter share. What sort of a say is that going to give us? Especially if Big Brother here starts shoving his oar in every five minutes. And are we going to have to pay out three quarters of everything we earn?' He glanced at Val. 'No offence meant, Val, but that don't seem fair to me.'

'Nor to me,' she said. 'I wouldn't want you paying me, Tom.'

'I bet our Brian would,' he said bitterly.

'Seems to me you haven't been listening,' Brian said. 'When I say *we*, that's what I mean. I'd be working here too, running the place.'

'*Running* the place? *You?*'

'Helping to run it,' he amended, rather grudgingly. 'But look at it this way. I'm an engineer. REME. I've got all the experience with machinery—'

'Just a minute,' Ted interrupted. 'This machinery you'm talking about – it costs money. A lot of money. Where's that going to come from? And what would us need here anyway? How's it going to make so much difference?'

'I'm not talking about *buying* machinery,' Brian said. He lifted his chin and looked round the table at the faces with their mixture of emotions – some bewildered, some disturbed, one or two (Tom's in particular) angry. He made sure he had all their attention and then he said slowly, 'I'm talking about making it.'

'There was a stunned silence.

'*Making* it?' Ted repeated.

'How could we do that?' Tom demanded. 'You need all sorts to make machinery. You need a workshop, tools, people to do it ...'

'We could do most of that ourselves to begin with. Start small, expand as we go on. And we've got the workshops. Those barns. I told you this afternoon, they're just a waste of space – good manufacturing space.'

'You want to turn the farm into a *factory*?' Alice asked in horror. 'Brian, what in the world are you thinking of?'

'Not a factory, no. It would still be a farm. Just a different sort of farm. And we'd make a lot more money.'

'We'd need to,' Tom said sourly, 'if we're going to be feeding you two as well.'

'That,' Brian said heavily, 'is just the sort of remark I was talking about, and you can't pretend it was a joke.'

There was another uneasy silence. At last Ted said, 'This wants a lot of thinking about.'

'I don't see that it wants any thinking about at all,' Tom said. 'The whole idea's completely nuts. Where are we going to store the feed? What about the herd? And the horses?'

'The horses will be surplus to requirements,' Brian said. 'They can go.'

'*Go?*' Val exclaimed? 'Barley and Boxer, *go*? Where to?'

Her brother shrugged. 'Where most old horses end up, I suppose. You've got to admit, they're both getting on. You've had them since I was a kid.'

'But they've always lived here! They're part of the family.'

'They're part of the farm. They're equipment, the same as a piece of machinery would be.'

'They're not the same as a piece of machinery! They're *horses*. They know us and love us. And we love them.'

'Look,' Brian said, 'that's just sentimentality. There's no room for that these days. The world's changed since the war.'

'And not for the better, it seems to me. Not if people are going to start killing their horses that have worked faithfully for them for years and years.'

'I didn't say they had to be killed. There's still a few years' work in

164

them. Someone would buy them to use – someone who couldn't see further than the end of their own nose. Machinery won't take over in five minutes, but it's going to happen, and if we can be there at the start, we can make good money.'

'We're not selling Barley and Boxer,' Val said stubbornly. 'Not if I have any say in it.'

Brian turned to his father. 'That's another thing I wanted to discuss. Just who has the say in what goes on on the farm? Because if we have to have this sort of thing every time we want to make some small change—'

'You're not *talking* about small changes!' Val broke in, but he ignored her.

'I agree with Tom on this. We got to settle who runs the place and who makes the decisions. Seems to me that ought to be the ones who do the work.'

'Well, yes,' Ted said uncomfortably. 'That makes sense. All the same …'

'What I want to know,' Tom said, 'is when *anyone* decided Brian was staying here? I don't remember you saying anything about that, Dad. We all thought he was just coming here for a bit of leave, before he found himself a job in Civvy Street. And even if he was going to stay, why should he suddenly start telling us what we're going to do and how we're going to farm? I thought you and me got all that sorted out between us.'

'We do. But maybe 'tis different now.'

'Now that big brother's come back, you mean?' Tom said. 'I don't see why it's any different at all. If Brian wants to work here, we decide – you and me, I mean – if there's enough work for him. And then we tell him what it is, and if he don't like it, he knows what to do.' He turned his head and looked his brother in the eye. 'Like it or lump it.'

Brian shrugged. 'You might at least let me tell you the rest of my ideas.'

'If they're all as crack-brained as the ones you've already—'

'All right, Tom,' Ted interrupted. 'You've had your say. Brian's right, we ought to hear him out.' He nodded at his elder son. 'Go on. And the rest of you keep quiet for a bit and listen.'

Brian raised one hand and spread the fingers out, ticking them off as he spoke. 'First, the horses. They don't have to go straight away.

It'll take a bit of time to get it all set up. But you can get a ploughshare to tow with the tractor and do the work they do in half the time. In fact, ploughshares could be the first thing we'd make.'

'In the barns?' Val asked, struggling to remain calm as her father had directed.

'Yes, and in the milking parlour. That's a good big size and it's one of the best buildings we've got. We just need—'

The whole family seemed to erupt at once. 'The *milking parlour*? But what about the cows?'

'That's the point,' Brian said. 'And this is where we could get the money to set up the manufacturing sheds. We sell the herd.'

The family gazed at him, dumbfounded. Tom found his voice first. '*Sell the herd?* But that's where we get most of our income.'

'That's what I'm telling you,' Brian said patiently. 'If we made agricultural machinery, we'd get a better income. We woudn't *need* cows.' He gave a triumphant sweeping glance around the table. 'Think what it'd mean. Proper working hours. No more morning and afternoon milking. No more getting up at five in the morning every day, summer and winter, Christmas included. A proper family life.'

'I thought us already had a proper family life,' Alice said. 'It's always seemed all right to me, anyway. And milking's part and parcel of it. It wouldn't seem like a farm with no beasts around.'

'Oh, there'd be a few beasts,' Brian said. 'But not milking ones.'

'Beef, you mean? But then we'd still need feed in winter.'

'Not beef exactly. Store cattle. Young bullocks we'd bring up and then sell on. Or heifers – they could be out on the moor most of the time, like the sheep. And we could grow silage and store it under tarpaulin in one of the fields. I'm not saying we shouldn't be farmers just the same.'

'Hardly the same,' Val remarked quietly, but Brian took no notice. He went on eagerly.

'I'm telling you, Dad, we'd be right there at the start. There's farmers using machinery now – harvesters like I said before, ploughs, harrows, all sorts. Shearing gear, run by electricity. We could make all of those. That's why it's important we keep the farm going, have a few animals, so that people will take us seriously. They'll see we know what we're doing. It makes sense, don't you see?'

'It could make us bankrupt,' Tom said sourly.

Brian turned on him. 'The trouble with you is you've never been able to see beyond the end of your own nose. You did a few years in the army because you had to, and then back you came running to the farm. To Mummy and Daddy. Too scared to make your own way.'

'And you were too selfish to see what needed doing back here!' Tom flashed. 'Don't you think Dad wanted you back? D'you think I'd have had a chance if you'd decided to take over? I would have been the one looking for a job then.'

'Now that's not true,' Alice said sharply. 'I don't know how many times we said to both you boys there was always a place for you here. And there still is.'

'I don't think so,' Tom muttered, scarlet-faced. 'Seems to me there's only room for one, and if it's going to be Brian, then I'd better start reading the Jobs Vacant pages in the *Western Morning News* straight away.'

'Tom! You don't mean that!' Alice turned to her husband in distress. 'Tell him, Ted.'

Ted shook his head and laid both hands palm down on the table. 'I reckon there's been more than enough said at this table tonight,' he said heavily. 'I don't want to hear no more from any of you until I've had a good think about it all and chewed it over with your mother. I don't want no talk of going or staying, nor of selling the cows and least of all about the horses. They've been good workers all these years and there's no question of them going, so you can dry your eyes, Val, and put your hanky away. As to the rest, as I said, I'll have to think about it. And that's all there is to it.'

The family glanced sideways at each other. When Ted spoke in that tone, there was no argument; even Brian seemed to recognise this. But Val looked at her brother and saw the triumph on his face. He thinks he's won, she thought. If Dad said he'd think about something we wanted when we were little, we knew we were halfway to getting it. So is Brian halfway to getting what he wants?

Tom also saw the expression on his brother's face, and thought the same. I'll never be able to stay here if Brian takes charge, he thought. Because that's what he'll do. He could never stand being the underdog, especially with me. Whatever Mother says, there's not room for two of us.

He glanced at Joanna and she saw his look and squeezed his hand.

He knew what she was saying. She understood what he was thinking and she was telling him that whatever happened, they would face it together. Even if it meant leaving Burracombe and starting a new life somewhere else.

We could emigrate, he thought. Go to Australia. There's plenty of opportunity there. They're crying out for people, and they've got millions and millions of sheep.

Val drew in a deep ragged breath. She glanced at her mother and said, 'I ought to go home soon. Christopher'll be wanting his supper.'

'Yes, you better had, maid,' Alice said, her voice tight. 'And you'll pop in tomorrow with that knitting pattern for the jumper you made for Luke, will you? I'd like to be getting on with it soon for your father's birthday.'

'Yes, I'll come in the morning.' Val stood up and tried to speak brightly. 'Well, cheerio, everyone. Thanks for the tea, Mum. Bye, Gran.' She bent to kiss Minnie's wrinkled cheek. 'Bye, Tom, Jo ... bye, Brian, bye Margret ... Bye, Dad.' She pulled on her coat, opened the back door and slipped quickly out into the yard.

As she walked with rapid footsteps along the farm track towards the village street, Luke appeared, his tall, rangy figure unmistakable in the moonlight.

'Hello, love. I thought you might be along soon. Christopher's fast asleep. I left Jacob keeping an ear out for him.' He kissed her and drew back, feeling the wetness of tears on her cheeks. 'What's the matter, darling? You've been crying.'

'It's just the cold air. I'm OK.' She smiled at him but turned her head away quickly, knowing that her smile looked forced. She brushed past him and walked quickly along the track, holding herself tightly to stop the tears coming. But they would not be stopped. Apart from the shock of Brian's plans for the farm, his reproach to the whole family had cut her to the heart, leaving her feeling lost and floundering. Genuine though her apology had been – even though she hadn't known what she was apologising for – she knew that it had not been accepted. Her brother had thrust it aside in his determination to make his point. Well, he had made it and now she did not know what to say to him any more. The jokes and teasing that had been part of their family life had been turned upside down and destroyed, and each word must now be examined before being spoken.

Luke caught her arm, forcing her to stop. 'There's something wrong. Tell me, darling – what's happened? Is someone ill?'

She knew she would have to tell him, but if she began to speak now, her tears would overwhelm her. She shook her head blindly and looked up at him with piteous eyes.

'Val!'

They turned quickly and saw Joanna hurrying towards them. Bemused, Luke stared from one to the other. Val waited, brushing the tears from her cheeks with the back of her wrist, and Joanna came to a stop beside her.

'I just wanted to say, Brian was talking well out of turn there,' she said breathlessly. 'He had no right to say that. Nobody's criticised him or Margret, and Tom was right when he said he seems to have lost his sense of humour. Don't you let it upset you.'

As Val had feared, the tears came gushing forth. She covered her face with both hands and Joanna gave a little whimper of dismay and began to cry too, while Luke held his wife's shoulders as she wept against him.

'What on earth is all this about?' he asked. 'What's been going on?'

'It's Brian,' Joanna said. 'He says we've been criticising them and making them look small. He won't even tell us what we've said or done, just says we've all got to stop it. And he wants to change the farm. He wants to change everything.'

'I just don't know what to say to him any more,' Val said miserably. 'I feel I'll have to walk on eggs whenever they're around, in case something I say upsets them. He doesn't seem the same brother any more.'

'Well, I didn't know him all that well before he went to Germany,' Joanna said, 'but he always seemed so jolly then. He certainly dished out plenty of teasing himself. But this evening – well, he's destroyed the picture I had of him, and the new one doesn't seem half so nice.' She shook her head. 'But I just wanted to say, I thought he was talking out of turn and you mustn't let it upset you.'

Val smiled shakily. 'Thanks, Jo. But I reckon it's her more than him. She's obviously been complaining to him about us. And that's another thing – she seemed nice enough at first. We all liked her. Why go behind our backs like that and whine about things he must have known were really jokes? Why couldn't he just tell her?'

Joanna shrugged. 'There's no knowing what goes on between a

married couple. Maybe she's got a bit more hold over him than it seems. Well, we'll just have to be extra polite and make sure we don't give her any more cause to take offence – though that's not going to be easy, since we don't know what cause she had to start with! But what we *don't* want to do is upset Mother any more than she already is. He's her son, and she's pleased to have him home for a while, so we've just got to make the best of it. As for all this business over the farm – well, I don't know what's going to happen about that. Tom's furious. Anyway, I'd better go back now. Good night, Luke.'

Val nodded and hugged her sister-in-law, the tears coming to her eyes again. She hooked her arm through Luke's and they began to walk slowly on along the track.

'What in God's name was all that about? I thought you were just going for a family get-together.'

'So did I. But Brian's obviously decided to stay on the farm. He's got all sorts of plans for it – selling the herd and turning all the barns into factories, as far as I can make out.'

Luke stopped and stared at her in astonishment. '*What?* You're not serious?'

'I think *he* is. He's got it all worked out. The horses, too – he wants to sell the *horses*. Barley and Boxer – they've been with us almost all their lives.' She started to cry again.

'I can't believe this,' Luke said. 'What does your father say about it? Does he agree with all this?'

'He'd never heard a word about it until this evening. Nor had Tom. Nobody even thought Brian wanted to stay. But he wants to take over and change everything. He says horses are out of date and it'll be all machinery from now on. Can you imagine it, Luke? It'll be horrible.'

'I don't know,' he said thoughtfully. 'I've read about it in the newspaper. I think it's going to happen – but not all at once. Brian sounds as if he's trying to go too fast.'

'You agree with him, then? You're on his side?'

'Of course not! I'm not on anybody's side who upsets you like this. But that wasn't what Joanna was talking about anyway. What's all this about criticising?'

'Oh, just what she said,' Val said drearily. 'Apparently we've all been criticising and making Brian and Margret feel small and unwelcome, when what we thought we were doing was making jokes. The way the family always have. I mean, we *know* Tom teases – it doesn't mean anything. And Brian used to do it as much as anyone. More.'

'Oh, one of those. He can dish it out but he can't take it himself,' Luke said grimly. 'I've known a few people like that. Think they're wildly funny and got the best sense of humour around, but can't take a joke when it's directed at them. I've noticed he doesn't even laugh at other people's jokes, just looks down his nose. The trouble with your big brother, Val, is that he likes to be the centre of attention and when someone else gets a laugh he feels sidelined.'

'That's stupid.'

'I know. And maybe that's when he feels small. But it's not what anyone else has done, it's his own problem with himself.'

'So what can we do about it? It's like I said to Joanna – I'm frightened to say anything now in case it's misconstrued. And if he stays, it's going to be awful.'

They walked the last few hundred yards to the cottage, where Jacob was sitting in Luke's armchair listening to the wireless. He assured them that Christopher hadn't stirred and then went back next door.

Val went to the kitchen to make some cocoa, thankful to be in her own cottage, with her husband and baby son and the warm, loving sense of acceptance and genuine affection. She thought sadly about what had happened that evening.

However hard the family tried, the atmosphere in the farmhouse was not going to be easy from now on. Brian's words and his refusal to accept any apology or to concede that no offence had been meant would hang in the air like a layer of acrid smoke, creeping into every conversation and making everyone feel ill at ease. Nobody could, any longer, act or speak naturally. Nobody could be who they really were.

There'll be a row in the end, she thought. The sort of row that could split the family right down the middle.

Chapter Twenty-Three

'Does anyone know you're out?' Terry whispered, holding Patsy close against him.

'No. My sister was fast asleep. She never wakes up. And Father was snoring his head off.'

'Oh Patsy ...' He kissed her again. 'I've missed you so much.'

'I've missed you too. It seems like months. We can't go on like this for four whole years. And even then, Father won't just give in. He says as long as his children stay living at home, they live under his rules. It'll be just as bad.'

'It won't,' he said. 'You'll be able to get married then. He can't stop you.'

'He wouldn't stop us now if we did what I want us to do,' she whispered.

He stroked her cheek, staring into the darkness. 'I dunno, Patsy. It's a big thing to do. You know the trouble it starts. What about your mum? What will she say?'

'She'll say it's a disgrace,' Patsy said in a low voice. 'But she'll get over it. People do. And this is *our* life, anyway. Mother and Father – they've had theirs. It's not right for them to stop us living the way we want to.'

'All I really want to do,' Terry said miserably, 'is be like other boys and girls. Go out together for a year or two, get engaged and then get married, right and proper, with you in a white frock and everyone throwing confetti. Everyone *pleased* about it.'

'But it's not going to be like that. You know it isn't. Father's going to keep me a prisoner for four years, never letting me out of his sight, and you'll get fed up with waiting and find someone else. I wouldn't blame you if you did. Who'd want my dad for a father-in-law anyway? Who's ever going to want *me*?' She began to cry and he pulled her closer.

'Patsy, don't. Don't cry. We'll work something out, we will. Only I'm not sure—'

'It's the only way!' she cried, forgetting to keep her voice low. 'If I tell them I'm having a baby, they'll *have* to let us get married. And I'd tell them the minute I knew for sure, so people would think it was a seven-month baby. Terry, we could be married in a few weeks' time – by Easter – and be together for *ever*. We'd never have anything to worry about again.'

'My dad says there's always something to worry about. Where would we live? And I'm only an apprentice – I don't earn enough to keep a wife and baby. I just can't see how we could do it.'

'We could live with your mum and dad. They like me, don't they? And there's that room at the back that they only use for putting stuff. With your bedroom as well, there'd be plenty of space.' She tugged at his coat. 'We wouldn't need much money and I might even be able to go on working at the Barton. Miss Hilary wouldn't mind me taking the baby.'

'You don't know that. You don't know any of it.'

'I'm sure she wouldn't mind. Or your mum might look after it while I was at work. It wouldn't be any trouble. Terry, it's the only way. It's not just the waiting. You don't know my father. He can be so nasty. I'd have a really miserable life. You don't want that, do you? You don't want to be going to the pictures or local dances or out for walks of a Sunday afternoon knowing I was trapped at home, doing housework and cooking there as well as at the Barton, working all the time and never having any fun?'

'No, of course I don't. But ...'

'It'll be bad for a while,' she whispered, pressing close. 'When we have to tell them, there'll be an awful row. I know that. But then it'll be over and we'll be married. I won't be Patsy Shillabeer any more, I'll be Mrs Pettifer, and people will have to respect me. And we'll be together. We can do as we like and nobody can tell us not to. We can go to the pictures every night of the week and come home whenever we like, and nobody waiting up.'

'Not if we've got a baby,' Terry pointed out. 'People with babies can't go out every night.'

'But if we lived at your house, there'd always be someone to look after it. Anyway, it would be asleep. And I don't really mean we'd *want* to be out every night, just that we could, if we wanted to. We wouldn't have to ask anyone's permission.'

Terry was silent. Patsy pressed against him again and whispered, 'Isn't that what you want, Terry? Or don't you really want to get married at all?'

'Of course I do! You know that.' His head was swimming and he hardly knew what to think. He was conscious only of Patsy's nearness, of the shape of her body against his – the lovely soft curves against his leanness, the whisper of hair against his cheek, the scent of her skin that seemed to fill his head with perfume. 'I just wanted it to be all above board. I wanted a proper wedding for you.'

'I'd rather just get married now, with a few people there, than live like a prisoner for four years,' she said. 'Please, Terry. Please love me now. It might not even happen,' she added. 'But at least we'll know what it's like to love each other. Terry ...'

He was lost. With a groan, he pulled her down beside him on to the hay and Patsy sank willingly into his arms.

Alice had never known such a strained atmosphere in the farmhouse before.

Tom and Joanna were spending less and less time with the family and more and more in their own sitting room. Alice tried to tell herself there was nothing wrong with that – with a young family they needed time to themselves. And it was true that with Brian and Margret about the place, the kitchen did get a bit crowded at times. But we used to have Val and Jackie at home as well, she thought, and it never seemed cramped then. There was always such a nice family feel about it, even when Jackie was in one of her huffs.

They'd had several letters from Jackie now, all full of her doings in America. Joe's daughters had made her welcome and shown her around Corning, and soon they were going to take her to New York itself. The houses were wonderful, with two or more bathrooms in each and all sorts of modern appliances – vacuum cleaners, washing machines, gleaming new cookers, even swimming pools in the gardens. And she'd found herself a job in the offices of the glass factory.

'She's never going to want to come home,' Alice had said to Ted. 'Us have lost her.'

'She promised to come back before the summer,' he reminded her, with a squeeze of her shoulders. 'And whatever else our Jackie might do, she do always keep her promises.'

Alice had nodded, but she kept to herself the fear that Jackie might only come home for a short while before going back to America again. But there was nothing to be done about it now, and she was more concerned about the atmosphere that Brian had caused when he told the family off for being unkind to him and his wife.

Alice could still scarcely believe he had said this. As if we would be, she thought. Why, we bent over backwards to make things nice for them, and glad to do it too. Decorated two rooms for them, made the best meals we could to show them we were glad to have them here, treated them like royalty. And then to turn round and say we were making jokes at their expense, when Brian knows perfectly well us have always been a family for jokes, and him more than anyone. Val's right, he've changed. And it's changing us too. It's driving a wedge into the family. And it didn't take much brain power to work out what – or who – had changed him.

Yet she could not understand why Margret, who had seemed so pleasant at first, should have wanted to come between them like this. Was she jealous? Was there more they could have done to make her feel at home? Minnie had been a bit sharp once or twice over the war, it was true, but surely that hadn't been enough to upset her so much. And any other remarks that had been made were really nothing more than affectionate family banter. Surely Brian could have explained it to her, rather than create this rift. Or he could have mentioned it quietly to them, separately – just said that Margret didn't really understand their friendly teasing. They would all have respected that. He didn't have to make a thing about it at the beginning of a family discussion.

Alice wondered if it was something in the German woman's own background that had caused her attitude. She herself didn't have much idea what it had been like to live in Germany during the war. They'd been bombed too, every bit as heavily as Britain, and they must have had food shortages at home and all the fear and worry of their men being sent off to fight. Perhaps we haven't been understanding enough, she thought. But we really have tried to make her feel like one of the family, and this bad feeling seems to have gone too deep now to mend. I don't know what we can do abouit it.

As it was, Tom and Joanna had even started to have some of their meals in their own room as well as sit there of an evening, and that meant Robin and Heather weren't seeing so much of their grandparents as they were used to. And Val had stopped popping in at odd times. She still came, of course, to see Minnie and to have a cup of tea, but it was amazing how often she managed to be here when Margret was out somewhere else. And Luke hardly came at all. He'd called in once and found Brian there, and the air had been electric, like it was before a thunderstorm. Alice had been sure there was going to be an argument, but Brian rarely took much notice of Luke and shortly afterwards he and Margret had left to go for a walk. Which, since just before Luke and Val had arrived they'd been talking about having a game of cards, seemed a bit pointed.

And then there were these new ideas about the farm. Selling the dairy herd, giving the barns over to making machinery. Turning the whole place into a factory. That wasn't farming. It wasn't what she and Ted had built up for their children. It wasn't what they wanted to leave as their legacy to Burracombe.

'It isn't just the farm,' Ted had said to her later, in their bedroom. ''Tis the whole village. What do you think people will say when they find they got a factory on their doorstep? Factories mean noise and smell, a lot of coming and going. Deliveries and such. It would change the whole place.'

'We can't do that,' Alice had said, horrified. 'All that clatter and lorries backwards and forwards. Why, the whole of the lane from the main road would be a deathtrap for anyone walking along it. And who's going to work here anyway? Would there be folks coming out from Tavi? I don't think us'd like that.'

'Oh, he've got an answer for that. With fewer beasts about the place, we'd not need so many farmhands. Our Norman, for a start, he'd be laid off, so according to Brian he'd be glad of a job in the factory. And there'd be others too as time went on – our own electricians, that kind of thing. He don't reckon there'd be any problem finding workers.'

'Your Norman would never want to work in a factory. He gets claustrophobia going down the shed, Cissie told me.'

'Well, he works in the milking parlour all right, so maybe it's just small spaces he don't like. The thing is, he'd lose his job here. I don't see how I can do that, Alice, not to my own cousin. But Brian says there'll be less call for farm workers anyway, as more and more folk go over to these machines he wants us to make.'

'What exactly *do* he want us to make? Big things like tractors and harvesters like he was telling us about – they'd be too much for us, surely.'

'Yes, it's more the smaller sort of agricultural machinery like sheep clippers and crushes – that sort of thing. But once he got the bit between his teeth, there's no knowing what he might come up with next.'

Alice was silent for a moment. Then she said, 'We aren't going to do it, though, Ted, are we?'

He looked at her. 'I don't know, Alice. I honestly don't know.'

'The trouble is,' Tom said, 'a lot of what he says makes sense.'

Joanna turned from folding Heather's nappies and stared at him. 'Whatever do you mean?'

'What Brian says. Farming *is* going to be more mechanised. It makes sense – tractors can pull a plough or harrow faster and easier than horses. You can do the job in a third of the time with only one man. All the jobs on a farm can be done better by machine.'

'But that's horrible,' Joanna said. 'It's so soulless. A farm without animals isn't a farm at all. Even if you only grow crops, you still need animals.'

'Not if you use machinery,' Tom said. He sat down on the bed and took off his socks. 'I can see it coming, Jo. It's partly the war that's done it. A lot of machines and vehicles were invented and improved to fight the war, and now they're being used for peace. Wars have always done that, one way or another.'

'Wars do a lot of bad things,' she said grimly. 'Strikes me this is one of them.' She came and sat beside him. 'You're not really thinking of doing this, are you? Turning the farm into a factory?'

'Not just like that, no. Of course not. But we have to move with the times.' He turned and put his arms around her. 'We've got our family to think of. Robin and Heather. If that's the only way farming can be successful, we'll have to consider it. We can't let ourselves fall behind.'

'But I don't want to be in a race. I just want to stay here and farm.

Why can't we do that, Tom? People will always want food.'

'We can still produce food. Just in a different way. Even the milking – why are we still doing that by hand when we could be using a machine? Think of the extra time that would give us.'

'I'm not sure it would. You've still got to bring the cows in, wash their udders, hook them up to the machine. I don't see that it would save any time at all. And the cows wouldn't like it anyway.'

'They get used to it. And the machine draws the milk out faster. It doesn't get tired, either!' He sat forward, his elbows on his knees, thinking. 'It would mean only one of us was needed in the shed instead of two or three.'

'That's just what your dad was saying – Norman would lose his job. How could we do that?'

'He wouldn't,' Tom said slowly, 'if we went into production of agricultural machinery like Brian wants.'

Joanna stared at him. 'You really mean it, Tom? You want to do this? But you and Brian don't get on. Look at the way he spoke to us all the other day. Val was really upset.'

'I know. I don't see how it could work. And I don't want to get rid of the dairy cows either. It's our way of life. But – whatever we may think about it, Jo, he's brought up something we can't just brush aside. Now it's been said, we've got to think about it. And there's another thing – the farm itself.' He looked at her.

'What's going to happen to it later,' Joanna said slowly. 'That's what you mean, isn't it? You four inheriting it together.'

'It's going to be a real problem,' Tom said. 'Bad enough that Val and Jackie won't get anything, as far as I can see, not if their inheritance is all tied up in the farm. You heard what Val said – she wouldn't want to get paid, and neither would Jackie – and anyway, we couldn't afford to do it. But if Brian has his way and brings in all these changes, he's going to be top dog and I don't know as I can stomach that.' He shook his head and met her eyes again. 'I agree with him that we're going to have to think about more machinery. We might even think about making some ourselves – a few sheep clippers, that sort of thing. But I don't want to see the farm turned into a factory, and I don't reckon I can spend the rest of my life working here under Brian's thumb.' He fell silent, while Joanna watched him anxiously, and then he said heavily, 'We might even have to move away.'

Chapter Twenty-Four

Miss Kemp stood in front of the assembled school, looking very grave.

'I'm sorry to tell you, children, that there seems to be someone here who is stealing.'

Some of the children turned and looked at Billy Culliford, who went very red and looked as if he might cry.

'I'm not going to go into details,' the headmistress continued. 'But several children have come to me and said that small items – a toy car, a few marbles, even pennies – have been taken from their coat pockets or their desks. Now, I don't need to tell you that stealing is a very serious matter.' Here Miss Watkins, standing beside her, nodded her head severely. 'You're all quite big enough to understand that we don't take things that belong to other people. But it's also very serious to accuse someone else of doing that if you don't know absolutely for certain that they did. Do you understand? If you're not sure what I mean, please put your hand up and I'll explain it again.'

No hands went up and she waited a moment, then continued. 'Good. Now, I am hoping that whoever has done this will come and tell me, or Miss Watkins, quietly by ourselves, and we can sort it out without any more trouble. It's much braver to admit when you've done something wrong, isn't it? We all know that.' Again she waited and the children gazed back at her. With a small sigh she said, 'That's all for now. Please think about it. One of you knows that you did this, and all you have to do is come and tell me. Nobody else will know and I shan't tell any of the other children. It will be just between you and me.' And your parents, she thought. I'll have to tell them. But we'll cross that bridge when we come to it. 'I'll be here in the classroom all through dinner time, so all you have to do is slip quietly through the door whenever you feel ready. Now, off you go and have your dinner, and I hope that by the end of the afternoon we will have sorted it all out and need never mention it again. Meanwhile, it might be better if you don't bring toys to school, or any money except your dinner money. And don't leave anything in your coat pockets. If we don't put temptation in the way of whoever is doing this, they might forget such silly behaviour.'

The children filed out in silence, but as Miss Kemp had expected, there was an outburst of chatter the moment the door closed behind the last one. I hope they don't pick on little Billy, she thought. There's no proof at all that it was him.

Miss Watkins said, 'I'm surprised you didn't say who the money was stolen from. It might have helped the children to know that.'

'In what way?' Miss Kemp asked, more sharply than she had intended. 'I'm not trying to turn them into little detectives, or asking them to spy on each other.'

Miss Watkins sniffed. 'In my opinion, you don't need to. Billy Culliford looked the picture of guilt. Didn't you see how red he was?'

'Of course I did. But I didn't think it was guilt – to me, he looked like someone who knew he would be accused even if he was completely innocent, and the way the other children stared at him proved that. In fact, I'd like you to go out into the playground now and make sure he's all right. I don't want him frightened or bullied.'

'If you ask me,' Miss Watkins said, 'you're making too much of those Culliford children. A poor background, with no example set by their parents, they're bound to get into trouble. Billy's not too young to help himself to other people's property if he's a mind to, and he's not too young to be as sly as his sisters. Young Betty's got a way of looking at me sometimes that makes me want to smack her.'

'I hope you'll do nothing of the sort!' Miss Kemp exclaimed, horrified. 'The rule here is that if the children do anything really naughty, they're sent to me – and I never smack them! And just looking at you is not enough, Miss Watkins. Please remember that.'

'It is when it's dumb insolence,' the teacher retorted. As she left the room, she added, 'I've always believed in discipline wherever I've taught. It does no good to let children get away with bad behaviour.'

She went out, leaving Miss Kemp seething. If I had my way, I'd sack her this minute, she thought, but she knew that such action was impossible. But she would broach the matter with the governors at their next meeting and make sure there was no possibility of the woman being taken on permanently.

Burracombe had always been such a happy school and now it was being sullied – partly by the new teacher, who was so unpopular with both children and parents, and partly by this outbreak of petty theft. Somehow she was going to have to deal with both and restore the pleasant, cheerful atmosphere the school had always enjoyed.

She ate her sandwiches and drank a cup of tea at her desk, but nobody came timidly through the door to confess, and when the children filed back for their afternoon lessons they were subdued and quiet. An air of tension hung over the classroom all afternoon, and when she read them a chapter from *The Wind in the Willows* for the last quarter of an hour they listened without their usual expressions of enjoyment. One or two of the younger ones put their heads down on their arms and went to sleep. They were all clearly thankful when she rang the bell and they were allowed to go home.

'Well, your little talk seems to have had some effect, anyway,' Miss Watkins remarked as they watched the last child stump out of the playground in his Wellingtons. 'They've been as quiet as mice all afternoon. A great improvement.'

Miss Kemp stared at her. 'They were quiet because they were upset! I'd far rather hear some cheerful chatter, even if I do have to ask them to stop talking sometimes. And nobody has come to confess.'

'Nobody will. We don't need a confession anyway – we know perfectly well who's been taking things.'

'If you mean Billy Culliford,' Miss Kemp said frostily, 'I must ask you to take that back. In fact, I must ask you not to say any such thing about *any* of the children. We don't know who it was. We have no proof at all. Until we do, we must treat them all as innocent. I'm hoping that now we've brought it out into the open, it will stop anyway.'

'And whoever did it will never be punished. That's how people grow up to be thieves.'

'Please! I don't want to hear that word again. These are children, Miss Watkins, some of them very young children, still learning about the world. Whichever one it was has probably had a shock and is worrying about being found out. That's quite enough punishment and they'll probably never do it again. I doubt if we'll hear any more about it.'

'Well, I beg to differ. Justice is justice and should be seen to be carried out at any age. What about the children who have lost their possessions? Joey Cotter was in tears over his toy car.'

'He shouldn't really have brought it to school at all, but I do take your point, Miss Watkins. We have to consider the victims as well.' Miss Kemp sighed. 'It's very difficult, but perhaps it's just one of life's lessons we all have to learn at some time. Joey will learn to be more careful with his possessions, and it's my hope that whoever did this will have learned that their behaviour is not acceptable. But I still don't want anyone to be under a cloud of suspicion. That will poison the whole school.'

'It's the stealing that poisons the school,' Miss Watkins said, and hurried out of the playground to catch her bus.

Miss Kemp locked the school door and walked across to her own cottage. She felt weary and depressed. Of course there had been a little pilfering from time to time – it was bound to happen. But this time it seemed more serious, and her assistant's attitude, though probably correct in the eyes of many people, worried her. It was almost as if Miss Watkins took pleasure in finding fault with the children – especially little Billy – and wanted nothing more than to punish them. Her remark about the quietness of the children that afternoon was also disturbing. She seemed to prefer them sitting in neat rows, as subdued as trapped mice, rather than cheerfully enjoying their lessons as they used to with Stella.

Not for the first time, Miss Kemp thought longingly of those afternoons when Stella had taken a dozen fish-paste pots into the lobby to fill them with water for a painting session. Or the times when the school had rung with the voices of the infants' class singing a favourite song. Or the laughter that had pealed out as she read them a story.

There had always been something going on at the other side of the partition, and the children had always left cheerfully, sometimes waving a damp painting, sometimes still singing. Now, more and more, they left with an air of relief, and she knew that some of them were still hanging back on their mothers' hands when they arrived in the morning, reluctant to come in.

There was something very wrong at Burracombe school.

'I really don't know what we can do about it,' Basil said, his pink face corrugated with concern. 'She had such good references.' He looked down at the papers in his hand. '*The children learned quickly under her tuition ... excellent behaviour in class ... good pass rates in their examinations* ... I can't think what can be going wrong.'

'Exams,' Miss Kemp said thoughtfully. 'That implies that she was teaching the older children. Do any of them mention her work with infants? I have to admit, I was so anxious about poor Stella at the time that I didn't really take it all in.'

'No, they don't,' he admitted, reading through the letters again. 'They don't say anything about the ages she taught.'

'Perhaps that's the problem. She might do very well with older children, particularly in some of the rougher areas in cities. She's never actually been in a country school, has she?'

'No. London ... Portsmouth ... Liverpool ... She does seem to have moved about rather a lot.' He looked up. 'I'm beginning to think we've made a very bad mistake.'

'We didn't have much choice, as I remember it,' Constance Bellamy pointed out in her gruff voice. The meeting was being held in Basil's study, and the only member not present was Colonel Napier, the fourth of the school governors. 'Nobody else answered the advertisement – it's always difficult to fill a vacancy in the spring term – and as Basil says, we were all at sixes and sevens after Miss Simmons's accident. Grace and Mrs Warren filled in admirably, but we couldn't go on imposing on them. It was Miss Watkins or nobody.'

'I'm beginning to think we'd have been better off with nobody,' Miss Kemp said gloomily.

They were all silent for a moment or two, then Miss Bellamy said, 'Aren't we getting things a little out of proportion? I know you're not happy with Miss Watkins, but she is only here provisionally. We can appoint her permanently if we like, or if we don't want to – and it seems likely that we won't – we can advertise for someone else to start after the summer term. The new teachers will be coming out of college then and we shall probably get someone just as good as Miss Simmons. It's only a few weeks until Easter, and the summer term will surely be easier. The winter always gets people down.'

'The children will probably settle down after half-term,' Basil said, looking at Miss Kemp hopefully. 'And it seems to me that however difficult she may be, Miss Watkins is not our main problem. That's the much more serious matter of the stealing that's going on.'

'I know,' Miss Kemp said. 'And I've been hoping that after my little chat with the children a few days ago it would stop. But ...'

'It's happened again?'

'I'm afraid so. Yesterday morning. You know that we always count the dinner money on a Friday so that it can be paid after school. Miss Watkins and I do it together so that there can be no mistake, and we bring all her children into my room while one of the older children reads them a story. It's a little crowded, but it never seems worth taking down the partition just for that short time and I think they rather enjoy squeezing into the desks together. Anyway, yesterday there was rather a lot of coming and going. Two of the girls needed to go to the lavatory and the Crocker twins thought it would be funny to go together and swap jumpers – at least, we think they swapped jumpers – and the coke delivery arrived in the middle of it all, and we lost count three times. And when we finally did finish, we were one and threepence short.'

'One and threepence?' Basil echoed. 'Are you sure?'

'Yes. We counted again once each and checked it against the numbers. There should definitely have been one and threepence more.'

There was a short silence.

'That's rather different from the odd penny or couple of marbles, which might actually have been lost anyway,' Basil said at last. 'And you think it was all there when you began?'

'I'm sure it was. Since I lost my old purse, I keep the money in a tin in my desk all through the week, and the desk is locked whenever I'm out of the room. I can't see how it could have been taken before we put it on the table to start counting.'

'Do you have any idea who could have taken it?' Miss Bellamy asked. 'The children were mostly sitting in their desks while this was going on, weren't they?'

'Most of them, yes. Except for the two girls who needed to go to the lavatory, and the Crocker twins.'

'The Crocker twins ...' Basil said thoughtfully, tapping his pencil against his front teeth.

Miss Kemp looked unhappy. 'I know. It's easy to suspect them of any mischief that happens, but I really think that's all it ever is with them – mischief. I don't think they'd steal.'

'Do you think *any* of the children would steal?' Constance asked shrewdly. 'We all like to think the best of Burracombe children, but *somebody* is doing this.' There was another pause and then she asked, 'Where was Billy Culliford sitting?'

Miss Kemp looked even more unhappy. 'In the front row. But I really don't think we should . . .' Her voice trailed away.

'Miss Kemp's right,' Basil said firmly. 'We mustn't suspect anybody without evidence. I oughtn't even to have mentioned the Crocker twins. And I assume that Billy wasn't the only one in the front row.'

'No, both his sisters were with him. They tend to look after him quite a lot. And Wendy Cole was there as well, and – let me see – Joey Cotter and Robin Tozer. They've struck up quite a friendship. And Derek Barnicoat, one of the older boys, but I can't believe it was him. He's never put a foot wrong the whole time he's been in the school.'

'It needn't necessarily have been someone in the front row,' Constance said. 'Not if there was all that moving about. Were you out of the room at all, Miss Kemp?'

'Yes, when the coke arrived. I had to go out and make sure it was dumped in the right place and not scattered all over the playground – the children are quite capable of doing that themselves – and I had to sign the delivery note. But Miss Watkins was there.'

'She didn't go out of the room?'

'No, we never leave the children alone with the money. Not that we'd suspect them of stealing it – well, not until now,' she finished sorrowfully. 'She did have to go to the back of the room once, though, to see to one of the children who felt sick.'

'It seems to have been quite a morning,' Basil observed. 'So she didn't have her eye on the money just then. Someone could have slipped out and taken it.'

'But the other children would have seen them,' Constance objected. 'They couldn't have done it unnoticed.'

'Well, they could,' Miss Kemp said, looking even more unhappy. 'Apparently a squabble broke out between two or three of the boys over by the window. Miss Watkins put a stop to it at once, but naturally all the children turned to look. Someone could have done it then. In fact, that's what we think must have happened.'

'And it must have been someone who could do so quickly,' Constance said, and they looked at each other, the same thought in all their minds.

'Someone in the front row,' Basil said soberly.

Chapter Twenty-Five

It was David's voice on the phone. Hilary gripped the receiver tightly. She had been thinking about him all day, carrying out her daily routine like an automaton while her longing for him grew until it was almost unbearable. Always strong, today it threatened to overwhelm her, and in the end, after seeing her father to bed, she decided to break her own rule and telephone him.

'Hilary?' he said doubtfully. 'Is it really you?'

'Yes. I had to speak to you, David. I tried not to ...'

'What's happened? Is it your father?'

'No. It's just me.' Her voice quivered and broke. She pressed her free hand to her forehead. 'I wanted to talk to you so much. I want to see you. I want to be with you. David, I don't think I can bear this ...'

'Oh my darling.' His voice softened. 'Sweetheart.'

'I know I shouldn't be doing this. I've tried so hard to be strong – not to think about you. I've told myself it's over, there's no chance, no future for us. But I can't believe it. I don't even care about the future – I just want to see you *now*. It's as if now is all we've got – as if the future doesn't matter. Maybe won't even happen.'

'Darling, of course it will happen. Nothing stays the same for ever. Something will change. Sybil—' He broke off, and then added quietly, 'I can't wish her dead, darling, even though it might be best for her, the way she is.'

'No, of course you can't.' The first storm of tears was subsiding and his quiet voice was calming her. Just to hear him again ... She groped in her pocket for a hanky and mopped her face with it. 'How – how is she now?'

He sounded weary. 'Much the same. She just lies there unconscious, not responding to sound or touch, or anything, but still alive. She's being kept alive through a drip ... It's pretty awful, actually.'

'Oh David.' Shame washed through her. 'I'm being so selfish. I shouldn't have rung you.'

'Yes you should. Don't go now, Hilary. Don't put the phone down. It's doing me good to hear your voice.'

'Even weeping at you?' she asked with a tiny, unexpected flicker of humour.

'Even weeping. Darling, I feel just the same as you do. There's not a minute in the day when I'm not thinking of you and longing for you. This exile we've imposed upon ourselves ... it's not doing any good. It's making things worse.'

'I know.'

'I think we should meet,' he said flatly.

'Meet? But—'

'I have to go to London next week. I'll be there on Wednesday. I could stay overnight and come back on Thursday. Could you meet me then? Thursday? Just for a few hours?'

'I—'

'Please,' he said urgently.

'I could,' she said after a moment. 'I can leave Father for a day. But I can't stay overnight.'

'Just a few hours,' he said. 'Just to see you again – touch you, hear your voice without all these damned miles between us.'

'Sybil ...'

'Sybil won't know I'm gone. She doesn't even know I'm here. I've got nurses in day and night – I had to, so that I could go on working. I'm not going to be doing anything wrong, darling.'

You are, she thought. Just meeting me, even for a walk in Hyde Park, is wrong. Talking to me now is wrong. Calling me darling is wrong ... But they had gone too far for such scruples now, and what hurt could they cause anyone by meeting? If they had known years ago how precious their love was, they would have been together from the start. It was Hilary's engagement to Henry – who had been killed before she had a chance to see him again – and David's to Sybil, which his sense of honour had forbidden him to break, that had stood in their way. If we had had the courage then, she thought, we would never have been in this position now.

But they had not had the courage, and they were in this position now, and you couldn't make excuses for doing wrong because of a mistake made years ago.

'I'll come on Thursday,' she said. 'I'll come on the train, the one that gets to Paddington at eleven. I'll have to catch the four o'clock back. We'll only have a few hours.'

'Five,' he said. 'Five hours of heaven. I'll meet you there.'

Hilary put down the phone and found that she was shaking. She leaned both her elbows on the desk and held her face in her hands, tensing her body to stop the trembling. Tears trickled from her eyes and slid down her cheeks.

Thursday. Five days. In five days' time she would see David.

And then it would be worse than ever, because they would have to part again, and each time they parted, she felt as if another small piece of her had died.

'You didn't come to see me after all,' Charles Latimer said to her next morning, after church.

Hilary had been standing just outside the door, contemplating a broad swathe of snowdrops under the yew trees. She turned and smiled at the doctor.

'I'm sorry. I didn't want to waste your time. There's really nothing the matter with me.'

'That's not how it looks to me,' he said, scrutinising her face. 'You look tired. Are you sleeping properly?'

'Yes, of course. Well – most of the time. I do have the occasional bad night.'

'And I imagine that last night was one of them.'

Hilary looked at him ruefully. 'Do I look that awful?'

'Not awful, no. But tired and – something more than that. Are you worried about your father?'

'No more than usual. Less, in fact. He seems to be doing really well and he's actually taking a bit of notice of what he's been told.'

'The estate? The house?'

'Travis and I are managing very well between us, and we've got a new housekeeper coming at the end of next week. Honestly, Charles, everything's fine.'

'Come and see me anyway,' he ordered her. 'I'm worried about you,

Hilary, and it won't do your father or the estate any good if you crack up. Tomorrow morning, first thing, or else I'll come to you – and what will that do to your father?'

'All right,' she agreed with a sigh and a small smile. 'Just to keep you happy.'

'I'm more interested in keeping you happy,' he told her, and Hilary turned away, tears suddenly stinging her eyes.

A moment later they were brimming again as a voice hailed her from the lychgate and to her astonishment she saw her brother and Maddy standing there, waving cheerfully. They came up the path and Maddy threw her arms around her, then drew back in surprise.

'You're crying! Whatever's the matter?'

'It's not Dad, is it?' Stephen came to stand beside Maddy, putting his hand on Hilary's arm and giving her a searching look before kissing her cheek.

'No, it's not Dad. It's not anything – I was just so surprised to see you. And thrilled. Why didn't you let me know you were coming?'

'We didn't know till last night. At least, I didn't know. Stephen did a bit of wangling and got a twenty-four-hour pass. He's got to be back at eight this evening, so we thought we'd dash up to beg a bit of lunch with you and then go in to see Stella. He's going to take me back as far as Dorchester and then I'll catch the train. Is that all right? You don't have to give us a meal. A sandwich would do.'

'Don't be ridiculous! We're having roast pork and there'll be plenty for you. But will you have time? It sounds an awful rush.'

'We may have to skip pudding,' Stephen said. 'But I've been feeling guilty about you and Dad. I know I haven't been around much lately.'

'You can't help that. You're in the RAF. Dad will be pleased to see you anyway, and maybe you can manage a bit longer at Easter.'

'Yes, maybe,' Stephen said with a glance at Maddy, who giggled and looked away.

Hilary felt her eyebrows go up a little. 'What's going on? You look like the cat that's swallowed the cream, both of you.'

'Two cats, then,' Stephen said, and they both burst out laughing. Hilary didn't know whether to feel amused or annoyed. She marched past them, saying briskly, 'If you've only got a couple of hours, we'd better get home. I'll need to get the vegetables on early and Dad won't be happy with just a hello and goodbye. Come on.'

190

They fell in step beside her and all three walked through the village, waving and stopping for a word with almost everyone they met. Hilary's impatience grew. And where was Stephen's car?

'It's at the house,' he said in answer to her question. 'We knew you'd have walked to church. We just left it there and walked back. Dad probably knows it's there by now, if he's looked out of the window.'

'Well, we'd certainly better get back as quickly as possible then. And I do wish you two would stop giggling. You're like a pair of five-year-olds.'

'Sorry,' Stephen said with an attempt at solemnity. 'But you always did say I'd never grown up.'

'I thought you'd got past five, though,' Hilary said. 'Seven at least.' She glanced at him and felt her mouth tug itself into a grin. 'Oh, all right. I'm being a grouch, I know.'

'We took you by surprise,' Maddy said penitently. 'We're sorry. Only ...' She looked at Stephen and just managed to stop the giggles breaking out again. Her eyes danced. 'We mustn't say anything yet. Not till we're all together.'

'So there *is* something going on?' Hilary said. 'What? What's happened? I could do with a bit of good news.'

Stephen gave his sister a sudden more serious look. 'Why, what's the matter? Come to think of it, you do look a bit off colour. You're all right, aren't you, Hil? And Dad's OK?'

'Yes to both. Of course I'm all right. When wasn't I? And Father's doing very well. He's been sensible for once and he's almost back to normal. Charles is very pleased with him.'

'He didn't look so pleased with you when we saw you in the church-yard,' Maddy said with unexpected perception. 'He looked almost as if he was telling you off!'

'Well he was, in a way,' Hilary admitted. 'He wants me to go and see him in his surgery. Apparently he thinks I look tired too.'

Stephen studied her more closely. 'It's more than that,' he diagnosed. 'I've been wondering for some time if there's something bothering you. Is it the estate and everything? I really ought to be here to do more to help.'

'You can't be. Anyway, it's not that.' She bit her lip as she realised that this was practically an admission that there was something. 'And I don't want to spoil this news you've obviously got to tell us, so let's get a move on. Whatever it is that's turning you into giggling children, I want to know what it is.'

They had reached the house by now and the three of them almost ran up the steps to the front door. Hilary went straight through to the kitchen, saying, 'Dad's probably in the morning room. You go in and say hello, and I'll make some coffee.'

'I'll come and help,' Maddy said. 'Your father will want to see Stephen first.' She gave Hilary a searching look as they went into the kitchen. The aroma of roasting pork filled the air and the vegetables were ready in their pans. 'Please don't mind me saying this, but you do look as if there's something wrong. Stephen's thought so for some time. It's not so much the way you look as the way you *are*, somehow. You know that if there's anything we could do to help ...'

Hilary sighed. Her hand on the kettle, she said, 'All right, there is something. But it's nothing anyone can help with. I just have to battle it out on my own.'

Maddy frowned. 'Is that really true? Wouldn't it help to talk about it? I tried to manage on my own after Sammy was killed, but all that happened was that I turned into a selfish monster. I expected everyone to know how I was feeling without me having to say, and then when they did say they knew how I felt, I told them they couldn't possibly know. I was horrible to them. I seemed to be thrashing about in a dark locked room and nobody could reach me. I didn't know where the door was, I suppose.'

Hilary looked at her. 'I hadn't thought of it like that. But what happened to you was very different from ... from what's bothering me. I don't think anyone *can* help. Anyway, let's not worry about it now. You've come with news of some sort and I want to hear about that. If it's good news, it'll be more help to me than anything else could be.'

'Oh, it's good news all right!' Maddy said, her smile breaking out again. 'At least, we think so!' She looked suddenly anxious. 'But I'm not sure now that you or your father will agree.'

Hilary felt baffled. They made the coffee, put some shortbread on a plate and carried the tray into the morning room, where Stephen and his father were discussing the situation in Vietnam.

'The French are in a bad way,' Gilbert stated. 'They're crying out for aid from America. If they don't get it soon, they're going to be massacred.'

'It depends what sort of aid America gives, though,' Stephen said. 'You know some people are talking about the nuclear option. I don't like the idea of that.'

'Not after what happened in Hiroshima and Nagasaki,' his father agreed. 'Ah, here's coffee. We'll talk again later, Stephen. Pity you don't have more time.'

Hilary suppressed her resentment at the obvious implication that only men could discuss these matters. It was a major advance that her father even thought that Stephen was capable of doing so. She set the coffee down and said, 'Lunch will be sharp at one today. Stephen and Maddy want to go to Plymouth to see Stella.'

'And we've got some news,' Maddy said, almost quivering in her desire to break it. 'We hope you'll be pleased.'

Hilary poured coffee and handed it round. Her hand was shaking. She wasn't sure that she and her father would be pleased. The sudden doubt that Maddy had expressed in the kitchen was gnawing at her mind. More sharply than she intended, she said, 'Well come on, don't keep us in suspense any longer – out with it.'

The two looked at each other. Then Stephen said, 'I'm being posted to Cyprus.'

Hilary and her father stared at him, then at Maddy, whose face was a picture of excitement.

'*Cyprus?*' Hilary said at last. 'But – how long for?'

'The rest of my time in the RAF, I suppose. The whole squadron's going, of course. We heard a few days ago.'

'But – you've got nearly two years to do! You'll be there all that time?'

'Seems like it.' He turned to Hilary apologetically. 'I'm really sorry I won't be around to give you any help you need. But I've been lucky to be as near home as I have been all this time. And if anything happens – they're pretty good over compassionate leave.'

'If I peg out, you mean!' Gilbert said abruptly. 'You might as well say what you mean. And there's no need to apologise – you're in Her Majesty's Armed Forces. If anyone knows what that means, I ought to.'

'But what about you, Maddy?' Hilary asked, bewildered. 'You'll be alone all that time.'

'No I won't.' Her face was pink with suppressed delight. 'I'll be going too! That's what we want to talk to you about. We want to be married as soon as possible. Then we can get married quarters and I can go to Cyprus with Stephen. Isn't it wonderful!'

'Wonderful,' Hilary echoed faintly. Her mind was already buzzing with the implications of what she had just been told. A wedding to plan ... Stephen overseas ... Stella ... Her mind fastened on the last thought. 'But what about Stella? She may be still in hospital.'

'Oh, you don't know, do you? I had a letter from Stella on Wednesday. She's hoping to come out of hospital soon and she's going to stay with Grace and Basil. At least until Dottie comes home and she can manage the cottage stairs. And Dottie will be home soon. We won't get married without her.'

Hilary shook her head, trying to clear her muddled thoughts. 'So when do you want to get married, then?'

'Well, we thought Easter. The squadron isn't going until just after that. It gives us plenty of time to arrange everything.'

'Eight weeks,' Hilary said, counting on her fingers. 'It's not very much time.'

'You only need three weeks for calling the banns. And we'll have to make sure Basil can manage it then. That's all there is really.'

'But what about the reception?' Hilary almost wailed. 'There are invitations to be sent, a guest list, catering. And the cake and your wedding dress, and – oh, you've no idea how much there is to think about!'

'Of course we have,' Maddy said. She moved closer to Hilary and touched her arm. 'You mustn't worry about a thing. Stephen and I will do it all. Don't you remember, I contacted everyone about Stella's wedding after the accident, and let them know it was postponed. If I could do that, I can certainly send invitations to our friends and family for *our* wedding! Not that I've got much family anyway – mostly people in the village, and Ruth and Dan from Bridge End, and the Budds from Portsmouth.'

'What about Fenella?' Hilary asked. 'She's your adopted mother, after all – won't she want to be involved in the organising?'

'I'm sure she would, but it would be difficult for her, now she lives in France, and Jacques isn't very well. I'm not sure they'll even be able to come. No, let me have your list and I'll see to it. I'm doing that kind of thing all the time for the Archdeacon.'

'I suppose so. But we still have to think about the reception, and I don't see how you can do that when you're miles away in West Lyme. And we'll have to do something special.'

'I'll take that on,' Gilbert declared. 'And don't look like that, Hilary. We'll have it in Tavistock, at the Bedford Hotel. You can take me in one day, as soon as we know the time of the wedding, and I'll talk to the manager. We're old friends. He'll know the form.'

'But menus ...'

'He *runs a hotel*,' Gilbert said. 'He'll know just what to do. And I think I'm fit enough to discuss a menu. It will give me something to occupy my mind.' He rose from his chair and came over to kiss Maddy's cheek. 'It's very good news, my dear. I'm delighted for you both. Stephen's a lucky young man.'

'I'm lucky too,' she said, turning pink again. 'But we honestly don't want to be a lot of bother.'

'You're not being any bother. Stephen's only going to get married once and I'm sure Fenella and I both want it to be a suitable wedding. I'll write to her and make sure she's happy with what I propose. We're old friends, from the days when my wife was alive and Fenella used to come and stay with us. The announcement had better go in *The Times* immediately,' he said to Hilary. 'See to it in the morning. And you two ought to see Basil this afternoon, before you go to Plymouth. Better still, telephone him now and get him round here to talk about the date. Ask Grace as well, Hilary – we'll celebrate with a sherry.'

'But Grace will be cooking lunch!'

'They can stay and have it with us. Don't suppose she's got the potatoes on yet. Ring them now.'

'No, Father.' Hilary could feel all control slipping away from her. 'Sunday lunch is special. We can't ask Grace to abandon theirs and come over here. Not to mention the fact that we've already got two extra and I need to peel more potatoes for them!' She jumped up. 'And if you're to get to Plymouth at all, I'd better make a start now. But Dad's right,' she added to Stephen. 'Seeing Basil and getting the date confirmed is the first thing to be done. Why don't you go round to the vicarage now and settle that? Then we'll all know what we need to do.'

Stephen looked at Maddy. 'That's probably the best thing.' He gave Hilary an apologetic look. 'We seem to have dropped a bit of a bombshell in your lap.'

Maddy stood up too. She looked at Hilary and said, 'I'm sorry if we're giving you a lot of trouble. We really don't want to. You – you are pleased for us, aren't you?'

Hilary saw the doubtful expression on her face and inwardly cursed herself. 'Of course I am! I think it's wonderful. And it won't be any trouble at all – it doesn't even sound as if I'll have anything to do. Though I dare say something will crop up!' She kissed Maddy. 'I'm absolutely thrilled for you, although we'll miss you terribly while you're away. And having another wedding to look forward to is going to make us all feel better. Now, off you go to see Basil, and when you come back, lunch will be ready. One o'clock sharp, remember. You don't have much time.'

She watched them go, then turned to her father. 'Well! That was a surprise. And you seem pleased.' In fact, she thought, he looked more alive than he had for weeks.

'I am. I'll be glad to see them safely married, even if it does mean losing them for a year or two. Maddy's a nice young woman and she'll settle Stephen down. Cyprus will be a good start for them.'

'I hope so.' She loaded the tray with the coffee cups and carried it back to the kitchen. There were extra vegetables to prepare, and places to be laid at the dining table, but as she went about her work, her mind was busy with thoughts of what would need to be done.

And like a thread running through all these thoughts was the image of David and the overriding sadness that she seemed unlikely ever to celebrate a wedding day with him.

Chapter Twenty-Six

'And there's really nothing else troubling you?' Charles Latimer said, his keen eyes probing Hilary's face. 'No other reason why you're not sleeping well, why you're losing weight and looking altogether more fragile than I like to see you?'

'I've been anxious about my father, of course.'

'Of course. But no more than usual, I think, especially as he's mending so well. And the news about Stephen and Maddy is good. An Easter wedding – you're not worried about that, are you? It'll mean more work for you.'

'Not a lot,' she assured him. 'Maddy's determined to do most of the organising herself and Father says he'll arrange everything with the Bedford Hotel. It'll give him something to occupy his mind for the next few weeks. Anyway, I didn't even know about that when you spoke to me yesterday.'

'Which is virtually an admission that there was already something else on your mind,' he observed. 'Hilary, my dear, I don't want to press you if you don't want to tell me, but it could help you to talk about it. Bottling things up often makes them worse, and you know it would be entirely confidential.'

'I know.' She hesitated, knowing that her reluctance stemmed mainly from a guilty conscience. 'I suppose – I suppose I'm afraid of losing your good opinion of me,' she said, very quietly.

The doctor's eyebrows rose a little. 'Are you likely to? Hilary, I'm a doctor. I've seen a great many things in my time, even here in Burracombe, and if I thought less of my patients because of their failings, I would have very little opinion of anybody at all. Besides,

197

who am I to judge? The point is, we are all human and all fallible, you and I just as much as anybody else.'

Hilary smiled faintly but found it hard to agree. Charles Latimer had been her doctor and her father's friend since she was born. He had brought her into the world, had tended her through all her childhood illnesses, had treated her mother before she died, had looked after her father during his recent heart attacks. She could not think of anything he had ever done that revealed him as a fallible human being. Certainly nothing like the situation she found herself in now.

'Remember that we don't know half as much as we think we do about our friends,' he said gently, observing her doubts. 'You've always lived by very high standards. If you think you're falling short of them now, that's as likely as anything else to trouble your mind.'

'I don't know who I should talk to,' she said. 'You or Basil.'

'Either of us is as discreet, but it's your health I am concerned about. Basil might be the one to talk to about your soul, if that's what's worrying you.'

Hilary smiled wryly. 'And if my soul is cured, will I still need to come to you? Or the other way about? Oh Charles ...' Suddenly, without warning, she burst into tears. Covering her face with both hands, she sobbed, 'I don't know what to do! I just don't know what to do!'

Charles Latimer waited for a few moments. Then he touched her arm gently and said, 'Tell me about it, my dear.'

Hilary nodded. She found a handkerchief in the pocket of her coat and mopped her face. Then, still shuddering with sobs from time to time, she told him the whole story.

'It's as if I couldn't help myself,' she said wretchedly. 'I *knew* it was wrong, yet I still went on. And I still shall go on,' she added, raising her head to look the doctor in the eye. 'I've tried not to contact him, but I just can't manage without at least hearing his voice ... seeing him once in a while ... even if we don't take it any further than that. Well, we won't – we've agreed that. Not while Sybil is so ill.'

'And is she likely to get better?'

Hilary looked at him miserably. 'It doesn't seem like it. David says she might go on like this for years.'

'She might indeed.' He tapped his teeth thoughtfully with his fountain pen, then asked, 'And can you?'

'I don't see what else we can do. David won't leave her now – I would never ask him to. And there's not going to be anyone else, for either of us.' She felt the tears spring to her eyes again and dabbed fiercely with her hanky. 'I just can't see any end to it.'

'It doesn't often last that long,' he said. 'But nobody can really tell.' His eyes were kind. 'It's no wonder you are so troubled.'

'And there's no real medicine for it, is there?' she said dejectedly. 'Even Basil wouldn't be able to help me feel better. Because I shouldn't have got myself into this situation in the first place.'

'Only you can know that. The point is that you *are* in this situation now, and since you can't go back to where you were, you have to deal with it as it is. And my job is to look after your health.' He drew his prescription pad towards him. 'You're quite right, there's no medicine to help you decide what to do, but I can give you something to help you sleep better, and something to build up your strength a bit. That will help you to cope with your difficulties. And I do believe that talking helps, so if you want to come again, just to do that, please feel you can do so, at any time. Or go to see Basil. He won't judge you.'

'Thank you,' Hilary said gratefully. She hesitated, then said, 'You've been so kind, I have to be honest with you. David's coming down to London from Derby this week and he's asked me to meet him. I'm going on Thursday.' She met his eyes. 'It will only be for a few hours, during the day. Just to talk. Just to see each other.'

Charles nodded and handed her the prescription. 'Derby? Is that where he practises?'

'Yes. He works with his father. He's David too – David Hunter. It must be quite confusing for their patients!' She sighed. 'That makes it all the harder, really – that he works with his father. Even before Sybil's stroke, it would have been difficult for him to leave.'

She left the surgery with her prescription and realised, to her surprise, that she did indeed feel a little better. She'd spoken to Val about the situation, of course, but somehow talking to an older person, one who might be expected to disapprove yet didn't appear to, had a different effect. She walked home feeling that even if there still was no light at the end of the tunnel, the tunnel itself was a little less dark.

Charles Latimer sat for several minutes at his desk, deep in thought. It was almost inevitable that something like this would happen to Hilary, after all her years of frustration in caring first for her mother and then her father, and no doubt losing all hope of ever finding a partner for herself. And equally inevitable that when it did happen, it would hit her very hard indeed.

He sighed. Then he got up and went to his bookshelf and took down the latest publication of the Medical Register.

David Hunter, he thought, leafing through the pages. David Hunter ... I wonder ...

'David!'

Suddenly unaware of other people, Hilary ran through the barrier and into his arms. He caught and gripped her tightly against him, so close that it was moments before they could even kiss. Then she laid her face against his chest and broke into tears.

'Hey!' He cradled her again him. 'Hey, darling, don't cry. It's all right. You're here. We're together.'

'Sorry.' She sniffed, rubbing her eyes with the back of her hand. 'I didn't mean ... I didn't even know ... Oh *David*!'

'Let's get away from here,' he said, letting go of her and then tucking her hand into the crook of his arm. 'Come on, darling – we'll find somewhere to sit and talk.'

They went out to the taxi rank. Rain was coming down in sheets, so Hyde Park was out of the question. After a moment's hesitation, David suggested one of the big museums and Hilary nodded, not caring where they went as long as they were together.

'Natural History, I think,' he said. 'We can lurk behind one of the dinosaurs.' They got into the taxi and set off, sitting so close together that Hilary felt she could sense the beating of his heart through the thickness of their coats. She inhaled deeply, trying to draw in the scent of him, the mixture of wool and male skin and a faint tinge of sweat.

'Goodness,' she said as they got out of the taxi and looked up at the imposing edifice of the Natural History Museum. 'I'd forgotten it was so enormous. Mother brought us here when we were children, before the war. I remember a huge whale – or was it a shark? And cases and cases of butterflies.'

'Let's get inside,' he said, taking her arm, 'before we get soaked through.'

They half ran up the steps and through the entrance, then paused, awed despite themselves by the huge skeleton of a dinosaur that awaited them, its long skeletal neck bent as if to sniff them as a dog might sniff strangers to its home. For a few minutes they gazed at it, then David looped his fingers gently around Hilary's wrist and drew her into one of the semi-alcoves that ran along the side of the great hall.

'Sweetheart, how are you?'

'All the better for seeing you!' she answered, with a little laugh that was almost a sob. 'Oh David, I've missed you so much.'

'I know.' He twined his fingers around hers. 'It's not easy, is it?'

'Easy! It's the hardest thing I've ever known. I just don't know how I can go on like this. And it must be so much worse for you – seeing Sybil day after day, just lying there. It's horrible.' She paused. 'I feel really sorry for her too, you know.'

'So do I. I would never have wished this on her. She was so full of vitality. I know our marriage was a sham, but that was probably no more her fault than mine. We were both too young and we got pushed into it. I think her parents saw me as a good catch, someone who would tame their wild daughter and give her a house full of babies to keep her out of trouble. It didn't work out that way.'

'She's been tamed now,' Hilary said wryly.

'Yes, but not as anyone would have wanted.' He looked at her. 'I wish I could give you some hope, my darling.'

'I've given up hoping for hope. It's not your fault, David. It's just life. It deals some people pretty rough cards. We're lucky compared with a lot. We've got our health. We're not poor. We've got homes and friends and family. We've even got each other. I mean, we both know we've got someone to love and who loves us. Even if ...' Her voice broke and she turned away.

David caught her shoulders and turned her back to face him. 'It'll come right one day,' he said forcefully. 'I know it will.'

'How?' She stared at him hopelessly, her eyes brimming with tears. 'There's only one way, David, and we can't wish for that. And even then – can you imagine the problems? You live in Derby, I live in Devon. Hundreds of miles apart. How could you give up your practice? It might be easier if you didn't work with your father, but he must expect you to carry it on. And how can I leave the estate? There's no one else to take it over.'

'The French boy?' he hazarded. 'Robert? Isn't he the heir?'

'Not any more. He doesn't really want it and Father's decided to change his will and leave it to me and Stephen equally, with a bequest to Rob and his mother. And Steve's going to Cyprus soon – he told us at the weekend – and even when he comes out of the RAF he won't go back to Burracombe. He and Maddy will probably emigrate.' She spoke drearily as she envisaged a future where both she and David were hopelessly trapped in their different lives, able to meet only occasionally. 'We'll be no more than pen friends.'

'Don't talk like that! Of course we'll be more than that. We'll find a way. Something will change – something we've never even dreamed of.'

'I can't imagine what it would be,' she said, and he smiled.

'That's what I mean! Now look, nobody can see us here – give me a kiss and we'll try to forget our problems and enjoy the day. It's too precious to spend being miserable. Let's not bother about dinosaurs and sharks and things. Let's go somewhere nice for lunch and just be together.'

'That's the best idea yet,' Hilary said, smiling. 'I've wept over you quite enough for one day. And I'm hungry – lunch would be perfect. We can talk about something quite different. I'll tell you about the crime wave that's hit Burracombe!'

For the rest of the day they talked determinedly about other subjects. Hilary told him about the outbreak of pilfering at the school – 'everything points to little Billy Culliford, but Miss Kemp really doesn't want to believe it' – about her brother and Maddy's plans to get married at Easter – 'they broke it to us on Sunday. Goodness knows how we'll get everything ready in time, but Maddy says she'll do most of it and it seems to have given Father a new lease of life' – and about Patsy Shillabeer's romance with Terry Pettifer – 'I feel really sorry for her. I thought my father was a bit of a tyrant, but he's a teddy bear in comparison!'

In return, David told her about a sailing holiday he had enjoyed with friends when he was a medical student, and about a year he had spent in a hospital in Australia. 'That's a country I'd like to go back to sometime,' he said thoughtfully. 'They're really forging ahead and they're crying out for people to go there and work. Teachers, nurses, doctors.' He stopped abruptly, and Hilary looked at him over their roast lamb.

'Is that what you'd like to do? Emigrate to Australia?'

He looked at her, his eyes losing their faraway expression, and reached quickly across the table to take her hand. 'It was once, when I felt there was nothing for me in England. But not any more. Now, everything I want is here.'

And at once they were back again in their own world, face to face with the impossibility of their situation.

Later, as they left the restaurant, they saw that it had stopped raining. They walked slowly back across Hyde Park towards Paddington, hand in hand, confident of being anonymous.

'I don't think,' Hilary said quietly, as they stood for a moment watching the ducks on the Serpentine, 'that I have ever felt so frustrated in my whole life.'

'I know,' he answered, squeezing her hand. 'And we can't even be sure when the next time will be. Goodness knows when I'll be able to come to London again.'

'I don't want to go home.'

'Neither do I.'

They stood staring at the birds without really seeing them at all. Hilary drew in a deep, shuddering breath and turned to him. 'Oh *David ...*'

He took her in his arms and drew her close, folding her against him, his hand cradling the back of her head and his fingers in her hair.

'We can stop now if you want to, Hilary,' he said huskily. 'If it's all too much for you ... I'll understand. And I won't ring you, or even write, if that's what you really want. I've no right to ask you to wait for – for something that may never be. And I have to do all I can for Sybil. So if you want to be free ...'

'Free?' she echoed, with a half-laugh that turned quickly to a sob. 'I'll never be free now.' She lifted her head away and looked into his eyes. 'Whatever happens to either of us now happens to us both,' she said quietly. 'Your troubles are mine. From now on, we share everything.'

Chapter Twenty-Seven

When Dottie Friend arrived home from America, the entire village rejoiced.

'Us was afraid you might decide to stop there,' Alice Tozer told her when she met Dottie on her way to the village shop on her first day back. 'I know that's what our Joe had in mind when he took you off with him.'

'It might have been what he had in mind, but that's all it was,' Dottie declared, hanging her basket on one arm as they walked along together. 'I told him from the start I'd be coming back to Burracombe. 'Tis where I belong to be.' She didn't tell Alice what heartache it had caused them both to part, and how often she wished she had been able to tear herself away from her roots and stay in America with the man she had kept in her heart all these years. But she could never have settled there, not for good, and it was too late now for Joe to return to Devon. They had chosen their paths, and both had enjoyed a good life. It was enough now to know that each remained special to the other.

'Well, and we'm all very pleased to hear it,' Alice said, unaware of these thoughts in Dottie's mind. 'You must come up to the farmhouse one day soon and tell us all about it. And what about our Jackie? How's she getting on there?'

'Why, don't she write to you?' Dottie asked, knowing that Alice had never stopped being anxious about her younger daughter.

Alice snorted. 'Oh yes – a letter every week, all about what she's doing and how wonderful 'tis there and what smart houses they all live in. But it's what she *don't* tell us that Ted and me would like to know.'

Dottie laughed. 'I know what you mean! Well, you don't need to worry too much about your Jackie. If any young girl had her head screwed on the right way round, 'tis her. And Joe and his girls keep an eye on her. She won't go far wrong.'

'I don't want her going wrong at all,' Alice said a trifle grimly. 'So do you reckon her'll be coming home when she said she would?'

Dottie hesitated, then said, 'I don't know, Alice, and that's the truth of it. Well, no – I think she *will* come back. Been talking about Stella's wedding, she has. But I'm not sure she'll stay here.'

'Not stay here?' Alice exclaimed. 'Why, what in the world do you mean, Dottie? You don't think her'll go back to America again?'

'I wouldn't be surprised. Oh, she's not said as much, not to me at any rate, but – well, I just noticed one or two things and all I can say is, I wouldn't be surprised.'

Alice walked in silence for a moment or two. Dottie stole a glance at her and saw that her lips were pressed tightly together and her eyes were bright, as if with tears. She said gently, 'Don't take on about it, maid. Like I say, she's never said a word and I'm certain to be wrong.'

'What things?' Alice said, as if she hadn't spoken. 'What things have you noticed?'

Dottie wished she had never mentioned it. 'Alice, 'tis probably nothing. I'm making too much of it—'

'What things, Dottie?'

'Oh – just that she's got herself a very good job, working up at the glass factory. Secretary to one of the high-ups. And I did hear tell they've been seen together a time or two outside of working hours, and—'

'What?' Alice broke in. 'She's running around with one of the men from the factory? Why's our Joe never said anything about this?'

'It's not like that, Alice. She's not running around. He's a respectable man.'

'He must be older than she.'

'Well, yes, a few years. But that's—'

'And married? Don't tell me he'm married, Dottie.'

'No, he's not married. He was, but—'

'*Divorced?*' Alice said, horrified. 'Oh Dottie!'

'Not divorced neither,' Dottie said firmly. 'His wife died in an accident. They'd only been married a few months, so there were no kiddies. And he and Jackie aren't *running around*. He's taken her to one or two big dinners, that's all. Things to do with the glass factory.'

'She'll never come back here now,' Alice lamented. 'Not after living that sort of life. Oh, I knew we should never have let her go, and my Ted'll say the same when I tells him about this. I tell you, Dottie, the Tozer family has never been the same since Joe came over, and I'm beginning to wish he never had.'

'Don't say that,' Dottie said uncomfortably. 'Joe's a good man. He'll look after your Jackie. But you got to remember, her's a grown woman now and if you've let her fly a bit earlier than you wanted, you did it because you trusted her. You just got to go on trusting her. You can't always keep your children close by. Anyway, tell me about your Brian and his wife – Peggy, isn't it? How are they liking it back here?'

'Oh, you mustn't call her Peggy!' Alice exclaimed. 'Only Brian's allowed to call her that. You should see the look he gives us if we happens to slip up.' She sighed. 'To be honest with you, Dottie, it's been a bit of a disappointment. He's changed. I know it's being away in Germany all this time, and then marrying a German girl – it was bound to make a difference. But he just don't seem the same Brian as we used to know. He – and her, too, both of 'em – well, they'm so touchy. Us can't make a joke any more without wondering if us is upsetting one or t'other of 'em. And it's causing such an atmosphere. Our Val hardly ever comes up to the house these days. I have to go down there if I wants to see young Christopher.'

'I'm sorry to hear that. Perhaps it'll be better when they move on – I dare say he's looking for a job. They'll want a place of their own then and everyone'll feel easier.'

'I'm not so sure about that either,' Alice said. 'Talking about staying on the farm, he is, and wants to make a lot of changes too. I don't know how it'll all end up, Dottie, I don't honestly.'

The two women arrived at the shop and met Maggie Culliford coming out. As usual, she had a cigarette hanging out of her mouth, and she looked tired, her skin dull and sallow. Her hair was tangled and her shabby brown herringbone tweed coat had a button missing just where her stomach was most swollen.

'Hello, Maggie,' Dottie greeted her. 'And how are you getting on? Not long to wait now, I see.'

'Too long,' Maggie responded. 'Not till July. I've never started to show this early before. Doctor says he thinks I got my dates wrong, but I told him, when you've had as many kids as I have, you don't have dates. And how did you like America, Dottie? I thought we might be seeing you in films.'

'That'll be the day! It was very nice, but I'm glad to be back. Everyone's in such a hurry over there. I'd rather be in Burracombe, where folk have got time to pass the time of day with each other.'

'Talking of time of day,' Alice said, 'I ought to be getting my few bits and pieces and going home. Mother's making suet crust pastry for a meat pudding, and we need some more flour. You'll have to excuse me, Maggie.'

'I've got to go home anyway. Our Billy wouldn't go to school again this morning and I've left him by himself. Arthur was meant to be home, but he's not appeared yet. I don't know where he've got to, I'm sure.'

She went off down the village street, with Freddie in the pushchair and Jeanie clinging to the handle. Alice and Dottie looked at each other.

'D'you reckon she means he never came home all night?' Alice asked. 'What d'you make of that?'

'What *can* you make of it?' Dottie responded. 'Been caught poaching again, I'd guess. And why won't Billy go to school?'

Alice shook her head. 'They've had a lot of trouble there since Billy Culliford started. Money missing, toys the kiddies took and left in their coat pockets – even someone's sandwiches one day, I heard. And a lot of the little ones don't like the new teacher either. Our Joanna had the same trouble with Robin for a while, saying he had tummy ache every morning. From what I can make out, Miss Kemp's at her wits' end with it all.'

'That's a pity. It was always such a happy school, especially when Stella was there. Not that I'm surprised to hear about Billy Culliford, mind. Going the same way as the rest of them, I dare say. What chance has he got, with a family like that? Though the little girls seem to be a bit better, I must say.'

They did their shopping and then strolled back together as Alice brought her friend up to date with all the other goings-on in Burracombe. By the time she was back in her own cottage, Dottie had heard all about Mrs Ellis's mother's progress, Jennifer Kellaway's pregnancy and the romance between Patsy Shillabeer and Terry

Pettifer, nipped smartly in the bud by Percy Shillabeer. She already knew about Stella's improvement, having kept in close touch by letter all the time she was away, but hadn't yet heard about the plan for Stella to stay with the Harveys when she came out of hospital. It was disappointing to know that she wouldn't be coming to Dottie herself, but the little woman was sensible enough to realise that the cottage was too small and the stairs too steep for an invalid who needed to be able to practise her walking. She hoped her lodger would return as soon as she was able, for at least a few weeks before her Whitsun wedding.

That was something to look forward to, she thought, smiling as she stood in her own kitchen unpacking her basket. As soon as she'd done that, she would make a cup of tea and sit down to write to Joe. It had been hard to leave him, and she would miss him sadly, but she was sure now that it was the right thing.

As she'd said before, Burracombe was her home.

'So you do come home sometimes,' Maggie greeted her husband as she came through the door into the small, cluttered living room. 'I was beginning to think you'd got another woman somewhere. And what about this fire? It's like an icebox in here.' She threw on a log from the pile by the hearth.

'Another woman? Not much chance of that,' Arthur said, not getting up from his battered armchair. 'One's enough for me.' He gave her a shifty glance and she felt her forehead crease with suspicion.

'What is it? What's happened?' The same thought that Dottie had expressed came immediately to mind. 'You've not gone and got pinched, have you?'

'It weren't my fault,' he blustered. 'It were that new keeper over to Staddacombe. All I had was one rabbit for our dinner and he acted up like I'd got a coachload of pheasants. Him and his underkeeper, they got me by both arms and chucked me in their van and took me down to Tavistock police station for the night. Up in front of the magistrate by ten o'clock I was.'

Maggie stared at him in dismay. 'So what's going to happen?'

'Dunno. Got to go to court on Friday. But I can't see getting away with less than a month.'

'A month in prison? And what am I supposed to do?' She swept a shaking arm around, indicating the small room, the open-mouthed children. 'That'll be a month with no money coming in – not that you brings much as it is – and no food on the table for these little'ns. And what about the rent? And all the other bills?' She sat down at the table and began to cry. 'What am I going to *do*?'

Arthur watched her uncomfortably. 'I'm sorry, maid. I only wanted a rabbit you could make a dinner out of. It's not as if I was bringing home a dozen to sell at back doors.'

'You would have done, though, if you'd not been caught!' she retorted. 'How many snares had you set? He'll find 'em, sure as God made little chickens, and he'll lay the blame with you. Won't matter then whether you had one in your pocket or twenty. And Squire won't be on the bench either, not with his health as it is, so you won't get no leniency from him.'

'I'm sorry,' he said again. 'I never meant to get caught.'

'Well of course you never!' She raised her head, her pale face blotched with tears. 'What am I going to do?' she whispered. 'All I've got in my purse is a few bob. That's not going to feed us for a month. And you won't have nothing to give me when you come out, neither. Arthur – what are we going to *do*?'

The desperation in her voice frightened the two small children, who began to cry. Footsteps sounded on the stairs and Billy appeared at the door, his eyes wide. 'What's the matter? Mum – why are you crying?'

Maggie took no notice. Completely absorbed in her despair, her shoulders racked with sobs, she ran her fingers through her tangled hair, then rubbed both hands over her face, smearing it with green lichen and dirt from the log she had picked up. Her eyes were reddened and her nose was beginning to run.

She stared wildly around, first at her three children and then at her husband. Then, resting her elbows on the table, she said in broken tones, 'The workhouse, that's where we'll end up – just like my dad. The *workhouse*.'

Chapter Twenty-Eight

'I just saw Dottie in the village,' Alice said, dumping her basket on the kitchen table. 'And you'll never guess what she told me.'

'Dottie's back?' Minnie exclaimed. 'Oh that's good. I was never sure whether our Joe would persuade her to stay.' Her eyes grew dreamy. 'Do you realise, Alice, if all had gone like me and Ted's father thought it would all those years ago, Dottie would have been my daughter-in-law and your sister-in-law, *and* a Tozer!'

'I suppose she would.' But Alice was not to be diverted for long. 'What I was going to say—'

'And did her have a good time? What did she think of America? How did she get on with the journey? Not too seasick, I hope. And what about our Jackie?'

'That's what I'm trying to tell you!' Alice said, exasperated. She began to unpack her basket. 'Here's that flour you want. She said our Jackie's going about with a man – an American!'

'Well, that makes sense,' Brian commented, coming down the stairs as she spoke. 'I don't suppose she'd find many English boys over there.'

'It's not a boy, it's a man. Quite a bit older than her. He's been *married*.'

'Been?' Minnie repeated. 'Not divorced, is he?'

'I asked that, of course, the minute Dottie told me. But she says not – says he was widowed young, only been wed a short while so there's no kiddies. But the point is, he's too old for our Jackie. He's one of the bosses at the glass factory. *Her* boss. He must getting on for thirty at least. Maybe more. And suppose it gets serious?' She flapped her hands in agitation. 'Oh, I knew this would happen! And whatever Ted is going to say, I don't like to think.'

'Hold hard, Mother, nothing's happened yet,' Brian said, picking up the copy of the *Western Morning News* that Alice had laid on the table. 'So the girl's having a bit of fun. Where's the harm in that? What did you expect, anyway? Our Jackie's had boyfriends before, hasn't she?'

'Yes, but they were Burracombe boys – Roy Pettifer and Vic Nethercott. We've known them all their lives. They're our sort. What's this American like? That's what I'd like to know. And what's he got in mind, going about with our Jackie? He must know she's only nineteen. And he must know she's coming back to England soon too. What's he thinking of?' She crimped her lips so tightly that her mouth looked like a Cornish pasty. 'I just hope she has the sense to look after herself.'

'You mean you hope she doesn't find herself with a bun in the oven,' Brian said, shaking out the newspaper, and both women stared at him in horror.

'Brian! I won't have that sort of language in my kitchen, and in front of your grandmother, too! You ought to be ashamed of yourself. Apologise this minute.'

'Oh come on, Mum, there's nothing wrong with that. I could say a lot worse if I was in the mess. Anyway, it's what you meant, isn't it?'

'It's not what I meant at all,' Alice said, although she knew it was. 'I'm just worried in case she gets too fond of him and he lets her down.'

Brian grinned. 'Maybe you should have thought of that before you let her go. You must have known she'd find herself some romance.'

'I hoped she'd be a sensible maid,' Alice said primly. 'And I hoped our Joe would look after her too, as he said he would.'

'And I'm certain he is,' Minnie said reassuringly. 'Brian's right, the maid just wants to enjoy herself and you can't expect a young woman nineteen years old not to have an eye for the boys. Especially not Jackie.'

'What do you mean by that?' Alice demanded, firing up. 'Our Jackie's always been respectable.'

'All I'm saying is, I don't suppose there's anything to worry about. The maid knows how you expect her to behave and she won't let you down. But you knew there was a risk of something like this happening.'

'I know, and that's one of the reasons Ted and me didn't want her to go. But she held us over a barrel about it. Threatened to run off to London if we didn't let her go, and said we'd never see her again. And she meant it, too.'

'If you ask me,' Brian said, laying the newspaper flat on the table and shoving a bag of apples to one side to make room for it, 'you've only yourselves to blame. You've spoilt her. You let her have her own way ever since she was a baby, so it stands to reason she wouldn't take notice of you now.'

'And you're an expert on bringing up children, are you?' Alice asked angrily. 'Seeing as you've had so many of your own!'

Brian raised his head and gave her a look. Then he stood up, folded the newspaper and walked towards the staircase door.

'I'll read this upstairs,' he said over his shoulder, 'seeing as Peggy and me don't qualify for a room of our own, like Tom and Joanna do.'

Minnie and Alice were silent as they listened to his step go heavily up to the room above. They looked at each other.

'Maybe I shouldn't have said that,' Alice admitted, brushing her hand across her eyes. 'But I'm really worried, Mother. And to have him laying down the law like that – well, I've had enough of it, I have really.'

'I know, my flower. But you don't really know there's anything to worry about, do you? Joe'll know all about it and he won't let anything happen. He'll make sure 'tis all above board. Why, I dare say he knows the young man as well as we know Roy and Vic.'

'Maybe he do, and maybe he don't,' Alice said. 'But I'm going to write and ask him. And if '*tis* all above board, then you tell me this.' She gazed at her mother-in-law and her eyes filled with tears again. 'Why hasn't our Jackie written and told us herself? Is she ashamed of him? What's wrong with this man that she's never thought fit to mention him?'

By that afternoon, Dottie had spoken to almost everyone in the village. After her shopping trip, she had walked round to the Bell Inn to tell Rose and Bernie that she was home and arrange to start working again behind the bar. As it turned out, Bernie had a bad cold and Rose was only too glad of a hand there and then, so it was past two o'clock before she left. By that time, half the village men had been in for their dinner-time pint, and on her way home she ran into half the women going to their WI meeting.

She had only been indoors for an hour when Felix knocked on the door.

'Well, you're not slow to smell the baking!' she greeted him, holding out her arms. 'And since when did you have to knock before coming into this house?'

'I was being polite,' he responded, wrapping his arms about her small round figure in a bear hug. 'And you're not slow to start baking. You can't have been back any time at all.'

'Last night. And I've been behind the bar all dinner time, but I've got to get some food into the house, especially if you'm going to come visiting. Sit you down there at the table and I'll take the first batch out of the oven. Scones and rock buns. And how be you, Felix, and how's our dear Stella? Coming home soon, I hear.'

'The week after next, we hope. She's going to stay with Basil and Grace at first.' He spoke a little anxiously, afraid that Dottie might be offended, but she simply nodded.

'That's sensible. Her couldn't manage my stairs, not with her leg still in plaster. When do they think that will come off?'

'Tomorrow. They want to be sure the bones have set properly before they let her out, and she's got to do a lot of exercises. The district nurse will call in every day. Grace and Basil are going to turn their morning room into a bedroom for her, and they've got that little bathroom on the ground floor as well. It will be ideal. We didn't really know where else she could go.'

'She'll be well looked after there, and I'll be popping in to see her most days. In fact, I reckon Grace Harvey might live to regret her kindness, with people knocking on the door all day wanting to see Stella.'

'They're used to that,' Felix said. 'Only usually it's Basil they want to see. I think he may have his nose put out of joint! Anyway, the real reason I dropped in was to ask if you'd like to go in to the hospital with me this evening. It will do Stella a lot of good to see you and she'll want to know all about your trip.'

Dottie turned from the oven, her face pink with pleasure. 'Tonight? That'd be master grand, Felix. I was thinking of going in on the train tomorrow, but if you'm sure ...'

'Of course I'm sure.' He watched as Dottie loaded a plate with scones and rock buns, still steaming, and put a pot of jam and a dish of butter on the table beside them. The kettle was already singing, and she made the tea and brought the fat brown teapot to the table. Felix stretched his arms luxuriously.

'I didn't realise until this moment how much I'd missed you.'

'Well, isn't that what I've always said?' Dottie said sardonically. 'Cupboard love. It's my baking you've missed, not me at all!'

Felix flushed to the roots of his dark auburn hair and laughed. 'I didn't mean it like that! Honestly I didn't.' He caught her eye and grinned. 'Well, not entirely. It's the whole thing of being here, in your cottage, with the warm fire and the smell of baking and the atmosphere that you seem to create – of kindliness and hospitality and good down-to-earth common sense. You'd make any house feel like home, but this cottage is the homeliest place I know. You make me feel that everything is going to be all right.'

'And so 'tis,' Dottie told him. 'Now, my handsome, tell me all about your wedding plans. And what's this I hear about Maddy? Getting married at Easter, so Alice Tozer said, but she didn't seem to know any more than that. Is it just a rumour?'

'No, it's true. Hilary told me herself. She and her father didn't know until Sunday last week. It's happened very suddenly. Stephen's being posted to Cyprus, you see, and if they get married, Maddy can go with him.'

'Cyprus! But there's all sorts of trouble there. Will it be safe for the maid?'

'Oh yes, they wouldn't allow wives if it wasn't safe. Anyway, now that you're back, I expect they'll come and tell you all about it themselves. The wedding's fixed for Easter Monday, that I do know, and Colonel Napier's arranging the reception.'

'But what about Fenella Forsyth? Maddy is her daughter, even if she is adopted.'

'They're doing it between them, I think. He's on the spot, so he can make all the arrangements, though I expect Fenella will pay. Not that that's any of my business,' he added hastily. 'The main thing is that Stella will be there. And you too. Maddy wouldn't have dreamed about getting married without you there.'

'Oh, I expect she would,' Dottie said drily. 'Young women don't

214

let things like that stop them getting wed to the man they love. And nor should they. But I'm glad I will be, all the same. And what about her weddding dress? Will her be expecting me to make that, alongside Stella's and the bridesmaids'? Though they'm mostly finished now.'

'Don't ask me,' Felix said, holding up his hand. 'Not my department. All I have to do is sit beside Stella and enjoy the whole thing. It will be a nice change from officiating.' He got up from the table and gave her a kiss. 'I must go now. Thanks for the tea and cakes, Dottie. It's a real joy to have you back, and that's *not* just cupboard love! I'll be here at about a quarter to seven to collect you for the hospital.'

'I'll be ready.' She hugged him and saw him out of the door, then went back to her cooking, thinking of all the news she had received about the village that day, good and bad. Two weddings to prepare for – that was good, very good indeed. But the situation at the school, with an infant teacher the children didn't like and one of them pilfering from the others – that wasn't good at all. And thinking about that led her to thoughts of the Culliford family. Maggie hadn't looked at all well this morning, and if it was her Billy doing the stealing, she would have even more to worry about.

Dottie had never had much time for the Culliford family, but the sight of the young woman that morning, looking unkempt, pale and wan, had touched her heart. She wasn't a bad maid, and even Arthur wasn't really bad. They'd never had enough money to live on, and it must be hard for a mother in that position, useless though she might be.

I'll go round and knock on the door tomorrow, she thought. Just to see how they are – give them a friendly word. I could take a dozen rock buns with me. I don't suppose those kiddies see cake on the table from one Christmas to the next.

Whatever their parents' failings, it wasn't right to let the children suffer. And what was a village for, if people didn't rally round in times of trouble?

A dozen rock buns was hardly enough to divert Maggie Culliford from her troubles. She opened the door to Dottie's knock, her face even paler than before, and stared vacantly at her visitor. Guiltily, Dottie thought how seldom she had come to this door, and almost never with gifts in her hand. More likely the parish magazine or collecting for Remembrance Day poppies. And Maggie had always found a ha'penny or two to put in the tin, she thought, even though I just took it that she wanted poppies for the little ones. Well, and why not? They get little enough, poor toads.

'I just brought a few buns round,' she said, holding out the paper bag. 'Forgot I hadn't got a lodger no more and made too many. And if there's anything I can do ... well, you let me know, all right? You got enough on your hands without baking cakes.'

Maggie gave a short laugh. 'I never been one for doing a lot of baking. But thanks, Dottie. The little'ns can have them for their tea.'

'And you have one yourself,' Dottie told her. 'You'm looking thin, Maggie.'

'Thin?' she exclaimed, putting her hand on her stomach. 'I'm swelling up like a balloon.'

'Well, so you will, but that don't stop you being too thin if you don't eat enough. Eating for two, you ought to be, and I don't reckon you'm even eating enough for one.'

'Two? I wouldn't be surprised if I shouldn't be eating for three, the way I'm going. I said yesterday, I never been this big so early on before. And how I'm going to be able to buy anything at all if my Arthur gets sent down, I just don't know.'

'Sent down?' Dottie repeated, horrified. 'But why?'

'Why d'you think? Caught poaching over on Staddacombe land, he was. That's why he never came home the night before last. Spent the night in the cells in Tavi. Up in front of the magistrate in the morning and court case next week. He'll get a month inside for certain.'

'Oh my stars,' Dottie said in real distress. 'I'm so sorry. Whatever are you going to do?'

Maggie shrugged hoplessly. 'I don't know, do I? We got no money behind us, nothing set aside for a rainy day, as they say. Seems every day's a rainy day in this house. There's a few bits and pieces in the cupboard, but not enough to see us through a whole month. I reckon we'll end up in Bannawell Street.'

'Bannawell Street?' Dottie stared at her. 'You mean the workhouse?'

'What else can we do? I can't watch the poor toads starve to death.'

'But you know what happens in there. They separate the children from their mothers. You might never get them back. Once they see how you'm living here ...'

'Don't think I don't know that,' Maggie said bitterly. 'I've been going over and over it in my mind all night. My father went in there, you know, come the end of his life, and I used to go in to see him. I know just what it's like. It's not like in that story we learned at school – *Oliver Twist* – and you won't starve in there, but it's not a place you want to see your kiddies go.' Her hands covered her stomach. 'They might even take this one away, when 'tis born.'

'But Arthur will be out by then. You'll be able to come back home.'

'They'll have seen what it's like,' Maggie said, without hope. 'We'm done for this time, Dottie. And just as if all that isn't enough, we got our Billy in trouble at school. Four years old and branded a thief. What chance do any of us have?' She looked at the paper bag in her hands. 'Thanks for the cakes. I reckon I better go inside now or my Freddie'll be falling in the fire. I can't be doing with any more trouble.'

She closed the door and Dottie turned away, deeply troubled. The Cullifords had never been a credit to Burracombe, but they were part of the village just the same. There had been Cullifords here for generations, handing down their useless ways from father to son, and never marrying a woman who could have hauled them into respectability, but didn't every village have a family like that? And whatever they'd been in the past, Dottie had thought things were improving. The two little girls, Shirley and Betty, were doing really well at school, thanks to Stella, and Billy could be the same with a sympathetic teacher.

I suppose he just wanted to help, she thought, trudging back to her own cottage. Thought the odd penny or ha'penny here and there would pay for a loaf of bread or pint of milk. Four years old – what could he know about right and wrong? Especially with a father like Arthur Culliford. And yet you had to give even Arthur a bit of credit. Called up into the army when war broke out, a bit of a hero at Dunkirk by all accounts before he was captured by the Germans and kept in a prisoner-of-war camp for the duration. And what had there been for him when he did come back? A job? A comfortable home?

Dottie could remember the day Arthur Culliford had returned to Burracombe. There had been a few before him – soldiers mostly, but one or two who had gone into the Royal Navy, and Jack Pettifer, who had been an aeroplane mechanic in the Royal Air Force. There had been a party atmosphere in the village – red, white and blue bunting, a Union Jack here and there, and a crowd to meet them when they got off the bus, proud in their uniforms or demob suits. But there had been nothing like that for Arthur Culliford. Dottie had happened to walk down her front path just as he was passing – a gaunt, ill-shaven wreck of a man, dragging a stained and dirty kitbag. He'd given her a curt nod as she stared at him, then shambled on down the road to his own cottage and pushed open the peeling front door. And Dottie had known that not even Maggie was there to greet him, for she was cleaning for Joyce Warren and wouldn't be home for another half-hour. Not even a cup of tea ready for the poor man, she'd thought, and gone indoors, disturbed and wondering if she ought to go after him.

But she hadn't, and the thought had haunted her ever since.

The workhouse? Over my dead body, she thought with sudden determination. I'll not see that family in the workhouse. If we all pull together, the whole village can help. Maggie Culliford might be a poor mother in some ways, but she does love her little ones and she don't deserve to lose them like this. It won't cost much for us all to give a bit here and there to keep them fed, and it wouldn't take too much effort for a few of us to get together and give the cottage a bit of a clean and smarten up. I could even give that poor woman a few lessons in cooking a decent dinner.

She went through her own door, struck by the difference in the two cottages and ashamed that neither she nor anyone else had ever really given much thought to the Cullifords and their problems.

Chapter Twenty-Nine

Ted was just as perturbed as Alice when he heard about Jackie's latest escapade, but he was also inclined to put his trust in his brother to look after her. 'Our Joe's got two daughters of his own. He'll keep an eye on her. And after all, she is with family now – not like when she was in Plymouth, living with a stranger. She could have been up to all sorts and us'd never have knowed.' He fished under the pillow for his pyjamas.

'She was with Jennifer Kellaway. You can't call her a stranger.'

'Not now, no, but when our Jackie was staying with her she was Jennifer Tucker and us didn't know all that much about her. And when she went to live in at the hotel, she could have been out all night for all we knew.'

'Ted! You're not saying—'

'I'm not saying anything. Only that she's probably better looked after in Corning than she might have been in Plymouth, that's all.' Ted took off his shirt and vest and put on his pyjama jacket. 'And to be honest with you, my dear, I'm more worried about the farm than I am about Jackie. I reckon we can trust her to be sensible.'

'The farm? Why?' Alice looked at him from her pillows. 'Is it what Brian's been saying?'

'It is.' He pulled on his pyjama trousers and got into bed beside her. 'I been talking to Tom about it. Trouble is, Tom reckons a lot of what Brian says is right – partly right, anyway. Horses have had their day. Machinery's going to be used more and more and us got to move with the times if us wants to go on making a living.'

'But we have moved with the times! We've had a tractor since before the war.'

'Yes, but do we use it enough? We still use those old horses first and foremost and only get the tractor out when it's a job they can't do. That's no way to run a business, Alice.'

'It's a *farm*, not a business!'

'That's just it. That's what our Brian keeps telling me – that we don't look at it the right way. I know the farm's our home and has been for generations back, but 'tis still a business. 'Tis how we make our living, same as a shop or a factory.'

'A factory!' Alice seized on the word. 'That's what he wants us to be, isn't it? A factory, making machinery; with no animals in the barns. Noise and smells and smoke and goodness knows what-all. Is that what you really want, Ted?'

'No, of course it isn't. And I don't reckon us needs to go that far. Turn over one of the outbuildings into making a bit of shearing gear, I wouldn't mind that, but go the whole hog like Brian wants – no, that ain't my idea of a good farming life.'

There was a short silence. Then Alice said, with tears in her voice, 'I'd miss the horses, Ted. I like going out of a morning and seeing their friendly old faces looking out of the stable doors. I like hearing them whinny when I go over with some apples for them. They've been here for such a long time. It's their home too, and they've done good service. You wouldn't get rid of them, would you? You wouldn't send them down the knackers' yard – old Barley and Boxer? You couldn't.'

'No, I couldn't,' he admitted. 'Not till their time comes, anyway. But when it does … well, I don't reckon I'll be looking for any more Shires. And us got to look ahead to that time. Us got to think about what we're going to do.'

'This is all Brian's doing,' she said sadly. 'I don't like saying this about our own son, but since he came back nothing's been the same. One way and another he's managed to upset the lot of us. And we didn't even know he was thinking of staying till he come out with all these ideas. We never thought he was that interested in the farm.'

'I still don't think he is,' Ted said. 'Not as a farm. He's looking at it different from us. And I can't say I like it.'

'So what are we going to do? Tell him you'll run the farm your way, you and Tom? Or let him stay on and take us down a road us don't want to go?'

'What you'm really saying,' Ted said slowly, 'is should we let him stay and take over, or tell him it's time he moved on? Tell our own son there's no place for him here no more.'

'Oh Ted,' she said, her eyes filled with distress. 'That's an awful thing to do.'

'I know. But that's what it comes down to, isn't it?'

They looked at each other for a long minute, and then Ted blew out the candle and lay down. Alice moved closer to him and he put his arms around her, and together they lay staring into the darkness, waiting for sleep to come.

'I wants a word with you,' Minnie said. She was sitting upright in her armchair by the fire, her wrinkles set in an unfamiliar stern pattern and her eyes snapping between narrowed lids. Brian, who had been lounging in his father's chair, reading the *Sunday Express*, grunted but didn't move. Margret was still in bed and the rest of the family had gone to church.

'Brian!' she said sharply. 'Did you hear me?'

'Sorry, Gran, I was reading the football results.'

'Never mind them. I got something to say to you.' She waited while he laid the paper down. 'It's about what you said the other day.'

'What was that, Gran?' His eyes strayed towards the newspaper again.

'You know full well what it was, and leave that paper alone while I'm talking to you. You caused a lot of upset, saying what you did.'

'Well, the others caused a lot of upset saying what *they* did,' he said in an injured tone. 'Peggy's been in tears over it once or twice. She's not used to being teased and laughed at.'

Minnie made an impatient sound. 'Don't be dafter than you have to be! You know very well 'twas all meant in jest. Nobody's been deliberately unkind to either of you. Why should they be?'

'Why?' he repeated. 'Well our Tom's always been jealous of me for a start, and he's been one of the worst.'

'Jealous of you? Why in heaven's name would you think that?'

'Because I got away, of course, and made my own life, while he's stuck on the farm. Stands to reason.'

'It don't stand to any such thing,' she retorted. 'Tom's happy to be here and so is Joanna, and we'm all happy to have them. Are you sure it isn't you who's the jealous one?'

Brian flushed but said nothing. Minnie went on.

'Anyway, leaving that aside, there was still no call for you to say what you did. It's left the whole family at sixes and sevens.'

'Don't we have the right to say if we're feeling upset?' he demanded. 'Are we supposed to just say nothing and put up with it?'

'No, not if you've good cause. But when 'tis just a matter of a bit of joking and larking about, the sort of teasing that goes on in any family—'

'It doesn't in Peggy's,' he said quickly.

'And that's the problem,' Minnie said. 'It has done in ours, as well you know, and 'tis no more than what you might call affectionate family banter, which we all understand and don't take offence at. You was always the best at handing it out in the past, so you should know. But maybe you don't find it so funny when someone hands it back to you. So instead of explaining to Peggy that nobody meant anything by it, and helping her to understand that 'tis all done out of affection, you've made her an excuse for protecting your own feelings. Either way, it don't suit you and it don't suit this family, and you've upset everyone else more than anyone's ever upset you by making a joke or two.' She paused, but as Brian opened his mouth she held up a wrinkled hand and continued. 'Nobody knows how to go on any more. We'm all so polite to each other now it's as if we were a bunch of strangers. Every word got to be watched, even our Tom's afraid to make a joke, and it just ain't natural. There's an atmosphere in here sometimes you could cut with one of Ted's wood axes, and it's upsetting your mother and father.'

'Well, if we're making things so bad, maybe we'd better go,' Brian said sullenly, and picked up his paper again.

'I never said that! But since it's you who started it, maybe it'd be a good idea for you to do something about it. And *leave that paper alone while I'm talking to you*!' She grasped the stick that stood beside her chair and thrust it across the space between them, knocking the newspaper out of his hands, and Brian stared at her in shock. 'Tell your wife that there's no harm in a bit of joking and teasing when there's nothing meant by it, apologise to your sister for upsetting her so much she hardly ever comes here any more unless you'm out, and give us a bit of a smile now and then. 'Twon't crack your face in half. And you might as well stop your bragging too, while you'm at it.'

'*Bragging?*' he echoed. 'What bragging?'

'Why, all the times you tell us how good you are at being a soldier or a driver or all the other things you think you'm the bee's knees at,' she said. 'I don't know whether it's because you think you need to impress us, or what it is, but we'm your family, and you don't need to do it. And there's another thing ...'

'Only one?' he asked sarcastically, but Minnie took no notice of his tone.

'Yes, only one, and it's not something I want to say much about, because I don't know all the ins and outs. It's these plans you've got for the farm.' She gave him a straight look. 'When you first came home, you and Margret, us thought 'twas just for a holiday. Your demob leave. As far as any of us knew, you'd be looking for work, the sort of work you did in the army, engineering work that you'm good at. It never crossed anyone's minds you'd want to stay here and turn the place into some sort of factory.'

'I just want to see it make a bit of money, that's all.'

'It's making enough for us to live on.'

'But how long for? You don't understand these things, Gran. Times are changing and the farm has to change with them.'

'Your father knows that. So does Tom. But they also know how fast it should change, and what changes would be best – not just for us, but for Burracombe as well. You'm trying to move too fast. And you'm taking quite a lot for granted, too. Has your father ever said he wants you to stay? Or did you just decide that for yourself?'

'You're saying I'm not wanted! That's it, isn't it?'

'I'm just saying you ought to think about what you're doing,' she said quietly. 'There might be better ways for you to go. Places where people think the same way as you. Ask yourself whether you might not like that better than stopping in a place where your wife's not happy. Because she's not, is she? Not really.'

They stared at each other for a long moment. Then Minnie said, 'Anyway, I think I've said enough for the time being. Just you think about it a bit. That's all. And now you can make me a cup of tea. It's a long time since I give anyone a piece of my mind like that and it's made me thirsty.'

Brian got up and did as he was told. He filled the kettle and put it on the range, then stood staring out of the window as he waited for it to boil. At last he spoke, a grudging note in his voice.

'I never meant to upset anyone, Gran. I just wanted things to go nice and easy for all of us.'

Her voice a little softer, Minnie said, 'I know, Brian. But you went about it the wrong way, don't you see? Telling people off and not even listening to their answers just ain't fair. Our Val tried her best to make things right by apologising, even though her had nothing to be sorry for, but you never even listened to her. You just left bad feeling, and being all together as we are, there's been no chance to clear the air. Anyway, the kettle's boiling, so make me that cup of tea and then maybe you'd better take yourself out for a long walk. The football results will still be there when you come back.'

He grinned reluctantly and poured boiling water into the pot. He made Minnie's tea and gave her a slice of fruit cake to go with it, then went to the door.

'I'll go up to the Standing Stones for a bit,' he said. 'Tell Peggy I'll be in for dinner, and maybe we'll go to the pictures in Tavistock later on – it's time we had an evening out.'

After he had gone, Minnie sipped her tea, wondering if her words had had any real effect. Brian had been away for a long time and it was naturally difficult for him and his wife to slot back in. While a family stayed together, there was a place for everyone, but if someone had been away for some time it was as if their space closed over. The Brian-shaped hole had disappeared and a new one had to be made, and that meant effort on everyone's part.

Well, I've done my best, she thought. I just hope I haven't made things worse by speaking out, that's all.

Chapter Thirty

'Y ou're *what*?'
Percy Shillabeer rose from his chair at the kitchen table, his face almost black with fury. At the other end of the table his wife stared in frightened horror from him to her daughter. Her eyes were already reddened with tears.

'You're in the family way? You'm *expecting*?'

'Yes, Father,' Patsy said, standing her ground, although her voice shook. 'About seven weeks' gone, we reckon.'

'Seven weeks? You can't tell that soon.'

'I can. I missed my time of the month, and I've started feeling sick in the mornings.' She glanced at her mother. 'You heard me this morning, didn't you?'

'Yes, but I thought 'twas something you ate. I never dreamed ... Oh Patsy, are you really sure? I mean, *could* you be? It's not true about it happening if a boy just kisses you, you know.'

'I know *that*,' Patsy said scornfully. 'I seen enough farm animals. And I am sure.'

'You and Terry ...?'

'Yes,' she said. 'Yes, we have.'

Percy Shillabeer shoved back his chair. Eyes bulging, he came round the table like a bear, growling deep in his throat, and grabbed Patsy by both shoulders, shaking her so violently that her head lolled. Patsy screamed in fear and put up her hands, trying to ward him off, but he was too strong for her, and her flailing fists did not even reach his body. As her mother too screamed and begged him to let go, he thrust her away from him and she staggered and fell against the dresser, sending half a dozen cups crashing to the floor.

'Now look what you done, you dirty little trollop!' he panted, standing over her. 'That was your mother's best tea service.'

'Patsy!' Ann Shillabeer gave her husband a frightened look before scuttling across to her daughter. Patsy was crouching against the dresser, one hand to her temple, tears running down her white face. 'Are you all right, maid?'

'All right?' Percy bellowed. 'Bringing disgrace on the family with her dirty ways and you ask if she'm all right? No, she ain't all right! And 'tis your fault as much as hers,' he added, rounding on his wife. 'Always been soft on her, you have, and this is the result. I knew there'd be trouble one day – that's why I took her out of Pillar's and brought her home, and this is where she ought to have stopped. But no, you would have her go and work at Burracombe Barton – and that's another thing. What's that Hilary Napier been thinking of, letting such things go on under her roof? I'll be going over there first thing in the morning and telling her what I think of her, see if I don't.'

'No, you mustn't!' Patsy cried as her mother felt the bump already forming on her forehead. 'Miss Hilary didn't know anything about it. And we never did anything at the Barton, anything at all.'

'So where did you get up to your tricks, then? A bit cold in the woods, this time of year.'

'In our barn,' Patsy said, facing him. 'That's where. In our barn, while you were snoring your head off indoors.'

'*What?*' Once again he advanced on her, but this time his wife stood between him and the frightened girl. He caught her shoulder and tried to pull her aside, but Ann stood her ground.

'Leave her alone, Percy. If you touch her now, you'll do something you regret. Take it out on me if you like, but Patsy's expecting a baby and I won't have you hurt her.'

'Damn you, woman, you don't have to tell me she's expecting a baby!' For a moment she thought he was going to strike her to the ground with one blow of his huge fist, but then he drew in a deep ragged breath and turned away. Breathing hard, he went to the fireplace, leant his head on the mantelpiece and thumped the big stone lintel instead. Patsy huddled into her mother's arms, weeping, but then Ann herself thrust her away.

'You needn't think I'm on your side, for all that. Your father's right, you've brought shame and disgrace on the family. And where's young Terry? Don't he have the nerve to face up to what he've done? Frightened to come over and admit it, is he?'

Patsy stared at her mother in shock. While feeling the bump and holding her in her arms she had seemed like a refuge; now her face and voice had hardened and Patsy felt suddenly very alone.

'He wanted to come,' she said, her voice shaking. 'I wouldn't let him. I told him that if he was here too, Father would half kill him.'

'And so I would,' Percy said, turning abruptly from the fireplace. 'And still will, when I get the chance.' His fingers strayed to his waist. 'I'll take my belt to him and give him the thrashing of his life, and I daresay Jack Pettifer will want to take a turn too.'

'And what good will that do?' Ann asked hopelessly. 'Our Patsy will still be in the family way. Everyone's going to know.'

'They won't,' he said curtly, coming back to the table. 'They won't, because there'll be no baby.'

'Percy!'

'I don't mean that,' he said irritably. 'Of course there'll be a baby, but 'twon't be here in Little Burracombe. Nor in Burracombe neither,' he added with a glower at Patsy. 'There's homes and places where young women can go, places miles away where nobody will know them. They has their babies and then they give them up to be adopted by some respectable family who can't have their own children.'

The two women gazed at him. Ann returned to her place at the table, but Patsy stayed where she was.

'I won't go to one of those places.'

'You'll do as you'm told!' he snarled, looking ready to break out again. 'And don't you look at me like that, neither. You'm my daughter and what I says goes.'

'And this baby's my daughter,' she retorted. 'Or my son. And *I'm* the one who says what'll happen to it.'

'Why, you little—' He was on his feet again, but Ann jumped up too.

'No, Percy! Don't start again! Don't you see, hitting the maid won't help. Us got to sit down sensible and talk it over. See what's to be done.'

'I've already said what's to be done,' he growled, but he sank down on to his chair again. 'We'll find out about a place first thing tomorrow. You can say she've gone off to work for a friend of Hilary Napier's, and she'll be gone before anyone knows any different.'

'But suppose Miss Hilary won't agree to that?' Ann asked doubtfully.

'She'll agree all right, seeing it was under her roof it all started.'

'I told you, we never—'

'I know what you told me, you cheeky little cow, but 'twas at the Barton you two met, wasn't it? Don't tell me no different. So Hilary Napier's got some responsibility in the matter, and if she've got a shred of decency, she'll put the story round like we asks her to.'

'Like *you* ask her to, you mean,' Patsy said, feeling that her father was so angry with her now it hardly mattered how she spoke to him. 'I'm not asking her to tell lies for me, and I don't think she will anyway.'

'So perhaps you got a better idea?' he demanded scornfully.

'Yes, I have. Let Terry and me get married.'

Percy stared at his daughter. '*Get married?* Is that what this is all about?'

'Yes, of course it is. We knew you wouldn't let us, not till I was twenty-one. You wouldn't even let us see each other, to walk out together. So we decided—'

'*Decided?* You done this deliberately?'

'Oh *Patsy* ...' Ann said with deep reproach.

'Well, what else could we do? I don't want to stay here being a skivvy and never having any life till I'm twenty-one. I love Terry and he loves me. If you'd let us see each other like other boys and girls do, we'd have waited a few years, but you wouldn't. And it wasn't Terry's idea neither, so you don't have to take it out on him. It was mine. I had to persuade him.'

'Oh, and I bet *that* took some doing!' her father said with bitter sarcasm. 'A young chap like him, needing to be persuaded? Pull the other one, Patsy, it's got bells on.'

There was a brief silence. Then Patsy said abruptly, 'So can we get married then?'

'*No you bloody can't!*' her father yelled, smashing his fist on the table. 'I'll not be taken for a fool by my own daughter. You'll do as I've already said – you'll go to one of these homes where they'll look after you and make you work until the child's born, and then it will be adopted. If you do that, you can come back here afterwards and we'll say no more about it.'

'Say no more about it?' Patsy said sceptically. 'You'll never stop reminding me.'

'Patsy, don't talk to your father like that. You know he only wants the best for you.'

'No he doesn't! He just wants to save his own name in the village. He doesn't care a bit about me or about my baby.' She turned to her father. 'This is your *grandchild*. Doesn't that mean anything to you?'

'No,' he said stonily. 'It don't. Because 'tis no grandchild of mine. Get wed in the proper way, when you'm old enough, to a chap I think is good enough for you, and I'll welcome any grandchildren that come along. But this one – no. I'm never going to see it. I don't even want to know what it is.'

Patsy stared at him, then burst into tears. She ran from the room and up the stairs, and Ann turned to her husband.

'Oh Percy. Whatever be us going to do?'

'I've told you. I've told you both. The maid goes away, out of Devon if I has my way, and no one the wiser.'

'But if Terry's willing to stand by her ... It's not that uncommon, Percy. Plenty of people get married a bit quick and then have a seven-month baby. Everyone knows the truth but nobody says nothing, as long as the girl's got a ring on her finger. Couldn't you see your way to letting them wed?'

'And be made a laughing stock? Never! We've always set a lot of store on bringing up our children as decent God-fearing people, and here's our eldest going the ways of the Devil when she's barely seventeen. What are people going to say? No, the only good thing to come out of this is that she's told us early enough that no one will have noticed. She can go by the end of the week if we can arrange it, and nobody any the wiser.'

'Terry will know. He might tell people.'

'Not when I've finished with him he won't,' Percy said, fingering his belt again.

Ann was silent for a while; then, her voice quivering, she said, 'But Patsy's right, in a way. This is our grandchild. It might be the only one we'll ever have.'

Her husband stared at her. 'Don't talk so far back! She'll have more, when the time's right. And what about all the other kids? Us'll have more grandchildren than us has hot dinners by the time we'm seventy.'

'We don't *know* that,' she argued. 'We don't really know anything. But this don't seem right to me – not when her young man's ready to stand by her. And 'tis his babby too, when all's said and done.'

'Said and done? There's been enough said and done in this matter.' He rested his head on his hand and sighed. 'Get us a cup of tea, will you, girl.'

Ann hastened to do as he asked. A cup of tea might soothe them both, she thought. And perhaps then Percy would be willing to talk some more, even to give way a little.

Ann Shillabeer was as angry and upset as her husband over Patsy's behaviour. But inside her daughter was a tiny being, no bigger than a plum, that was going to turn into a baby. Her grandchild. The thought of never looking into that little face, feeling the tiny fingers curl around hers, seeing the first smile, was a pain in her heart.

I don't know what we'm going to do, she thought, sweeping up the broken china as she waited for the kettle to boil, but us have got to do *something*.

Terry Pettifer knew that Patsy intended to tell her parents soon, but he had no idea just when she would pluck up the courage. He was at home in his father's shed, mending a pair of shoes for his mother and feeling almost as sick as Patsy had begun to feel in the mornings. At every sound outside he started, convinced that it was Percy Shillabeer come to thrash the life out of him.

We never ought to have done it, he thought miserably, cutting a piece of leather to fit the sole of the left shoe. I knew it was wrong but I let her persuade me. And I did want it so bad ... But we ought to have waited. I ought to have been strong.

The door opened suddenly and he jumped back, dropping his knife and almost knocking the cobbler's last off the bench. His brother Bob looked in, raising his eyebrows at the expression on Terry's face.

'Cor, Terry, what's the matter with you? Think I was a ghost?'

'You made me jump, that's all.' Terry bent to pick up his knife and turned his attention back to his task, avoiding Bob's eye. His brother came in and closed the door.

'It's not all, though, is it? There's something bothering you, Terry, and I reckon I know what it is. It's young Patsy, isn't it?'

'What makes you think that?' Terry blustered.

Bob laughed. 'Come on, Terry – you can't fool me. I known you all your life, remember? And us works together all day. You've been like a cat on hot bricks these past few days. Your mind's not on your work, neither, and that's dangerous. I thought you'd know by now you don't fool about with electricity.'

'I haven't been fooling about.'

'You haven't been taking proper care either.' Bob leaned against the bench and looked at his brother. 'Out with it now. Given you the push, has she?'

'No!' Terry met his eye. 'Not that we can see much of each other, the way her dad keeps her on a chain.'

'Is that it, then? Can't you go over and speak to him? Ask if you can see her on Sundays or something? He'd probably be all right if you went about it the right way.'

'He wouldn't,' Terry muttered. 'He'll never be all right – not now.'

'What d'you mean?' Bob looked at him more closely. 'Here, you haven't gone and got her in trouble, have you?' Terry didn't answer, and Bob sighed with exasperation. 'Oh, you *fule*!'

'It wasn't like that! It wasn't me – it was her. She kept on at me, said it would be the only way he'd let us be together. She got me to go over there and meet her in their barn after her mum and dad had gone to bed. She ... she's going to tell them soon and then we'll be able to get married.'

'*Married?* You really think that old tyrant will let you get married? Have you lost whatever bit of sense you ever had, Terry? Old man Shillabeer will never let you marry her now. You know what he's like – fire and brimstone aren't in it with him. He'll kill you before he lets you near his maid again.'

'He'll kill me anyway,' Terry muttered. 'I knew it was wrong, but ... I dunno, I just couldn't seem to help it. And she was so sure ...' He looked at his brother in bewilderment. 'What am I going to do, Bob?'

Bob pushed some of the tools and scraps of leather aside to make room to half sit on the bench. 'Buggered if I know, Terry. What do you *want* to do?'

'Well, I want to marry her, of course.'

'And where d'you reckon you'd live?'

'I thought ... well, here. Till we could afford to rent somewhere, anyway.'

'And when the hell's that going to be?' Bob demanded. 'You're just an apprentice, Terry. How can you *afford* to get married? How can you afford to support a wife and child? Patsy won't be able to work. How far gone is she anyway?'

'Seven weeks, she thinks.'

Bob stared at him. 'But that's no time at all. Are you sure?'

'Yes. She's being sick of a morning and – you know ...' Terry looked at him miserably. 'I knew it was a daft idea, but I just couldn't think straight.'

'Strikes me you didn't think at all.' Bob sighed. 'But there you are, what's done is done. And you reckon she's going to tell her folks soon?'

'She might be doing it now, for all I know,' Terry said, more accurately than he realised.

Bob blew out his cheeks. 'No wonder you jumped a mile when I opened the door. Well, if she's telling her mum and dad, I guess we'd better tell ours.'

Terry looked agonised. 'Do I have to?'

'Of course you have to, you dumb cluck. You don't want old man Shillabeer coming over breaking the good news, do you? And if you think Patsy might be doing it now, we'd better do it now too. Come on.'

'You mean you'll help me?'

'I'll come with you. I don't know as I'll be much help.'

Terry looked at the piece of leather in his hand. 'I was doing Mother's shoes.'

'You can do those after. Come on. No time like the present.' Bob laid his hand on his young brother's shoulder. 'Don't look so down in the mouth. You been all sorts of a fule, but 'tis no worse than a lot of young chaps have done before, and at least you want to marry the maid. There's plenty found themselves tied to a girl they hated the sight of before even the banns were called.'

'That's not going to happen to Patsy and me,' Terry said, laying down his tools and following Bob out of the shed. 'We'll *always* think the same of each other.'

'You've got Patsy Shillabeer into trouble?' Jack Pettifer laid down his newspaper and stared at his son. 'My stars, I never thought you'd have the luck with your looks.'

'Jack!' Nancy Pettifer reproached him, setting aside her darning. 'That's no way to talk. It's not as if you were much of an oil painting yourself.'

Jack sported the same gargoyle features as his sons. With his long, rubbery face he would have been quite at home on the corner of the church tower, pulling faces at the congregation as they went in to pray. It was a common belief in the village that past Pettifers had indeed been the models for the carved stone creatures that adorned the cornices, and the family took a certain pride in the jokes that were aimed at them.

'It's no laughing matter anyway,' Nancy went on. 'You ought to be ashamed of yourself. And so should you, Terry. What in the world were you thinking of? The Shillabeers are a decent, God-fearing family. Percy Shillabeer will be over here after your hide the minute he finds out.'

'He'll find out soon enough,' Terry said. 'Patsy's telling them herself. She wants them to know as soon as possible.'

His mother frowned. 'Why's that, then? Maids usually try to keep it secret as long as they can, feared of what'll happen to them. How far gone is she?'

'About seven weeks, we think.'

'*Seven weeks?* She've just make a mistake, that's all, and got into a panic. Next thing you know she'll be telling you it was a false alarm and asking you to be more careful next time. And *you* can tell *her* there won't be a next time. One fright's enough and let's hope you've both learned your lesson. You've been a silly pair of fools.'

'No we haven't. We wanted it to happen, Mother.'

'*Wanted* it to happen?' Nancy had been about to pick up her darning again, but she dropped it back on the table. 'Whatever foolishness be you talking now?'

'We want to get married. Old man Shillabeer wouldn't even let us see each other. He comes over every afternoon to walk Patsy home from work at the Barton, and she's not allowed out in the evenings. We can't even walk out on Sundays. We couldn't think of any other way, Mother.' He stared desperately at both parents. 'I wasn't that keen when she suggested it, but—'

'*She* suggested it? Patsy Shillabeer? She always seemed such a little mouse.'

'She's not, not when you get to know her. And we do want to get married. I didn't mind waiting, if we could just see each other properly and get engaged in a year or two, and get married when I've finished my apprenticeship, but he won't hear of her even walking out until she's twenty-one. That's four years! And I don't reckon he'd let her then, either. He'd find some way of keeping her at home. He's making a slave of her, Mum.' He turned to his father. 'I know I can't get married either, without your signature, but you'll let us, won't you? You won't see him turn her out, not when she could be properly married and live here with us?'

'Oh, so you got it all planned, have you?' his father commented. 'And what be you going to live on, then? An apprentice don't earn much.'

'I'll pay you back when I've finished. It won't be for long. I've only got another two years to do and the babby will be just over a year old. We can find some rooms in Tavi, maybe. Please, Dad – Mother. Patsy and me – we love each other. We *got* to be together.'

He gazed at them beseechingly, and Jack and Nancy looked at each other. Then Jack said, 'I dunno, boy. This isn't something us can decide all in a hurry. It wants thinking about. And you got to take your responsibility too. You can't expect me and your mother to put everything right for you. You take the pleasures of a man, you got to take on the responsibilities of a man.'

'I know,' Terry said, subdued. 'And I didn't do it for pleasure.' He heard Bob snort behind him and turned scarlet. 'I mean – I knew 'twas wrong, but it was only so that we could get married and be together.'

'And to my mind,' Jack said heavily, 'that was more wrong than if you just got carried away like many another boy and maid before you. You did it deliberate, to make someone else do what you wanted them to do. That don't seem much short of blackmail to me, whichever way you looks at it. And using an innocent baby to get your way too.'

Terry stared at him, horrified by both his father's words and his suddenly stern tone. 'I never thought of it like that.'

'Well think of it now. I'm disappointed in you, Terry. You done something very wrong here. Percy Shillabeer might be an old tyrant, but he've got a father's rights and responsibilities, and if he chooses to bring up his children his way, it ain't for us to argue. All he wanted was to look after his daughter, and he'll have every right now to say she needed it. And every right to come over here and give you the hiding of your life. I might be minded to give him a hand, as well.'

Terry looked wildly from Jack to Nancy. 'I never meant no harm. I never thought of it ... I knew 'twas wrong, but—'

'But you did it anyway,' Jack went on. 'And that's always been your trouble, Terry. You don't stop to think. Well, maybe this will teach you a lesson.'

There were tears in Terry's eyes now. He said plaintively, 'So you won't help us, then?'

'Now I never said that, did I?' Jack's tone softened and he got up and put a hand on his son's shoulder. 'I said it needed thinking about and talking about, and that's what me and your mother will do, same as we've always talked through any problems us have had. I won't say I'm not sorry it's happened, but I've had my say about that now and us have got to look forward. And there's Percy Shillabeer and his good woman to consider as well. They'll have their own ideas.' He turned to his wife. 'It might be a good plan for us to go over there, Mother, and get round the kitchen table for a bit of a chinwag, see what us can sort out. I don't want old Perce to think Pettifers don't put their hands up when there's trouble in the family.'

'I don't know that that's a good idea,' Terry ventured. 'You don't know Mr Shillabeer. He've got a real temper on him.'

'Don't know Percy Shillabeer? Why, I've knowed him all my life. Went to school together, us did, played marbles and conkers and kicked a ball about down the fields. I don't say us was ever best friends, but I know him well enough. And he knows me.' His fingers touched to his cheek. 'Give him a black eye once, I did, over Mary Jane Ellacombe, and he darn near broke my nose. It wasn't even worth it, either – she went off with Jacob Prout's cousin that lived in Mary Tavy and now she's a bitter old shrew with never a good word to say about nothing.'

'You never told me about that,' Nancy remarked, picking up her work again. 'Surprising the things that come out years after, isn't it?' She looked up at her sons. 'Well, don't just stand there playing statues. Put the kettle on, Terry, and make some cocoa, and then you can both go to bed. Me and your father got some talking to do.'

Percy Shillabeer, however, had his own ideas and they did not include round-the-table discussions with Jack and Nancy Pettifer.

'Your mother and me have been talking it over,' he said to Patsy next morning when she came downstairs after a sleepless night. She glanced at her mother, wondering just how much say she had had in this discussion, recalling that she had heard the deep rumble of her father's voice late into the night, with few pauses for her mother's lighter tones. Ann looked back at her with red-rimmed eyes and Patsy's heart sank. Then she remembered that she had never expected this to be easy, and squared her shoulders as she waited for her father's next pronouncement.

'Way we see it,' he said, 'you got two choices. Us can't stop you having this baby but us can say what's to be done next.' He took a long drink of tea from the big enamel mug he always used at breakfast time. 'Now, I hope you know I'm not an unreasonable man, but 'tis my duty to look after you. You don't seem to think you need looking after, but to my mind what you and that Pettifer boy have done proves you do. So this is what me and your mother have decided.' He gave her a heavy scowl. 'Well sit down, maid. No need to stand there like a stuffed dummy.'

Slowly, keeping her eyes on her father's face, Patsy lowered herself on to a kitchen chair. She had already been sick twice and still felt queasy. She wished she could go back to bed, pull the covers over her head and shut out the sound of her father's voice.

'You've brought disgrace on this family,' Percy went on. 'Your mother and me, we've always been good God-fearing Christians, going to church twice on Sundays and able to hold our heads up in front of our neighbours. You've spoilt all that. You've broke the Ten Commandments. You've committed fornication and you've not honoured your father and mother, and all through your own sinful desires and selfishness. You'm not fit to be part of a decent family.'

Patsy listened in horror. Powerful as her longing to be with Terry might be, her father's influence had been with her all her life, and she had not realised how much his anger would affect her. She had never considered how his religion would colour his response; nor had she understood how that same religion, instilled into her since the moment she was baptised, would strike fear into her own heart.

'But the Lord says we must forgive,' he went on, booming as if he were in the Chapel pulpit where he had preached before going over to the Church of England. 'And that's what we'm willing to do. We've

236

talked and thought and prayed for you, for your eternal soul, and for ourselves.' He looked at his wife, who nodded faintly. 'And we'll forgive you, and we'll help you.' He paused, and Patsy's heart gave a little jump. She turned her eyes from her father to her mother, hope already beginning to blossom, but what she saw there made her shiver, and the hope shrivelled.

'Two choices, I said, and this is what they are. You can go away, like I said last night, to a place where they'll look after you and make you work until the babby's born, and then you can sign it over for adoption and come home and no more said about it. I'll not have you going out to work again, mind,' he added forcefully. 'You've shown you'm not to be trusted out of this house, so this is where you'll stop until we find a man who's willing to take you on. A *decent* man this time – that's if there is such a man ready to take on soiled goods. Not that we'll put it about. There's not to be a word said about it, you understand? Your mother and me want to be able to hold up our heads same as us always have.'

There was a long silence. Then Patsy said, a quiver in her voice, 'You said there were two choices.'

'You want to know the other one?' He glanced at his wife, whose reddened eyes brimmed with more tears. 'Right then, and remember you asked for it.' His eyes fixed on her face. 'You can get married.' Patsy drew in a sharp breath and opened her mouth. 'You can get married,' he repeated, raising his voice. 'You can have what you want. But if you do' – and now he was speaking slowly, as if each word needed to be fully understood – 'if you do, you'm no daughter of mine. Nor your mother's. You don't have no brothers, nor no sisters, and you never come near this house again.'

Chapter Thirty-One

Arthur Culliford was sentenced to one month in prison. He was taken to Exeter, and Maggie, who had attended the court hearing with Basil Harvey, came home in tears of despair.

'It's the workhouse for us,' she repeated over and over again as he drove through the lanes. 'They'll take the kiddies away and I'll never see them again. We'd be better off dead.'

'Maggie!' Basil exclaimed, shocked. 'You mustn't say such things. People are never better off dead.'

'You can say that because you've never been in this position,' she told him bitterly. 'But what about all them starving children in India? What about the poor buggers who come home from the first war with no arms or legs and got turned out to beg on the streets? There was a bloke in Plymouth used to sell matches, blind he was, give his sight for his country and that was what he come to. I bet he thought he'd be better off dead than stood there in rain, sleet and snow trying to sell a few matches that nobody wanted.'

Basil could find no easy answer. After a moment he said, 'I think we have more compassion these days, Maggie. And you and your children are not going to end up in the workhouse. I promise you that.'

'Promises!' she echoed scornfully. 'Like piecrust, my old granny used to say, easy broken. Shall I tell you what I got in the house? Four shillings and sixpence, that's what I got in my purse, and half a loaf of bread and a packet of marge in the cupboard, along with a box of cornflakes, a couple of tins of baked beans and a bag of potatoes. That ain't going to keep my lot going till breakfast time tomorrow, let alone till the end of the month. Us can't live on air.'

'There'll be more than that soon,' he told her, feeling on surer ground. 'Grace said she would spend the morning making a beef casserole for your dinner. We'll call in at the vicarage on the way home and collect it and it will be nice and hot when you get home. And Dottie's promised a cottage pie for tomorrow, and I wouldn't be surprised if she doesn't manage a few buns as well. You're not going to starve.'

Maggie stared at him. 'They'm doing that for us? That's proper kind, that is.'

'Yes, and it's not going to stop there. The whole village is going to rally round and help while you're in this trouble. Once Arthur comes home again, it will be his responsibility to look after you, of course, but none of this is your fault and certainly not the children's, and nobody wants to see you suffer.'

Maggie sniffed and rubbed her sleeve across her nose. 'I can't hardly believe it. Nobody's ever had a good word to say for us. Why should they want to help us now?'

Basil knew very well why. The whole village – most of them, any-way – felt rather guilty about the way they'd treated Maggie and her family in the past. It was true that the cottage always looked unkempt, the garden a mess of rubbish and Maggie herself down at heel, her housekeeping as slovenly as her appearance. It was true that, until Stella had taken an interest in Shirley Culliford, the children had been dismissed as turning out no better than their parents. It was certainly true that Arthur was feckless and irresponsible, never able to hold down a job for more than a few weeks and preferring to roam the fields and woods poaching for his family. But there was no real harm in any of them, Basil had argued. Arthur had never committed any worse crimes and he might not even have poached so many pheasants if he hadn't had a family to feed. Whatever his and Maggie's shortcomings, they loved their children. And who could know what those years as a POW had done to him?

Besides, what was poaching, when all was said and done? No more than an age-old way for poverty-stricken country-dwellers to feed their families on birds and rabbits bred to grace the tables of the already overfed rich. Men had done this for centuries, sometimes risking their lives and always risking their freedom for a rabbit or two for their own pot and often their neighbour's. They had been thrown into jail, transported thousands of miles, even hanged. And always there was a family left to starve without them. Thrown, as Maggie was dreading, on the mercy of the parish, to end in the workhouse; or turned out of the village altogether, to wander begging from place to place, hounded like mangy animals.

Well, things were better these days – but how much better? Glancing sideways at Maggie's tear-stained face as he drove, Basil wasn't sure. Arthur would not be hanged or transported, but to hear a young mother, expecting another new baby as she spoke, say that the family would be better off dead was a shock. Maggie was right – you could starve to death within a month, and a family could not live on air.

'The village wants to help you because you're part of Burracombe,' he said gently, answering both her question and the one that had formed in his own mind. 'And perhaps this is a chance for us to help you get back on your feet again. Some of the other mothers have said they'll help look after the little ones. And Dottie and Mabel Purdy and one or two others are willing to come and help you sort out the cottage – that's if you'll let them. I've got some distemper in my shed, left from when we did the kitchen at the vicarage. Jacob Prout says he wouldn't mind slapping it on your walls one day when he's got nothing else to do. That's if you don't mind, of course.'

Maggie shook her head speechlessly as more tears poured down her face. At last she gasped and choked out, 'Mind? Why should I mind? I'll think I've died and gone to heaven.'

Basil felt close to tears himself. Heaven indeed. To some people that was a place of palaces, of white light and blue skies and glittering thrones, with winged angels in flowing garments playing on golden harps. That wasn't his own idea of heaven. But neither was it a tiny, tumbledown cottage filled with children, scrubbed clean by willing villagers and with freshly distempered walls.

And yet ... Wasn't Maggie's vision much closer to the heaven he believed in – a modest home surrounded by friendship and compassion, by an expression of the love for his fellow men that he had been taught mattered more than anything else on earth?

It was Dottie who had brought all this about. Still haunted by the memory of Arthur Culliford's return to the village after the war, and struck afresh by Maggie's despair, she had gone straight round to the vicarage and poured the whole story out to Basil Harvey. Grace was there too and had immediately offered to make a casserole. 'They can eat it whenever they're ready and it will be full of vegetables – more vegetables than meat, to tell the truth, but it will be so good for the little ones. And Maggie. She needs to keep her strength up.'

'I'll talk to Bernie Nethercott too,' Dottie had said. 'Us could get some of the regulars at the Bell to help. It only needs a bit here and there to keep that poor soul and her little'ns going. Folk could bring a few bits and pieces to put in a box by the door. I reckon us could surprise Arthur when he comes home. Might even put a bit of heart into him to get some proper work.'

'You might have a problem persuading some of them,' Basil warned her. 'Arthur Culliford's not the most popular man in the village.'

'I'll persuade them,' Dottie said darkly. 'You don't argue with the woman that serves your beer!'

She was right. As Basil had said, some of the regulars looked down their noses a bit when she broached the subject that evening, but when they saw the look on Dottie's face and heard the tone in her voice as she took their orders, they soon backed down. And Maggie wasn't a bad girl, after all. Had a rough deal in life, what with that father of hers and then having to get married to Arthur Culliford when she was only just out of school, that was their opinion.

It wasn't, however, only Maggie who concerned Basil and his wife. When Basil returned to the vicarage after taking Maggie home from court, they discussed the matter of Billy Culliford and the stealing.

'You can't call that poor little boy a thief,' Grace said. 'He's only four! How can a child that young be branded as a criminal?'

'I agree,' Basil said. 'But even at four he must learn the difference between right and wrong. He might not actually *understand* that it's wrong to take other people's property, but he can certainly be taught to *know* it.'

'Children do understand that they own certain things, like toys, and feel upset when someone takes them away,' Grace agreed. 'But Billy obviously also realises that things are very wrong at home and that money is a part of it. He may have felt that helping his mother was more important than the dinner money, when the school seems to have plenty of it. Seeing those pennies piled up as Miss Kemp and Miss Watkins counted them must have been just too much for him.'

'The question is,' Basil said, 'what is to be done about it?'

Miss Kemp was asking the same question. Since the dinner money had disappeared, nothing else appeared to have been taken and she was beginning to hope that the little spate of pilfering had ended. Perhaps Billy was too shaken by what had happened to his father to risk it. She thought of him lying awake at night and wondering in terror if he too would go to prison, and her heart ached for him.

'We must be very careful with the Culliford children,' she said to Miss Watkins. 'The girls are old enough to understand what's happened, and that's bad enough, but heaven knows what poor Billy is imagining. The poor child looks terrified out of his wits.'

'I dare say it will do them all good,' the younger woman said. 'Teach them what happens to thieves. From what I've heard about their father, he's got away with it for far too long.'

'That's not for us to judge,' Miss Kemp said with some asperity. 'Our concern is the welfare of the children in our care. Nothing that's happened is their fault and they're clearly upset and frightened. I don't want them picked on or teased about this, so please keep an eye on the children in your class, and on all of them when you're on playground duty. And give Billy and his sister a little extra attention – *kindly* attention.' She added the last two words almost without meaning to, realising as she spoke them that the implication was that she didn't think her assistant would necessarily be kind. Horrified, she wondered if this were really true. If so, didn't she have a duty to speak to the governors again? How could she knowingly work with a person she thought might be less than kind?

Miss Watkins's sharp eyes seemed to read her expression.

'I hope I know how to be kind to small children,' she said stiffly. 'I've never had any complaints before. My references were all very good, as I'm sure you know.'

'Yes, of course,' Miss Kemp said. 'But I don't think you've worked with the infant class before, have you? They do sometimes need an extra-gentle hand, especially when they're having difficulties at home.'

Miss Watkins made a peculiar little half-shrugging motion with one shoulder, which seemed to say that she thought she understood this as well as anyone, and turned to go. 'Unless there's anything else you wish to discuss?' she enquired with just the right amount of exaggerated politeness to fall short of insolence.

'No, there's nothing else,' Miss Kemp said with a sigh. 'You'd better go now, or you'll miss your bus.'

She watched the other teacher depart. It was now mid March and the lanes were brightened with small wild daffodils, with the hawthorn hedges showing a tinge of green above them. In another month it would be Easter and they were still no nearer to finding a permanent teacher. It looked as if she would have to work with Miss Watkins for another whole term.

She turned to tidy her desk and put on her own coat, and found a small face peering at her from the classroom door.

'Hullo, Janice,' she said in surprise. 'Why haven't you gone home yet? Your mother will be wondering where you are.' She looked more closely as the child limped into the room. 'Why, you've been crying! Whatever's the matter?'

'Please, miss,' Janice said in a wobbly voice, wiping her nose with her sleeve. 'I know I shouldn't have brought it, but I wanted to show my friend – I haven't ever had one before and it was so new and shiny – and I looked after it ever so carefully, I did really, but when I went to take it out of my pencil box, it was gone. And I don't know what my mum's going to say. She *told* me not to bring it to school.'

'What did she tell you not to bring?' Miss Kemp asked, her heart sinking. 'What was it, Janice?'

'Please, miss, it was my half-crown that I got for my birthday last week. My uncle in Plymouth gave it to me. I told Rosie Friend I'd got one and she wouldn't believe me, so I had to bring it. And then some of the others wanted to see it too. I hid it in my pencil box and now it's *gone*.' She burst into heartbroken sobs. 'And I was going to buy a baby dolly with it that I saw in Tavistock, and now I'll never have another one, never!'

She broke down completely, weeping until she was almost sodden, while Miss Kemp gazed at her with dismay. Half a crown. It was a lot of money for a small child to have, and the largest sum that had disappeared so far. She felt almost like breaking down herself and weeping along with the child.

Gathering herself together, she produced a handkerchief and bent to dry the child's woebegone face. 'Now stop crying, Janice. You'll make yourself ill. You probably haven't lost your half-crown at all. I expect you put it somewhere else and forgot. Let's have a look, shall we? Have you tried your coat pocket?'

'I've tried everywhere,' Janice said miserably, and after they had searched for a quarter of an hour, Miss Kemp was forced to admit that she had. But she would not give up yet.

'Go home now, it's getting late. We'll look again tomorrow and ask the other children if they've seen it. Do you want me to walk home with you?'

'Yes please.' The little girl sniffed, and her hand stole into the head teacher's.

They walked slowly along the village street, Miss Kemp matching her speed to Janice's lurching gait. As they walked, she found herself growing more and more angry with whoever was doing this. The pilfering that had gone on up to now was bad enough, but to steal from a child who had nearly died and been crippled by polio was despicable. She could scarcely believe that any child in the school would have done such a thing, let alone Billy Culliford, the youngest of all.

And yet ... if you were a child, she asked herself, living in what amounted to no more than a hovel, with never enough to eat, never any new clothes or toys, wouldn't you perhaps feel that someone like Janice Ruddicombe, crippled though she was, who came from one of the better houses in the village and never wanted for a new frock or a bag of sweets, had more than she needed? Might you not be tempted when you saw that bright, shiny half-crown?

And at only four years old, would you really think very much about Janice's condition? Billy probably barely understood why the little girl had to wear that big surgical boot. Children of that age tended just to accept things without question. And his own problems would have seemed very much worse to his young mind.

I'll have to talk to the whole school again tomorrow, she thought sadly. And I wouldn't be at all surprised if they feel they've had enough and turn on little Billy. It's like a poison, seeping through everything, and I'm not sure I know how to handle it.

Chapter Thirty-Two

Stella returned to Burracombe in style, travelling in the Napiers' silver Armstrong-Siddeley with the dark blue leather seats. Hilary drove and Felix sat beside her, so as to give Stella plenty of room in the back, where she reclined like a princess, wrapped in Hilary's fur coat and a cocoon of blankets.

'I feel like Queen Victoria going on a state visit. You'll have to watch out, Felix, or I shall demand this all the time.'

'I'll be happy to give it to you all the time,' he said as they drew up in front of the vicarage. 'I'm going to treat you like a piece of rare porcelain.'

'Goodness, I hope not! I just want to be a normal person again and able to run about like a two-year-old. Oh look, there's Basil! And Grace.'

The vicar and his wife were hurrying down the steps almost before the car had stopped. Basil pulled open the door and fussed about, wanting to help yet not knowing quite how, while Felix and Hilary eased Stella from her nest and stood her on the gravel drive.

'I can walk a bit,' Stella said, as they handed her a pair of crutches. 'But I still need quite a lot of help. If I can just lean on you, Felix ...'

Between them they got her indoors and into the big front room, which had been organised into a bed-sitting room, with a comfortable reclining chair in the window, a small table with two upright chairs in one corner, and a bed on the other side of the room. The bookshelves in the fireplace alcove had been cleared and furnished with some of Stella's own books and some new ones that she hadn't read. A wireless set stood on one shelf and the mantelpiece was covered with cards and pictures made by the children to welcome her back.

Hilary and Felix helped her in and eased her into the reclining chair. Then Hilary gave her a kiss and departed, saying that she needed to get home to her father.

'Oh, how lovely,' Stella exclaimed, resting back and reaching out to have the pictures brought to her. 'Look at these. The children must have spent hours working on them. How are they all getting on, Basil? I've missed them so much.'

'They've missed you too,' he told her, and his pink forehead creased a little. 'We all have.'

'But they're getting on better now with Miss Watkins? I thought Miss Kemp seemed a bit worried when she came to see me last week.'

'They're doing very well,' Basil assured her hastily, but Stella gave him a quizzical look.

'You don't sound as though you're telling the truth,' she said, and then covered her mouth with her hand. 'Oh, I'm sorry – I didn't mean you were lying!'

Basil smiled uneasily and Grace, coming in with a tray of tea and some of Dottie's shortbread, said, 'You might as well tell her, Basil. She's going to hear it from someone anyway.'

'Hear what?' Stella asked, alarmed. 'What's been happening?'

'It's nothing really – just a little boy wanting to help his mummy and going too far.' Basil explained about the pilfering. 'Everything points to it being Billy, although no direct accusation has been made yet – not by Miss Kemp or the governors, anyway. It's understandable – the Cullifords are going through a dreadful time and he obviously wants to help. But someone is going to have to talk to him and try to make him understand, and we'll have to see his mother as well.' Basil sighed. 'And we can't leave it too long.'

'Poor Billy,' Stella said feelingly. 'I wish I could help. I'd offer to speak to him myself, but I don't really know him. What do his sisters say?'

'We haven't talked to them about it. We've been trying to decide what's the best course of action.'

'You know,' Grace said thoughtfully, 'I wonder if in fact Stella might be just the right person to talk to him. The fact that she doesn't know him could be an advantage. She knows his sisters, after all. And he will certainly know of her – Miss Kemp says the children never stop talking about her. She says she feels quite sorry for Miss Watkins, having this paragon held up in front of her all the time.'

'I don't think she feels very sorry for her now,' Basil said. 'I get the impression that our Miss Kemp has developed a hearty dislike for her assistant.'

Stella listened in dismay. 'But that's awful. It was always such a happy school.'

'It was a happy school while you were there,' Grace corrected her sadly. 'The vital ingredient is missing, I'm afraid.'

'That's not entirely true,' Basil said. 'The atmosphere was just as good while you and Mrs Warren were helping out, despite the children being so anxious about Stella. Look how successful the nativity play was.'

'But what's going to happen?' Stella asked. 'You can't let Miss Watkins stay if she's making the children unhappy. And what about Billy?'

Felix, who had been sitting quietly in a chair he had drawn up as close to Stella as he could get, intervened.

'I can tell you one thing that's going to happen, my darling. You're going to stop worrying about it. I'm sorry to sound harsh, but the school really isn't your problem any more. You've left, and your main job is to get better and marry me.' He took her hand as she turned to him and began to protest. 'I mean it, sweetheart. There'll be many more problems in Burracombe school over the years, and you won't be able to take them all on your shoulders. It's just because you still feel close to the children that you're worrying now. But Miss Kemp and the governors are more than capable of dealing with it. They might wish you were still there, as I'm sure they do, but they know that you can't be, and they know they can find a solution – as they did before you ever came to Burracombe.'

Stella stared at him. Her eyes filled with tears.

'It's just because I love them all so much,' she whispered. 'I can't bear to think of them being unhappy.'

'I know, and neither can I. I know the children well too, you know, from all the times I used to go in and chat to them. But we've both got to step back. Our lives are going to be over the river, in Little Burracombe, and we'll learn to know and love the people there just as much. It doesn't mean we have to abandon all those we love here – just that we need to stand back a little.'

247

Stella looked up at Basil and Grace. They glanced at each other and nodded.

'Felix is right,' Basil said quietly. 'You have to let them go and look forward to your own new life.'

'I suppose so,' Stella said sadly. 'But it's terribly hard. I don't think I ever realised just how hard it would be.'

Hilary had left home early that morning, before Patsy had arrived. She'd eaten her breakfast in the kitchen and then laid the breakfast room table for her father, leaving Mrs Curnow to cook his bacon and eggs when he came down later.

The new housekeeper had settled in well. She was built rather like a cottage loaf, Hilary thought, with a dumpy round body and a round head. Her hair was very thin and wispy and kept short, which added to the impression, but her plain face was always cheerful and smiling, and she had a forthright way of expressing herself which both Hilary and her father enjoyed.

'You just leave the Colonel to me,' she'd told Hilary. 'I'll make sure he eats his breakfast properly. And it won't matter if you're not home for lunch. I'll poach that fish you brought home from Tavi yesterday, with a bit of mashed potato and some nice greens. Ernest Crocker brought in some purple sprouting yesterday, that'll put a bit of colour on the plate. I always think white fish and mashed potato need some colour to make them look appetising. Did I see some oranges in the bowl on the sideboard yesterday?'

'Yes, I bought half a dozen. They're nice at this time of year.'

'I'll take one of they then, if 'tis all right with you, Miss Hilary. A few slices simmered and then laid on the side of the plate will make all the difference, seeing as there's no tomatoes to be had yet. And that nice lemon sponge pudding for afters, that separates out to make a cream under the sponge. Mrs Kellaway told me he likes that.'

'He does, but I'll be home by lunchtime. I'm only going to fetch Stella Simmons from the hospital and take her to the vicarage. She's being discharged at ten o'clock.' The doorbell rang and Hilary glanced at the kitchen clock. 'That must be Felix. I'd better be making tracks.'

She departed in a flurry of scarves, boots and gloves, taking extra rugs and her fur coat for Stella. Mrs Curnow, left alone, took Hilary's plates to the sink and then looked up as Patsy came in.

'Why, whatever be the matter with you, maid? You look as if you've been crying your eyes out.'

'I have.' Patsy dumped her bag on the table and began to unwind the long knitted scarf from around her neck. The March wind was cold this morning and her nose was red as well as her eyes. Fresh tears welled up in them now, as she took off her coat and gloves. 'Oh Mrs Curnow,' she sobbed. 'I hardly know what to do. It's awful!'

'My dear soul, what in the world's happened?' The housekeeper bustled over and took Patsy's coat and scarf, then pushed her gently into a chair. 'You sit there, maid, and I'll bring you a cup of tea. There's still some in the pot. Just you have your cry out and then you can tell me all about it.'

Patsy sobbed while the tea was poured and brought to her. The housekeeper sat down opposite her and reached across to take her hand. Her round face was full of concern.

'What is it, maid? Is somebody ill?'

Patsy shook her head. 'No.' She snuffled, pulled a hanky from her sleeve and blew her nose. 'No, it's nothing like that. It's ... it's ...' She began to cry again.

Mrs Curnow reached across to pat her shoulder. 'Now come on, maid, it can't be that bad. If nobody's ill, there's nothing that can't be put right, that's what I always say. Now, dry your tears and drink some of that tea before it goes cold, and tell me what 'tis, and let's see if us can't find a way to make it better.'

'It'll never be better,' Patsy wept, but she wiped her face as she'd been told and blew her nose again and drank some of the tea. Then she looked up at the housekeeper with a face so filled with woe that the little woman began to think it must be something really serious. But you could never tell with these young girls; they took everything so hard and could never believe it wasn't the end of the world when little things went wrong.

'Is it that boy you're fond of?' she asked gently. She hadn't met Terry, but she'd heard about the romance and the lengths Patsy's father had gone to to make sure the two didn't meet.

'Yes.' Patsy sniffed, glad not to have to introduce the subject herself. 'We want to get married.' Her voice rose to a wail and more tears began to flow.

'I see. And your father won't let you, is that it? Well, you are very young to be thinking that way. In a year or two—'

'No! You don't understand. He says we *can* get married, but . . . but . . .' And now she put her head down on the table, on her folded arms, and began to cry again in earnest.

Mrs Curnow stared at her, bemused. She waited a while, but before she could speak again, the kitchen door opened and Colonel Napier put his head round it.

'Oh, so you *are* here. I thought the place had been deserted. Am I to get any breakfast this—' He broke off. 'What on earth's the matter with young Patsy?'

'Trouble at home, I think, sir. I'm sorry about your breakfast – I'll bring in your coffee now, and some milk for your cornflakes. You just sit there, Patsy, I'll be back in two shakes of a duck's tail.'

The Colonel withdrew hastily and Mrs Curnow bustled about, filling the coffee pot and pouring milk into a jug. She put them on a tray and carried it out, returning a moment or two later to start frying bacon and eggs. She glanced over her shoulder at Patsy.

'Have you had any breakfast, maid?'

Patsy shook her head. 'I can't eat in the mornings. It makes me feel sick.'

Mrs Curnow laid down the slice she was using to turn the bacon. 'Ah . . .' Their eyes met and Patsy nodded. 'Well, no wonder you'm upset. You've been a silly girl, haven't you? But you'm not the first, not by a long chalk.'

'I suppose that's what people will think,' Patsy said miserably. 'But it wasn't like that, not really. I mean – it wasn't an accident.' She gave Mrs Curnow a swift glance. 'I wanted it,' she whispered. 'I wanted it so that Father would let us get married. I *made* Terry do it.'

There was a long silence. Mrs Curnow laid a slice of bread in the pan and fried it in the bacon fat. Then she put it all on to a warm plate and set another tray.

'I'll take this in to the Colonel, and when I come back you can tell me all about it. I can see there's more to this than meets the eye. And find yourself a dry biscuit to go with that tea. I always found that helped with morning sickness.'

Patsy did as she was told. The small activity helped her to overcome her weeping, and when Mrs Curnow returned, she was back at the table, nibbling a cream cracker and gazing hopelessly into her tea.

'Now then,' the housekeeper said briskly, sitting down again. 'Tell me what's the matter. Not an accident, is that right?'

Hilary was as appalled as Mrs Curnow when she came home after delivering Stella and Felix to the vicarage, and heard the story.

'I've got to choose between Terry and my baby, and my whole family. And if I don't get married, I've got to give my baby away!'

'But that's dreadful. It's inhuman.'

'It's Father,' Patsy said drearily. 'He says it's his right. I'm supposed to do as he says until I'm twenty-one, and even after that if I stop at home. But I *won't*,' she added, raising swollen but defiant eyes to their faces. 'I won't stop there. He won't be able to make me, once I'm of age.'

'But you're talking about leaving now,' Hilary said gently. 'If you get married, you'll be your husband's responsibility. Your father will give up all those rights when he gives you away. That's what's meant by that part of the wedding service.'

Patsy looked at her, and she added rather hastily, 'Not that that's a good reason for getting married. You've got to be very sure that this is what you want, Patsy.'

'I am sure. We're both sure.'

'Even when you know what your father's conditions are?'

With another flash of defiance, Patsy said, 'He's a bully. He makes Mother do everything he says, and she's miserable all the time. He'll do it to me too. I'll never get away.'

'And if you do, how will you feel knowing you'll never see your mother again?'

'I reckon we'll see each other,' Patsy said. 'He can't be in the house all the time. He's got a farm to see to. And she goes to Tavistock to the market every Friday.' But her voice trembled and Hilary knew that she wasn't nearly as sure as she pretended.

What a cruel thing to do, she thought. Whatever Patsy chooses, she's going to lose people very important to her – either Terry and their baby, or her entire family. It doesn't sound as if her father will be much loss, but what about her mother and the other children? And what would all this do to poor Mrs Shillabeer? What kind of a life did she have already with that dreadful man?

'You really must see Terry,' she said. 'You can't just let your father decide everything. And where are you going to live? What do his parents think about it?'

'I don't know. He was going to tell them.' With a hopeless shrug she said, 'I don't even know if he's done that.'

Hilary made up her mind. 'I said I couldn't interfere, but now I think you need help. Take some time off – the rest of the day if you need it. Go down to the Pettifers' cottage and ask when Terry will be there. You have to talk about all this. Does he come home for his dinner?'

'Sometimes. If he's working in the village. But not if he's in Tavi, because he and Bob don't have time.'

'Well, if he's not coming home today, ask if he can come tomorrow, and you can see him then. Is that tea cold? I'll make some more.'

'I'll do that,' Mrs Curnow said, but Hilary shook her head.

'You've got your own work to do. But you can make this poor child some toast – she looks as if she hasn't eaten for a week. And maybe a boiled egg. Do you think you could manage that, Patsy?'

The girl nodded and whispered a thank-you. Hilary busied herself making a fresh pot of tea and Mrs Curnow put an egg in a saucepan and began to slice bread. A silence settled on the kitchen, and Patsy began to feel as if the situation were not quite as hopeless as it had seemed. If she could only see Terry and talk to him, know that everything was all right ... Because whatever she said, she knew that there was a kernel of dread, deep and hard and icy, in the base of her stomach.

Suppose Terry did take fright and refuse to marry her? What in the world would she do then?

Chapter Thirty-Three

'**O**f course I'm going to marry you,' Terry said. He and Bob were doing some work at Joyce Warren's house, so they had both come home for their dinner. Patsy had approached the house nervously, unsure as to whether Nancy Pettifer even knew what had happened, but when the door opened, the motherly woman took one look at her and enveloped her in a huge warm hug.

'You poor little maid. Come you in here. Terry's told me and his father all about what's happened, and I won't say you haven't both been very foolish, but what's done is done and now we got to look forward. Now, Terry will be here soon for his dinner. You'll stop and have some with us, won't you?'

'Thank you, Mrs Pettifer, but I don't want to put you to any trouble ...'

'Trouble? Why, 'tis no trouble at all. We'm having Cokers.' She meant the sausages made by Bert Foster, the butcher, which everyone said were the size of Alf Coker's huge fingers. 'There's plenty to go round and plenty of mash to go with them. You sit down over there. Here they come now,' she added as voices were heard at the door. 'Terry! Visitor for you.'

Terry came in somewhat anxiously, half afraid that it might be Percy Shillabeer who had come to lay about him with a horsewhip. He saw Patsy and strode across the room at once, pulling her into his arms and holding her close as she wept against his chest. In a few moments she had sobbed out the whole story, and his anxiety turned to fury at her father's harshness.

'We'll get married the first minute we can,' he declared, settling her into a chair and wiping her eyes gently with his own handkerchief.

253

'That's if it's what you want, Patsy. I don't like the idea of you being separated from your family like this – specially your mother.'

'I've got to choose, though, haven't I?' she said. 'It's them, or it's you and our baby.' Tears overflowed again. 'I never thought it would be like this,' she whispered.

'Neither did I. I knew there'd be trouble, of course ... but to say you either got to give it up or never see your mother again, nor the rest of the family ... Nobody ever thought he'd do anything like that. I'd rather he horsewhipped me.' He looked at her seriously. 'You got to be really sure, Patsy. Once we'm wed, there'll be no going back.'

'I know. And I am sure.' She gripped his fingers with hers and looked at him steadily. 'I'm never going to give you up, Terry, and I'm never going to give up our baby neither. I know it's going to be hard and I'm really sorry for Mother, but she's had me for seventeen years after all. I'd have had to leave home sometime.'

'But not like this,' he said.

'No, not like this. But he was always going to make trouble. He'd got in mind that I'd always be there, to help look after the little ones and then look after him and Mother as they got old. I don't reckon I'd ever have got away.'

Nancy Pettifer, who had kept Bob out in the scullery while they were talking, put her head round the door.

'Dinner's ready now. I'll bring it in. Give me a hand with the plates, Bob, and Terry, you put a chair to the table for Patsy. And I want to see all that finished,' she told Patsy as she set a plate of sausage and mash in front of her. 'You'm looking too thin and pale for my liking. Eat up now, and we'll talk after.'

'Terry and me'll have to be going back to Mrs Warren's by one o'clock,' Bob said, tucking into his dinner. 'You know what she's like for timekeeping.'

'That's all right. We'll have time for a cup of tea before you go. Come on, maid, eat up. Feel a bit sick in the mornings, do you?'

Patsy nodded. 'I can't face anything until about eleven o'clock.'

'Well, you must eat well the rest of the day, then.' Nancy looked at her younger son. 'You're going to have to take care of this maid. Having a baby is no picnic, as you'm about to find out.'

Terry glanced uncomfortably at Patsy and she gave him a smile. ''Tis all right, Terry. As long as we can be together, it will all be worth it.'

Nancy looked at them both, feeling a surge of pity. They'm just children theirselves, she thought, with no idea what life is really like or what it might hold for them. Poor little tackers. Well, we must do whatever we can to help them, because it seems certain that Percy Shillabeer don't mean to, and that wife of his is a poor beaten-down little body who never learned to stand up to him and never will now. It's a sad business all round, and all because the stupid man couldn't see the sense of letting his daughter grow up in her own time.

By the time Terry went back to work, it was all settled. He and his parents would go over that evening to see Percy Shillabeer and arrange the wedding. Someone would also have to go to see Felix at the vicarage to make sure of a date, for Nancy and her husband were determined it should be a church wedding. 'You won't be the first bride to stand at the altar in the family way, and there's plenty of seven-month babies born. People might click their tongues and watch your shape for a bit, but you'll be decently wed long before there's anything to see. And if your father's of the same mind when he's settled down a bit and got used to the idea, then you and Terry will live here with us. It just means a bit of shaking up, that's all. Bob's room is the biggest, so he can move into Terry's for you.'

'Here!' Bob protested. 'What about asking me about that?'

His mother gave him a look. 'You'm over twenty-one and ought to be thinking of settling down with some nice young maid yourself. But while you're here, you have whichever room me and your father sees fit to allow you, and be thankful for it!' She smiled to show that she didn't really mean such harshness and he grinned back to show that he understood.

'I've always wanted his room anyway,' he remarked. 'Got a better view out of his window than I have.'

'That's settled then.' Nancy looked kindly at Patsy. 'But the hope is that your father might come round a bit, especially after the babby's born. It usually does pan out that way, you know. Babbies bring their love with them and there's not many men can turn their backs on their own grandchild.'

Patsy smiled back gratefully but said nothing. She thought that Nancy Pettifer was judging her father by her own standards, which were, she reflected, a deal kinder than his. Few people other than his own family really understood just how strict and unbending Percy Shillabeer could be. And if any man could turn his back on his own grandchild, he was that man.

'The week beginning April the twelfth,' Felix said thoughtfully. 'That's Holy Week.'

'Do that mean they can't get wed then?' Percy Shillabeer asked, looking ready to start another argument.

'No, not at all, but the church will be very bare that week. A purple altar cloth, no flowers, no bells, and we couldn't have it on Thursday or Good Friday because of services. You might prefer to wait. Easter Monday's a very popular day for weddings. I do have one that day, over in Burracombe, but I could easily do another, and there will be lots of flowers still in the church from Easter Day—'

'Don't matter about flowers,' Percy broke in. 'Us won't be having any of that nonsense, whatever day it is.' His expression made it clear that this wedding was to be no celebration, to his mind at any rate. 'Us'll have it on the Wednesday.'

'It is a working day,' Felix pointed out. 'You might find that not many people are able to come.'

'Nobody's being invited. You don't seem to understand, Vicar. Our Patsy's been a sinful young woman and her got to get married because of it. Us won't be asking a lot of nosy folk to see our shame.'

Felix looked at him. Then he said, 'I'd like a word with Patsy alone, if you don't mind, Mr Shillabeer.'

'I do mind. I'm her father and got responsibility for her until I gives it up to the young fool she shares her sinful ways with.'

'And I am the vicar you're asking to conduct this wedding,' Felix said firmly. 'I have responsibilities too. Both legal and Christian ones. Now, I must ask you to leave us for a few minutes.' He held Percy's eye until the farmer, glowering, got to his feet and lumbered out of the room. Then he turned to Patsy. 'Now, my dear, don't be frightened. I want to help you. Tell me, do you really want to get married to Terry Pettifer? If you don't, all you have to do is say so. Nobody can force you.'

'But I do,' Patsy said. 'That's why we did this. It wasn't Terry's fault,' she added. 'It was my idea. He didn't want to do it at first, said he'd never ask a respectable girl like me, but I talked him round in the end.'

Felix felt his eyebrows go up. He looked at her again, thinking that he'd always taken her for a little mouse of a girl, coming obediently to church with her family every Sunday, helping her mother with the smaller children ... Another thought struck him. 'And Terry wants to marry you?' he asked, still wondering if this was going to be his first experience of a shotgun wedding.

'Of course he does!'

'Well I'll have to talk to him as well,' Felix pointed out. 'It's my duty to see you both. I'll need to see the two of you together, with nobody else present.'

Patsy nodded. 'You'll tell Father that?'

'I will.' Felix went to the door. 'You can come back in now, Mr Shillabeer. I was just reminding Patsy that I need to see the bride and groom together, on their own, before I can agree to call the banns. You'll arrange that, will you?'

Percy Shillabeer scowled. 'I don't want them two on their own before they'm decently wed.'

Felix repressed the desire to comment that not much harm could come of it now, nor was anything untoward likely to happen in his study, and merely said, 'Let me know when to expect them. It will have to be quite soon.' He hesitated, then said carefully, 'You don't think it would be wise to wait a little – just to be sure? Marriage is too big a commitment to rush into.'

Patsy looked panic-stricken, but her father said harshly, 'Us don't have time to wait, Vicar. I'm sorry if it turns out bad for them, but they should have thought of that before they did what they did. I'll not have folks talking, and I'll not have any grandchild of mine born out of wedlock.'

Felix nodded and saw them out. He watched them walk down the drive, stiff-backed and at least a yard apart, and sighed before closing the door and going back inside.

What a horrible man, he thought. What a bully. No thought whatsoever of his daughter, still barely more than a child herself. No consideration for his wife and her feelings about the matter. And certainly no Christian charity towards the innocent child.

Every Sunday morning and again every Sunday evening, Percy Shillabeer led his family into the church and sat them in the pew they always occupied. During each chant and hymn his voice boomed out above every other member of the congregation. His head nodded agreement at the words of the psalms and gospels, especially those of St Paul, which talked of sinfulness and punishment. He listened with attention to the sermons and occasionally praised Felix as he gave his hand a firm shake at the door on his way out. 'That was better, Vicar. Put the fear of God into them. 'Tis the only way.'

Felix had always felt dismayed rather than flattered by these words, and wondered what he had said to make Shillabeer misunderstand him so completely. His God was not one to be feared; rather to be loved and feel loved by. To respect, to obey, but never to fear.

Percy Shillabeer's God was clearly very different. But then, Felix thought as he walked slowly and sadly back into his study and marked the Wednesday of Holy Week in his diary, Percy Shillabeer was no more a true Christian than were the Romans who had sentenced Jesus to death, nearly two thousand years before Patsy Shillabeer was to be married.

Chapter Thirty-Four

'It's nearly all organised,' Maddy told her sister, her face alight. 'Easter Monday. We can even have a proper honeymoon – Stephen's got a fortnight's leave. We're going to Bridge End to see Ruth and Dan Hodges and their new baby, and then we'll go to Portsmouth to see the Budds in April Grove, and then we'll have a week all to ourselves somewhere. We thought perhaps the New Forest, or the Isle of Wight, but we haven't decided yet. We might just tour around in the car.'

'It sounds perfect,' Stella said. 'And it will be lovely for you to see the Budds again. Uncle Frank is going to give me away, you know, since he and Auntie Jess looked after us so much during the war. Have you decided who you're going to ask to give you away?'

'Yes, the Archdeacon is going to do it. I thought of asking Mr Harvey, but since I've been at West Lyme they've been so good to me I feel they're almost my family. And Felix and Mr Harvey can do the service together, so he won't be left out.'

'And Fenella will be here too?'

'Oh yes, Jacques is better now so they're both coming. She wouldn't miss it for anything. Especially as we haven't seen much of each other over the past two or three years, since she married Jacques and settled in France. It will be so good to see her again.' Maddy hugged herself with glee. 'It's all going to be gorgeous!'

Stella smiled. It was good to see her sister back to her old bubbly self. She had been so low-spirited after Sammy's death, withdrawing into herself and unable to overcome her grief, and then, just as she was getting better, Stella's accident had upset her all over again. Now, having finally realised that she loved Stephen Napier after all, she had put all her unhappiness behind her and seemed ready to dance through life as she had always done. Stella felt unexpected tears in her eyes and brushed them away.

Maddy looked at her with dismay. 'What is it, darling? Have I upset you? I'm being a selfish pig again, prattling on about my own wedding when you've got to wait for yours. I'm sorry! Let's talk about something else.'

'You haven't upset me at all,' Stella said, laughing. 'I'm just so pleased to see you happy. The last few months have been hard for you, I know.'

'Not as hard as they were for you. It was dreadful seeing you lying there so white and with all those bandages and plasters on, and tubes sticking out of you.' Maddy shuddered, and Stella took her hand.

'Don't think about it. It's all over now and I'm going to get quite better. Tell me more about the wedding. What about bridesmaids?'

'Well, you, of course. And Linnet. She's going to come with Auntie Jess and Uncle Frank, since Ruth won't be able to come, having just had the baby. That's all. I'm not having a whole flock, like you are.'

Stella laughed. 'You know I didn't really want that many. But it's nice to be able to please so many people.' She hesitated. 'It's not long until Easter. You do know I may not be able to walk much by then.'

'Yes you will. It'll give you something to aim for,' Maddy said hard-heartedly. 'But if you can't, Felix can push you in your wheelchair. He may have to wear a pink frock, of course,' she added thoughtfully, and they both dissolved into giggles.

'What's all this mirth?' Felix enquired, coming into the room just then, but at the sight of him both girls immediately imagined him in a pink bridesmaid's dress and went off into fresh howls of laughter. He sighed, rolled his eyes and sat down in a chair on the other side of Stella, fondling her hand and waiting patiently for the storm to subside.

'You never laugh at me like that,' he said plaintively, and for a moment there seemed to be a danger that one or both of them would suffer a seizure. Eventually Stella calmed herself, wiped her eyes and explained that actually they were laughing at him, but when she tried to explain why, the paroxysm gripped them both again and eventually they gave up.

'We'll never be able to tell you,' Maddy gasped at last. 'Because every time we do, we'll think of you in ... ohhh!'

'For goodness' sake!' Felix exclaimed, losing patience. 'I think I'll go out and come back in again when you've both grown up a bit. And I may be gone some time! Don't you realise there's nothing more irritating than people who can't control their giggles and can't tell you the joke? It never turns out to be that funny anyway,' he added grumpily.

They stopped at once, and Stella gazed at him anxiously. 'Felix, I'm sorry. We weren't really laughing at you, and you're right, it wasn't all that funny anyway.' She turned her hand over in his and twined their fingers together. 'Is something the matter? You look rather upset.'

'Well yes, I am in a way. It's nothing to do with *us*,' he added hastily. 'It's just a wedding I've been asked to do.'

The two girls looked at him. 'You've been asked to do a wedding, and you're upset?' Maddy probed delicately.

'It does sound odd, doesn't it?' he agreed. 'And I can't really say much about it, although I suppose everyone will know eventually. It's Patsy Shillabeer and Terry Pettifer, and it's going to be a few days before yours, Maddy.'

'Well, I know Terry slightly,' Maddy said, wrinkling her brow. 'He's Bob Pettifer's younger brother, isn't he? Bob was a couple of years below me at school. But I don't know Patsy.'

'She lives in Little Burracombe – that's why I'm doing the wedding. She and her father came to see me this morning.'

'But surely they're very young?' Stella asked. 'If Bob's two years younger than Maddy, he can't be much more than twenty-one, so how old's Terry? And isn't Patsy the girl who's working at the Barton now? Hilary told me about her – she's only seventeen or eighteen.'

'Yes, that's right,' Felix said, and closed his lips.

The sisters glanced at him and then at each other. The story seemed plain enough, and as Felix said, everyone would know eventually why Patsy and Terry were getting married so quickly. But why should it make Felix look so disturbed?

However, they knew he didn't mean to say any more and it would be wrong to press him. Maddy suspected that he might tell Stella more when they were alone, but even if he did, Stella wouldn't repeat it. She felt a small pang of jealousy at the thought, but then scolded herself. After all, hadn't Stephen told her things that she would never repeat to anyone else, even her sister? It was the right and natural way of things.

'So tell me what you've been talking about,' Felix invited. 'That's if you can, without falling about like hysterical schoolgirls. Weddings, I should imagine.'

'Of course,' Stella said with dignity. 'What else is there to talk about? But mostly we've been talking about Maddy's. Basil's going to start calling the banns on Sunday, you know.'

'*If anyone knows just cause or impediment ...*' Maddy said dreamily. 'I love those words. I've always wanted to know what would happen if someone said they did. What would you do, Felix?'

'Don't ask,' he said, shuddering. 'Stop the wedding and investigate, I suppose. It must be every vicar's worst nightmare.'

'Oh no,' Stella said. 'The worst nightmare would be having the corpse push the lid off its coffin in the middle of the funeral service. I can't imagine anything worse than that.'

'I can,' Maddy said demurely. 'I can imagine a vicar in a frilly pink cassock, carrying a bridesmaid's bouquet.' And then both girls were off once more and Felix rose to his feet.

'I told you I'd go if you started that again, and I shall. Actually, I only popped in for a minute anyway.' He bent to kiss Stella and then ruffled Maddy's hair. 'It's good to see you laughing again, darling,' he said to his fiancée. 'And take no notice of me. Giggle all you like. It's the most beautiful sound I've ever heard.'

He went out, and they looked at each other again.

'You don't think he was really upset, do you?' Maddy asked a little doubtfully.

'Not about us, no. But he does seem a bit perturbed about this other wedding he's been asked to do. It's as if he thinks neither of them really wants it – and maybe they don't. It must be very difficult for him to perform the service if he thinks that's the case.'

Maddy nodded. Then her brow cleared and she said, 'Well, there's nothing we can do about it, and we may be quite wrong anyway. Let's go back to talking about bridesmaids – and not male ones either! What colour would you like to wear? I want you and Linnet both the same, so you can choose.'

'Your father won't pay out for a wedding dress,' Ann Shillabeer said sadly, looking at her daughter's meagre wardrobe. 'Not that you could wear white anyway. Oh *Patsy* ...'

'I'm sorry, Mum,' Patsy said, tears starting down her cheeks again. She seemed to have done nothing but cry this past week, since confessing to her parents. 'I never wanted it to be like this.'

'*Couldn't* you have waited?' Ann asked yet again. It was her constant refrain, even though she knew the answer. She looked at her daughter beseechingly. 'It wouldn't have been so long.'

'It would. Four years. That's nearly a quarter of what I've lived already. And you know what it would have been like, Mother. Never allowed out, never having any fun, treated like a skivvy ... I'd never have got away.'

'That's not why you'm doing it, though, is it? You know what they say – out of the frying pan, into the fire. And you've only knowed Terry a few weeks, all told. You don't want to ruin your life.'

'I won't be. I'd be ruining it if I did what *he* wants.' She could barely say the word 'Father'. 'I'd lose Terry *and* our baby. I wouldn't have anything left.'

Ann Shillabeer sighed. She looked through the few clothes hanging in the cupboard and brought out a pink frock that Patsy had worn to a Sunday school party a couple of Christmases ago. It hadn't been new, it was a hand-me-down from one of her cousins, but it was the palest colour there. 'This is pretty. You looked ever so nice in it that time.'

'It won't fit me now. I've grown since then. What about my green one?'

'You can't wear green! That's an unlucky colour.'

'It'll have to be my blue one, then.' Patsy took it out. It was plain and uninteresting and she wore it every Sunday to go to church, but it was the only one left. 'What does it matter anyway? Nobody's going to be there to see it.'

'But it's your *wedding*,' Ann said. 'I do want you to look nice on your wedding day.'

Patsy dropped the dress on her bed. 'And what sort of a wedding will it be, with just you and him and Terry and his mum and dad? And Bob, to be best man and stand witness. Who's going to care what I look like?'

'Witness!' Ann exclaimed, forgetting about the dress. 'You'll need another witness. Two, you got to have, one each, to make sure it's all legal.'

'Can't you do it?'

'I don't know. I think it has to be someone else.'

'I'll ask Miss Hilary, then,' Patsy decided. 'She's been good to me, even though I've only been working there a few months. And if she can't do it, I'll ask Mrs Curnow.'

Ann Shillabeer looked doubtful. Neither of these would be to her husband's taste, but Patsy had to have some say in her own wedding. And when the young vicar had talked to the couple the other day, he'd made it very clear that he wouldn't marry them at all if he felt that there was any suspicion of either of them being forced. If Hilary Napier were to be there, he would know for certain it was above board.

'What are you going to wear, anyway?' Patsy enquired, and her mother sighed.

'My grey costume that I wear to church, I suppose. I don't have nothing else. But I could put some flowers on my hat – that would be all right, wouldn't it, even though there's none in the church? And maybe we could make a bit of a headdress for you as well, just to dress you up. And I know your father said there was to be no flowers, but you can carry a bunch of primroses, can't you? He can't stop you doing that, not once you'm in the church.'

Patsy looked at her mother, hearing the catch in her voice and realising suddenly what this meant to her. Her eldest daughter's wedding – she must have looked forward to this day for years, seeing herself in a new costume with a new hat, making a cake weeks beforehand and inviting people back to the house for a ham tea and sherry. Instead it was to be a hole-and-corner affair, with no guests, no flowers, no celebration at all; and worst of all, Ann was forbidden ever to see her daughter again, or the grandchild Patsy was going to produce. In fact, *any* of the grandchildren she produced.

'I'm sorry, Mum,' she said again. 'I never thought it would be this bad. I never thought he'd stop me seeing you.' She moved towards her mother and they hugged, their tears mingling. 'We *will* see each other again, won't we? He can't stop us for ever, surely? Even *he* couldn't stop us seeing each other for ever?'

Chapter Thirty-Five

M aggie Culliford felt as though she had been stopped from seeing Arthur for ever.

'How can I go all the way to Barnstaple to visit him?' she asked Dottie, accepting yet another batch of home-made buns. 'I know there's a bus, but it takes hours, and I can't sit that long, not in my condition. And I can't take the little'ns. They don't think of that when they sends husbands and fathers to jail.'

Dottie thought that the husbands and fathers might have thought of it before they went breaking the law, but she didn't say so. Maggie had enough to put up with without people coming over all righteous about it. She was pleased with the way the village had rallied round – the boxes in the pub and village shop were never empty for long before someone dropped in a tin of baked beans or a pound of sausages, and Bob Pettifer and his cousin Roy had made a good job of doing up Maggie's kitchen, once Dottie and Mrs Purdy had given it a thorough scrub – but Maggie still had all the children to cope with, as well as getting bigger and heavier by the day herself.

'How's your Billy now?' Dottie asked. 'Got over that spot of trouble at the school, has he?'

Maggie stared at her. 'All round the village now, is it? Folk saying my Billy's a thief, taking after his father and all the rest of it? Oh, you needn't trouble to deny it – I know what Burracombe's like. It was bound to happen, with all the kiddies going home and telling their mothers and fathers about it. Well, you can tell 'em from me, it's all lies. My Billy never took a thing. How can you be a thief when you'm only four?'

'He may not have realised it was wrong—' Dottie began, but Maggie broke in harshly, her voice full of indignation.

'He never *done* it, I tell you! Where are the toys he's meant to have took, for a start? Wouldn't he have brought them home and played with them? He's never brought a thing here that wasn't his. And what about the money? Wouldn't he have wanted to buy sweets or summat? I tell you, my Billy never took so much as a farthing, and as long as he keeps being blamed, there's someone in that school who really is a thief and getting away with it!' Her voice cracked and she turned away, tears brimming from her eyes, and thrust the bag of buns back at Dottie. 'Here, take your charity and don't bother coming back with more. And we'll manage without they boxes you got in the pub and Jessie's shop, too. I'm not being beholden to folk who call my little tacker a thief.'

'Oh, don't do that,' Dottie exclaimed in distress. 'I never meant no harm. 'Tis only what us've heard and you know we all want to help. Look, why don't you have another word with Miss Kemp? She's a fair woman, she wouldn't see a child accused if he's innocent.'

'She's coming round here tonight,' Maggie said sullenly. 'To tell me I can't send Billy to school no more, I dare say. All right, Dottie, I'll take the buns and thank you for them, and for the work those two boys are doing here too. Don't think I don't appreciate it. But it do stick in my craw that folk are helping with one hand and calling my Billy a thief behind my back.'

'I can see that,' Dottie said. 'But don't throw people's kindness back in their faces – think of your little ones.' She paused, then said quietly, 'Folk don't like to see one of theirselves in trouble, Maggie, and you and Arthur are as much a part of Burracombe as any of the rest of us.'

Maggie's eyes filled with tears again. 'You're a good woman, Dottie. Friend by name and friend by nature, I reckon.'

'Well, when you got a name like mine, you got a duty to live up to it,' Dottie said briskly. 'Now, why don't you let me take your two little ones for a walk while you have a bit of a rest? We'll go down to the ford. It's a lovely spring afternoon; they can splash about in the water and we'll take a couple of the buns for a picnic.'

She set off with Freddie in the pushchair and Jeanie trotting alongside. Maggie watched them go and then went back into her cottage, quiet for almost the first time she could remember. The floors had been scrubbed clean and the place smelled of the fresh distemper that Bob and Roy had slapped on the walls. It was a sunny yellow, and to Maggie the whole place looked like a palace. She sank into the sagging armchair and leaned back, her hands resting on the swell of her stomach. In two minutes, she was fast asleep.

'I'm really concerned about the Cullifords,' Hilary said as she sat with her father and Travis in the estate office next morning, having their weekly review. Gilbert had insisted that he was able to start taking part in estate matters again, and Charles Latimer had agreed, provided it did not stretch to what he called 'gallivanting'.

'I should hope walking along the passageway to my own office doesn't count as gallivanting,' Gilbert had retorted and so for the past two weeks he had been back in his chair behind the big desk, making it quite clear that he was firmly in charge once more.

'The Cullifords?' he said now. 'He's in Barnstaple prison, isn't he? How long's he got to go?'

'Two weeks, I think. Poor Maggie's finding it very hard, with all those children and another on the way, not to mention this trouble at the school.'

'That's the little boy stealing, isn't it?' Travis said. 'Sounds as if it's a case of like father, like son.'

Hilary flushed angrily. 'That's just the trouble with people round here! You've no proof – I don't think there *is* any proof, it's all just circumstantial – but you're ready to condemn a four-year-old child out of hand, just because of what his father's done! Not that Arthur Culliford has ever done any stealing that I know of.'

'Hey, hold on,' protested Travia, holding up his hands. 'No need to fly at me like that.'

'I think there's every need,' she retorted. 'Perhaps while we're talking proverbs, we might also remember another one – give a dog a bad name. Or better still, innocent until proven guilty.'

There was a short silence, Hilary, breathing rather quickly, looked down at the papers in front of her. After a difficult start, she and Travis had learned to work together and grown to respect and like one another, but there was still the occasional spat between them and she knew he had never had much time for Arthur Culliford.

'Sorry,' he said at last. 'I was out of order. I apologise.'

Hilary looked up and gave him a brief smile. Gilbert, who had said nothing during the interchange, cleared his throat and said, 'Is anything being done to help the family?'

'Yes, Father,' she said, glad to have something more positive to talk about. 'The village has really turned up trumps. Dottie Friend and Mabel Purdy scrubbed out the entire cottage and threw away no end of rubbish, and Bob and Roy Pettifer got together and distempered every room. There's still a lot needs doing – the roof needs attention and the window frames are rotting away, Dottie says – but it's a world better than it was. Quite frankly, I don't think the place is fit to live in, but where else can they go? Maggie's terrified of the workhouse.'

'No question of that.' Gilbert thought for a minute or two and then slanted a look at them from under his bushy eyebrows. 'Nowhere else on the estate, is there?'

'Not at present, no.'

'You're not suggesting giving them an estate cottage?' Travis said. He glanced quickly at Hilary. 'Look, I'm not without sympathy for the family – it probably isn't the wife's fault Culliford is what he is, and it certainly isn't the children's – but he's not the estate's responsibility, and if we house him without giving him a proper job—'

'Then give him one,' Gilbert said tersely. 'I seem to remember telling you before to give him work wherever you could, simply to prevent this sort of thing happening.'

'I did give him work, cutting hedges, tree-felling, that kind of thing, but in my opinion you'll never prevent a man like that from poaching. It's in his blood.'

'Precisely. It's been in his blood for generations. And you know why that is as well as I do – because if men like Arthur Culliford hadn't looked after their families in their own way, they'd have starved.' Gilbert glowered at his estate manager. 'We live with all sorts in a village, but I'll not see any of them starve or suffer as it seems to me this family is suffering. You can say they shouldn't have so many children, you can say what you like, but they do and they have, and it's not for us to judge. They may come to some good yet.' He paused, then added more quietly, 'You may not know this, but Arthur Culliford had an uncle who served under me during the First World War. He was a ne'er-do-well at home, but in the army he was a hero. He died saving another man under fire. Should have had a medal, but all he got was a mention in dispatches. And Arthur himself was taken prisoner at Dunkirk and a POW for the rest of the war. That was no picnic, believe me.' He paused again, and when Hilary, who had been watching him with some alarm, began to speak, he waved a hand to silence her. 'What I'm saying is, you never know what's in a man until he's up against it, and when Edward Culliford laid down his life I told myself I'd never see any of that family in want.'

There was a long silence. Gilbert was breathing heavily, and Hilary moved closer to her father and patted his hand. She had never heard this story before and realised that this explained the leniency he had always shown towards Arthur Culliford.

'Now then,' Gilbert said at last. 'This is what I intend to do. Who owns that cottage? I forget.'

'I think it's part of the Staddacombe estate,' Hilary said. 'From the days when they owned several places in Burracombe.'

'But that's who took Culliford to court, isn't it?' Travis exclaimed. 'No wonder that poor woman's so afraid of being evicted.'

'They wouldn't dare,' Gilbert said contemptuously. 'It would bring it to everyone's notice what a wreck the place is. Well, we'll buy it from them. Shouldn't cost more than two or three hundred, the state it's in.'

'Buy it?' Hilary echoed.

'Yes, buy it. That'll give them some security. We'll have the roof attended to and any other structural repairs that need doing, and charge them a reasonable rent, something they can afford. And I want Culliford in regular work.' His eyes turned to Travis.

'That's all very well. I can give him the work, but is he going to turn up for it? Is he going to make a decent fist of it? The man's not reliable, we all know that.'

'He will be, when Maggie's finished with him,' Hilary said. 'She's had a terrible time lately – a bad fright over his going to prison and what it could mean to them all, and the worry over her little boy. Whether or not he's guilty,' she added. 'And she's pregnant as well. It's no wonder she's collapsing under the strain of it all. If Dottie Friend hadn't whipped the rest of the village into shape, I dread to think what might have happened.'

The two men were silent for a moment. Then Travis said, 'Very well. I can employ Arthur as an odd-job man, filling in wherever he's needed. I just hope he doesn't let you both down.'

'I don't see why he should. He's a countryman through and through, and knows the fields and woods like the back of his hand.'

'You can say that again,' Travis remarked wryly and they all laughed. The tension was broken and they went on to speak of other matters.

In the afternoon, Hilary went to see Maggie to tell her the good news. She could see the difference in the cottage the minute she stepped through the door, and she could smell it too. The aroma of ingrained dirt that had pervaded the air on her previous visit had been replaced by the scents of carbolic, fresh paint and distemper. She drew in a deep breath and smiled at the tired woman.

'The cottage looks lovely, Maggie. And you're looking better too. Is that a new maternity smock?'

'Val Tozer as was passed it on to me, and a couple of others too. I must say, it's nice to be able to wear something pretty instead of one of my Arthur's old shirts – not that he've got much use for 'em now, where he is,' she added bitterly.

'It's very hard for you,' Hilary said gently. 'But my father and I want to help.' She told Maggie of her father's plan and the woman's eyes opened wide. 'It does mean Arthur working regular hours, though,' she warned.

'He's never been one for that,' Maggie said. 'Always liked to come and go as he pleases. But I'll make sure he changes his ways from now on.' She wiped tears from her eyes. 'Look at me. Always piping my eye over one thing or another. But you know, folk have been so good to me just lately. I don't understand why. Up till now, nobody's had a good word to say for any of us.'

'I think we all feel sorry about that,' Hilary said quietly. 'And nobody blames you for what Arthur did. But once he's had his punishment and come home, we'll put it behind us, and if you really think he can turn over a new leaf . . .'

'He'll turn it over all right. I'm not going through this again. Mind you, he's a good man in his way, and never done nothing to hurt nobody. A few rabbits, or a pheasant here and there – what's that to anyone else, even your father? *You* ain't going to starve through it, are you?'

'No, we're not,' Hilary admitted, feeling rather ashamed. 'All the same, we do make it possible for pheasants and rabbits to thrive—'

'For rich folk to eat, that can afford whatever meat they like, now 'tis off ration.' Maggie shook her head. 'It don't make sense to folk like

270

Arthur and me. He only did what he thought was best for his family.' She gave Hilary an odd look, half shame, half defiance. 'I know what they says about us – having kiddies us can't afford. But us only has what the good Lord sends, and if He reckons there ought to be more Cullifords in the world, who are we to argue? And they'm all born out of love. Every one of them.'

'I'm sure they are,' Hilary murmured, embarrassed. 'Even so—'

'But I'll tell you one thing,' Maggie continued, ignoring her. 'Something I made up me own mind to do.' She looked at Hilary. 'I'm going to make a bargain with him. I'll give up the fags if he'll give up the booze. Save us a hatful of money too, that will.'

'That sounds a marvellous idea. It'll be good for both of you – I've heard that doctors are saying now that tobacco's really quite harmful. It might be a good idea for you to give up anyway.'

'Oh, I shall. I just won't tell him that till he agrees!' Maggie laughed, and Hilary laughed with her. And I wonder how long it is since these cottage walls have heard that, she wondered – two women, laughing together.

She gathered up her coat and bag and stood up. 'I'll let you know how things go,' she promised, and glanced around the room. 'Once the legal side of it's over, someone will come and see what needs to be done. The roof's quite bad in some places, I noticed.'

'Lets in rain, it do, right over where our Billy's bed was. And in the scullery as well.'

'Haven't you told your landlord? He should have seen to that.'

Maggie made a face. 'And have the rent put up? No, 'tis better to put a bucket on the floor and say nothing.'

'Well, it won't be like that when the cottage belongs to us,' Hilary said firmly. 'No, don't get up, Maggie. You keep the weight off your feet while you've got the chance. I'll come in and see you again soon.'

She walked up the village street thinking about the poverty she had just witnessed. Clean and fresh though the cottage was now, there were ugly patches where damp seeped incessantly through the walls, and the furnishings were threadbare and stained. It was overcrowded too, with all the children Arthur and Maggie had produced, and she hoped, despite Maggie's words, that the baby on its way now would be the last one. But the Cullifords were only in their thirties and obviously capable of producing many more. They needed advice, Hilary thought, but would they take it? There was only so much interfering you could do in anyone's life.

And then, as always, her thoughts turned to David and the situation they were in. We'll never have any children, she thought sadly, and she felt just then that she would rather live in poverty with the man she loved than in the finest mansion in the land, with money to spare. Because through all Maggie's misery and despair, there shone one fact: that she and Arthur Culliford loved each other.

Chapter Thirty-Six

'**E**ngaged? Our Jackie's *engaged*?'
　　'That's what she says here.' Alice slapped the letter down on the kitchen table and covered her face with both hands. 'I knew this would happen! I *knew* it! Let that girl out of our sight for five minutes and she loses all sense and reason. I *told* you, Ted!'

'Did you?' Ted searched his memory. 'I thought it was me that was set against her going.'

'Well, we both were. But her's so headstrong there weren't much us could do about it. And your Joe was no help, giving her ideas ...' Alice shook her head. 'What be us going to do about it, Ted?'

'What *can* us do? She's the other side of the Atlantic. And Joe promised to keep an eye on her.'

'That shows just how much *his* promises are worth.' Alice picked up the letter again. 'It's this man she've been seeing. Older than her, and been married once already.'

'Widowed, though. You can't blame him for that,' put in Minnie, who had been sitting in her chair listening.

'I can blame him for chasing after a young girl of nineteen,' Alice retorted. 'Especially one he knows is thousands of miles away from home and family. Oh, I *knew* this would happen,' she repeated despairingly. 'I knew it!'

Ted took the letter and read it himself. 'She don't seem to think there's a thing wrong with it,' he said unbelievingly.

'Well maybe there isn't,' Minnie said. 'She's only engaged, after all.'

'*Only engaged?*' Alice repeated. 'Mother, what are you saying? *You* know what being engaged means – it means you've promised to *marry* someone. Our Jackie's promised to marry some man in America, some man who's older than her, been married already and what us don't know a thing about. And you say *only*!'

'I can understand you being upset,' Minnie acknowledged. 'But you know as well as I do, plenty of young girls get engaged and then never marry the chap. I did myself.'

Ted gazed at his mother. '*You* did? I never knew that.'

''Well you wouldn't, would you? I never told you, and your dad never talked about it. It was a young chap from Okehampton, come down to Goosey Fair one year. He used to come on the train to see me, at weekends. It only lasted a few months. The point is, being engaged isn't the same as being married. You can break it off.'

'And the other point is that not everyone does break it off,' Alice retorted. 'The next thing we know she could be married and us not even set eyes on the chap. You'll have to do something, Ted. What are the laws about getting married in America?'

'I don't know, do I? And what can I do anyway?'

'You can get on to that brother of yours, that's what you can do. He must know about these things. It could be like that place in Scotland – Gretna Green – where girls can get married at sixteen without their parents' say-so. *Sixteen!* Have you ever heard anything so ridiculous? And you don't want her ending up like Patsy Shillabeer and *having* to get married, do you?'

'Of course I don't. But from what I hear, Patsy Shillabeer done that deliberate.'

'And if you ask me, I don't blame her,' said Brian, making them all jump. 'Anything to get away from that old father of hers. What's all this about, anyway?'

'Brian! Where did you spring from? I never heard you come in.' Alice waved the letter at him. 'It's our Jackie. Engaged to that American, or so she says. And pleased as a dog with two tails about it, too! Never a thought about how we might feel.'

'Well that's our Jackie, isn't it? I told you you'd spoiled her.' He read the letter and grinned. 'Attagirl, Jacqueline!'

'Brian! Your father and me are really worried.'

'Well there's not much point in that now, is there?' He gave the letter back. 'I told you before, you ought to have thought of this before you let her go.' He went out of the kitchen and up the stairs, whistling.

'Let her go!' Alice repeated. 'It wasn't so much a case of *letting* her go as being *forced* to. Oh Ted ...' She gazed at the letter again, as if it might magically say something different this time. 'You've got to talk to Joe.'

'You're a better hand with a letter than I am. You write to him.'

'I will. I just wish letters didn't take so *long*.'

'The sooner you write it, the sooner it'll get there,' Minnie said. 'Or you could send a – what do they call it? A cable. Like Joe sent when they got there first.'

'That's the same as a telegram, isn't it? I suppose us could.' Alice chewed her lip. 'You can't say much, though, can you?'

'You can say enough to get Joe to send one back. Tell him – I dunno – tell him he's got to write and tell us what he knows about this man. Tell him Jackie's not to get married without you and Ted being sure 'tis all right.'

'Tell him she's not to get married at all,' Ted broke in. 'She's still under twenty-one, surely we got some say in it.'

'That's just what I was saying,' Alice said. 'We might not, now she's in America. The laws are probably different there.'

'But she's still English!'

'Oh I don't know.' Alice rested her head on her hands again. 'We need to ask someone who knows. Mr Harvey – or maybe Mr Warren, he's a lawyer. We could ask him.'

'The best person to ask is Joe,' Minnie said firmly. 'Send him a cable and ask what's what. And don't get in too much of a tizzy over it, flower. Her's only engaged so far, and us don't know that they're planning a wedding next week, as it were. You know what they say – there's many a slip 'twixt cup and lip.'

Alice nodded, only partly reassured. She found a pencil and an old envelope in the drawer of the big table.

'What shall I write? How many words are you allowed?'

'As many as you can afford, I reckon,' Ted said. 'But just bear in mind that this might be only the first. There'll be a deal of sorting out to do before us have finished with this, I reckon.'

'And there's something else you might think about too,' Minnie observed, and they both looked at her. 'There's been plenty of young women got married at nineteen or twenty and had a good life with the man they love. And plenty got married to a man a few years older, too.

After all, we don't *know* how old this chap is – only that he've been married and lost his wife. He could still be only three or four years older than Jackie. I don't reckon Joe would have let her walk out with him if there'd been anything wrong.'

'Dottie,' Alice said. 'We'll ask Dottie. It was her told us about him in the first place. She's met him, she'll know. I'll go down straight away and ask her.'

'Do the cable first,' Ted said firmly. 'We need to send that, whatever Dottie has to say. Ask Joe to write and tell us everything he knows. 'Tis no use relying on Jackie, her's up on cloud nine with it all, and she'll only tell us what she wants us to know anyway. It's Joe we need to ask.'

Alice nodded and began to jot down words. With the three of them making suggestions, the cable was finally completed and she copied it on to a fresh sheet of paper.

'I'll take it down to the post office to send. That'll be better than doing it on our phone. You never know if they get it right when you'm talking to someone you can't see.' She got up and put on her coat. 'And I'll pop in to see our Val as well, and then go and talk to Dottie. We'll get this sorted out, one way or another.'

She went out, leaving Ted and his mother together.

'What d'you reckon?' he asked at last.

The old woman pursed her lips thoughtfully. Then she said, ''Tis in the lap of the gods, Ted, that's what I think. There's precious little anyone can do when a young couple decide to go their own way. You just got to trust Jackie's own judgement. Her's a sensible maid, at bottom, and you've done your best in bringing her up. And when you let her go to America, you knew you must be letting her go in other ways too. I don't reckon you can do anything about this but hope for the best.'

'That's what I think too,' he said. 'I was against her going and I don't like the way it seems to have turned out, but us got to trust her. And Joe's got daughters of his own. He's not going to let her go astray.'

They nodded at each other in reassurance. But deep down, both were still aware of a nagging worry. Jackie was, as everyone said, headstrong – and she was still only nineteen. They might hope for the best, but each of them also feared the worst.

*

Easter was well on its way before the Tozers received a reply from Joe. Meanwhile, Ted had been prepared for more discussions about Brian's plans for the farm. He and Tom had talked about them between themselves and, in a more guarded way, with other farmers they met at Tavistock cattle market. Some agreed with Brian that farming must move with the times and that machinery was the way to go; others, mostly older ones, pursed their lips and shook their heads.

'I know we all got tractors these days,' said one, speaking more or less for them all. 'Had 'em since before the war. They'm getting on for twenty years old now and still working all right. But there's still jobs horses can do better.'

'And what about when the machinery goes wrong?' another chipped in. 'Got to have it repaired then, and what's that going to cost?'

'And what does it cost to replace a Shire horse?' Brian asked when these conversations were reported to him as the three men finished milking. 'What happens if it's ill or breaks a leg? It can't work then. As for machinery going wrong, that's the whole point of what I'm saying. It'll want someone handy to do the repairs, same as a village garage mending your car. That's where we'd come in.'

'You mean we'd be a repair shop?' Tom asked. 'When you talked about it first off, you were all for making the stuff in the first place.'

'We could do both,' Brian said, but Tom shook his head.

'You're talking daft. How could us do all that? Build farm machinery *and* repair it? That means two separate operations. A lot of buildings – more than we've got with our barns – and a lot of men.'

'And a lot of money put into it in the first place,' added Ted. 'It's pie in the sky, Brian.'

'I'm not talking about doing it all at once. Build up gradually – repairs to start with—'

'Repair machinery folk haven't got yet?' Tom asked. 'I would have thought manufacture would come first.'

'They'll get their machinery from other places.'

'So by the time we've got going, we'll be in competition with people that have already cornered the market.' Tom shook his head. 'Dad's right. It's pie in the sky. And there's something you seem to have forgotten altogether.'

'What's that?' Brian asked sullenly.

'We're *farmers*. We're not interested in running a factory. We might not even be allowed to set up something like that in Burracombe. There's laws about such things, you know. Or maybe you don't, having been away for all these years.'

Brian threw him a look of scorn. 'It's no use talking to you. I can understand Dad being a bit behind the times, but I thought you might have more gumption. You're as set in your ways as an old man. I can see Burracombe's going to be the same in fifty years as it is now.'

'And none the worse for that,' Ted said tersely. 'You'd better make your mind up to it, Brian. Tom and me know how we want to run this farm, and it's not your way. Setting aside the old barn to make something small – shearing tools or the like, that we understand – would be one thing. What you'm suggesting is something else and it's not what we want. We've talked it inside out, and your mother too, and we'm all in agreement, and that's an end to it.'

Brian stared at him. 'And what about Margret and me?'

'What about you?'

'Don't we have no say in our own future?'

'You got all the say you want,' Ted said quietly. 'But it don't seem to me your future's here. Look, you went into the army the same as Tom did, but you stayed there. You made it your job. Tom did his bit in the war and then he come home and made the farm his job. And that was the way we expected it to stay. I don't see as how you can march in now and decide the farm owes you a living, and I don't see how you can start upsetting the apple cart by wanting to change the way we work and live.'

'So you're saying there's no place for us here?' Brian was reddening with anger.

'I'm saying you ought to have been able to see that for yourself.'

'But if we did what I'm talking about – if we expanded – there'd be plenty for all of us. You're sitting on a gold mine, and you don't even realise it!'

'I'm sitting on a farm. I'll farm it until I die, and then it'll be passed on.'

'Passed on to who? There's four of us, in case you've forgotten.'

'Passed on to whoever I think's fit to take it on!' Ted bellowed, losing patience at last. 'Those of you who chose to go different ways will get whatever I think you deserve, but the farm stays a farm and whoever's farming it at that time – it might be young Robin, or even baby Heather for all any of us knows – is the one who'll carry the responsibility. And that's what it is – a responsibility. Not a parcel of money to be shared out and spent four different ways. And it's *my* responsibility to see that it's looked after when I'm gone. That's all I'm saying about it. I don't want to hear another word.'

He marched out of the milking parlour, leaving the two brothers together. Tom turned away and began to swill the floor with water. Brian watched him for a moment, then said, 'I can see I'm no use here. I might as well bugger off.'

'Might as well,' Tom agreed, and began to whistle through his teeth. Brian bunched his fists and for a moment looked as if he might lash out. Then he turned abruptly and walked to the door.

'All right, daddy's boy. You got your way. It don't matter to me anyway – I've been putting out feelers and I've got another chap interested in what I want to do. Peggy and me are going up north, Gloucester way. You'll be buying machinery from me before you've finished, and don't expect a discount!'

Chapter Thirty-Seven

By the time the Easter holidays began, preparations for both Maddy and Patsy's weddings were complete, although the brides were looking forward to them with very different feelings. For Maddy, the world seemed filled with sunlight, each spring flower blooming especially for her and the birds singing as if in celebration. She left the Archdeacon's employment in West Lyme, having trained another girl in his ways, and returned to Dottie's cottage to dance through the days in a haze of happiness, her mind filled with white lace and bouquets. She spent most of her time at the vicarage, where Stella was still in residence, the two sisters aware that their time together now was short and they must make the most of it.

'It's only for a year,' Maddy said, to console herself as much as Stella. 'Or maybe two. And it's lucky that Stephen's posting has been delayed so that we can both be at your wedding too. I was afraid I'd have to stay behind and be a grass widow for six weeks!'

'And I'll be so busy learning to be a vicar's wife that you'll be back almost before I know you've gone,' Stella said. 'We'll both be old married women by then. We might even have children.'

'They'll be cousins,' Maddy said. 'Doesn't that seem funny. Oh Stella, I'm so happy now! To think I might have sent Stephen away and lost him for ever. I very nearly agreed to marry Russ Tozer, you know.'

'Really? When was that?'

'After your accident, when you were so ill. He was so good to me – all the Tozers were, but Russ took special trouble. He told me he fell in love with me the moment he first saw me,' she added in a low voice.

'Oh Maddy. The poor man. I mean' – she added hastily – 'not

because he fell in love with you, but because you didn't fall in love with him. Was he very upset?'

'I think he was, because for a while I did think . . . But he understood too. He knew I was still getting over Sammy. People do sometimes fall in love after something like that, and then realise it's not the right person. Russ saw that it was Stephen after all, and stepped back. He's a very generous man,' she added thoughtfully. 'I think if I had married him, I would have had a happy life. Just . . . not quite as happy as I'm going to be with Stephen.'

'Like Dottie and Joe,' Stella agreed. 'Joe had a happy life with Eleanor, but I think he still believes there would have been something extra with Dottie. She told me about it one day, when I first came to the vicarage. He asked her again to marry him when he was here, you know, but she wouldn't. She said she was too much part of Burracombe to move away now. All she'd agree to do was go for her holiday.'

'Poor Joe,' Maddy said. 'And poor Dottie, to have missed all those years of happiness. And children, too. I often used to wonder why she never had any. She was such a lovely mother to me.'

Patsy's feelings were very different.

'Only a few days now,' her mother said. 'Are you really sure, my dear? You don't have to go through with it if you don't want to.'

'And what'll happen to me then?' Patsy asked. 'Sent off to a mother-and-baby home miles away with nobody I know around me, and the baby taken away as soon as he'm born, and never know who his mother was. Anyway, I've told you a hundred times, Terry and me love each other and we want to get married. If Father had let us see each other properly, this would never have happened.'

Ann Shillabeer sighed. 'But you'll be losing me and all your family. And I'll be losing you. Don't you think I'll feel the same? You were my baby once.'

'But I'm not now,' Patsy said. 'And you've had me all these years. I'm grown up now, old enough to get married, and I reckon Terry will make me a good husband. Better than *he's* been to you.' She still could not bring herself to mention her father by name. 'Anyway, you won't be losing me. You might not see me much, but I'll be over here to visit you whenever I reckon it's safe. You'll still be my mum.'

Ann brushed away tears. 'And Nancy Pettifer don't mind you moving in there?'

'No, she says she's looking forward to hearing the patter of tiny feet around the house. I told her, it'll be a while before that happens! And Bob says he'll move out of his room so me and Terry can have it. They're giving us a double bed for a wedding present,' she added, blushing.

'I wanted to talk to you about that,' Ann said. She went to the kitchen dresser and pulled open a drawer, taking out a brown envelope. 'Your father says you're not to have anything from us, but I can't let you get married with nothing at all. So I want you to have this.' She handed the envelope to Patsy, who took it wonderingly and looked inside.

'Mother! There must be fifty pounds in here!'

'Just over. I've been saving it from the housekeeping.'

'It must have taken you years! You can't give us all this.'

'I don't see why not. It was meant for your wedding all along. It'll help to buy some of the things you'll need for the baby.'

'Oh *Mother*,' Patsy said, and hugged her. 'I *will* come and see you,' she promised. 'As often as I can. You're not losing me and you're not losing your grandchild. But I won't ever come when *he's* here. And I don't want my baby seeing him – ever. As far as I'm concerned, my baby will only have one grandfather, and that's Mr Pettifer!'

At the Cullifords' cottage, Arthur returned from prison to find his home transformed.

'Who done all this, then?' he demanded, standing in the middle of his living room.

'Half the village,' Maggie told him. 'Dottie Friend and Mabel Purdy scrubbed out, with a few of the others, and Bob and Roy Pettifer and Bob's friend Reg did most of the distempering. Like it, do you?'

'Like it? It's like living in the middle of a blooming sunflower! Who picked out yellow? Why couldn't it have been a nice blue, or green?'

'Because yellow's what the vicar had to spare after he'd had his kitchen done, and he let us have it for nothing, that's why. And nobody charged for their labour so 'twas all done free. And you didn't ought to look a gift horse in the mouth, Arthur. We got some good friends in this village, and never knew it till now.'

'Well they never showed it before.' But he looked round again and grinned. 'A real palace it is now, and you'm keeping it nice too, Maggie. And what's that I can smell?'

'Beef casserole,' she said. 'Dottie Friend's been showing me a few things to cook. All fresh, too, none of it out of tins. She's been real good to me. None of this would have happened without her.'

'Ah, Dottie's a good sort.' He looked around again, shaking his head in wonder. 'I'll drop in at her place and say thank you. I'm sorry if I was a bit offhand, Mag, but it took me by surprise, coming in here and seeing it all so different. And I hear I got to go and see the Squire tomorrow morning. What's that about, then? Going to give me a job, is he?' He laughed, to show what an incredible idea this was.

'More than that,' Maggie said mysteriously. She longed to tell him about the cottage but had been sworn to secrecy by Hilary. The Squire wanted to give him the news himself. 'And I'm coming too. We got to put on our best, same as on a Sunday. Dottie's coming to look after the little'ns.'

He looked at her properly for the first time. They'd hugged and kissed as soon as he had arrived, but since then he'd been more taken up with the transformation of his home.

'Reckon you'll make it? You look ready to pop to me. And where did you get that smock thing you'm wearing?'

'Val Ferris give it to me. I've got three – one to wear, one for spare and one in the wash. Made them herself, she said. I reckon I might learn a bit of needlework as well.'

'You'll never have time,' he said, and then, 'How's our Billy? Got over that spot of trouble at school, has he?'

Maggie sighed and sat down, suddenly dejected. 'I dunno, Arthur. I dunno what be going on there, and that's the honest truth. Miss Kemp come round here one night last week, said she thought he'd better not go back after the holidays. How am I meant to manage then, with four kiddies under five? I told her, he'll be going in September anyway, like it or not, so what's the difference, but all her said was he wasn't quite ready yet.'

'They'm still blaming him for all that stealing, then?'

'Of course they are. You only got to be called Culliford … though I got to say, she've been good enough to our Shirley and Betty. But that was more Miss Simmons's doing than hers.' She thought for a moment. 'Mind you, I don't think she *wants* to blame Billy, not really.

283

She just can't see who else it could have been.'

'I'll go up the school and see her,' he began pugnaciously, but Maggie put her hand on his arm.

'Don't do that, Arthur. It won't do no good. And I don't want to set that other woman against him any more than she is already. I reckon it's her that's half the trouble. None of the little'ns like her.'

'Well,' he said, 'if it happens again and our Billy gets the blame, I want proof. And I'll have a word with him myself. I don't want any of 'em ending up where I just been.' He looked at the clock on the sideboard. 'Since Dottie's took the little'ns out of the way for the afternoon, and it'll be a good half-hour before Billy and the girls come out of school, why don't you and me go upstairs and say hello properly? Or d'you reckon you'm too big for a cuddle now?'

Maggie laughed. 'That sounds like something you'd say to one of the boys! As if I'd ever be too big for a cuddle ...'

Chapter Thirty-Eight

O n the last day of term, with all the clearing-up to be done, Miss Watkins telephoned Miss Kemp from Tavistock to say she had fallen off her bike and broken a bone in her wrist.

'I've sprained my ankle too, and got bruises all over me. The doctor won't hear of me coming to school.'

'Oh dear,' Miss Kemp said in dismay. 'What a nuisance for you. I hope you're not in too much pain.'

'Well I'm bound to be, aren't I?' came the ungracious reply. 'But the worst of it is I can't collect the things I wanted to take away for the holidays. I'll have to come one day next week, when I can find someone to bring me.'

'There's no need to do that,' Miss Kemp said, thinking that the worst of it was actually the fact that she would have to clear both classrooms on her own. 'I'll bring them over to Tavistock for you. I'm coming in on Sunday morning anyway. There's not all that much, is there? Mostly things in your desk, I should think.'

'I can't ask you to do that. I'll come and collect them myself. You can open up the school for me, I suppose.'

'Well, yes, but—'

'I'll let you know when I'm coming,' Miss Watkins said as the pips began to sound to signify that she had had her money's worth in the telephone kiosk, and she hung up.

'It's really rather a nuisance,' Miss Kemp said later to Basil when he called in to wish all the children a happy Easter and remind them of the service on Easter Day. 'I'm planning to go away on Monday to stay with a friend in Penzance, and I won't be back until Thursday, so I'll have to ask someone else to come and open up specially. I'd far rather have taken her things over to her. There can't be much – just personal things that she keeps at school. I don't know why she was so insistent on collecting them herself.'

'Well why don't you do that anyway?' he suggested. 'It'll be a fait accompli then. You've got a key to her desk, haven't you?'

Miss Kemp hesitated. 'I don't like to use it without her permission.'

'It's only a school desk,' he said. 'There can't be anything valuable in there, and we won't look at anything private. After all, I'm here as a witness that you don't steal anything!'

'Don't joke,' Miss Kemp said. 'Stealing is a very sore point here! Well, I suppose it makes sense.' She opened her own desk and took out a bunch of keys. 'Come along, then.'

Together they went into the infants' classroom, where the teacher's desk stood on a low platform at the front. It was, as Miss Kemp had expected, firmly locked, and after a moment's hesitation, she fitted her key into the hole and turned it. She lifted the lid and they looked inside.

There was an initial gasp from them both, and then a long silence.

'Well,' Basil said at last, 'that solves the mystery, doesn't it? And now we know why Miss Watkins was so insistent that she come to collect her things herself.'

'Except,' Miss Kemp said quietly, 'that they are *not* her things ...'

'They were all there,' Basil told the hastily convened meeting of school governors later that day. 'The missing toys, a hanky with Wendy Cole's name embroidered on it, which she'd never even said she'd lost, and a few coins which add up to the dinner money and Janice Ruddicombe's half-crown. Even the old purse Miss Kemp lost months ago. A pathetic little collection to have caused so much trouble.'

'But why in God's name did she do such a thing?' Gilbert Napier demanded. The meeting was being held in Basil's study, and Gilbert had walked there, Charles Latimer having told him that sensible exercise would strengthen his heart muscles. 'She can't have wanted the toys, and she hasn't spent the money – not that there was much to spend.'

'Less than five shillings,' Miss Kemp confirmed. 'She certainly didn't need it. As for her reasons, I can't begin to imagine what they could have been.'

'If you ask me,' Constance Bellamy said in her gruff, forthright manner, 'they're simple. The woman's a kleptomaniac. Can't help stealing.'

'Well there's one thing that is obvious,' Gilbert declared. 'She's not fit to be a teacher and we don't want her in our school. We'll sack her immediately.'

'Don't you think we ought to speak to her first?' Basil said. 'Ask her to a meeting with us all and give her a chance to defend herself?'

'Defend herself? What possible defence could she have?'

'She might say the things were put in her desk by someone else. We could never prove otherwise.'

They looked at each other. Miss Kemp said, 'She always keeps her desk locked, even when she's at school. I told her when she first came that there was no need, but she said she'd been the victim of pilfering herself at another school and didn't intend to let it happen again. And then it started here ... I don't think there's any chance that one of the children could have done it.'

'At another school?' Gilbert said. 'And I wonder who was responsible there. It might be a good idea to have a word with her previous head teachers, just to see. Anyway, it's clear what's happened here. She's a thief, plain and simple. She's stolen from small children, and to make herself even more despicable, she's let one of them take the blame. A *four-year-old*! Quite frankly, I don't even want her in Burracombe again. She's not fit to walk the village street.'

'I'm sure we all agree with you,' Basil said. 'But I still think we have to pay due attention to the principle of innocent until proved guilty. You're a magistrate. We must at least interview her.'

Gilbert frowned but nodded. 'You're right, of course. We'll call her in immediately. I'll send Hilary over to Tavistock to fetch her in the car tomorrow.'

'Bit hard on Hilary,' Constance said. 'One of us would be better. Why don't you go yourself, Gilbert? She'll never dare argue with you.'

'Hm. Yes, all right. Where does she live?'

'Chapel Street,' Miss Kemp said. 'She's got rooms in a house about halfway up.'

'I'll go first thing. At least she's not likely to run away, if she's got a sprained ankle. Ten thirty be all right for the rest of you?'

They all nodded, and Constance said, 'What do we propose to do, apart from sacking her? Do we want to involve the police?'

'The police?' Miss Kemp said in dismay. 'Oh, I don't think so, do you?'

'She's committed a crime, and it may not be the first time. Do we really want her to go to yet another school and do the same thing there?'

'No, of course not ...' Miss Kemp thought for a minute, then shook her head. 'I'd really rather not involve the police. It would be frightening for the children and it would get into the papers – the *Tavistock Times* or *Gazette* at least, and maybe even the *Western Morning News* – and could lead to quite a nasty scandal. But what I could do is write to the county authorities and tell them what's happened. They'll hold an internal inquiry, and if they find her guilty, she'll not be allowed to teach again.'

'Well, that's something,' Constance said. 'Pity nobody did it before.' She looked around the little group. 'If that's all for now, I want to get home. There's a lot to do in the garden now that the planting season's almost upon us. I'll be here at ten thirty tomorrow.'

'There is just one other thing,' Miss Kemp said. 'Billy Culliford. That poor child has suffered considerably through all this. The other children think he's a thief, and I myself have been to his mother and suggested he's not yet ready for school. On top of all the other trouble the family has had ...'

'My God, yes!' Gilbert said. 'They're due some recompense for this.'

'I don't know what we can do, though,' Basil said thoughtfully. 'Apart from an apology, of course. Maybe some flowers for Mrs Culliford ...'

'That would certainly be something,' Miss Kemp agreed. 'But Billy is the one who was wrongly blamed.'

'A toy,' Constance declared. 'Something he can play with but would never ordinarily be able to have. What about a scooter?'

They looked at her. 'A scooter?'

'Yes. It'll be something he can use and enjoy and that the others will see. Give the child a bit of independence, too. Why not present it to him on the first day of next term, with an explanation as to why? You'll have to tell them about Miss Watkins anyway, even if you don't say outright that she was the thief – they're bright enough to

288

put two and two together – and you can give it to him as a public apology. We'll all come along too, won't we?' She looked at the other governors, and they nodded.

'It's a good idea,' Gilbert stated. 'The Cullifords have come through a bad patch, but I think they're turning the corner now, and this will help them along. And I propose we pay for this between ourselves. It'll be a present from the governors.'

'Just before we all go,' Basil added as they prepared to leave, 'there is one more thing we'll have to discuss very soon. And that's the appointment of a new teacher. Miss Kemp will be all on her own again next term. Grace and Mrs Warren may help out, as they did before, but we really need someone permanent. Someone more like our dear Stella.'

'We'll never find anyone like her,' Constance said gloomily. 'Never in a million years.'

'I tell you, I don't *know* how they got there,' Miss Watkins said belligerently. 'Someone did it out of spite, to incriminate me, that's what it is. What would I want with kids' toys and a bit of dinner money? It doesn't make sense.'

'It certainly doesn't,' Basil agreed. 'But I don't think we're looking for things that make sense, are we? The facts speak for themselves. The items were in your desk and your desk was locked. I was with Miss Kemp when she opened it.'

'And what right did she have to do that? Prying into my personal affairs!'

'I wasn't prying—'

'That's enough,' Gilbert snapped. 'Miss Kemp, you have no need to defend yourself. You're head teacher, and the school and all it contains is your responsibility. And that includes your assistant's desk. You had every right to open it.'

'Well, that's the first I've heard of that!' the assistant teacher declared, her face an unbecoming shade of red. 'I thought I was entitled to some privacy.'

'And the children are entitled to an honest teacher!' Gilbert snapped, losing patience. 'I presume, from all you've been saying, that you kept your desk firmly locked at all times, to guard your privacy. Is that the case?'

'I thought I was entitled—'

'*Is that the case?*' he roared, and Basil and Miss Kemp looked at him in alarm.

'Yes it is!' the teacher shouted back. 'I could see what little scally-wags some of the children were. Coming from poor homes, rags on their backs – and that Billy Culliford, his father's a *jailbird*! Of course I kept my desk locked.'

'None of my children come to school in rags—' Miss Kemp began indignantly, but Gilbert waved her to silence. He leaned forward and said in a tone so low it was almost a growl, 'In that case, how do you suggest those stolen items were put into your desk by someone else? Is there a Houdini in your class?'

Miss Watkins stared at him. Her mouth opened and closed again. She looked desperately from side to side and at last pointed towards Miss Kemp and said sullenly, '*She* had a key.'

Miss Kemp and Basil each drew in a shocked breath. Constance Bellamy snorted her contempt. Gilbert Napier stared at the flustered woman with deep loathing, and then leaned back.

'I suggest you retract that insinuation. You're in quite enough trouble already.'

'Oh yes!' Miss Watkins retorted. 'Don't blame her, will you? Just because she's been here for years, knows everybody, got all her own favourites. People do go funny when they reach her age, you know. And she's had it in for me right from the first day I came here. I knew she'd do something to get rid of me. It's always the same – just because I'm not a pretty young girl like that other teacher everyone thinks is the bee's knees, I'm not worth bothering with. It happens every time, every school I've ever been in, and I'm fed up with it!' She glowered at them. 'All right, I did it! I took the things! And why not? That boy should never have been at school in the first place. Four years old! I'm a teacher, not a baby-minder. And his mother with too many already and another on the way – it's disgusting. Well, you needn't bother to give me the sack – I know that's why you brought me here. I'm resigning. And you needn't wonder what to put in my reference, either, because I won't need one – I've had enough of teaching. I don't care if I never see another child in my life!'

She was on her feet, her face crimson as she glared at the four school governors. They stared back at her, shocked and dismayed by her outburst, and then Gilbert waved at her to sit down again. For a moment she seemed about to defy him, and then she sank slowly back on to her chair. Her mouth quivered and tears began to seep down her cheeks.

'I think that's all we need,' Gilbert said quietly, and Miss Kemp realised why he was a good magistrate. 'We'll expect your resignation in the post on Monday morning, together with an admission that neither Billy Culliford nor any other child was responsible for the outbreak of stealing. We've already agreed that we will not involve the police at this stage, and that you will not be provided with references for any other post. Miss Kemp is going to write to the county education authorities to inform them of what has happened and it will be up to them to decide how to deal with it. We ourselves will not be discussing this matter with anyone who is not directly involved.' He paused, and his eyes raked her face with a scorn as sharp as a razor. 'You may go.'

Miss Watkins stood up painfully. 'And how am I going to get home, me with a broken wrist and a sprained ankle? You didn't mind bringing me here, did you? Maybe you can take me back.'

'I'll take you back,' Basil said quietly, and offered her his arm to help her from the room.

The others were silent for a moment as the two went out.

'What a very unpleasant woman,' Constance said at last. 'We made a bad mistake there.'

'I'd rather run the school on my own than take on anyone like her again,' Miss Kemp said. 'But thank you both for standing by me. And now I have another task to do which can't be put off any longer.'

'What's that?' Gilbert enquired, and she smiled at him.

'Why, go and see Billy Culliford and his parents, of course, and tell them that we're sorry for what's happened and will be more than happy to welcome Billy back in school next term.'

Chapter Thirty-Nine

L ittle Burracombe church was dim and quiet that April morning. The air was filled with early birdsong and the lanes were bordered with primroses and violets, while the hedges were greening up with pale unfolding hawthorn leaves and camellias shone like red and pink lanterns from village gardens. But there were no flowers in the church and no music playing on the organ, and the members of the tiny wedding party were sombre as they made their way up the churchyard path and stood at the head of the aisle before Felix.

He looked gravely at the two young faces. Patsy was wearing the blue dress she had worn to Sunday services a hundred times or more, embellished with new buttons and an embroidered collar. In her hands she carried a bunch of primroses with a few violets twined amongst them, and on her shining fair hair she wore a small straw hat with some more primroses tucked into the ribbon wound around its crown.

Ann Shillabeer wore the grey costume he had also seen every Sunday since he had come to Little Burracombe, but she too had a few flowers in her hat. Her eyes were reddened, tears seeping out of them even now, and she dabbed them with a small lace handkerchief that he guessed was normally only for show. He gave her a kindly smile, and her lips quivered in reply.

Nancy Pettifer looked almost defiantly festive, in a purple dress that clashed violently with the ginger hair she had passed on to her sons and a wide-brimmed hat decorated with scarlet camellias. It almost hurt Felix's eyes to look at her, but he understood why she had done it. She wanted to show the Shillabeers that someone, at least, thought this wedding a joyful occasion and that Patsy would be warmly welcomed in her home. Her husband too looked smart in his best suit, with two or three Lenten roses fastened to his lapel, and his sons Bob and Terry looked the same. In contrast, Felix thought that Percy Shillabeer would have worn working clothes if he'd thought he could get away with it. He was tidy enough in his Sunday suit, but it wasn't his best one by any means; the sleeves and trouser turn-ups were frayed, and to cap it all, he wore a black tie. When Felix saw that, his heart hardened towards the man and he could hear the anger in his own voice as he began the words of the marriage service.

Hilary stood in one of the pews on Patsy's side, a little way back from the front. She felt the sadness of the occasion, and the cruelty of it, and wondered if the young couple could ever be truly happy after such a start. Would Patsy come to blame Terry for separating her from her family? Would Terry resent Patsy for having trapped him into this marriage? They're just children themselves, she thought pityingly, and prayed that they would be given strength to keep their love alive through all the difficulties ahead.

'Who giveth this woman to be married to this man?' Felix asked, and Percy Shillabeer stepped forward and took his daughter's hand. He passed it to Felix as if it were something he'd rather not have touched, then stepped back, rubbing his own hand with the other. Felix turned to Terry and asked the age-old questions: 'Wilt thou have this Woman to thy wedded wife, to live together after God's ordinance in the holy estate of Matrimony? Wilt thou love her, comfort her, honour, and keep her in sickness and in health; and, forsaking all others, keep thee only unto her, so long as ye both shall live?'

Terry took a deep breath. He looked steadily at Felix and then turned his eyes upon his bride.

'I will.'

And as he spoke his own words, making that holy vow, it seemed to Hilary that a small miracle took place. The bare church, the sombre group, the chill of the spring morning all fell away, and there were only two young people and a priest, performing a rite that would transform them and stay with them for the rest of their lives. And then Terry's face was lit by a single sunbeam, striking through the east window above the altar, and it seemed that his eyes and his whole expression shone with love.

They'll be all right, she thought with sudden certainty. Nothing can touch them now. They've moved beyond Percy Shillabeer's reach and they can start to live their own lives.

She looked at Felix, and he glanced up at the same moment and caught her eye. Neither smiled, but each knew that they were sharing the same deep confidence and relief; and then Felix turned to Patsy.

'Wilt thou have this Man to thy wedded husband, to live together after God's ordinance in the holy estate of Matrimony? Wilt thou obey him, and serve him, love, honour, and keep him in sickness and in health; and, forsaking all others, keep thyself only unto him, so long as ye both shall live?'

'I will,' Patsy said clearly, and the circle was complete.

It was completed again a few days later, when Maddy Forsyth married Stephen Napier in Burracombe church. The scene now was very different – an April noon, with the sun at its highest, the church filled with flowers, the organ playing and the bells ringing out in joyous delight. Stephen and his best man, Jeremy, sat nervously in the front pew, while Fenella Forsyth, the famous actress who had adopted Maddy during the war, was in the front on the other side of the aisle, elegant in a dress of shimmering amethyst, with her husband Jacques beside her. The church had filled with friends, family, neighbours and villagers, until every pew was tightly packed with brightly coloured spring dresses and costumes, and silvery grey morning suits.

Travis and Jennifer Kellaway were about halfway back, Travis tall and straight beside his wife, who was now five months' pregnant and beginning to blossom in her maternity dress of dark blue, brightened by the carnation pinned to one shoulder. As Hilary glanced round at them, she caught Jennifer's eye and smiled, seeing the contentment in the other woman's face. Love had come late to Jennifer Tucker, as she had been when she first arrived in Burracombe, but it had come true, and the thought touched warmly in Hilary's heart.

Stephen wore his RAF uniform. His fair hair had been brushed until it shone, his face was pale and his hands trembled. Hilary, sitting behind him, felt sorry for him and envious at the same time. If only it were David sitting here waiting for me, she thought longingly. But in the last weeks there had been no chance even to meet him, nothing but the secret late-night phone calls, and Sybil's condition had not changed. Nor ever would, Hilary thought. She'll live on like that for years, for the rest of all our lives, and if she feels and understands anything at all, she must be the most despairing of all of us, for she's been condemned to a living hell.

The meandering tune of the organ changed suddenly and swelled in triumph to the familiar notes of Mendelssohn's 'Wedding March'. The congregation rose, and Hilary saw Stephen shaking, and leaned forward slightly to touch his shoulder and give him a quick smile. Then they all turned to watch as the bride made her way up the aisle to where Basil Harvey and Felix waited to perform the service together.

She looks absolutely beautiful, Hilary thought. Such a simple white dress, yet it shimmers as if sprinkled with fallen stars. And Stella too – *walking*, albeit rather slowly – and Ruth and Dan Hodges' little girl, Linnet, both wearing sky blue and carrying bouquets of lily of the valley, Maddy's favourite flower.

The Archdeacon looked proud to have Maddy on his arm, Hilary thought. He and his wife had been so good to Maddy, helping her through that terrible time after her fiancé Sammy had been killed, that they had become almost a second family to the girl who had lost so many of her own. Yet she had been blessed with people who wanted to look after her – Fenella Forsyth, the glamorous stage and film star sitting across the aisle from Hilary now, Dottie Friend, who was resplendent in a new dark green costume she'd made herself, the American Russell Tozer who had almost won Maddy's hand; and finally Hilary herself and her brother Stephen. Not to mention their father, Gilbert, who sat beside her looking sternly proud of his son. Yes, she thought with sudden surprise, proud! She must remember to tell Stephen that ...

The wedding service continued, with almost everyone there shedding quiet tears as Maddy and Stephen completed their vows and kissed before proceeding into the vestry to sign the register. Hilary witnessed again, the second time in less than a week that she had performed this office, and she took a moment to remember Patsy's wedding and to think of the contrast between the two – one so plain and painful, one so colourful and joyous, yet with a common thread. And that was the love that had drawn both couples together, each through their own separate difficulties, linking them with the strength of a chain woven of steel. It had shone in Terry and Patsy's faces last week, and it shone in Maddy and Stephen's today, and there were surely few present at either ceremony who could have been untouched by it.

Later that night, Hilary drove her father home to a house that seemed oddly empty without Stephen. Oddly, because he was hardly ever there anyway, and when he did come back he would have Maddy with him, but they were both very aware that a major change had taken place. Both were tired too, and when Gilbert said he would go straight to bed, Hilary nodded and offered to bring him a hot drink in about a quarter of an hour.

Only one more wedding to go now, she thought – Stella's, at Whitsun. As she had promised to do, Stella would be able to walk up the aisle to Felix, and although she would not be back to full strength for some time, she would then be able to take up the reins of her new life as a vicar's wife. Three weddings, each very different; three happy brides and grooms; three new lives beginning in Burracombe.

And still no sign of a new life for herself, with the man she loved and longed for.

She took her father his drink and found him already in bed, tired but insistent that he had not done too much. 'It's healthy to be tired,' he said. 'And I don't mind telling you, Hilary, I was proud of Stephen today. He's turned into a fine young man, and Maddy will make him a good wife. He'll do well now.'

'I know, Father.' She bent and kissed him, and he caught her hand and looked into her eyes.

'I've not always been fair to Stephen,' he said gruffly. 'Nor to you. And this damned illness of mine – well, it's given me time to think. We need to have a talk, you and I.'

Hilary stared at him, wondering what he had in mind. But she could also see that he looked pale and tired, and she knew that this was not the time for serious discussion.

'Later,' she said quietly. 'Later. There's plenty of time for talking, Father. All the time in the world.'

Chapter Forty

The third wedding in Burracombe that year was perhaps the greatest celebration of all. The whole village had watched and rejoiced as Stella Simmons appeared amongst them once more, taking faltering steps from the vicarage to the village street and, first with the aid of two sticks and then just one, walking a little further each day.

'You'll be skipping along like a two–year–old before us knows it,' Alice Tozer beamed at her one day. 'It does my heart good to see you. It can't be easy, having to do all they old exercises and learn to walk all over again.'

'It's not,' Stella admitted, resting against Dottie Friend's garden wall. 'But it's worth it, and in a year's time it will all be in the past and I'll be too busy even to think about it.'

'You must be main busy now,' Alice remarked, 'with a wedding to get ready. Only a few weeks now.'

'Four.' Stella nodded. 'And Maddy and Stephen will be home today from their honeymoon. They're only staying a day but they promised to come and see us before they go back to White Cheriton. They'll be off to Cyprus straight after my wedding.'

'You'll miss her then,' Alice said, and sighed. ''Tis all change, it seems. Young people moving away from the village, living in foreign parts ... It seems strange to me.'

'It's not that new,' Stella pointed out. 'Ted's brother went to America all those years ago, and didn't Miss Bellamy's brother emigrate? Or was it her sister?'

Bu Alice wasn't listening. Her mind was on her own daughter. Stella saw the expression on her face and asked gently, 'What's the news of Jackie?'

'I wish I knew! The maid tells us nothing. You know she've gone and got herself engaged, I suppose?'

'I did hear about it.' It had been a subject of much gossip in the village when the news first got out, but Stella didn't want to upset Alice by saying too much. She said, 'Do you know much about the man? Dottie says she met him and he seemed very nice.'

'So she told us, and our Joe thinks he's the bee's knees. But that isn't the point!' Alice burst out. 'The point is, he's American, and say what you like, they'm different from us and got different ways. And Ted and me – us don't *want* our Jackie living all those thousands of miles away from us with a man we've never even set eyes on!'

'But you will meet him, surely. She won't be getting married yet, anyway.'

'Who knows what she'll up and do?' Alice said grimly. 'Only been over there five minutes and she tells us she's engaged. Next thing is, she could be telling us they'm wed. And how are we going to meet him if they don't come over here? Ted and me have already paid out for her fare on that liner, us can't afford to spend any more. Not that us'd want to go anyway, not just for a lot of trouble that won't do any good.'

Stella gazed at her. It seemed as if Alice had given up hope where Jackie was concerned. She knew that the Tozers had been against the trip from the start, and this must have been one of the consequences they'd dreaded.

'It might come to nothing,' she said, trying to offer what comfort she could. 'Things that happen suddenly like that often fizzle out just as quickly. The next letter might tell you it's all off.'

'That's what we'm hoping. What I'm afraid of is that she'll get married quick and live to regret it.' Alice sighed. 'Dottie says he's a decent sort of chap, but me and Ted still can't help worrying.' She looked at Stella. 'But you don't want to hear all that. You got enough to be thinking of. I hear there's plenty going on over at Little Burracombe vicarage, too.'

'Felix is having some redecoration done. Reverend Berry and his wife hadn't had much done over the past few years. So we've been choosing wallpaper and paints – it's been quite fun, but a lot to think about, as well as getting ready for the wedding. I'm just going into Dottie's now, to have my dress fitted.'

'Then I mustn't keep you chattering here,' Alice exclaimed. 'And you must be tired too, standing about. You go on in, my bird. And come up to the farm sometime for a proper chinwag. Mother'd like to see you, I know.'

Stella smiled and went to the door, which was just opening. Dottie looked out, smiled at Alice and drew Stella inside. As usual, there was a smell of baking, and a wire rack laden with fairy cakes sat on the table.

'George Sweet asked me for a batch,' Dottie explained. 'He wants some tarts, too – lemon curd and raspberry jam. I've already done those, so I'll just put these out of the way and we can have a look at your dress.'

The dress was of oyster satin, fitted closely to Stella's slender figure and rippling out to a circle of rich cream and a train that would be carried by the two chief bridesmaids, Maddy and Val. Dottie, who had been accustomed to making sumptuous theatre costumes in her younger days, crawled around the floor at Stella's feet, her mouth full of pins as she made adjustments to the hem. She finished at last and sat back on her heels with a sigh of relief.

'That should be all right now. Let's get you out of it and I'll make us a cup of coffee.'

Stella laughed. 'You and your American ways! I bet it's not Camp now!'

Dottie wrinkled her nose. 'I never did like that stuff. Chicory, it is, not proper coffee at all. If there was one thing Joe taught me, it was how to appreciate coffee. Not that I don't still like my cup of tea in the afternoon, mind, but I do seem to have got into the habit of enjoying coffee in the mornings.' She made the coffee in a blue enamel jug with a lid, which Stella had never seen before.

'You've grown very sophisticated, Dottie,' she smiled. 'You'll be buying a refrigerator next.'

'I might even do that too. I never realised how useful they can be. I've always been happy enough with my meat safe outside the back door, but you can keep things so much longer in a proper icebox – that's what they call them there. You don't have to boil the milk over-night in hot weather, and the butter keeps nice and cool, and cream will keep nearly a week. Not that they have proper clotted cream, not like ours. I showed the girls how to make it, though.' She handed Stella her coffee. 'And how are you feeling, flower? No regrets?'

'Not about the wedding, if that's what you mean. I do regret making

Felix so unhappy when I said I couldn't marry him, though. I really did think it would be wrong at the time.'

'Then there's nothing to regret,' Dottie declared. 'You did it for the best of reasons – for his sake – even if you were wrong! Anyway, 'tis in the past now and best forgotten.'

Stella nodded. 'That's what Felix says. And now I'd better go. Grace will have lunch ready.' She looked around the little room and added, rather diffidently, 'You know I'd like to be married from here, don't you? Would it be all right if I came back for the last week?'

'Why, of course it would, my bird!' Dottie exclaimed, her face pink with pleasure. 'I didn't like to mention it. I thought you'd decided to stay up at the vicarage.'

Stella smiled and shook her head. 'I'm comfortable there, and Basil and Grace are very good to me, but this is home. And Maddy was married from here. It seems the right place.'

'It's been a pleasure to have you both,' Dottie said, and kissed her. 'If ever I'd had daughters of my own, I'd have chosen you two. It's just a shame you had to be separated for so long as little girls.'

Stella made her way back to the vicarage, warmed by the love of the little woman. And as she walked along the street, greeting and smiling at the other villagers she had come to know so well, she reflected that Dottie wasn't the only family she and Maddy had found here. The whole of Burracombe had become their family.

It really was a very special village.

Maddy and Stephen returned from their honeymoon glowing with happiness, and called in at Dottie's cottage, the vicarage and, of course, the Barton. They paid no more than a flying visit to each house, but somehow a good many of the villagers seemed to be about in the lanes to be waved and smiled at, and all agreed that they looked as happy as larks. Their next visit would not be until the day before Stella's wedding, and then they would be off again, this time to Stephen's posting in Cyprus.

'Good to see the boy settled,' Gilbert remarked to Hilary when they had departed. 'Shown a bit of sense at last. Young Madelaine is a fine addition to the family.' He sighed. 'Pity they seem set on going to Canada when he leaves the RAF.'

'It's a while yet,' Hilary answered. 'Things can change a lot in that time.' Even for herself and David, she thought wistfully.

'So when are you off to London again?' Gilbert asked, making her jump as if he had read her thoughts. She looked at him, wondering whether to tell him the truth. Ever since his words after Stephen's wedding, she had been debating this, yet she could not bring herself to broach the subject. Once she had told him, there would be no going back, and she still feared the effect the story might have on his health.

'Next week,' she answered. 'Just for the day.' She and David had agreed not to court temptation by staying overnight. They would meet as before, walk if the weather was good, have lunch somewhere, walk again and then part. The parting was so painful that she wondered if it were worth it, but as soon as he was out of sight she began to long for the next time.

They managed two more meetings before Stella's wedding. The second was only a few days before, and this time David was to stay the night at a hotel, for a meeting early next morning. Hilary was torn with the longing to stay with him and almost gave in. They stood together at Paddington railway station, their hands gripped together, and Hilary leaned her head against his shoulder.

'David ... I can't go ... I *can't* ...'

'I don't want you to go,' he murmured into her hair. 'But you've got a lot to do at home. Stay next time, darling. We'll make it soon. Stay with me then.'

She looked up at him, her face wet with tears. 'You know what we agreed.'

'I know. I just don't think I have that kind of strength.' He looked exhausted, his skin pale, dark patches beneath his eyes. She thought of what awaited him at home, of all he had to bear. Would the relief of being able to love her ease his burden, or would guilt make it all the heavier? How could she know?

A whistle sounded and she gave him an anguished glance. 'I'll have to go. My train ...'

'Yes.' He gave her a gentle push. 'Go now, darling, before I change my mind and take you away for ever.'

'Don't say such things!' Half laughing, half in tears, she turned away and ran for the barrier. In a moment she was through, and when she looked back, he was gone.

And at once, as it always did, the yearning began.

Chapter Forty-One

'Only two days to go,' Felix said. 'I don't know how I am going to wait.'

'Of course you do,' Stella laughed at him. 'We've waited so long already – what's another two days?'

'An eternity, that's what. And I'm not even going to *see* you again until then. Honestly, darling, it's just a superstition that the groom mustn't see the bride the day before the wedding. What possible difference can it make?'

'It's probably so that he doesn't distract her from all the things she has to do. I'll be far too busy to see you. Anyway, you might change your mind if you do.'

'Nothing will change my mind,' he said forcefully. 'Before you go, let's just have one last look around the house to make sure it's exactly as you want it to come home to after our honeymoon. I don't want you wishing you'd never said "I do" because the curtains don't match the carpet or something.'

'It would be too late to change it now, even if they don't,' Stella said, but she allowed him to lead her by the hand into each of the rooms in the rambling vicarage, up the stairs to the bedrooms, and even into the attics. They came to a halt in the kitchen and she said firmly, 'And now I really must go. You can't find any other excuse to keep me here.'

'After Monday, I won't need one,' he told her. 'You'll be mine, for ever and ever.'

'Amen,' she responded, and reached up to kiss him. 'And you won't need one, because I'll never want to leave. Now I really am going. Goodbye, darling. The next time you see me, I'll be walking up the aisle to marry you. And that's a promise.'

He regarded her anxiously. 'Are you sure you want to walk back to Burracombe now? I don't want you overtiring yourself.'

'Quite sure,' she said firmly. 'I shall enjoy it. And you've got plenty to do yourself. You're having visitors tomorrow, remember? All those bishop uncles of yours, and their wives.'

She set off down the narrow lane towards the Clam, pausing to look over the bridge at the foaming water below. There had been quite a lot of rain in the last few days and the water was brown and bubbly as it swirled under the bridge. Years ago, a father and his young son had drowned here, and she thought of the sadness that must have gone on for a lifetime afterwards in the family. She dropped a twig over, as if in memory, and watched it swirl away.

Coming up the other side, into Burracombe itself, she met Arthur Culliford. He was cutting the hedge that bordered the lane and gave her his half-sheepish grin, as if he wasn't sure she wanted to acknowledge him. Stella smiled and paused to ask how Maggie was.

'Her baby must be almost due. Is she keeping well?'

Arthur screwed up his face. 'Well enough, I s'pose, considering she'm carrying twins.'

'Twins?' Stella exclaimed. 'Goodness me! Are you sure?'

'That's what midwife says. My Maggie's at her wits' end with it. Five kiddies under five! I dunno how she's going to manage. I tell you this, though.' He fixed Stella with a look that made her feel as if it were all her fault. 'There'll be no more after this. We always reckoned we'd take what the good Lord sends, but seems to me he'm just playing us for fules and I had enough. How am I supposed to feed all that lot, eh?'

'I don't know,' Stella murmured. 'It must be awfully difficult.'

'Difficult!' He returned his attention to the hedge. 'At least I'm in regular work now, thanks to the Squire, but it still don't pay enough to feed all those mouths. I dunno what we'm going to do, and that's a fact.'

'How's your Billy?' asked Stella. 'I was really sorry to hear about what happened, but at least everyone knows now that he's not a thief.'

'Never was, was he? But that's folk for you. Always ready to think the worst of a Culliford.'

Stella escaped at last, feeling somewhat battered by Arthur's obvious anxiety. She thought of the little cottage, already overcrowded, with two more babies soon to be added. How could they possibly live healthily in such circumstances? How would poor Maggie manage?

A new voice hailed her as she came into the village, and she saw Hilary Napier turning into the Barton drive, a shopping basket over her arm.

'Have you walked all the way over the Clam?'

'I have, and enjoyed it. Well, until I met Arthur Culliford. Did you know Maggie's having twins?'

'I did hear that. The poor woman must be in despair. I don't know how she manages as it is.' Hilary frowned. 'I think I ought to talk to Father about it. We don't want Arthur going back to poaching and ending up in prison again.' She looked at Stella. 'But you mustn't worry about it. You've got a wedding in two days' time.'

'I know.' Stella beamed at her. 'And I couldn't be happier about it. I just want everyone to be as happy as I am. I know it's silly.'

'It's not silly. It's sweet.' Hilary smiled at her. 'And you deserve to be happy, after all you've been through.'

'You'll be there, won't you?' Stella asked. 'I want all my friends there.'

'Of course I'll be there.' Hilary glanced at her watch. 'I'm sorry, I'll have to go – I promised to get Father's supper early so that he can play chess with Charles Latimer. And I expect Dottie's waiting for you.'

Stella smiled and walked on into the village, while Hilary turned to continue up the drive. She sighed wistfully as she thought of Stella's wish. If only, she thought, if only ...

She and David had met the day before yesterday, as planned, but Hilary had not stayed overnight. Instead, she had come home as usual on the four o'clock train, her heart breaking as she said goodbye, but unable to bring herself to make love with him while his wife lay so ill and helpless at home. A Sybil who was so dependent on her husband was very different from a Sybil who had been cheating him for years. Hilary could not have put the difference into words, but it was there and she couldn't overcome it.

'How long can we go on like this?' he'd whispered as he held her in his arms. 'I don't know how I can get through the days without you.'

Hilary had been unable to answer. The only option was too cruel to say aloud. She shook her head, held both her hands to his mouth, then kissed him. 'Oh my love, my dear, dear love ...'

And then, once again, they had parted, and she did not know now when she would see him again. They had said nothing, made no plans. It was all too hard, too impossible.

She took a deep breath. For the next few days she must once again set her worries aside. Tomorrow, visitors would be arriving, for they were to put up some of Felix's relatives at the Barton, and the day after that would be taken up entirely by the wedding.

The rainbow wedding, when Stella would stand at last before the altar and marry Felix Copley.

'It were a lovely service,' Dottie Friend said afterwards, as they gathered in front of the church door for photographs. 'And though I says it meself, the frocks do look a picture. And Stella says some of the photos will be in colour too.'

'They don't come out all that well, though,' Ivy Sweet said disparagingly. Like nearly all the villagers, she had come to the church, but she wasn't invited to the reception at the Bedford Hotel in Tavistock. She was clearly affronted by this. 'My niece had colour pictures at her wedding and the colours didn't look anything like they really were. And sometimes they'm just coloured in and don't look no better than a kiddy with a box of crayons could do.'

Dottie didn't bother to answer. She was sure that Felix's parents, who were paying for the wedding, would have made sure the photographer was the best they could find, and she happened to know that he had come all the way from Exeter so was bound to be good. She moved away and then heard her name being called.

'Dottie! Come over here, we want you in the family photo.'

'But I'm not family,' Dottie protested as Maddy took her arm, leading her back to the main group.

'Of course you are! Weren't you as good as a mother to me during the war? And haven't you looked after Stella ever since she first came to the village? Anyway, you've got to be in the photo or it will be all clergymen, and they make it look more like a funeral!'

Dottie laughed and allowed herself to be dragged into the group. It was true that many of Felix's large family were clergy and dressed today in what Felix irreverently referred to as 'working gear', which did mean that there was rather a lot of black.

'Stand there,' Maddy commanded, placing Dottie beside Stella.

'And Uncle Charles and Aunt Mary beside you.' The doctor and his wife were no relation to Maddy and Stella, but Maddy had proclaimed them an honorary uncle and aunt a long time ago. 'And Felix's family all around us, because we're sharing them now. Where's Stephen? I must have Stephen with me.'

Stephen emerged from the crowd to stand close beside his wife, gripping her hand in his. 'You seem to have taken over,' he said with a grin. 'I wonder what the poor photographer thinks of you stealing his job.'

'He's pleased as Punch,' Maddy declared, pinching his arm. 'I think he may offer me a job before the day's over.'

'He'd better not try,' Stephen said, looking at the young man busy with his camera and tripod. 'I hope you've told him you belong to me.'

'I didn't have to.' She smiled into his eyes. 'Now stand still while I make sure everyone's in position.' She raised her voice. 'Look at the camera, everyone. Janice, your rosette's twisted – let me fix it. There.' She looked down at the little girl. 'You're not getting too tired, are you?'

'No, miss,' Janice said. Her eyes were shining, and Maddy remembered that when Stella had announced to her class that they could vote for one girl to act as her bridesmaid, she had given them all two votes – one because most of them were sure to vote for themselves, and one for someone else. To everyone's surprise and delight, Janice had been the outright winner.

Maddy smiled at her sister. 'You look absolutely beautiful.'

'I'm just happy,' Stella replied. 'When I think of all I could have thrown away ...' She shivered, and her new husband, who had been talking to his father on the other side, put his arm around her.

'You're not cold, are you, darling?'

'No, just thinking of what I could have lost if you'd taken notice of me when I said I couldn't marry you. I'm so glad everyone made me see sense.'

'It wasn't easy,' Maddy reminded her. 'But we had to be cruel to be kind. Anyway, don't let's think about that now – the photographer will be getting impatient, and I'll lose my job!' She cast a final assessing eye over the gathering and slipped back to her own position. 'Smile, everyone! Say cheese!'

'Cheese!' they all repeated obediently, and the photographer clicked his camera.

'Right, that's enough,' he said. 'You can stop smiling.'

'I hope not!' Felix exclaimed. 'I don't want any long faces at my wedding. But if you've really taken enough photos, we can go to the reception now. I'm starving!'

'I've never known a time when you weren't,' Stella said. 'I think I'm going to be grateful for those cookery lessons Dottie gave me.'

'Not half as grateful as me,' Felix said as they made their way down the church path to the lychgate, where Tavistock's smartest taxi awaited them. Maddy, Val and Dottie followed, all helping to tuck the flowing satin train around Stella so that it didn't get crushed on the journey, and the couple drove off to the cheers of the waving crowd.

'There they go,' Hilary said, watching the car disappear down the track that led to the corner of the road and into the village itself. 'We'd better follow them. We'll give them a few minutes' head start so they can be ready to greet us as we arrive.'

'I'm so glad it's all gone well for them,' Val said, coming to stand beside her. 'It was awful back in January when Stella was so badly hurt and saying she wouldn't marry Felix because she couldn't be a proper wife to him.'

'I know. The poor man was distraught. But between us we made her see sense, didn't we? And now look at her. No more than a limp, and Charles says even that will probably go eventually.'

'And how are you?' Val asked, giving her friend a keen look. 'It can't have been easy for you watching them standing at the altar looking so happy.'

Hilary hesitated, then said honestly, 'No, it wasn't. But I couldn't begrudge it, could I? And it's something I'm going to have to get used to – seeing other people happy when I can't be. It's not as if my life is that bad, after all. I'm really very lucky.'

Her voice shook, despite her words, and Val moved closer and touched her arm. 'It'll come right for you too one day, Hilary. It has to.'

'Will it?' Hilary's lips twisted a little. 'I'm not so sure, Val. I don't think it ever will – not really. Anyway, let's not think about that now. Let's just be happy for Stella and Felix. And you'd better go – the taxis are lining up and you're matron of honour, remember? You have duties to perform!'

She watched Val pick up her skirts and hurry down the path to join the rest of the bridesmaids. In a moment Hilary would join her father to drive to Tavistock in their own car, but for a brief space she stood alone, needing the respite of solitude to gather her feelings and get them under control.

She drew in a deep breath and turned to see her father coming towards her. She summoned up a smile and put out her hand. For the rest of the day she would think only of the wedding of her friends. There would be time later to reflect on all that had happened since January.

The Bedford Hotel seemed to have put on a special effort to welcome Stella and Felix and their wedding party. There were pink and white roses on each side of the big doors at the top of the steps, and more in the main function room. As the taxi stopped outside to let them go inside, the bells of St Eustachius' church, just across the road, rang out in a merry peal and Stella looked at Felix in surprise.

'Oh, how lovely. Fancy the Tavistock team ringing for us.'

'Well, I'm not sure they are, actually,' he said with a grin. 'I think they've got a wedding of their own to ring for. But it's certainly very opportune.'

They went inside and just had time to make sure they were ready for their guests before they began to arrive. Dottie, with Frank and Jess Budd, came first, and Stella made them stand beside her, repeating Maddy's assertion that they had all been as good as parents to both girls when they were small bewildered children orphaned by the war. The bridesmaids arrived next like a billowing bouquet of sweet peas, and then Felix's parents. The line was then complete and the rest of the guests were allowed in, to kiss, shake hands and offer all their good wishes to the radiantly happy couple.

'Good to see you again, Frank,' Dan Hodges said, shaking the hand of his old friend from Portsmouth. 'I'm a bit out of me depth here.'

'You're not the only one,' Frank answered. 'All these bishops! But they seem a friendly lot – don't stand on ceremony. They tell me the Bedford's laid in a case or two of whisky specially!' He grinned and turned to Ruth, who was standing beside Dan. 'And how are you keeping, Ruth? And the little one? Must be a few months old now. Must say, I was a bit surprised to hear old Dan still had it in him at his age!'

'Three months.' Ruth smiled. 'He's lovely, thank you, Frank, and the image of his father. My sister's looking after him.' She looked at Jess. 'We'll have a chat later. Come on, Dan, we're holding up the queue.'

They moved on into the big room and accepted a glass of sherry. The tables were laid in a big horseshoe formation and there was an easel with a plan showing where everyone was to sit. One of Felix's uncles, who was acting as master of ceremonies, rapped on the table with a small gavel and the buzz of conversation stopped as they were directed to their seats. Ruth and Dan made their way to their table and shook hands with the Tozers. They all sat down, Dan still feeling out of place in such surroundings, and Ted picked up a knife and fork and stared at them dubiously.

'I dunno why us has to have such a master lot of cutlery to eat one dinner,' he remarked. 'Bit unnecessary, if you asks me. And look at all these glasses. However many drinks be us going to have, for goodness' sake?'

'Ted!' Alice reproved him. 'Behave yourself. You knows very well you use the cutlery from the outside in and the glasses are for whatever sort of wine you wants, and water.' She looked at Ruth and lifted her eyes to the ceiling. 'Men! You can't take 'em anywhere.'

'And if you do,' Ruth agreed solemnly, 'you have to take them back again, to apologise.'

The four of them burst out laughing and Dan relaxed. He would get on all right with Ted, he knew, and from now on they could all just sit back and enjoy the rest of the day.

From the top table Maddy, who had been anxious about Dan, saw them laughing together and she too relaxed, knowing that they would enjoy each other's company. She turned to Stephen and smiled.

'Isn't it lovely to see everyone so happy.'

'It's a happy occasion,' he said, squeezing her hand. 'But what's best of all, for me, is seeing *you* so happy. There have been times when I thought I'd never see that again. And I really never thought it would be because of me. I'd just about given up all hope.'

'But you never did, quite,' she said quietly. 'You were always there, waiting until I was ready. I really don't deserve you, Stephen.'

*

It was over at last. The newly-weds, radiantly happy, had left for their honeymoon in Wales and a good many of the guests were still at the Bedford Hotel, enjoying each other's company and picking at the buffet that had been provided for the evening. Ruth and Dan and the Budds had returned with Dottie and the Tozers to Burracombe, where Bernie Nethercott was giving his own party at the Bell Inn. Some people had simply gone home, Janice Ruddicombe and her parents among them, while the smaller bridesmaids from Felix's family were asleep like bright flowers in big armchairs in a corner of the Bedford lounge.

'What would you like to do, Father?' Hilary asked. 'Stay a bit longer, or go home?'

'Home,' he said. 'I'm not up to these late nights now. It's been a long day. But what about you, my dear? Don't you want to stay on?'

She shook her head. 'I've had enough. I'm ready to go too.'

They made their excuses and left. It had been a good day, she thought as she drove back, but a painful one as well. So many people seemed to have found happiness in Burracombe – Stella and Felix, Stephen and Maddy, even Patsy and Terry, who were now living with his family – yet still it eluded her. And the partings from David were worse every time. She could see no end to it.

I must just get used to it, she thought, and be happy for everyone else.

They went indoors and she sent her father straight up to bed with the promise of a cup of cocoa in half an hour's time. Fit and well he might be, but he still needed to take care, and he did look tired. She pottered about in the kitchen, feeling deflated after the excitement of the day, and put a shot of brandy into his drink before carrying it upstairs.

Gilbert was sitting up in bed. He took the mug of cocoa and sipped it. Then he set it on the bedside table and looked at his daughter gravely.

'It's been a good day,' he said. 'Almost as good as Stephen's wedding day. And they've made me think.'

'Have they, Father?'

'Yes. They've made me think about you, and all you've given up.'

Hilary looked at him in surprise and opened her mouth to speak, but he held up his hand.

310

'Let me finish. I've been wanting to say this for some time. I know you enjoy running the estate and I know I've always told you you should find a husband. Maybe I haven't told you in the right way. It doesn't have to be an either/or. Not for you. You're a very capable woman, and you could do both – if only you find the right man.'

'Yes,' she said in a low voice. 'But that's the hard part, isn't it?'

He looked at her, still with that grave expression. 'I've seen the happiness in these young people's eyes. I'd like to see it in yours too.' He reached out and took her hands. 'I'd like to see the same thing happen to you, my dear. It's not right for a young woman to live alone as you do. You've not been happy lately, I know – you've not been happy for a very long time. Promise me something.'

'What, Father?' She looked at him with some alarm. There was a difference in him tonight – a change in his colour, in his eyes and voice. Don't leave me now, she thought in sudden panic. Don't slip away before we've had a chance to say all we need to say to one another. He'd wanted to talk after Stephen's wedding, but somehow they never had. Why did we never find the time? Was this what he wanted to say?

'Promise me to take your chance, if one comes along,' he said. 'They don't come often – some say they only come once. But if it comes – if it already has come – take it with both hands and keep hold of it. Don't let me stand in your way, any more than I have already.' He glinted a look at her again, and she saw the old Gilbert there, arrogant, sure of himself, confident that he was right. 'Promise me, Hilary.'

'I promise,' she said softly, wishing even as she made it that she could keep the promise, and she kissed him again. 'Good night, Father.'

If only, she thought as she left the rom and closed the door softly behind her, she could keep it. But he didn't know what he was asking. Nobody, other than Val Ferris and Charles Latimer, knew about David, and even they could not fully understand the anguish that dwelt in her heart.

She went downstairs, still disquieted. I'll ring Charles, she thought. He'll probably be home by now. It might be just tiredness, but there was something different about Father tonight – something I've never seen before.

She went into the office and laid her hand on the telephone, but before she could pick it up, it rang, startling her so much that she almost knocked the receiver from its cradle. She caught it, and lifted it to her ear.

'Hello? Burracombe Barton.'

'Hilary? Is that you? It's David.'

She had known his voice the moment he spoke. She gripped the receiver tightly, her heart leaping, and whispered, 'Yes. Yes, it's me. David—'

'I've been trying to ring you all day,' he said urgently. 'Hilary – it's Sybil ...' His voice was shaking and he had to pause a moment to control it. 'She died,' he said at last in a flat, unbelieving tone. 'She had another stroke, a massive one, and we couldn't save her. Hilary, Sybil has died ...'